A
Million
Little Things

#1 *NEW YORK TIMES* BESTSELLING AUTHOR

SUSAN MALLERY

A
Million
Little Things

MIRA

MIRA

ISBN-13: 978-0-7783-3091-2

A Million Little Things

A
Million
Little Things

Chapter One

"My name is Zoe Saldivar and I just had stupid sex with my ex-boyfriend."

As Zoe spoke, she carefully pulled on the rope dangling from the attic door in her ceiling. The mechanism was very stiff and if it snapped back in place too hard, the door would be stuck forever. Or so the building inspector had told her when she'd been in escrow for her house.

"Not that the sex was stupid," she continued. "It was okay. I want to say I was drunk, but I wasn't. I even knew better. And I do know better. I was weak. There. I've said it. I had stupid ex-boyfriend sex in a moment of weakness."

The ladder lowered into place in the small hallway of her house. Zoe put her foot on the first step and then looked at Mason, her oversize marmalade cat.

"Nothing?" she asked. "You don't want to offer any advice at all?"

Mason blinked.

"Is that disinterest or are you giving me a pass?"

Mason yawned.

"I can't decide which is worse," Zoe admitted. "The stupid sex or the fact that you're the only one I have to talk to about it."

She climbed the narrow, rickety steps up to the surprisingly spacious attic. So far she hadn't put much up there—mostly because hauling anything large or heavy on those stairs was nearly impossible. But she had found a home for her luggage and the new seasonal flag collection she'd bought at a recent beach craft fair. Her mom had always loved celebrating every holiday and season. Now that Zoe had her own house, she wanted to follow suit.

She turned on the light and ignored the innate creepiness of being in an attic. This one was open and didn't smell too musty. But hello, it was still an attic.

She moved the four-foot flagpole to the attic opening, then returned to pick out the "spring" flag she would hang. She held it up and smiled at the beautiful woven bouquet of brightly colored flowers.

"Perfect."

Something creaked.

Zoe turned in time to see Mason heading up the stairs.

"No!"

The last thing she needed was to have her cat disappear into some dusty corner for several hours while she tried to coax him out.

Mason gave her his best green-eyed "who me?" stare before jumping into the attic.

He was a big boy. Eighteen pounds of muscle, and okay, maybe too many cat treats. Regardless, when he bounced, the stairs bounced, too. Then they rose with astonishing speed before snapping into place. The final *thunk* of the attic stairs coming to rest shook the house. Silence followed.

Zoe and Mason stared at each other before the cat strolled off to begin exploring, his tail held high. As if everything was fine. But she knew better.

Don't close the attic door hard. It's warped from age and humidity and needs to be replaced. If you let it snap shut, it's going to get stuck.

The inspector's words came back to her. Words she'd duly noted but hadn't done anything about. She'd had her mind on things like painting and new window coverings. I mean seriously, they were attic stairs. How much could they matter?

Only they mattered now. A lot.

Zoe let the seasonal flag slip from her fingers. She crossed to the attic door and gave a little push. Nothing happened. She pushed harder, with the same result.

She was not a mechanical person. She could change a lightbulb and tell her computer to update with the best of them, but anything more complicated was challenging. She understood the concept of the attic stairs. She pulled a rope and the trap door opened. Stairs unfolded. When she was done, she pushed the stairs back into their folded position and they gracefully closed.

What she didn't know was how to make that happen from the inside of the attic rather than the hallway. If she stood on the stairs and they opened, she would find herself tumbling down to the hallway below. That was unlikely to have a happy ending.

She knelt in front of the opening and put her hands on both sides of the stairs, then pushed down as hard as she could. There wasn't even a hint of movement. She was well and truly stuck.

She shifted until she was sitting on the attic floor and tried to figure out what to do. Calling out for help was pretty useless. There was no one home—mostly because she lived alone. Sure she had friends, but they wouldn't miss her for days. The same with her father. Her cell was downstairs and flagging down a neighbor would be challenging, what with the attic not having any windows.

She swallowed and told herself it wasn't getting any hotter up here. That she was fine, and yes, she could breathe. Everything was okay. Something moved in the corner and she

jumped, then pressed her hand against her suddenly thunder-
ing heart. Mason appeared. Was it just her or was he eyeing
her in a somewhat predatory way?

"You are so not eating my liver," she told him.

He smiled.

Zoe forced herself to her feet. If there was a problem, there
was also a solution. She would find it. If worse came to worst,
she would simply throw herself on the attic door and take her
chances with the fall. Better that than dying a slow, painful
death alone up here.

As she prowled the large space, she tried to think positively. She would be fine. This would be a great anecdote
for later. But her brain kept supplying her with awful stories
she'd read about people dying and not being found until they
were mummified. Because no one noticed they were missing.

Which could very well happen to her, she thought, horrified at the realization. She lived alone. She worked from
home. Her best friend was obsessed with her eighteen-month-
old son and rarely called. Zoe could very easily end up liver-
less and mummified. She'd seen the pictures in science class.
Mummified was not a good look on anyone.

Twenty minutes later she had collected her luggage, the
flagpole, two old musty blankets and, oddly enough, a metal
bow rake. The latter items had been left by the house's previous owner. If James Bond could kill someone with a fountain
pen, she could MacGyver her way out of the attic.

She placed the pole right by the opening and her smallest
suitcase next to it. The blankets were being held in reserve
in case she really did have to throw herself on the stairs and
hope she didn't kill herself when she landed. She would wrap
herself in them to help break the fall. But first, a more sensible approach.

She stood with the rake head pressed flat against the opening. She pressed down as hard as she could. The door shifted

slightly, then snapped closed. She rested for a second, then pressed down again, this time using her body weight for leverage. She felt the door give a hair, then half an inch, then a little more. She managed to kick the flagpole into the opening to hold it.

She straightened and shook out her arms. If she made it out of here, she was so going to have a serious talk with Mason. And maybe start working out. And get more friends. And one of those old people alert thingies.

When her arms felt less shaky, she went back to work. This time she got the door open enough to slide the small suitcase in the resulting space. The pressure dented the plastic, but allowed her to widen the opening.

Two suitcases and much swearing later, the attic door dropped to the open position and the stairs oh so gracefully unfurled. Mason trotted past her and made his way to the main floor, then looked up as if asking what was taking her so long.

"We are so having a talk about your attitude," Zoe muttered as she followed him down the stairs. "And tonight, there's going to be wine."

Four days after the attic incident, as Zoe thought of it, she stopped by Let's Do Tea for scones on her way to her friend Jen's place. One of the advantages of working from home was that her time was pretty much her own. If she wanted to get her work done at two in the morning, no one cared. The downside, of course, was the fact that no one would know if she was mummifying in her attic.

No matter how many times she reminded herself that she'd figured out a way to escape and now was fine, she couldn't shake the feeling of having stared down her own mortality—and blinked. Or maybe her general unease had nothing to do with attic near death. Maybe it was more about feeling so incredibly isolated.

All her old work friends had either relocated with the company to San Jose or found other work. Her dad was a great guy and local, but still her dad. It wasn't as if they were going to go shopping together. She worked at home and rarely had a reason to leave. Somehow in the past few months, she'd kind of lost the concept of having a life.

Breaking up with Chad was a big part of that, she told herself as she walked to the bakery counter to choose her scones. Not that it hadn't been the right thing to do. But now she was left at loose ends.

She picked out a dozen scones—buttermilk, blueberry and white chocolate chip—before returning to her car and driving the handful of blocks to Jen's house.

The mid-March air was cool, the sky clear. The Pacific Ocean less than a half mile away kept the beach community of Mischief Bay regulated, temperature-wise. Even in winter, it rarely got below sixty, although it could be damp.

She turned onto Jen's street, then pulled into the circular drive. The big, one-level ranch-style house sprawled across an oversize lot. The landscaping was mature, the roof on the newer side. In the land of escalating home prices, especially in this neighborhood, Jen and her husband, Kirk, had hit the housing jackpot.

Zoe wrinkled her nose as she remembered that good fortune had come at a terrible price. Almost two years ago, Jen's father had suddenly passed away. Jen's mother, Pam, had given the house to her daughter and moved into a condo. Zoe would guess, given the choice, Jen would rather be back in her small apartment and have her dad around. Zoe knew she would give anything to have her mother with her again.

"That whole attic thing has pushed me into morbid land,"

she murmured as she got out of the car. "Time for a mood shift."

She walked to the front door and knocked softly. A bright yellow hand-painted sign above the doorbell warned My Baby Is Sleeping.

A few seconds later, Jen Beldon opened the door. "Zoe," she said, sounding surprised. "Was I expecting you?" Jen, a pretty brunette with hazel eyes, groaned. "It's Thursday. I'm sorry. I'm a horrible friend. Come in."

Zoe hugged Jen, then held up the box. "I bring terrible food that neither of us should be eating, so that makes me a bad friend, too."

"Thank God. Lately all I want is carbs. The more, the better."

Jen led the way into the big, open kitchen. She put water in a kettle, then set it on the stove. After collecting a teapot from a cupboard, she scooped loose tea into a strainer.

"The days go by so fast," she said. "I can't seem to keep track of where I am, timewise. There are always a thousand things to do."

Jen wore a baggy T-shirt over black yoga pants. She had on white socks but no shoes. There were dark shadows under her eyes, as if she hadn't been sleeping, and the extra weight she'd gained carrying her eighteen-month-old son, Jack, was firmly in place.

"Kirk's so busy at work. I know he's happy, but his hours are erratic. And don't get me started on his partner."

"Still making you nervous?" Zoe asked sympathetically.

"Every single day. The man is a walking, breathing cowboy. He has no regard for the rules. I don't know why he hasn't been disciplined or fired."

Six months ago Kirk had left the relative safety of the Mischief Bay Police Department for a detective position at the LAPD. His partner was a reckless old-timer named Lucas.

Jen lived in fear that Lucas was going to lead Kirk into dangerous situations.

Zoe put the scones on a plate and set them on the table. She collected butter from the refrigerator, along with milk for the tea.

She glanced at her friend. "Should I ask about Jack?"

Tears immediately filled Jen's eyes. Her friend looked away, then back at her. "He's the same. Bright, happy, loving. I just wish…"

The kettle began to whistle. Jen turned and snapped off the heat, then poured the boiling water into the teapot.

Zoe took her place at the table and held in a sigh. Jack was a sweet baby who had reached every milestone exactly when he was supposed to. Rolling over, sitting up, crawling, reaching for objects. The only thing he hadn't done was talk. He rarely vocalized, instead getting his point across in other ways.

Jen had grown increasingly worried over the past few months, convinced something was wrong. Zoe didn't have enough experience to offer an opinion, but as every specialist Jen had been to had said Jack would talk when he was ready, she thought maybe her friend was making herself crazy over something that might not be a problem.

Jen poured the tea, then brought the baby monitor from the counter to the table and took her seat. "I'm still doing a lot of home testing with Jack," she said. "He does so well on nearly everything. I think he's bright. He's not regressing, at least not that I can see. I have another specialist I'm going to take him to next week." She sighed and reached for a scone. "Maybe it's nutritional." She waved the scone. "I'd never let him have this. I'm so careful with his diet." She sighed heavily. "I just wish I could sleep. But it's hard. I worry."

"Of course you do. You have a lot going on."

"Tell me about it. I had to let the cleaning service go. They were using a spray cleaner. Can you believe it? I told them they could only use steam and those special cloths I bought. What if the fumes from the chemicals are affecting Jack's development? What if it's the paint on the walls or the varnish on the floors?"

"What if he's fine?"

Zoe spoke without thinking, then wanted to call the words back. Jen's gaze turned accusing and her mouth pulled into a straight line.

"Now you sound like my mother," she snapped. "Look, I know it's not a big deal to you, but Jack is my child and I'm his only advocate, okay? I know there's something wrong. I just know it. If you had children of your own, you'd understand."

Zoe had been looking forward to her chocolate chip scone. Now she found herself unable to take a bite.

"I'm sorry," she said. "I only meant to help."

"You didn't."

She waited, wondering if Jen was going to apologize for *her* snipey remarks, but her friend only continued to glare at her.

"Then I should go," Zoe said quietly. She rose and started for the door.

Jen followed her. Before Zoe walked out of the house, Jen touched her arm.

"Look, I'm sorry. I just don't want to hear that Jack's okay from one more person. He's not and I seem to be the only one who sees that. I'm drowning and no one sees it. Please understand."

"I'm trying," Zoe told her. "Do you want me to come back next week?"

"What?" Jen's eyes filled with tears again. "No, don't say that. You're my best friend. I need you. Please come back. We'll do better next time. It'll be great. Promise?"

Zoe nodded slowly. The words were there, but they weren't best friends anymore. They hadn't been in a while.

"I'll see you then," she said and made her way to her car.

When she was driving away she realized that she'd never had the chance to tell Jen about what had happened to her in the attic or anything else that was going on.

Everything was different now, she thought. There was no Chad. Jen was slipping away. Zoe felt as if she was living in total isolation. If she didn't want to die alone, then she was going to have to make some changes in her life. Step one, she told herself, find a handyman to fix her attic stairs. Step two, get her butt out of the house and make new friends.

Jennifer Beldon knew that every mother thought her child was special, but in her case, it was genuinely true. John Beldon, who was named after his late grandfather and who went by Jack, was handsome, happy and oh, so bright. At eighteen months old he could walk and run, albeit unsteadily. He could stack large blocks, understand words like *up* or *down* or *hot*. He could laugh, point to objects she named, recognize the sound of his father's car pulling in the drive and kick a ball with surprising accuracy. He was careful with his grandmother's very odd and delicate little dog and even washed his hands himself—sort of—before meals.

What he didn't, couldn't or wouldn't do was talk.

Jen sat on the family room floor with Jack across from her. Classical music played in the background. The rug was organic cotton and plush enough to provide a little protection when there was a tumble. Sunlight streamed through steam-cleaned windows. As far as the eye could see, the nose could smell and the lungs could breathe, there were no chemicals of any kind.

She held up a simple drawing of a spider. Jack clapped and pointed. The second drawing had all the spider parts, but they were put together incorrectly, creating more of a random pattern than an insect. Jack frowned and shook his head, as if he knew something wasn't right. She showed the spider drawing a second time and got a happy grin.

"You are a smart boy," she said cheerfully. "Yes, that's a spider. Good for you."

Jack nodded, then patted his mouth with his palm. She immediately recognized the signal, then glanced at the clock on the wall. It was eleven-thirty.

"Are you hungry?" As she asked the question, her stomach growled. "Me, too. I'm going to make lunch. Want to watch?"

Jack laughed and crawled the short distance between them. Once he reached her, he stood and held out his arms for a hug.

She pulled him close and let the warmth of his little body comfort her. He was such a good boy, she thought, her heart overflowing with gratitude. Smart, loving, sweet. If only…

She pushed that thought away. The day was going well. She would focus on that and deal with the rest of it later.

She rose and together they headed for the kitchen. Jack made a beeline for the small activity table set up in the corner by the pantry. There were all kinds of things to keep him busy while she cooked. A giant pad of paper and chubby, nontoxic crayons, a blue-and-green "lunch box" that played music and talked about the various items he loaded in it. She'd wanted to put in a small play kitchen, but Kirk had objected. When she'd pointed out that it was perfectly fine for boys to cook, he'd insisted on equal time, with a play workbench, and even though their kitchen was large, it couldn't hold both toys and still leave room for her.

She carefully pulled the gate closed behind her, so Jack couldn't go exploring without her, then plugged her phone into the small speaker docking station. After starting Pandora, she scrolled to one of their favorite stations.

"In the mood for disco?" she asked with a smile.

Jack looked at her and grinned.

The Bee Gees' "You Should Be Dancing" started. She

moved her hips. Jack did the same—kind of—he was a little awkward, but still pretty coordinated for his age. She began stepping from side to side, moving backward toward the sink. Jack laughed and clapped his hands. She spun twice and he did the same.

Fifteen minutes later, they were sitting down to their meal. She'd pulled Jack's high chair close. Disco music still played from the overhead speakers.

His lunch was a small portion of tender chicken and a cauliflower-potato fritter modified from a recipe she'd found online. She used an air fryer to make sure it wasn't greasy, with eggs and a bit of organic cheddar acting as a binder. She made them smaller than the recipe called for so they were the perfect size for him to pick up. While Jack was pretty good with a spoon, she found that the meal went better when he could simply pick up everything on his plate.

She had leftover salmon from the night before and a couple of crackers. She probably should have made herself a salad, but it was so much effort. Kirk would tell her to buy one of those premade bags, which probably made sense, but seemed a little wasteful to her.

"Today is Wednesday," she said between bites. "It's nice that it's so sunny outside. We can go for a walk later and see the ocean."

Everything she'd read said to be sure to talk to Jack as if he were capable of understanding. Just because he wasn't talking didn't mean he wasn't hearing. She was careful to always use complete sentences and plenty of specific nouns. Lulu, her mom's pet, wasn't just a dog. She was a Chinese crested. Food was specific, too. Bread, apple, rice cereal. The same with his toys.

Every second he was awake, she knew where he was and what he was doing. She was always looking for opportunities to stimulate his brain, to help him grow. She knew all the warning signs of autism and except for his inability to speak, Jack didn't have any of them. But there was a reason he didn't talk and a thousand things that could still go wrong. That reality kept her up at night.

After lunch, Jack carefully carried his plate back to the kitchen. She took it from him and put it on the counter, next to hers. She drew the gate shut again and turned off the music. Because a child had to get used to quiet, as well.

She plugged in her earbuds and, as she did every day after lunch, tuned into the police scanner app. It was the usual barrage of chatter. Two officers being sent to investigate possible domestic abuse. Someone checking in with dispatch to see if they wanted breadsticks with marinara. She glanced at the counter to make sure she'd put all the food away. Seconds later, her entire body went cold.

The words came too fast for her to follow what was happening, but enough of them got through. *Two detectives. Shooter. Officer down.*

Kirk! Panic flooded her, making her heart race. She couldn't breathe, couldn't catch her breath. Even knowing she wasn't having a heart attack didn't stem the growing sense of dread. Her chest was tight and even though she was inhaling, she couldn't seem to get air into her lungs.

Crackers are a tasty snack.

The singing voice from Jack's toy cut through the growing fog in her brain. She glanced at her son, who pushed the square of plastic crackers into the lunch box, then laughed.

She hung on to the counter and told herself to stay calm. If Kirk was the injured officer, she would be getting a phone call. A squad car would show up to take her to wherever it was family went in times like this. In the meantime, she dialed Kirk's cell, but it went right to voice mail—as it always did when he was working.

She desperately wanted to turn on the TV, but couldn't.

Jack couldn't be exposed to the news. It was too violent. She didn't know what memories he might retain. Besides, everything she'd read or heard said to limit television at his age.

She carefully scraped the food into her composting bin, then put the plates in the dishwasher. She wiped down the counters, all the while listening to the scanner. There were no details, just more jumbled information. No mention of names. Just a repeat of what she'd heard before.

When the kitchen was clean, she reluctantly took out her earpieces. She didn't want to wear them in front of Jack. He needed to know she was paying attention to him. She was still having trouble breathing and was wracked by occasional tremors. Going to the beach was out of the question now. She had to stay home in case the worst had happened.

Jen took Jack into the backyard. She kept the slider open so she could hear if someone came to the front door. She had her cell phone in her pocket. For an endless hour, she played with her son, all the while waiting anxiously for some bit of news from Kirk. About one forty-five, they headed inside, where she gave Jack a light snack of pumpkin dip with a quarter of a sliced apple. When he was done with that, they went into his room to begin his afternoon prenap ritual.

She pulled the curtains shut while he picked out which stuffed animal he wanted with him. Winnie the Pooh usually won and today was no exception. She helped Jack take off his shoes, then got him into bed. She sat next to him and turned on the night-light/music box she played every afternoon. The familiar music made him yawn. One story later, he was already asleep. Jen turned on the baby monitor, then slowly backed out of the room. Once the door was closed, she ran into the family room and turned on the TV.

All the local stations were back to their regular programming. She switched over to CNN but Wolf Blitzer was talking about an uptick in the stock market. She raced to her desk and waited impatiently for her laptop to boot, then went to her local affiliate's website and scanned the articles.

She found one on the shooting, but it hadn't been updated in thirty minutes. There was no news beyond a suspect shooting at two detectives. The suspect had been taken into custody. There was no information on a downed officer—which meant what? No one had been shot? They didn't want to say anything until family had been notified?

She tried Kirk's cell again and went right to voice mail. She told herself he was fine. That he would be home soon. She needed to get moving, to tackle all the chores that piled up during the day. Jack's nap was only about an hour. The quiet time was precious.

Only she couldn't seem to move—mostly because her chest hurt and she still wasn't breathing well. Panic loomed, threatening to take her over the edge. She needed her husband. She needed her son to start talking. She needed someone to keep the walls around her from closing in.

Her eyes burned but she didn't dare cry. If she started, she might not stop and that would frighten Jack. She didn't want any of her craziness to rub off on him. She still remembered being little and having her mother always worry and how that had upset her.

She forced herself to stand. She had to plan menus for the next few days then create a grocery list. There was laundry and the sheets needed to be changed. She would just keep putting one foot in front of the other. Kirk was fine. He had to be fine. If he wasn't—

She sank back into her chair and wrapped her arms around her midsection. She was going to throw up. Or maybe faint. She couldn't breathe, couldn't—

Her phone chirped, notifying her of an incoming text message from Kirk.

She straightened and grabbed her cell off the desk. Relief poured through her as she read and she sucked a lungful of air.

Hey, babe. Did you want me to pick up something at the grocery store? Sorry, but I can't remember what you told me this morning. Love you.

Jen made a half laugh, half sob sound and typed back a response. Kirk was okay. Order was restored.

She stood and ran through her mental to-do list. Sheets, grocery planning and the list, if she had time. Then five minutes online looking for information on someone who could tell her why her little boy refused to talk.

Chapter Two

"It's not gonna happen."

Pam Eiland allowed herself a slightly smug smile as she rolled her shoulders back to appear more in charge. Because she knew she was right. "Oh, please, Ron. You're doubting me? You know better."

Ron, the blond, thirtysomething plant guy and part-time coach of the UCLA volleyball team, shook his head. "You can't grow bush monkey flower in a container. These guys like rocky soil, lots of sun and excellent drainage."

"All three conditions can be created in a container. I've done it before."

"Not with bush monkey flower."

What was it about men? They always thought they knew better. One would think after nearly two years of her buying plants he *swore* wouldn't grow in containers on her condo deck and then making them flourish, he would be convinced. One might think that, but one would be wrong.

"You said that about the hummingbird sage and Shaw's agave," she pointed out.

"No way. I totally told you Shaw's agave would grow in a container."

The man was incredibly intense about his plants. Intense

and wrong. "I'm going to buy the bush monkey flower and there's nothing you can do to stop me."

"You don't even have a plan," he complained. "You buy your plants based on the names."

That was true. "When my grandson asks me about my plants, I want to be able to say they *all* have funny names."

"That's a ridiculous reason to buy a plant."

"So says a man who doesn't have children. One day you'll understand."

Ron didn't look convinced. He collected the three one-gallon plants, shaking his head at the same time. "You're a stubborn woman."

"You're actually not the first person to tell me that." She handed over her credit card. "You'll deliver these later?"

"I will."

The words were more growl than agreement. Poor guy, she thought. He didn't take defeat well. He would be even more crushed when she showed him pictures of the flourishing plants.

After returning her credit card to her, he tore off the receipt for her to sign, then he held out his hands, palms up. Of course. Because Pam and her regular purchases were not the real draw for Ron.

Pam opened her large tote. "Come here, little girl."

A head popped out. Lulu, her Chinese crested, glanced around, spotted Ron, yelped with excitement then scrambled toward him. Ron picked her up and cradled her against his broad chest.

The tiny dog looked incredibly out of place against Ron's How's Your Fern Hanging T-shirt. Lulu was slim, hairless—except for the white plumes that covered the top of her head, her lower legs and tail—and wearing a pink sundress. The latter as much to protect her delicate skin as to make a fashion statement.

Ron held her gently, whispering into her ear and getting doggy kisses in return. It was an amazing thing, Pam thought. Lulu was a total guy magnet. Seriously—the more macho the guy, the more he was attracted to the tiny dog. Pam's friends teased her she should put that power to good use. Which was not going to happen. She was old enough to be Ron's...

She glanced at her plant guy. Okay, maybe not mother, but certainly his much older babysitter. Not that the age thing mattered. She wasn't interested in any man. She'd lost the great love of her life two years ago. While she would never forget John, the sharpest pain had faded, leaving wonderful memories. They were enough.

Ron reluctantly handed Lulu back. "She's a sweet girl."

"She is."

"You're wrong about the bush monkey flower."

"When I prove to you I'm right, I will mock you for your lack of faith."

Ron flashed her a grin—one she was sure sent hundreds of coeds swooning. "We'll see."

Pam put Lulu back in the tote, slung it over her shoulder and headed out onto the sidewalk. It was mid-March. She was sure there was a massive snowstorm happening somewhere in the country but here in Mischief Bay it was sunny and a balmy seventy-two. There were skateboarders practicing their moves in the park, people on bikes and mothers out with small children.

For a second she thought about calling her daughter and suggesting she and Jack join Lulu and herself for a quick lunch. An excellent idea in theory, if not in practice. Because Jen would obsess about Jack getting too much sun or not the right food. She would also fuss about the table being clean enough, and then point out that it was wrong for Pam to bring her *dog* into a restaurant. And while Lulu was technically not allowed, she stayed in her tote and never made a sound. Which was more than could be said for a lot of the human patrons.

The point being... Pam sighed. While she would very much like to spend an afternoon with her grandson the same couldn't be said about her daughter. Oh, she loved Jen. She would die for Jen or donate an organ. She wished her only the best. But—and this was something Pam hadn't admitted to anyone but Lulu—since Jack had been born, Jen wasn't very much fun.

She was obsessed with her child. Was he growing? Was he sitting up when he should? Did he maintain eye contact? Being around her was exhausting and stressful. And thinking that probably made her a bad person. She knew what it was to worry about kids. She'd been a bit of an obsessive mother herself. But nothing like this.

She reached into her tote and patted Lulu. "What do you suggest?" she asked her little dog. "Should we live with our flaws and go get ice cream?"

Lulu barked. Pam took that as a yes. She would, she promised herself, gird her loins and visit her daughter in the morning. But for this afternoon, she would enjoy the beach and the fun of repotting her bush monkey flowers. Later, there would be ice cream.

Off to later switch down.

Zoe wrinkled her nose. She wasn't sure where to place the blame. A faulty translation program or human error. Either way, the message was getting lost. She glanced at the second document open on her large computer screen and began to type.

To turn off the unit, press down on the power switch. After thirty minutes in standby mode, it will shut off automatically. Because if you're stupid enough to walk away without turning off an incredibly hot iron, we will do our very best to keep you from burning down your house. Personally I'm not sure you deserve that much consideration, but no one asked me.

Zoe allowed herself a brief fantasy that she would simply hit the send button. If only. Then she carefully and responsibly deleted the last two sentences and moved on to the next section of the instruction manual.

She translated more semi-English to the real thing. This week's work was small appliances. The week before had been some high-tech medical equipment. That had been more challenging. It wasn't so much that the original manuals weren't written in English, it was that they'd been written by people who spoke in code and abbreviations. Technicians in hospitals were busy with pressing problems. They didn't have time to figure out what they thought the instructions meant. They had to do their job and move on to the next patient.

Zoe made that possible. She translated manuals from their original gibberish to something easily understood. She knew that for the most part the average consumer never bothered cracking a manual, but if they happened to read one of hers, they would find easy-to-understand instructions written in a way that made sense.

She reached the bottom of the section, then rose to stretch. Too much computer time made her back stiff and her legs ache.

"Wasn't I supposed to be getting more exercise?" she asked out loud, then turned to Mason, who was asleep on the old club chair in the sunniest corner of her small home office. "Did you not want to talk about it now? Should I point out I'm the only person who feeds you, and I'm the only one who loves you? So if something happens to me, you're going to be swimming in regret."

She waited, but Mason didn't even twitch an ear. Right before she reached down to scratch him under the chin, he gave her a little *murr* of greeting and began to purr.

"Ha! I knew you were listening. And yes, I get how pathetic it is that we're having this conversation."

Her phone rang. Saved by the ringtone, she thought as she glanced at the screen, smiled and pushed the talk button.

"Hey, Dad."

"Why don't I ever see you? What are you hiding from me? Did you get a tattoo? Shave your head?"

She laughed. "Why does it have to be about my appearance? Is this a woman thing? Are you discriminating against my gender, assuming that we're all about how we look? Women have brains, Dad."

"Zoe, I beg you. No talk of female equality. It's barely ten in the morning." Her father chuckled. "As for your brain, I suspect you have too much of one. I'm checking up on you because I'm your father. Things are good?"

Zoe thought about "the attic incident" but decided not to mention it to her dad. He would worry and she didn't need one more thing in her life. Well, truthfully she needed a lot more things in her life, but his worrying wasn't one of them.

"I'm fine."

"What's going on?"

"Work."

"And when you're not working?" Her father sighed. "Please don't say you're hanging out with Mason. He's a cat. He does nothing but sleep and eat."

"Sometimes he poops."

"Yes, and it's a moment to be treasured by all of us." There was a pause. "Zoe, are you getting out at all? You're no longer going into an office and now Chad is gone. I'm glad you finally dumped him, but you're young. You should be having fun."

Uh-oh. She could hear the worry building up a head of steam. "Dad, I'm great." She emphasized the last word. "And busy." She desperately tried to think of something that would make her sound busy. "Oh, you know what? I'm having a barbecue next Sunday. You should come. It will be fun."

"A barbecue?"

"Yup. At, ah, four. You can bring a date, assuming she's age appropriate."

Her father laughed. "We have different definitions of that."

"Yes, we do and yours is icky."

"I never dated anyone younger than you."

"You don't get points for that. Most people would tell you dating someone younger than me shouldn't even be a consideration."

"You know I gave up young women years ago. I'm not seeing anyone, but if I were, I promise she would be age appropriate."

Zoe sank onto the floor next to Mason's chair. "Dad, you haven't had anyone in your life in a while. Why is that?"

"I want something more. I'll know when I find her. Until then, I'm happily single."

Zoe wondered when the change had occurred. If she had to guess, she would say it was when her mother had died. While her parents had been divorced for years, they'd always stayed friends. Her father had been nearly as devastated as Zoe by the loss.

"You need to get back to work, young lady," he said. "I'll see you next Sunday. Can I bring anything?"

She smiled. "The usual."

"Tequila it is."

Jen heard the garage door open and jumped to her feet. "Daddy's home!"

Jack's eyes widened and he clapped his hands together. For

a brief, heart-stopping second, she thought he was going to say something. Anything would be great. She so wouldn't care if *Da-da* was his first word. But he only laughed and got unsteadily to his feet before running toward the far end of the family room.

Jen was feeling a little giddy herself, but her excitement was more about knowing that her husband had made it safely through another day. His working for the Mischief Bay Police Department hadn't bothered her very much. Nothing bad ever happened in the small, family-oriented beach community. But the LAPD was totally different. There were over eight million people in the metro area and some days Jen agonized that too many of them were after her husband.

Kirk walked into the house. He and Jack rushed toward each other. She watched as Kirk scooped up his son and swung him around. Jack squealed and held out his arms and waved his hands. Then Kirk pulled him close and they hung on to each other.

Seeing father and son together always filled her with love and gratitude. Jack took after his dad—both with red hair and blue eyes. Her two men, she thought happily. As long as Kirk kept coming home.

He kissed Jack's forehead, then walked toward her. "How's my best girl?" he asked before kissing her on the mouth.

"Good."

She leaned into him for their ritual greeting of a family hug. Jack grabbed her hair and pulled her close. For several heartbeats, she allowed herself to feel only the perfection of the moment. This was everything she wanted, she told herself. They were all going to be okay.

Then Jack squirmed to be put down. Kirk stepped back and the spell was broken. He set his son down.

"How was your day?"

While there hadn't been anything scary on the police scanner in the past few days, she'd still had her share of worrying about Jack. Her panic attacks were getting more regular, at least one or two a day. But she didn't want to mention them to Kirk. He didn't need to be concerned about her. Not when he could be shot at any second. Telling herself he was a detective and not a beat cop didn't help her relax.

"Good. Jack and I went to the park and he met a little boy there. They played well together." Something that made her happy. She didn't want to put Jack into day care, but she didn't have any friends with kids. She knew the importance of socialization for a child his age. She was either going to have to suck it up about day care or get him in a playgroup. But that wasn't something she would worry about today.

Kirk headed for his study where Jen knew he would lock up his sidearm and badge in the small wall safe they'd had installed when Jack was born.

"I invited Lucas over for dinner," Kirk called from the other room.

Jen glared in his general direction. No doubt her husband had deliberately waited until he was out of sight to share that nugget.

"Tonight?"

He returned, his smile winning. "Yes, for tonight. Is that okay?"

Okay? No, it wasn't okay. It was never okay when Lucas came over, but it was so much worse when Kirk sprung it on her. She was a mess—she didn't have on makeup or nice clothes and she honestly couldn't remember if she'd showered that morning. She'd planned on a simple, healthy dinner, neither of which her husband's partner would appreciate.

But Lucas was Kirk's best hope at coming home alive every day. She drew in a breath and forced a smile. "It's fine, although I doubt he's going to want what I have ready for dinner."

"He said he would bring steaks."

"From where?"

Kirk looked blank. "The store?"

So just regular beef from an unknown source. Not the grass-fed, organic, certified meat she bought at a specialty store fifteen miles away.

"Wonderful," she said between gritted teeth.

He moved close. "Honey, you don't always have to have a family tree to eat a hamburger."

There were a thousand different responses to that condescending statement. "I want to give Jack the best start possible."

"I know and I appreciate all the work you do. But maybe it's okay to lighten up now and then."

Sure. Because it was always about her having to change, not other people. Kirk would let Lucas do anything he wanted. Jen knew he respected his partner, but there were times when she wanted to scream. Of course the need to scream wasn't limited to Lucas.

"I need to go get changed," she said. "Then figure out some sides for the steaks."

"You look fine. Lucas won't care."

She was sure that last part was true. After all, she was far too old to interest him. But that wasn't the point. "I'll be right back."

Fifteen minutes later she'd changed into jeans and a pretty blouse. After applying makeup basics, she'd pulled her hair out of its ponytail and brushed it. She needed highlights and a decent cut, but neither was happening today.

On her way back to the kitchen, she mentally reviewed the food in her refrigerator. She put away the free-range chicken she'd been marinating, then tested a couple of avocados for the salad. There was a bag of French fries in the freezer and organic frozen chicken fingers, because while Jack could eat ground meat, he wasn't ready for steak.

Kirk had already started the barbecue and wiped down the patio table. She'd just collected plates to take outside when he stuck his head in. "Lucas is here."

Jen mentally braced herself for the chaos that was to follow. Lucas was a larger-than-life character who dominated every room he entered. Despite her misgivings about him, from all that she'd heard, he had an excellent reputation on the force. He was a decorated veteran officer. He was also a completely selfish, egotistical man who didn't give a damn about anyone but himself. And he was her husband's partner, so there was no escaping him.

She walked out into the backyard. The gate was open and Kirk had walked out to greet his buddy. The incongruity of her handsome husband holding his toddler son and the ridiculously expensive two-seater convertible that pulled into their driveway was telling. Jen had no idea how Lucas could afford the Mercedes—it had to cost as much as he made in a year. Maybe more. But she hadn't asked, mostly because she didn't want to know.

She moved toward the gate. To do otherwise would signal her feelings and she didn't want to make things awkward for Kirk.

Lucas was around fifty, slim and tan. His hair was white, his eyes a startling deep green and his smile easy. She'd never seen him in anything but jeans, a long-sleeved shirt and cowboy boots. When he was working he threw on a sport coat. She supposed most people would say he was good-looking. She thought of him as more dissolute. He lived hard, drank often and had a string of incredibly young women in his life. Jen disapproved of him on principle and getting to know him hadn't changed her opinion at all.

"Hey, Jen," he called out to her. He nodded at Kirk and

winked at Jack who clapped happily. For reasons Jen couldn't begin to understand, her son adored Lucas.

"I come bearing gifts." Lucas walked around to the passenger side of his small car and pulled out a grocery bag, an Amazon box and a six-pack of beer. "Something for everyone," he joked as he walked to the gate and handed her the packages.

She stared at the Amazon box and told herself it couldn't be nearly as bad as she imagined—then hoped she wasn't lying. He turned back to Kirk. Jack laughed, then flung himself at Lucas, fearless at the midair transfer.

"How's my man?" Lucas asked, holding Jack comfortably. "High five."

He held up his hand. Jack smacked his palm against Lucas's, then laughed even more.

They went into the backyard. Lucas put Jack down and the toddler ran around, shrieking. Jen did her best not to roll her eyes. This always happened. Lucas overexcited the boy. Later, she would have trouble getting Jack to sleep.

Lucas took the Amazon box and the beer from her, then winked. A gesture of friendship or mockery? With him, she was never sure. He crossed to the built-in outdoor kitchen, opened a drawer and pulled out a bottle opener. After popping the top on two beers, he hesitated, then glanced at her.

"Did you—" he began.

"No. I'm fine."

Like most pregnant women, Jen had completely given up alcohol, but even after Jack was born, she hadn't gone back. She was too afraid her son might need her. She had to be alert and vigilant at all times.

Lucas stuck the rest of the six-pack in the minifridge, then drew a pocketknife out of his pocket. He slit the tape on the box and set it on the ground in front of Jack.

Her son squatted down and peered inside. Slowly, his eyes

widened and his mouth turned up in delight. He pulled out a blue-and-white... Jen squinted. What on earth?

"That is a genuine B. Woofer guitar," Lucas told him. He removed the packaging, then settled the strap on Jack's small shoulder. The guitar hung down to his thighs.

"You hold it like this," Lucas told him, placing his hands on the neck and body. "See these buttons? When you push them, they make music. They're called chords. I'm sure your mom will teach you all about them."

Jen listened in dismay as she heard a full chord being played by the guitar. Apparently every button was a chord. They could be played individually or together. While that would be an excellent way to learn music, the noise potential was terrifying.

"And over here?" Lucas pointed. "There are prepro-grammed songs. A bunch of different ones. If you push the little dog button?" He winked at Jen again. "You get dog songs. Cool, huh?"

Jack looked unsure as he pushed the yellow button with the note on it. Sure enough a song began to play. His eyes lit up and he turned toward her, wanting to share the joy of the moment.

Jen smiled even as she looked at her husband and mur-mured, "I'm going to kill him."

"It's a great toy."

"You're not going to be stuck home with it." She glanced back at the guitar. "Did he check out the age suggestions? That seems really advanced for Jack."

Kirk put his arm around her. "Honey, let it go for now. Later you can check it for small parts. Lucas is a great guy and he adores Jack. That should be enough."

Why? Why should it be enough? Why shouldn't Kirk's partner have to abide by the rules when he was at their home? Why did Lucas always make her feel like the most boring, traditional person on the planet? He was the frat boy, party guy and she was the house mother. It wasn't fair.

She wanted to stomp her foot, but that wouldn't accomplish anything. Instead she smiled tightly, murmured a quick, "Thanks, Lucas," then escaped into the kitchen.

The bag of groceries he'd brought contained three massive steaks, a large container of blue cheese potato salad and, kind of surprising, two jars of organic toddler food. Root vegetables with turkey and quinoa.

Kirk walked into the kitchen. He took the jar from her. "See. He's not all bad. You like this brand."

"Maybe."

Lucas walked in with Jack on his hip. Jen was grateful that the guitar had been left outside. She would put it away and bring it out only when Jack was rested. Teaching him about music would be good, she thought reluctantly. She was sure she'd read somewhere that music appreciation helped with math skills.

"Someone has a dirty diaper," Lucas said, handing Jack to his father. "Uncle duty only goes so far."

Kirk laughed. "I'll take care of it."

He reached for his son and carried him out of the room. Jen found herself alone with Lucas and unsure what to say.

"Thank you for the steaks," she began. "And the salad and baby food."

"I hope it's the right one. I know you want him only eating good stuff, so I asked a lady at the grocery store."

"Did you also get her number?" The words popped out before she could stop them.

Lucas leaned against the counter and raised an eyebrow. "She was married, Jen. I don't date married women. Plus, she was too old." His mouth twitched. "Probably thirty."

"How depressing for you." She faced him. "Why do they have to be so young?"

"They're uncomplicated."

"Whatever do you talk about?"

"Who talks?"

Her smile was involuntary. Fine—if he was going to sass her, she could sass right back. She folded her arms across her chest. "Great. So there's six minutes filled. What do you do the rest of the time?"

He winked. "I share my life's wisdom."

"You're full of crap."

"Maybe, but I'm having a great time." He lifted a shoulder. "One day they'll stop taking my calls, but until then, it's good to be me."

"Don't you ever get lonely?"

"Nope. That would require an emotional depth I don't have." He flashed her a winning smile. "Don't try to reform me. It's not going to happen. I like my life and don't see any reason to change."

Which was all fine and good, but she didn't like that he was so different from her husband. What if he tried to lead Kirk astray? What if Kirk was intrigued by all those young possibilities?

She glanced toward the hallway, then back at Lucas.

"I don't understand why you have to date twenty-year-olds, but that's not my business. What I need to know is that you'll take care of him. If something bad happens."

Lucas's smile faded. "You have my word, Jen."

Which could have reassured her, only she didn't know what his word was worth.

Chapter Three

Mischief in Motion was a well-known Pilates studio in town. The storefront was light and bright and probably appealing to people who, you know, liked exercise. Zoe had done her best to avoid anything that would make her sweat so she'd never ventured inside. Until today.

Not only did she have to work on her muscle mass, as demonstrated by the *attic incident*, she wanted to see if Jen's mom was still a regular. She and Pam had always gotten along, and Pam kind of reminded her of her own mother. These days, a little maternal TLC seemed like a good thing. And if a little Jen-focused advice was shared, as well, all the better. To be honest, Zoe had no idea what to do about her friend. They were drifting apart and she didn't know how to make that stop.

Wearing her newly purchased discount store Pilates workout gear—aka black leggings and an oversize T-shirt, she went inside to register for the class.

There were four women there already, along with a perky redhead behind a small reception desk. Zoe had a brief impression of scary-looking equipment, too many mirrors and very fit clients. She thought of her own jiggly thighs and told herself that everyone would be so focused on themselves, they

wouldn't notice her at all. And if they did, they were probably too polite to say anything. Besides, she was here to get
in shape and everyone had to start somewhere and—

"Zoe?" Pam spotted her and crossed the room. "What are
you doing here?"

"I, ah, wanted to start working out some, ah, more than I
am and I'd heard you mention the class so I thought I'd try
it. Is that okay?"

Pam smiled, then hugged her. "Of course it is. I haven't
seen you in forever. How are you?"

"Good." Zoe hugged her back, allowing herself a second
to feel the Mom-goodness that flowed from Pam.

"Come on. Let's meet everyone."

Pam led her around the studio, introducing Zoe as, "My
daughter's friend and mine, too," which made Zoe feel good.
She did her best to focus on names and faces rather than trim
thighs and killer abs. She would get there—eventually.

Nicole, the owner of the exercise studio, was an attractive
blonde who couldn't be thirty. Pam mentioned something
about Nicole's son and new husband. Talk about having it
all, Zoe thought, determined to be inspired rather than de-
pressed by so much success in one fit package.

The class started on time. By minute three, Zoe knew that
she was going to die—right there on the wooden framed reformer. She would simply stop breathing or rip herself in two,
by accident, of course.

Nicole offered her a kind smile. "It takes a little getting
used to. Just do the best you can."

Zoe nodded because she was too out of breath to speak.

It wasn't that they were doing anything especially vigorous.
Instead it was the slow and controlled movements that left
her gasping. She was expected to hold positions for counts of
ten, then lower slowly. Or stand on some stupid moving plat-
form with straps whose only purpose seemed to be to kill her.

Fifty minutes later, she rolled off the reformer and onto the ground. Other people stood and maybe she would too, one day. But for now, she had to wait for her muscles to stop shaking.

Pam crouched next to her. "You okay?"

"No."

Pam laughed. "I know it's hard at first. Everything is confusing. You might want to try a few private lessons first, to get the basic movements down. The classes move at a pretty fast pace."

"Uh-huh." Wow—two syllables. Zoe was so proud.

She sat up, then pushed to her feet. Her thighs shook but she managed to stay standing.

Pam's lips twitched.

"It's okay," Zoe said, still breathing hard. "You can mock me. I get it."

"You'll do better next time." Pam put her arm around Zoe's shoulders. "Do you have time for lunch? I'd love to get caught up."

"Sure. That would be great."

Pam plucked at her fitted black tank top. "We're not exactly dressed for a restaurant. Let's get takeout and go back to my place instead."

"Perfect."

As they collected their bags, a little dog popped her head out of Pam's oversize tote.

"Lulu!" Zoe dropped to her knees, then winced as her leg muscles complained. Ignoring them, she held out her hands and the adorable hairless dog jumped into her embrace.

"Hey, you," Zoe said, snuggling with the odd creature. Lulu was part canine, part fashionista, part alien and all rock star. Today she had on a white lightweight sweater with tiny purple buttons down her back.

Lulu gave her cheerful kisses, then settled in for a good cuddle.

"You bring her to class?" Zoe asked.

"I take her everywhere. She's quiet and enjoys getting out. So what are you in the mood for, lunchwise?"

Pam's condo was big and bright, with a view of the Pacific Ocean. The building style was modern, which could have clashed with Pam's more traditional furniture, but the warm woods and comfortable fabrics blended nicely with the sharp edges and sleek design.

Pam lifted Lulu out of her tote before washing her hands and setting the small dining table by the patio door.

"It's still a little cool to eat outside," the other woman said. "We'll do that next time."

Zoe liked the sound of that—the promise of another meal together. She washed her hands, then helped by putting out napkins and taking the take-out cartons from Wok's Up out of the bags.

"I have iced tea," Pam said as she opened the refrigerator. "Diet soda, oh and that organic juice Jen likes Jack to have."

"Iced tea is fine. Thanks."

They sat across from each other. Lulu settled in her bed by the sofa.

"This is nice," Pam told her as she reached for her carton of Honey-Spicy Shrimp. "I'm so glad you came to class today." She wrinkled her nose. "You're going to be sore. Drink a lot of water and take ibuprofen. It will help."

"I promise." No way Zoe was going to forget that. She wanted to be able to move in the morning. She glanced around at the condo. "This place is really nice. Do you like living here?"

"I do. It took me a bit to settle in. It was an adjustment for both of us." She nodded at Lulu. "John and I lived in our house for over twenty years. But this is better. Manageable. I like being close to everything. Plus, now that I'm traveling more with my friends, it's easier to leave a condo than a house."

"I know Jen loves the house."

After Pam's husband had died, she'd moved into the condo and had given the large family home to Jen and Kirk. Zoe couldn't remember all the details, but she was pretty sure that Pam had bought the condo from a girlfriend who'd gotten married and moved into her new husband's place.

"She does," Pam said. "I'm glad it stayed in the family."

Zoe scooped chicken fried rice onto her plate. "The garden is so pretty. I'd like to do something like that at my place. Maybe a few raised beds. I'm not sure."

"Jen mentioned you'd bought a house. Are you liking it?"

"I am. It's different. I'm responsible for everything, which is strange after always being a renter. But it's good."

Except for the killer attic, she thought.

Pam looked at her. "How are things otherwise?"

A simple question. The expected response was to say things were just dandy. Perfect. Happy. Or, you know, fine. Which was what Zoe *planned* to say. What came out instead was, "Everything is a mess."

Pam's expression turned sympathetic. "Tell me."

"I just… I don't know. I'm so confused." She put down her fork. "Chad and I broke up a couple of months ago. Or rather I broke up with him. I feel good about the decision. It was the right thing to do."

"But?"

"But it's hard. We were together nearly five years." She had the wherewithal not to mention how it had started, or the problems they'd had, instead adding, "He's divorced, with two kids. I suddenly realized I'd met them exactly twice. Twice! He kept telling me that they needed to adjust, but I started to think he was really waiting for them to grow up and be on their own."

"I'm sorry."

"Me, too. I feel like I've wasted so much of my life on him. I've made choices because of him. Some were good, but some I'm really questioning." She stared at her plate for a second, then looked back at Pam. "I bought my house thinking we would live in it together. I assumed that was where we were going. My house has three bedrooms. Three! I bought bedrooms for kids I've met twice. And my job—I'm not sure that was right. Quitting teaching. I make more money now, but I don't love what I do. And I'm home alone all the time."

She drew in a breath. "I had stupid breakup sex with Chad a few weeks ago and when it was over, I felt sick to my stomach. I'm done with him. Done. But I reacted out of loneliness. I want what everyone wants—someone to love, a family. I don't want Chad back, but I resent the time I wasted. It was such a bad decision."

"You're being too hard on yourself," Pam told her firmly. "You loved him and believed in him. When you figured out what was wrong, you dumped his sorry ass."

Zoe smiled. "Thank you for that."

"You did. You moved on. Now keep moving on. Are you dating anyone?"

"No. I want to, but I'm kind of stuck. I don't meet any guys. I was with Chad for so long, I've kind of forgotten what I'm supposed to do. I guess I could go to a bar or something."

Zoe held in a shudder at the thought. "What's worse than not dating is that I've isolated myself. I don't know how it happened, but it did. Last week I got stuck in my attic. The door slammed shut and I couldn't get it open. I didn't have my phone with me. All I could think was that I was going to die and no one would miss me for weeks."

Pam's mouth twitched. "Weeks? Really?"

"Okay, days. But I could still be dead and Mason would eat my liver."

"Mason is?"

"My cat."

"Cats do love liver. Tell me about your work."

"I translate manuals into readable English. Sometimes the translation from foreign languages is difficult to understand, or the manuals are written by people who are seriously technical. I take that gibberish and make it understandable."

"So what don't you like?"

"Being by myself all the time. The company relocated to San Jose. Because of Chad, I didn't want to go. They offered to let me work at home rather than lose me and I said yes." Zoe dropped her head to her hands. "I'm such a fool."

"Do you want to go to San Jose now?"

"Not really. But I really miss being in an office." She raised her head. "I think about going back into teaching, but I'm not sure."

"What grade was it?"

"Junior high English."

Pam winced. "That had to be tough."

"I know, right? Sometimes I think about getting my master's but I'm not sure about that either. I'm lost and confused and I miss my mom."

Pam reached across the table and squeezed her hand, then released her. "Of course you do. How long has she been gone?"

"It was a year last month."

"I'm sorry. It's hard. For what it's worth, the good memories are always with you."

"Thanks. I like thinking about her. I always feel like she's close by." Zoe swallowed. "Sometimes I think she's really disappointed in me."

"She's not," Pam said firmly. "It's not wrong to love someone. What gets us in trouble is when we make bad decisions based on that love. But you got yourself out of the relationship and you're moving on."

"I hope so."

"Are you close to your dad?"

Finally a subject that wouldn't embarrass her. "I am. He's great, but you know, a guy. There are things I can't tell him."

"Sure, because then he'll want to fix things, and possibly beat the crap out of Chad."

Zoe smiled. "He could probably do it. My dad's in good shape."

Pam grinned. "There's a visual for you to hang on to. For the rest of it, stop thinking and start doing. The next time a nice, appropriate man asks you out, say yes. Look into getting your master's. Figure out if you want to go back to teaching or not. As for being alone too much, make plans with your friends. What do you and Jen do together?"

Zoe bit her lower lip. Talk about an awkward turn in the conversation. Jen was Pam's daughter. Zoe couldn't say that Jen had become…

Pam sighed. "I know what you're thinking."

"I doubt that."

"Jen has become something of a killjoy."

Zoe stared. "You know?"

"Everyone knows. I can't decide if I feel sorry for her or if she needs a good smack on the back of the head. I worried about my kids, maybe more than most, but nothing like this. She is obsessed with Jack."

"The not talking," Zoe murmured.

"The organic food. The cleaning products. Every time I go over, she asks me the last time Lulu got a bath. The only thing wrong with her son is that she won't leave him alone for five seconds. He's not talking because he doesn't have to." She paused. "Is that too harsh?"

"Not to me."

"Well, I can't say any of that to Jen. She would never forgive me. You're not going to rat me out, are you?"

Zoe made an X over her heart. "I won't, I swear."

"Good. Now, how do you feel?"

Zoe considered the question. "Better. I need to stop wallowing and start doing." She leaned forward. "I'm having a barbecue on Sunday. Would you like to come?"

"I'd love to. What time?"

Pam parked her SUV, collected her tote and headed into the offices of Moving Women Forward. MWF was housed in a small business park on the edge of Mischief Bay, about three thousand square feet that had been donated by a former client. Because of the cramped and shared office space, Pam did as much work out of her condo as she could. But every week or so, she had a meeting at the offices, either with staff or clients.

She greeted their volunteer manning the reception desk, then walked back to Bea Gentry's office.

Bea, the director of the organization and one of the women who had recruited Pam two years ago, was about Pam's age. She dressed in pantsuits and always wore a cameo on her lapel. Bea's oldest boy and Pam's youngest son had been best friends through high school.

Pam sat across from her and let Lulu out of her tote.

"You're looking smug," Bea said by way of greeting. "What have you been up to?"

Pam laughed. "I'm shocked that it shows, but you're right. I'm feeling very good about things. I might have found the right woman for Steven."

"I can't believe you're even looking. My kids would kill me if I tried."

"Not if you got it right. Besides, Steven needs me to meddle. He's finally given up his flavor of the week, which is great, but he's not getting serious about anyone either. It's time."

She knew part of the reason for Steven's change in behavior had been the death of his father. John's unexpected passing had affected them all. Pam had been stuck in a kind of grief that had threatened to overwhelm her, while Steven had taken over the family plumbing business years before he'd expected he would. At first the responsibility had weighed on him, but he'd quickly grown into the position and now was doing a great job as president of the company. Which meant it was time for him to find the right woman.

"I wouldn't have gone looking for someone for him," Pam said. "But if I happen to run into her, then that's hardly my fault."

"Uh-huh. I'll remind you of that when you have a total disaster on your hands. Remind you and say 'I told you so.'"

Pam laughed. "That's not going to happen."

Lulu finished exploring the room and trotted over to Bea, who scooped her up and held her close.

"How's my best girl?" she asked in a soft voice. "I like the buttons on your sweater. It takes a very fashion-forward girl to pull that off and, of course, you do."

Lulu gave her a kiss, then relaxed in her embrace. Pam supposed there were people who would say her dog was spoiled, and while that might be true, Lulu was a faithful companion who had been by her side every second after John's death. The little girl had missed her dad as much as everyone else in the family.

Pam shook off the memories and reached into her tote. This time she pulled out a file. "Tell me about Filia," she said, opening the folder.

"We helped her five years ago, to get her nail salon up and

running, and now she's thriving. I think you're going to like working with her."

Pam was sure her friend was right. Bea had always done a good job of matching clients with coordinators. Moving Women Forward had a simple mission statement—they were there to help female entrepreneurs. That was it. A simple, clear vision. If a woman wanted to start a business, MWF was there to offer advice on everything from what to expect start-up costs to be to how to get a business license. If a woman already had a business up and running, MWF would provide mentoring, assistance with figuring out how to do payroll, manage employees and inventory. There were even cash grants and loans available. The services themselves were provided free of charge, but the client had to be accepted first, and that wasn't easy.

Over the past couple of years Pam had learned that a lot of people *said* they wanted to open a business, but not very many of them were willing to put in the hard work required to make it happen. MWF insisted that clients take the first steps on their own—to show they were serious.

"I have a few ideas," Pam said. "Her plans are ambitious. Let's see if she can put them into action."

Pam worked for MWF as a volunteer mentor. She took on a handful of clients every year. She was their point person. If she couldn't answer a question, she would find someone who could. If the client was applying for a grant through MWF, Pam helped with the paperwork, then was her advocate through the process.

Filia hoped to expand her nail salon into a day spa. According to her paperwork, the space next door to her salon would be available in a few months. The location was good and she was already at capacity with her nail salon. It seemed to be the next logical step.

"I'll let you know how it goes," Pam said. She stood and looked at her dog. "You want to stay with Bea?"

Lulu wagged her tail and gave a little woof of agreement.

"Then I'll be back in about half an hour."

"If she gets restless, I'll take her for a walk," Bea promised.

"Thanks."

Pam walked down the short hallway to one of the small meeting rooms. Filia, a petite, dark-haired woman in her late thirties, was already there. She stood when Pam entered and offered a nervous smile.

Pam introduced herself and they shook hands. They both sat at a small, round table in the center of the room.

Pam left the file closed. There was no need to get into the weeds just yet. Better that she and Filia get to know each other.

"Bea tells me you want to expand your business. Tell me about that."

Filia's brown eyes brightened. "I started my nail business five years ago with two girls. Now I have fifteen. We're open seven days a week. Walk-ins and regulars. A year ago, I started offering chair massages for clients, either before or after their nail appointments. Six months ago, I began selling a skin care line. It's doing well."

Filia leaned forward. "My younger sister moved in with my family two years ago. She went to school to be an aesthetician. She's worked for a big spa for several months now. She would come work for me and maybe a couple of her friends. I know how I want the space next door to be. I have some of the money, but not enough. I need to get a loan."

Pam nodded. None of this was new information. She also knew that Filia was married and that her husband worked as a gardener. They had a ten-year-old daughter. Both of them had a high school education, but they planned to send their daughter to college. It was the American dream in living color.

"The first thing the bank is going to ask for is a business plan," Pam told her. "Do you know what that is?"

Filia nodded slowly. "I created one the first time I came here. I can put together an updated one for the new business."

Pam opened the folder and pulled out several sheets of paper. "Wonderful. The bank will want to know that you can cover your bills, including payroll, and pay back the loan. Once you have the basics taken care of, they'll look at whether or not they consider you a good risk."

There was also the possibility of a low-interest loan from MWF, but Pam wasn't going to mention that just yet. First she wanted to see if Filia was committed to do the work necessary to even apply for a bank loan. Not everyone was. But she had a feeling that the woman in front of her was going to be someone willing to do the work to get herself where she wanted to be.

Filia took the paperwork and looked it over. She smiled. "This is much more clear than the books from the library. Thank you."

"I'm glad." Pam handed over a business card. "This is my contact information. Why don't you take a week or so to get the first draft of the plan together? Once you have that, we'll meet again and I'll go over it with you."

She would take as much time as necessary to get it bank-ready. Once Filia showed she was willing to do what had to be done, Pam would be with her all the way.

"Thank you for your help." Filia clutched the paperwork tightly. "I'm going to make this happen. You'll see."

"I'm excited to work with you."

"I feel the same way." Filia smiled. "When my day spa opens, you can have the first facial."

Pam laughed. "I can't wait."

Chapter Four

"Do you think he's warm enough?" Jen asked her mother as she pushed the stroller along the boardwalk. It was sixty-eight degrees, which wasn't cold, but they were at the beach and there was a cool breeze off the ocean. She had on a light hoodie, but her mom was only in three-quarter sleeves.

"He's fine."

"I don't know."

Jen hesitated, then decided they were close enough to the carousel that she could wait to check on Jack. It wasn't as if he was crying or anything.

There weren't a lot of people hanging out at the Pacific Ocean Park, otherwise known as the POP. A few mothers out with their young children. A handful of businesspeople taking a late lunch. Most everyone else was busy with their lives. Midday walks at the beach were a luxury—one she should be grateful for.

Jen had read an article that said a spirit of gratitude could help with anxiety. At this point she was ready to try nearly anything. She was exhausted from checking on Jack a dozen times a night. Not that he woke up—she was the one springing out of bed to make sure the reason there was no noise from the baby monitor wasn't that he'd stopped breathing.

She was tired of the vague feeling of impending disaster—a sensation that frequently blossomed into a full-blown panic attack. She hated the sense of being unable to catch her breath or knowing she was spiraling out of control and that in a very short period of time, she was going to lose it completely. So if gratitude would help, she was all-in.

Lulu trotted along at Pam's side. The little dog had on a T-shirt that proclaimed her Queen of Everything. In Lulu's case, that was probably true.

"You gave her a bath this week, right?" Jen asked, knowing Jack would want to play with the dog after he rode the carousel.

"I did because she gets a bath every week. You need to stop asking me that." Pam's tone was annoyed.

"I'm just checking."

"Monitoring. You're monitoring." Her mother shook her head. "I can't wait for you to have another baby."

A second child? Jen felt her chest tighten. "Why would you say that?" How on earth could she manage? She was barely hanging on with Jack. There weren't enough hours in the day. She couldn't do it, couldn't worry twice as much. She would explode—or maybe just shrivel up like an old, dead bug.

"You wouldn't have time to ask if I'd bathed Lulu." Her mother offered a sympathetic smile. "You need to get out of your head more, Jen. Everything's fine. You're suffering for nothing."

"That's harsh."

"I don't mean it to be. I wish you could believe me."

About Jack, Jen thought resentfully. That was what her mother meant. Pam wished Jen would stop worrying about her son not talking. Like that was going to happen. There was something wrong with Jack and everyone's lack of belief didn't change the truth.

"You worried, too," she said, knowing she sounded resentful. "All the time. Dad was forever calling you on it."

Her mother smiled. "I did worry, but you take things too far."

"I don't."

"If you say so. On another topic, I saw Zoe a couple of days ago."

The unexpected statement had Jen blinking at her mother. "My friend Zoe?"

"That's the one. She came to a class at Mischief in Motion, and then we had lunch. She's so sweet. I can't believe she locked herself in the attic. That had to be terrifying."

"What are you talking about?" Jen asked.

"Zoe accidently got stuck in her attic. The door's sticky and slammed shut. I would have freaked out, that's for sure. She didn't tell you?"

"Um, no, she didn't mention it."

Jen wanted to ask when this had happened and why she didn't know about it. Except she knew the answer to the second question. She didn't know because she and Zoe weren't talking very much anymore. Certainly not on the phone. They rarely went out together. Zoe still dropped by most Thursdays, but her last visit hadn't gone very well.

Guilt pressed down on her. Yet one more thing she was supposed to fix. Just not today, she told herself.

"So, Mom, where are you and your girlfriends going next?" she asked brightly, hoping for a change of topic.

"We're doing a long weekend in Phoenix in a few weeks, then my cruise in June."

"Where's the cruise?"

Pam sighed softly, making Jen wonder how many times she'd already asked that same question. It wasn't that she wasn't interested, she told herself. She was busy. She couldn't be expected to remember every detail of her mother's life.

"Northern Europe," Pam told her. "We start in Copenhagen and spend two days in St. Petersburg. There's a day trip to Moscow."

"That will be interesting."

"I'm looking forward to it."

Jen glanced down at Lulu and felt another stab of guilt. No doubt she should offer to take the dog while her mother was gone. Lulu was comfortable in the house and relatively well behaved. Only it was one more thing that Jen didn't have time for. Plus the dog would go to the bathroom out in the yard and then Jen would have to clean it up. There were germs to consider and it was all so exhausting.

They reached the carousel. Pam put Lulu in her large tote while Jen got Jack out of his stroller. Her son clapped when he saw the wooden horses circling round and round. He pointed.

"The blue one," she said. "I remember." The blue horse was her son's favorite.

They purchased tickets and waited for the carousel to stop. Once they reached the blue horse, Jen set Jack on the painted saddle and carefully strapped him into place. She stood on one side while Pam took the other. A minute or so later, the carousel began moving. Jack laughed and waved his arms.

"How is Kirk?" her mother asked.

"Good. Okay. I wish he hadn't joined the LAPD, but it's done now."

"What about his partner? Is he improving with time?"

"I wish." Jen grimaced. "Lucas is a character, and not in a good way. He's got to be fifty and his latest girlfriend is twenty-two. Whatever do they talk about?"

Pam raised her eyebrows. "I doubt they're talking."

"Oh, Mom."

"Don't 'Oh, Mom' me. I'm not kidding. Lucas and Kirk have stressful jobs. People deal with stress in different ways. That's his. Or are you concerned about something else?"

"He's a cowboy. I worry he's going to get Kirk into a bad situation. Or a dangerous one."

"I thought he was a good detective."

"He is. He's well respected. Kirk was really happy when they were assigned together. I just think he's a bad influence. All those women. Kirk's married."

"You think Lucas will try to influence Kirk into—" She glanced at Jack. "You think he's pushing Kirk to have an *a-f-f-a-i-r*?" She spelled the last word.

"I don't know. I hope not."

"Kirk wouldn't do that."

"Not every guy is as great as Dad."

"Is Kirk giving you reason to think he would do that?"

Jen wished she hadn't started down this path. "Not exactly. It's just, he's busy and I'm busy. We have Jack. Things are different now."

Her mother turned to face her. "Jen, are you and Kirk having regular sex?"

"Mom!" Jen glanced around, but they were pretty much by themselves on their side of the carousel. "We can't talk about that here."

"Why not? This is important. You can't let life and work and the baby come between you and your husband. Women show love through words and actions. Men are different. For a lot of them, sex is an expression of love. In a marriage, sex is bigger than a man having needs. Of course he does, but without lovemaking, there's often no way for him to demonstrate how he cares. You both need a strong, vigorous sex life."

"Stop, I beg you. I don't want to have this conversation with my mother."

"You'd better be having it with someone." Pam looked at her. "This is serious."

"I know."

"Your father and I always had a great sex life."

Jen squeezed her eyes shut. "Stop. You have to stop. No one wants to know this. I can't handle thinking about my parents' sex life."

"Fine, but just know this. Sex is an important part of any successful marriage. Don't forget that. Kirk sure hasn't."

"Fine. You're right. I get it. Can we please talk about something else?"

Her mother hesitated, then nodded. "I have a new client at MWF. I like her a lot."

"That's nice. What kind of business does she have?"

Pam talked about a nail salon, but Jen was only half listening. Part of her was still weirded out, thinking about her parents doing it. But the rest of her was more concerned about what her mother had said about men and sex. She and Kirk weren't doing it much at all. Between his job and Jack and her being tired all the time, they'd fallen out of the habit. To be honest, she didn't even miss it. But what about Kirk? What did he think?

Damn Lucas, she thought. Damn him and all those young women. She knew he was giving her husband ideas. She just knew it. If she didn't want to lose her husband to some young bimbo, she was going to have to do something. The question was what.

Four o'clock on Wednesday afternoon, Zoe sat in the shade of her patio and stared at her backyard. She'd always imagined the space with raised plant beds—the kind that would allow her to grow fruits and vegetables. But she had no idea where to place them or how to install them. She supposed she could ask some gardener person, but it seemed like the kind of project she should do herself.

Her phone rang. She glanced at the number and didn't recognize it.

"Hello?"

"Zoe? It's Steven Eiland, Jen's brother."

The information took a second to fall into place. Steven was also Pam's son. Zoe had met him several times, including Jen's wedding, where Zoe had been the maid of honor and Steven had been the best man.

"Oh, hi," she said. "What's up?"

"I was talking to my mom and she mentioned you'd bought a house. Congratulations on that."

"Thank you." Why on earth would Pam be talking to Steven about her and her house? Before she could ask, he answered the question.

"She told me your attic stairs are sticking and thought I might be able to help with that. I'm actually in the neighborhood. Mind if I stop by and take a look?"

The unexpected request caught her by surprise. She hesitated before saying, "Uh, sure. That would be nice. Thank you."

"Great. I have the address. See you in ten."

"Okay. I'll be here."

She hung up. That was odd—sweet of Pam, but strange. Still, Steven worked in the family plumbing business. No doubt he'd been raised to be handy. If nothing else, he could explain how big the job was going to be and what she should expect to pay when she hired a handyman. At least that way she wouldn't have to worry about being screwed by someone.

She scrambled to her feet and called for Mason. Her cat was lying in the sun and didn't bother so much as flicking an ear in her direction.

"I know you heard me," she told him. "Let me be clear. I won't be letting you in the house fifteen seconds from now."

The tip of his tail curled slightly. She had a feeling that was feline for "No one believes that. Least of all me." Sadly, he was probably right.

Zoe went into the house and wondered what she should

do to get ready. The stairs were where they always were and it wasn't as if she kept a bunch of stuff in the small hallway. Steven would have clear access to the attic.

She knew Pam was behind his offer to help. Talk about a sweet mom-thing to do. Jen was so lucky to have Pam in her life. Zoe allowed herself a couple of minutes of missing *her* mother, before hearing a knock at the front door.

She opened the door, prepared to greet Steven. After all, she'd known him for years. He was her best friend's brother. She knew Steven was a couple of years younger than Jen, worked in the family business and that he always had a different woman on his arm. Beyond that, she didn't know much of anything about him.

Now, as she looked into his blue eyes, she realized that what she'd apparently forgotten was how good-looking he was. Had he always been so tall? So muscled? Had his smile always been so sexy?

"Hey, Zoe. How's it going?"

She was aware of the sunlight kissing the top of his head and way he filled her until-this-moment-perfectly-big-enough doorway. He had on jeans and a long-sleeved shirt. She was in ratty cutoffs and an oversize T-shirt that might or might not have stains. Dear God, she hadn't even bothered to comb her hair! Or shower!

"Um, good," she said as she stepped back to let him into the house. She'd always been on the short side and next to him, she felt positively dainty. As he moved past her, she caught a whiff of something yummy—like soap and pine and man. Her stomach clenched, her heart rate increased and she had the strangest need to start babbling.

She was saved from the latter by a very loud *meow* emanating from the back of the house. Steven glanced in that direction.

"Someone's unhappy."

"It's Mason. Let me go let him in."

She headed for the kitchen and reached for the screen door on the slider. Mason looked up at her and meowed again, his tone implying he'd been trapped outside for days.

"You're not as charming as you think," she told the cat.

He sauntered in and headed directly for Steven. Most men she knew didn't like cats. Chad had always avoided Mason as much as possible and had complained about the ever-present cat hair. By contrast, Steven held out his fingers to be sniffed. When Mason rubbed the side of his face against Steven's hand, Steven scooped him up and held him close.

"Hey, big guy," he said, offering chin scratches. "How are things in the cat world?"

"You like cats?"

Steven smiled. "I like all animals, but cats have that cool factor. Dogs are all about the pack. Cats make you earn it."

"And Lulu?" she asked, her voice teasing.

Steven shuddered. "I don't know what to make of her. It's not the weird spots and wild hair I mind so much as the wardrobe. My mom spends way too much time planning what that dog's going to wear." He set Mason on the floor. "I'll admit it. I'm a guy who doesn't get dog fashion."

"A forgivable flaw."

"I'm glad you think so." He nodded toward the hallway. "Want to show me the problem stairs?"

"Right this way."

She started to get the step stool so she could pull them down, but he waved her away. "I can reach."

He drew down the stairs, and then pushed them up in place. After doing that a couple of times, he ran his hands along the edges.

"The wood is warped," he told her. "Probably from age and a couple of our wet winters. When wood swells, it doesn't always go back to its original shape when it dries out. A little sanding should take care of the problem. I can do it for you, if you'd like."

"Really? That's all it is?"

She was aware of them standing close together in the narrow hallway and did her best to keep from nervous babbling. And failed. "I'm so happy to hear that. Did your mom mention I got trapped in the attic when the stairs slammed shut? I didn't have my cell phone with me and kept thinking I was going to die up there and Mason would eat my liver. I would end up being one of those sad stories you read about on the internet." She made air quotes. "Single woman dead for eight months before anyone noticed."

Steven pushed the stairs back up into place before he turned to her. "Single? I thought you were involved. With that guy you were always with. What was his name?"

She wrinkled her nose. "Chad. We broke up a few months ago." No way she was going to mention the stupid sex. It was one thing to confess all to Pam, but that wasn't the sort of thing one admitted to a guy like Steven.

"You still dealing?" he asked.

The question surprised her. "No. It was my idea. I realized I'd wasted way too much time on him."

"Good."

A single word, but there was something in the way he said it. Or maybe it was how close they were standing or how tall he was. Zoe was once again reminded of her lack of Lulu-like fashion and possibly uncombed hair.

"I can fix the stairs," he told her. "Go back to my place and get a sander. It won't take long." He smiled. "Or we could go grab a drink and I could get my sander another time."

Her bare toes curled just the tiniest amount. "A drink would be nice. Give me five minutes to change."

She darted around him and headed for her bedroom. Once

the door was closed, she allowed herself a three-second victory dance, then ripped off her shirt and shorts.

She stared at the choices in her closet. Since working at
home, she hadn't had to worry about what to wear. She mostly
wore jeans or shorts with a T-shirt. She didn't want to put
on any of her sensible teaching clothes, which left her eyeing her date dresses.

"Not a date," she whispered. "But still nice."

She settled on a red short-sleeved dress with a flattering
V-neck. The style was simple—a modified A-line that followed the curves of her body. The color was deep and good
for her. She slipped it on, then raced into her bathroom.

She applied mascara, blush and lip gloss, then brushed out
her hair. She had a natural wave to her dark hair. Most of
the time she fought it, but right now she didn't have time.
She added a little volumizing spray, then went back into the
bedroom where she put on hoop earrings and slipped into
four-inch taupe heels.

She walked back into the living room and found Steven
on the sofa with Mason. The cat was stretched out, kneading
a pillow while Steven rubbed his face. Both males looked at
her. Mason gave her that slow I-love-you blink while Steven
quickly rose to his feet. His eyes widened slightly.

"You look great."

"Thank you."

"That was fast."

"I didn't do that much."

He motioned to the door. She picked up her bag and led
the way, carefully locking the door behind her.

"Olives okay?" he asked.

"Sounds perfect."

Olives was a martini bar near the business district in town.
While tourists sometimes wandered in, the place was mostly

frequented by locals. Zoe hadn't been in ages. Back in the day, she and Jen had often gone there for drinks and to talk.

Steven parked his Mercedes SUV and walked around to her side to open her door. The polite gesture surprised her until she reminded herself that not every guy was Chad, and wasn't that nice to know.

Once inside, they found a small corner table. Their server came over. Zoe ordered a lemon drop while Steven chose a vodka martini.

"You didn't say shaken, not stirred," she said when their server left.

"Bond and I are different kinds of guys." He leaned forward and smiled at her. "What are you up to these days? Last I heard, you were teaching at the same school as Jen, but you left."

"I did. I'd been working part-time as a manual writer. They offered me a full-time position after a particularly difficult week of teaching, so I said yes."

Which was all true, if not the complete truth. She'd also quit her teaching job on the foolish assumption that she and Chad were going to be married and starting a family. Working from home would have given her time to be a stepmom to his kids. But none of that had come to pass and she was living her post-Chad life now.

"What's the best part about what you do?" he asked.

"Good question." She thought for a second. "That I help people. Most consumers never read the instructions, but a few do and every now and then someone really needs to understand how to work an appliance or troubleshoot it. When they do, I'm going to help them." She smiled. "Some of my work is for medical equipment manufactures. I'm guessing those people really do read the whole manual."

He leaned toward her and lowered his voice. "You do realize that no *man* is going to read the manual."

She laughed. "I'm very aware of your gender's many flaws."

"Hey, that's not a flaw. We're born with intuitive knowledge."

"Is that what we're calling it?"

Their server returned with their drinks and the small plate of bruschetta they'd ordered.

"What's the part you like least?" Steven asked.

"I'm by myself all the time. I didn't realize how much I would miss people, but I do. I want to wander down the hall and talk to a coworker. When I was a teacher, I felt like all I did was talk to people, but now, there's no one." She sipped her drink. "Mason can be very charming, but he's not much of a conversationalist."

"I got that vibe from him. He's the strong, silent type of cat."

She smiled. "He'll appreciate that you got that."

"Any regrets on leaving teaching?"

She had plenty of regrets but they were mostly about Chad. "There are things I miss, but I'm not sure I want to go back. I like my job—I just wish it were different." She looked at him. "What about you? Do you like what you do? You're in the family business, so I'm not sure you could leave, but still."

"I'd always known I was the heir apparent and I was okay with that. I just didn't expect to have to take over so soon."

Right. Because his dad had died. "I'm sorry."

"Me, too. I miss Dad every day. He was a great guy. For a while I wasn't sure I could do it—run the company like he did. Then I figured out I wasn't supposed to. That I had to run it like me. Either we made it or we didn't."

"You made it."

His dark gaze settled on her face. "You can't know that."

"I kind of can." She held up one finger. "Jen would have mentioned if you were destroying the company." A second finger went up. "You don't strike me as the kind of man who would let himself fail. Not with something so important. It's more than your family's business. The company has what—a couple dozen employees? You certainly weren't going to put all those people out of work."

He looked both proud and a tiny bit uncomfortable. "Yeah, well, things are moving in the right direction."

"Your dad would be proud of you."

"That's what my mom tells me." His expression turned serious. "When he died, it was a shock for all of us. I wasn't surprised by that, but I didn't expect his passing to change me as much as it did. I guess I'd taken him for granted."

"It's a kid thing," she pointed out. "We assume they're always going to be there for us."

He nodded. "When I was little, I was happy that my parents were so connected. They were a unit. There was no playing one against the other. As a teenager, I was embarrassed by how close they were. It wasn't cool. But later, it was the best. How they loved each other. Jen, Brandon and I worried that Mom wouldn't be able to go on, but she's pulled it all together."

"She has. Pam is amazing."

"If I agree, you have to promise not to tell her."

Zoe laughed. "Because she can't have too much power?"

"You know it."

"I will keep your secret, but you owe me."

"Will fixing the stairs make us even?"

"It will." She lightly touched his arm. "I really appreciate you helping out with that. I have to tell you, when I got locked in the attic, I totally freaked out."

"Sure. Who wouldn't?"

He was nice, she thought happily. Honorable. When his family had needed him, he'd stepped up—even though he'd been suffering himself.

"Handyman skills and you like cats," she said, her voice

teasing. "Why isn't there a Mrs. Steven Eiland waiting for you somewhere?"

He sipped his drink. "Charming answer or real answer?"

"Real answer."

"I was pretty popular in high school and college."

"Ah. Why have one when you can have them all?"

"Pretty much. It got to the point where Mom wouldn't let me bring a girl home. She didn't want to start to like her only to have us break up in a week or two."

"You lasted a week? That is so impressive."

"You're mocking me. Here I am, baring my soul, and you're making fun of me."

"I am." She fluttered her eyelashes. "Deal with it."

He chuckled. "My folks kept bugging me to settle down. Or at least go out with someone for a month, but I never saw the point. Then my dad died and everything changed. At first I didn't have time to date the way I had, but when things calmed down at work, I found I didn't want to. I want what my parents had. The kind of love that lasts."

He looked at his mostly untouched drink. "Sorry about that emotional dump. I want to blame the vodka, but I haven't had enough. Either you're really easy to talk to or I'm turning into a woman."

"Do I get to pick?"

"Sure."

"You're not turning into a woman."

"I'm glad," he told her.

"Me, too."

For a second they simply stared at each other. Zoe found herself wanting to scoot her chair closer to his. She certainly wanted to keep talking to him. He was nice, kind, funny and he had a heart. Oh, yeah, there was the really sexy thing, too. Talk about the perfect guy. Was it possible her luck had changed?

"I'm having a—"

"Would you like to—"

They spoke at the same time. "You go," Steven said.

"I'm having a barbecue this Sunday. A few friends, nothing too formal. Want to come?"

"I would." He smiled. "I was going to ask if you wanted to stretch drinks into dinner."

She smiled back. "I would."

They stared at each other. She felt the tension crackling between them—something she hadn't experienced in what felt like forever.

"I should probably warn you that I also invited your mom to the barbecue, along with my dad."

"Parents. Interesting. I can handle it if you can."

"I'm up for the challenge."

Chapter Five

Jen backed out of Jack's bedroom and quietly closed the door. Later, just before she and Kirk went to bed, she would open it again, so she could hear him if he started crying. A backup plan, in case the baby monitor failed.

Instead of joining Kirk in the family room, she took a quick detour to their bedroom where she brushed her teeth, combed her hair and made sure the light makeup she'd applied earlier hadn't gotten all smudgy under her eyes. She debated changing into something provocative, but wasn't sure what to say if Kirk noticed.

Not that she *didn't* want him to notice. That was the point of her carefully planned evening. She'd been unable to stop thinking about what her mother had said a few days ago— about Jen and Kirk having a healthy sex life.

The truth was they didn't. Since Jack had been born, they rarely made love. She was usually so stressed she couldn't summon the enthusiasm, and in the past few months, Kirk had stopped asking. That was the part that made her the most nervous. How much of it was his being busy with his new job and how much of it was Lucas talking about his twenty-two-year-olds? Not that she was going to ask. Instead she would deal with the problem.

She went into the family room and found Kirk already sitting on the sofa, watching a basketball game. Instead of sitting in her usual seat at the other end, she settled closer to him. He smiled at her.

"Jack asleep?"

"Uh-huh. I start the music box and he's usually out in seconds."

"Best baby gift ever?"

She laughed. "Certainly one of the top ten."

He looked back at the game. The Lakers were up by six. Jen shifted so that her oversize shirt fell off one shoulder. She'd put on her sexiest bra, with the lacy strap. Hopefully the visual would—

"You okay?" Kirk asked. "You're fidgeting. Does your back hurt?"

"No. I'm fine."

She sighed silently. So much for her sexy move. She turned to him, prepared to snuggle closer, only he'd leaned forward, his elbows on his knees, his gaze intent on the television.

"Come on, come on! Don't blow it. Pass the ball. Pass it!"

Kirk had entered the game zone. She had a couple of choices. She could try to be less subtle, maybe kiss him or something, or she could simply accept it wasn't going to happen tonight. The danger with the first choice was he could give her that absent smile that said he wasn't the least bit interested. Not that she'd seen it very much, but the threat was always there.

In her head she knew that the best response would be to simply tell her husband what she was thinking. That she was very much in the mood. Considering how long it had been, he would probably turn the TV off so fast her head would spin.

But saying that didn't guarantee the outcome and while her head was very clear on the mature, straightforward action, the rest of her was less sure. What if he *wasn't* interested in her that way anymore? What if there was a twenty-two-year-old? What if...

"I'm going to go pay bills," she said, rising from the sofa.

"Okay. Is there ice cream for later?"

"Uh-huh."

She walked into the study and sat behind what had been her father's desk. According to her mother, her parents had gone at it, right up until her father's death. They'd been married over thirty years. How on earth had they managed to keep the spark alive that long?

She wasn't sure if the problem with her and Kirk was circumstantial or something more. To be honest, she didn't think she wanted to risk asking that question either.

Late Sunday morning, Zoe checked on the chicken marinating in her refrigerator. She'd decided to go simple with the menu for her barbecue. Grilled chicken, an assortment of salads, pinto beans cooked in a Crock-Pot—the recipe compliments of her mother—and desserts from Let's Do Tea. The drinks were equally simple. Sun tea, beer and margaritas made with Saldivar tequila.

Her father's family had emigrated from Mexico four generations ago. Over the years there had been plenty of non-Hispanic spouses until the Saldivar family was just like most in Southern California. A little bit of this, a lot of that, with a sprinkling of I-have-no-idea thrown in. But the family business—Saldivar tequila—kept them connected to Mexico.

The agave plants were grown in Mexico, but the company was headquartered in Southern California. The liquor was exported all over the world. She'd been at least twelve or fourteen before she'd realized that *liquor* didn't just mean tequila.

Her father and his brother had been raised to be in the family business. Her uncle ran the company, her father acted as the spokesman until just a few years ago. While Zoe enjoyed a margarita as much as the next person, she'd had no desire to join the family firm. Her cousins were doing just fine without her.

A little before eleven, her father showed up.

"I came early to help," he said as he hugged her, then passed over a bag of limes. Mariposa, his papillon, trotted in on his heels.

Miguel Saldivar was about six feet tall, with thick, graying hair and a trimmed beard. A lot of her friends had gone on and on about how handsome he was—which Zoe didn't get. To her, he was just her dad.

She bent down and scooped up Mariposa. The small dog relaxed in her embrace and offered a doggy kiss.

"How's my girl?" Zoe asked. "Are you keeping Dad in line?"

Mariposa wagged her tail.

"I have a friend with a little dog," she said, thinking of Pam. "You two could have a playdate."

"Mariposa doesn't hang out with dogs," her father said. "She's a people person, not a dog person."

Zoe thought about pointing out that Mariposa wasn't a person at all, but why go there?

"You came alone?" she asked with raised eyebrows. "No beach bunnies trailing behind."

"You're disrespectful. Where did I go wrong?"

She traded him the dog for the limes and started for the kitchen. "Maybe it was the time you showed me the pictures of you at the Playboy mansion."

"That was a hundred years ago."

"I was twenty. Most of the girls there were my age. It was a little creepy."

Her father winked. "You're jealous."

"Of the bunnies? No. They're not my type."

"There were handsome men there, I'm sure."

"Not interested in a guy who wants them. A ridiculous

standard, I know, but there we are." She put the limes on the counter. "I was thinking of serving vodka tonics to everyone," she said, knowing the statement would cause a quick change in topic.

As if on cue, her father crossed his arms over his chest and his gaze narrowed. "Zoe Elizabeth Saldivar, don't ever joke about that."

"Oh, Dad." She crossed to him, raised herself on tiptoe and kissed his cheek. "You have got to work on your sense of humor."

"I have an excellent sense of humor. Where do you think you got yours?"

"From Mom."

He grumbled something under his breath, then washed his hands. She got out a couple of small bowls. One would be for the lime juice. The other was for Mariposa. Heaven forbid his precious girl drink out of a cat bowl. Speaking of which…

Zoe left her father squeezing limes. She went into the living room and found Mariposa and Mason lying together in a patch of sun. The marmalade cat was about five pounds heavier than the papillon, and far more sturdy. Still, the two were friends. As Zoe watched, Mason tucked his head into the dog's chest so Mariposa could wash his ears.

"You two are weird," she announced before returning to the kitchen.

Miguel continued to squeeze limes. While he sliced, Zoe strained the liquid before pouring it into a large measuring cup. When her guests arrived, her father would make margaritas by the pitcher.

"How are things?" he asked.

"Good."

"You seeing Chad?"

"I told you, we broke up."

"You broke up before and took him back."

"Not this time. We are totally done."

"Good. I never liked him."

Her father had liked him just fine, until she'd dumped him. Which, she thought with a smile, was the sign of a good dad. Now he would dislike Chad forever.

Miguel eyed her. "You're happy without him?"

"I am, I swear."

"If you start to get lonely, let me know. I'll find you a nice guy."

"I'm so going to pretend you didn't just say that. I don't need my father finding me dates."

"Why not? I have great taste. I married your mother."

"Yes, and then you left her. Stay out of my love life and I'll stay out of yours."

"It's a deal. Now tell me who's coming to this party of yours."

Pam arrived at Zoe's a little after one. The house was small but charming. This block had yet to see too much change, which she appreciated. Too many of the older streets in town had been turned into McMansions—huge houses on tiny lots. She preferred the older style of the original bungalows.

There were already several cars in the driveway, so she parked down the street and walked back to the house, passing Steven's SUV. With luck, her plan was working. She looked forward to spying on the two of them. Surreptitiously, of course. Steven needed a woman in his life—but the right kind. From what Pam knew about Zoe, she was sweet and caring. Chad had been a disaster, but Zoe had recognized the problem and walked away before any harm was done.

Pam walked up to Zoe's partially open front door. She knocked once and let herself in. Through the back windows, she could see people milling around Zoe's pretty backyard. There was a covered patio, several large trees and an expanse of grass. She started for the sliding door at the back of the living room, only to be stopped by the rapid approach of a tiny barking dog.

Pam immediately set her plate of brownies on the coffee table before dropping to her knees and holding out her fingers to be sniffed.

"Look at you," she said in a soft voice. "You're a beautiful little girl, aren't you?"

The dog had big brown eyes and huge ears. Her face was multicolored, with splashes of white, brown and black, while the rest of her was mostly white.

She sniffed Pam for a second, before giving her a quick kiss. Pam rubbed the side of the dog's face a few times until she collapsed onto the carpet and exposed her belly.

"Ah, Mariposa, you're supposed to make them work for it, my love. Not give it away for free."

The words, spoken in a low, melodious male voice, had Pam looking up. Her gaze settled on a tall, broad-shouldered man with very handsome features.

"You must be my daughter's friend Pamela. She told me about you. I'm Miguel Saldivar, Zoe's father."

Pam blinked. Wowza. The voice, the face, the voice—they were all so appealing.

Miguel held out his hand. It took Pam a second to realize he was helping her to her feet. What on earth? She was perfectly capable of... Oh, right. He was being polite because nice men did that sort of thing. John had. He'd always been so considerate and polite.

The unexpected reminder of her late husband caught her off guard. Pain and longing sliced through her until she found it hard to breathe. Her reaction was as sudden as it was powerful. Miguel immediately crouched beside her.

"Pamela? You are not well?"

She forced a smile. "I'm fine. Is this little girl yours? She's beautiful."

Miguel stared into her eyes for a second. She had a feeling he was debating whether or not to accept the change in topic.

"She is. Mariposa is very spoiled, as you've already seen."

He held out his hand and she put her fingers on his palm. Together they stood.

He was taller than she'd first realized, with broad shoulders and a trim physique. She would guess he was only a few years older than herself. There was something about him, she thought absently. Almost a memory. As if they'd met previously.

Before she could ask about that, she heard a familiar laugh and turned to find little Jack running toward her. His arms were outstretched as he barreled into her. She caught him and pulled him up in the air.

"There you are," she said happily. "I've been waiting to see you."

Jen and Kirk followed. She greeted her daughter and son-in-law, then turned to find Miguel had gone into the back-yard. Pam looked back at Jen and noticed the dark circles under her eyes.

"How are you feeling?" Pam asked.

Jen shrugged. "I'm okay. I haven't been sleeping well."

Pam pressed her lips together to keep from saying something she would probably regret. While she appreciated that Jen was an attentive parent, her daughter was making herself sick with worry about things that were never going to happen. Or at least were unlikely to. She was in a constant state of alert about Kirk getting injured on the job. While being a police officer was certainly dangerous, Kirk was now a detective. He had experience and a partner. As for something being wrong with Jack...

Pam told herself not to go there. She didn't want to fight with her daughter, but she couldn't help worrying about her.

Jen was making things harder than they had to be. Pam had a feeling that whatever Jen had shared, there was so much more she wasn't saying. Jack's first few years were supposed to be wonderful, not terrifying.

They all went out to the backyard. Zoe had set up tables in the shade. There was a play area for the kids and a drinks station.

Zoe came over to greet them. She tickled little Jack and thanked them all for coming.

"Have I met your father before?" Pam asked her. "He looks familiar."

Zoe grinned. "He was the face of Saldivar tequila for years. You've seen him in magazine ads and on TV."

"Of course. I should have remembered."

Jen took Jack and set him on the ground. He ran toward two other children and Jen followed. Kirk went with her. Zoe leaned close to Pam.

"My father is very charming. He can't help it. Just so you're warned."

"Don't worry. I promise not to be swept off my feet by him." She appreciated the information—not that she was interested or anything, but the man was very appealing. She linked arms with Zoe. "All right. Introduce me to your friends. I want to find out what the current slang words are. I'm sure mine are all outdated."

The afternoon was sunny and warm. Pam enjoyed chatting with everyone. She took charge of Jack during dinner so Jen and Kirk could hang out together. Sometime after, she found herself sitting in a beach chair on the lawn next to Miguel.

He eyed her glass of iced tea. "You don't like margaritas?" he asked. "I made them myself."

"I like them just fine and I had one earlier. But I have to drive home."

"A cautious woman. Interesting. Tell me, Pamela, what do you do?"

She thought about correcting him—she always went by Pam. But there was something about the way the more formal version rolled off his tongue. It was nice, she told herself. Fun.

"I volunteer with an organization called Moving Women Forward. They support women entrepreneurs. I'm a mentor. I also take care of my grandson and spend time with my friends. I travel a few times a year, that sort of thing."

It wasn't a life that would change the world, but it was a very good one and she knew she'd been blessed.

"What about you?" she asked. "Zoe mentioned you'd worked in the family business. As the spokesman."

He raised one eyebrow. "Did she? I'm retired now. My nephew is younger, which has an appeal, I suppose. But he's hardly more handsome."

Pam laughed. "I'm sure that's true."

Miguel winked at her. "You're going to hear stories about me."

"Am I?"

"Yes. That I'm charming and fickle when it comes to women."

"You're saying neither is true?"

He touched his hand to his chest. "You wound me. Of course I'm charming. As for the women, perhaps years ago. After my divorce. I had a modest amount of fame and I might have used it to my advantage."

She would guess that was quite the understatement. "And now?"

"I have learned to appreciate different things. Maturity and wisdom bring their own kind of beauty."

Pam did her best not to snort. Talk about a line. Sure, it was a good one, but still. "Miguel, I promise I will only believe the good things about you."

"I appreciate that." He glanced around the backyard. "This reminds me of when I was in Rio many years ago. One of our distributors invited me to his home for a birthday party for his youngest daughter. She was turning seven and the whole family was there. So many generations celebrating together. I fear we are losing that."

"I know what you mean. I appreciate getting to hang out with at least two of my children, but not enough people do."

"How many children do you have?"

"Three." She pointed to Jen and Steven. "Brandon is in San Francisco." She smiled. "If I say he's a doctor, will you accuse me of bragging?"

"I promise I will not."

"Then he's a doctor. Brandon was one of those kids who makes you want to bang your head against the wall. If there was an easy way and a hard way, he would find the impossible way. But he's doing great now."

Miguel studied her. "You were a good mother."

"I like to think so but you can't possibly know one way or the other."

"I have a sense about these things. There is a determination about you. Whatever the problem, you would have seen it through to the end."

A lucky guess, she told herself, slightly surprised he would have figured that out about her.

"You are out of iced tea." Miguel rose and reached for her glass. "I'll be right back."

Pam watched him go, appreciating the view. Yes, he was a very interesting man. Charming and—

Steven dropped into the empty seat. He angled toward her. "Mom, you have to be careful. With Miguel. You've been talking to him for a while. Zoe's told me all about him. He's a player. I know he's charming and all that, but it's superficial."

"Oh, dear God." Pam stared at him. "First Zoe and now you? How incompetent do you think I am?"

"Not incompetent," Steven said hastily. "Just, you know, inexperienced. You were married to Dad for a long time and you're not used to…" He seemed to be searching for the right word.

"The ways of the world?" she offered dryly.

"Uh, sure." He shifted uncomfortably. "Mom, I love you and I don't want you to get hurt. You know, thinking that Miguel is really—"

She stared at him. "Go on."

"Um, nothing."

"You don't want me thinking that Miguel could possibly be interested in me? Is that it? Because I'd like to point out he's several years older than me, so it couldn't possibly be an age thing. Are you saying I'm not attractive enough? You think your mother is ugly?" She supposed it was wrong to torture him like this, but seriously, he'd started it.

Steven nearly whimpered. "Mom, I'm just—"

"Oh, I know what you are and what you're thinking. That I'm so pathetic I would think that Miguel was actually interested in me. That I'm so unsophisticated and backward that I would be swooning over the first man to bat his eyelashes at me. Let me tell you something, Steven Eiland. You and your generation didn't invent sex. I was doing it years before you were born. And while I might have been happily married for thirty years, I'm not an idiot. I understand exactly who and what Miguel is. Now, unless you want me to start talking about all the things I know that you don't—when it comes to what goes on between a man and a woman—I suggest you hightail it back to the other side of the party."

Steven swallowed and stood. "Yes, ma'am."

He disappeared at a pace just fast enough to let Pam know the message had been received. Honestly, what was with young people today?

Miguel returned with a full glass of iced tea. He put it down on the small table next to her. "Everything all right?"

She smiled at him. "Things are pretty great right now."

Chapter Six

The party started to wind down some time around seven. By seven-thirty, nearly everyone had left. Pam carried serving dishes into the kitchen and set them on the counter.

"That was a lot of fun," she said cheerfully. "Thanks for inviting me."

"My pleasure." Zoe looked at the last of her guests, still talking in her backyard. "I should do this more often. I had such a good time."

Pam leaned against the counter. "Did you talk to Jen at all?"

"A little. Why?"

"I don't know. I worry about her. She's so caught up with Jack. It's one thing to be a good mother, but another to stop having a life outside of your child."

Zoe didn't want to step on any toes, but Pam had started the conversation. "She's different," she admitted. "Since having Jack. I love her and would do anything for her, but I sometimes wonder how interested she is in our friendship."

"That makes me sad." Pam pressed her lips together. "If she was *happy* spending every second with her baby, I would be fine with it. But she's so stressed, all the time. I just..." She looked at Zoe. "Maybe we should talk to her. The two of us. Tell her that we're worried."

Zoe took a step back. "I don't think that's a good idea. Jen isn't going to take it well. She's going to assume we're ganging up on her."

"Not if we start by telling her we love her. She needs to hear the truth from people who care about her. I'll text you some dates and times. We'll figure out when we're both available and Jen is home. While Jack is napping would probably be best. I don't want her distracted."

Pam hugged her, then waved as she left the kitchen. "I'll be in touch. Bye."

Zoe held in a groan. She had a bad feeling about confronting Jen. Interventions went well when they were in a movie or on TV but she doubted real life was that tidy. She was running low on friends—she didn't want to lose one of the few she had left. But she also didn't want to offend Pam.

"You're looking serious about something," Steven said as he came into the kitchen and set a pitcher of iced tea on the counter. "Everything okay?"

"Just deep thoughts." No way she was going to drag him into this, she thought. Getting caught between his sister and his mother was the definition of a rock and a hard place.

"That's the last of the drinks from outside," he told her. "What else can I do to help?"

"You've done enough."

Not only had he been attentive to her friends, he'd kept serving bowls filled and drinks topped up.

She smiled. "You're an excellent kind of guest to have."

"My mom taught me to be handy." He started to say something, then seemed to change his mind. "Mason survive Mariposa?"

"He actually likes her. He always has, which is good. I would hate for my dad's dog to see my cat as a living chew toy."

"I'm pretty sure Mason could take care of himself. He's a

smart guy." He picked up a half-full bottle of chardonnay. "One more glass?"

"Sure."

She pulled two glasses out of the cupboard and he poured, then they both went into the living room and sat on her sofa. There was a single lamp on in the corner, but otherwise the room was dim. Zoe briefly thought about turning on more lights, but decided against it. She couldn't remember the last time she'd been in the semidark with a handsome, charming man. Chad didn't count because he'd turned out to be a total mistake. Which meant it had been years and years. She was due for some handsome-man-in-the-dark time.

"Your dad's nice," Steven said.

His tone was completely neutral, but she had a feeling he wasn't as calm as he acted. She decided to test the waters.

"He spent a lot of time with your mom today."

"I noticed. I hope she didn't…" He set his glass on the coffee table. "I tried to talk to her about him."

Zoe felt her eyes widen. "Wow. How did that go?"

"Not well. She told me—" He cleared his throat. "That doesn't matter. I hope he doesn't hurt her."

"Wouldn't they have to get involved for that to happen?" she asked gently. "Steven, you're sweet to worry, but there are a million steps between tonight and that. Yes, my dad was a bit of a player when he was younger. But less so now. And he's not a bad guy. When my parents got divorced, it was the most civil, friendly marriage dissolution ever. He and my mom stayed friends. The three of us were together when she died and he was as sad as I was."

"I'm sorry about your mom, but I'm glad you're telling me good things about your dad." He hesitated. "My mom and dad were together a long time. I worry about her being out of her element."

"That's really sweet and you have to let it go. Wait until

something happens before you get crazy. And for what it's worth, I kind of warned her off, too."

"You did?"

"Yes, but I have a feeling I was a lot more subtle than you."

"Probably." One shoulder rose. "I'm a guy. Subtle is hard for me. I just say what I think."

"That's not a bad quality," she told him. In fact, it was an excellent one. A man who said what was on his mind. How refreshing, and unlike Chad.

He angled toward her. "I'm glad you think so, because I'd like to see you again. Is that okay?"

Pleasure flooded her from her head to her toes. She smiled. "I'd like that a lot."

"Good." He rose. "Now I'm going to get out of here before I do something I shouldn't." He drew her to her feet. "Well, maybe just one thing."

He kissed her. Softly, gently. Just lips lightly touching hers. More promise than passion, Zoe thought, leaning into him. Which was exactly what she was looking for.

"Jen, you have to relax."

Until this minute, Jen had always liked Dr. Miller. Jack's pediatrician was intelligent, caring and good with both parents and children. Her staff was always so cheerful. Jen felt safe and cared for in the office. Or she had.

Dr. Miller, a gray-haired woman in her fifties, offered a sympathetic smile. "There aren't any more tests. Nothing else to be done. Jack is healthy and smart and affectionate. He'll talk when he's ready."

"But—"

"Medically, there's nothing else to be done." Dr. Miller's tone was firm. "Get him into a playgroup. Have him interact with other children. Once he hears them talking, he may get inspired. If nothing else, you'll have some other new moms to spend time with. That will help."

"Is this your polite way of telling me I'm losing it?" Jen asked, not sure if she was more hurt or angry.

"You're anxious. It's natural. You love your son and you're a good mom."

Jen noticed there was no firm "No" in those few sentences.

She wanted to stand up and start screaming—something that wouldn't help her cause. But she knew she wasn't the problem. There was something wrong with her son. Why couldn't other people see it? Why was she the only one?

"I don't want him in a playgroup," she said instead. "There are too many germs and sick kids."

"He needs to be exposed to a few viruses. Fighting them will strengthen his immune system."

Or kill him. But Jen didn't say that.

"Do you have help with day care?" the doctor asked.

"My mom looks after him sometimes. She's the only one I trust. I'm afraid of what would happen if he was in a day care situation or with a babysitter."

"Start with a playgroup. See how that goes. And think about finding some outside help with Jack. You need to get out more, Jen. Having a baby is wonderful, but it doesn't mean you have to give up being you."

Which all sounded really good, Jen thought bitterly, but wasn't the least bit helpful.

She collected Jack and walked out of the office, then down the hall to the waiting area. Frustration built inside of her. Why wouldn't anyone listen? Not that there was an answer. Jack's own doctor had given up on him. There was nowhere else to turn.

She felt the familiar combination of panic and tears building up inside of her. In a few minutes she wasn't going to be able to breathe and if she started sobbing, she wouldn't stop for several minutes. She had to get out of here. To the safety of being alone.

Just then her phone chirped. She checked the screen and saw that her mother had texted, asking if she could stop by later. Relief overrode panic.

Yes. Please do.

Jen drew in a breath. Having her mom around for an hour or so would help, she told herself. Even if Pam didn't believe there was a problem with Jack, she was a friendly face. She would listen and offer comfort and hugs. Exactly what Jen needed today.

"This is not a good idea," Zoe said, trying not to clutch her stomach and rock. She felt a little light-headed and sick. "Jen is going to be mad."

"No, she won't," Pam said firmly. "She'll appreciate our support. You agree that she needs to take a step back from her ridiculous helicopter parenting and start being a person again, don't you?"

"I wouldn't put it like that, exactly," Zoe said as she wondered how badly she would get hurt if she jumped out of the moving SUV.

"We agreed this was the right thing to do. We're being honest."

Zoe was starting to think honesty was far from the best policy, but before she could say that, they were pulling up in front of Jen's house.

For a second she thought about simply telling Pam no. That this wasn't a good idea. At the same time, she wondered if hearing from both of them was exactly what Jen needed. Wouldn't it be great if she could get her friend back?

Together she and Pam walked to the front door. Jen had

her hand-painted, baby-sleeping sign out. Pam knocked softly, then opened the front door and stepped inside.

"We're here," she called softly.

"Who's we?" Jen asked as she stepped out of the kitchen. She spotted Zoe and looked confused. "Oh, hi. Did I know you were coming by today, too?"

"Not exactly," Zoe admitted. Before she could say anything else, Pam took charge.

"Zoe and I want to talk to you."

Jen's expression turned wary. "Why is there a Zoe and you to begin with? What's going on?"

They were not getting off to a good start, Zoe thought anxiously. If this went badly, Pam would still be Jen's mother. That couldn't be changed. But friendship was much more fragile than a family bond.

"We've been talking," Pam said. "Let's go into the family room."

Jen looked like she was going to bolt. Zoe understood the reaction completely. Not only wasn't this going to go well, but she could tell that Pam was going to do all the talking. Which was probably for the best—Pam knew her daughter. But it also left Zoe agreeing through silence. Which meant being blamed for everything, too. She was going to have to speak up and soon.

"We love you, Jen," she said as soon as they were seated. "You're my best friend and you mean everything to me."

Jen didn't look reassured. "Then what is this about?"

"You're obsessed with Jack," Pam said bluntly. "You have too many rules. You're smothering him with your attentiveness. I get that you want to be a good mother, but you've gone way too far with it. It's one thing to have a schedule, but this household is run with NASA-like precision. Kids are tough, Jen. Lighten up."

Zoe held in a groan. That was not the right approach to

take, she thought, searching for a way to mitigate what had just been said.

"Lighten up?" Jen asked, her voice low and controlled. "Lighten up? What exactly is your complaint? That I care too much? That I worry? What kind of mother would I be if I didn't? You worried plenty, but I suppose that's okay?" Her voice rose. "My son won't talk. That's not normal. But all you can see is I worry too much? I'm his mother. I know him better than anyone. I'm with him every second of every day."

"That's the problem," Pam told her. "You need to get out and have a life of your own. You can't be defined by your children. You're constantly worrying about what might never happen, which means you don't get to enjoy all the good stuff right in front of you."

"You don't know what I'm going through," Jen told her.

"I had three kids. I think I know something. You're neglecting your marriage. That's not a good idea, Jen. One day Kirk isn't going to be so understanding."

Oh, God! Zoe wanted to cover her ears with her hands and start humming. She so didn't want to be hearing this, only she couldn't figure out how to quietly escape.

"You're a part of this?" Jen asked Zoe. "You think I'm stunting my son through my ridiculous concerns?"

"That isn't what I said," Zoe told her. "Jen, you're my friend."

"Not really. Not like this. I can't believe you ganged up on me with my mother. Who else have you been talking to? I thought I could trust you. I thought you were on my side." Tears filled her eyes. "You two had better get out. Just leave."

Zoe's stomach turned over. "I'm sorry. Jen, please understand. We just wanted…"

"You wanted what? To make me feel like shit? Well, you did. Congratulations." Tears spilled down her cheeks. "Get out now!"

Pam rose. "You're making a mistake, Jennifer. We only want to help you. I hope, with time, you can come to see that."

Jen pointed to the front door.

Zoe and Pam walked out to the car. "I'm going to throw up," Zoe said. "That was horrible. She's really upset."

"She'll get over it."

"You sound very casual."

They got in the SUV.

"Jen has always had a dramatic streak. You should have seen her in high school. Sometimes I get a little impatient with her. I know I shouldn't but she frustrates me." She started the engine. "I meant what I said. She's missing out on wonderful days, coloring them with her incessant fear that something bad is going to happen. Sure, it might, but what if it never does? She will have suffered for nothing. Worse, she will have missed out, and that makes me sad. I want more for her and for her relationship with Jack." Pam offered a smile. "Don't worry. She'll come around."

"I hope so."

"Thanks again for inviting me to your barbecue. It was fun."

"I'm glad you could come."

Pam glanced at her. "What do you think of Steven?"

"He's nice. Very—" Zoe felt her eyes widen. "You set us up? Is that why you had him call me about my attic stairs?"

"You're single. He's single. I gave a little push. If it works out, great. If not, no harm done."

Pam's smile was friendly enough, and on the surface, her sentiment was perfectly fine, but Zoe had a feeling that there was more to Pam than she'd realized. A determination and view of the world that were unique to her. She supposed everyone was like that. What was the old saying? That everyone was the star of their own life.

Pam was a powerful, self-confident woman who took control of most situations. Zoe hadn't expected that. Now she was caught up in Jen-drama in a way that might not end well. She also had to consider that if things went badly with Steven, there would be ramifications with Pam. Her seemingly sad, empty life had just taken a turn for the complicated.

Pam sat at her small kitchen table and stared out at the ever-changing ocean, phone in hand. Lulu was stretched out in a patch of sun, while Pam chatted with her friend Olimpia.

"The day trip to Moscow is going to be long," Olimpia was saying. "We'll have to make sure we take protein bars with us."

"They'll have food in Moscow," Pam teased, shifting her phone to the other ear. "I'm confident Russians eat just like we do."

"You know how the tours go. Rush, rush, rush."

Pam laughed. This always happened. About six weeks before their trip, Olimpia got crazy. In a couple of days she would calm down and be up for anything on the trip, but the pretravel jitters were always powerful.

Pam had met Olimpia, Laura and Eugenia two years ago on a Caribbean cruise. Pam had been recently widowed and was by herself. Olimpia and her friends had taken her under their collective wing and gotten her through a very rough time. As the three of them were also widows, they had understood what she was going through.

The three friends had become four friends. Now they traveled together a few times a year. Mostly cruises—like their upcoming Northern European jaunt in June—or weekends to hang out. They would all be in Phoenix in a couple of weeks.

"I'll make sure I bring the protein bars you like," Pam said.

"Only chocolate," Olimpia told her.

"Would I bring anything else?"

"No. You're very good to me. How are things otherwise?"

Pam sighed and told her what had happened with Jen. "We're still not talking. It's been three days of radio silence. I know it can't go on much longer."

"You should reach out to her."

"I knew you were going to say that." Pam also knew her friend was right. "I'll text her when we're done talking."

"I guess this means she won't be taking Lulu while you're gone."

Pam rolled her eyes. "She never takes Lulu. Not since Jack was born. Imagine the germs. She's a dog after all. Lulu will stay with my friend Shannon."

And while Shannon took excellent care of Lulu, she worked all day, so Pam also had to hire a dog sitter to spend a few hours with Lulu each afternoon. Yes, her dog was spoiled. She was also used to being with someone all the time. It wasn't fair to leave her alone day after day simply because Pam was going on vacation.

"I'm sorry about Jen," Olimpia said.

"Me, too. I wasn't tactful. I should have been more gentle. It's just she makes me crazy."

"I believe children are supposed to make us crazy. It makes them leaving easier."

"God always has a plan. You okay about the trip?"

"No, but I recognize my process. I'll be fine in a week or two."

"I'm still bringing protein bars. In case they try to starve us."

Olimpia laughed. "You're a good friend. Thank you."

"You're welcome. Talk to you soon."

They hung up. Pam allowed herself thirty seconds of pouting before she texted her daughter.

Checking in to see how things are going. I hope you know I said what I said with love. XO

Thirty seconds later, her phone rang. Pam smiled as she picked up her cell only to realize she didn't recognize the number on the screen.

"Hello?"

"Pamela. It is Miguel."

Pam felt an unfamiliar swirling in her stomach, which she refused to analyze. It wasn't the poor man's fault that he had a delicious voice.

"Hello, Miguel. How can I help you? Is something wrong with Zoe?"

"No. Not that I know of."

Oh. Okay. So why was he calling?

"I enjoyed our conversation at my daughter's barbecue," he told her. "I thought we could continue it over dinner."

She blinked a couple of times as she considered his statement. She was pretty sure he was inviting her to dinner, which was weird. Maybe he needed advice about redecorating or something.

"Um, sure. We could do that. When and where?"

He suggested a date and time. Pam checked her calendar and said she was free.

"I'll see you then," she said. "Goodbye."

After ending the call, she looked at Lulu. "That was very strange. I wonder if it's Zoe birthday and he wants help buying a present." Lulu didn't seem to have an opinion.

Curiouser and curiouser, Pam thought. Whatever the reason, she would enjoy the evening with a very attractive man. She smiled. When she met with her friends in Phoenix, she would have a fun story to tell, and wouldn't that be nice?

Chapter Seven

"Your dad said he liked me better than Chad."

Zoe picked up her wineglass, put it down and sighed. "Please tell me you're kidding." Although she was pretty sure he wasn't. She could see she needed to have a serious conversation with her father. There were personal boundaries he wasn't supposed to cross.

Steven smiled at her from across the table. They were having dinner in Redondo Beach. Kincaid's was a nice pier restaurant that featured great steaks and seafood.

"Your dad mentioned it at the barbecue." Steven grinned. "Something along the lines of a gruff 'you seem better than Chad.'"

Which was so like her father. "I'm going to kill him."

"I doubt that. You two get along great and he's a nice guy. So, Chad. You two were together a long time."

"Five years."

"Want to talk about it?"

She didn't. Mostly she wanted to forget everything about the relationship. Only he'd been a part of her life and she knew that she had to understand her past or she would be at risk of repeating it.

"We met on the 405 freeway when I got a flat." She held

up her hand. "I swear, that's exactly what happened. He pulled over and helped me. He said he was a master mechanic and he fixed my tire, then he invited me to dinner."

"Taking advantage of the situation. You have to respect that."

"An interesting way of looking at things."

"I'm an interesting guy. So you went out."

"We did. He was the perfect boyfriend, or so I thought. He was busy with work. He worked at a very upscale garage. They handle luxury cars with demanding clientele. So he was always traveling to work on cars in exotic locations."

Steven frowned. "They don't have local mechanics there?"

"Yes, well, it turns out they do. Chad wasn't traveling—he was married, with two kids."

She still remembered when she'd finally figured out the truth. How shocked she'd been. No, more than that. "I was devastated and humiliated. I thought I was so smart and to-gether. I thought he was the one."

Steven's gaze turned sympathetic. "I'm sorry."

"Me, too. It was horrible. I broke up with him immediately and that lasted about six months. Then he showed up on my doorstep and told me he loved me and couldn't live without me. More important, he was getting a divorce."

"Was he?"

She nodded. "I wouldn't believe him at first. He showed me the paperwork, took me to meet his lawyer, and when the divorce was really final, he had me speak with the judge. He meant it. He was all-in."

She wondered how the story sounded. Did she sound like she'd been sensible or had she been a fool? She knew the an-swer, of course, but from outside—how did it look?

"That's about when my mom died. I didn't have the strength to fight him anymore. I'm not saying that as an ex-cuse. I needed someone to lean on and he was there. So we got back together. I bought the house, foolishly thinking it would be our home. We planned how the bedrooms would be for the kids and what our life would be like. A few months later, I was offered the full-time job writing manuals. It was a lot more money than teaching and what with Chad and I getting married and starting a family, it made sense."

Steven stared at her. "You were engaged?"

"Only in my mind. One day I realized that I'd only met his kids twice in the past year. He said he wanted them to adjust after the divorce, which I got, but twice in a year? I pushed, he pushed back. I realized we weren't having the same relationship. He wasn't looking for things to be different between us. He liked the status quo. So I broke up with him again and that's it."

"He let you go?"

She thought about their last few conversations. "He's tried to win me back, but there's no point. We want different things. I thought I loved him, but now I'm questioning that. Love is supposed to be a positive thing. With him, my world got smaller, not bigger. I made so many bad choices."

"The house?"

"Not that. I really like it." She smiled. "Except when the attic tries to kill me."

"I'm going to fix those stairs."

"I wasn't hinting. I'll be more careful next time." She sipped her wine. "I wonder if I made the right decision quitting teaching. There are parts I miss and parts I'm grateful not to have to deal with. But I do wonder."

"You could go back."

"I don't know if I want to. So I'm thinking on it." She rested her hands on the table. "I hate that I was that girl. The one who built her life around a man. I thought I was smarter than that."

"You believed in him. He's the one who lied to you, Zoe. You have nothing to apologize for."

"You're being nice. Thank you."

"I'm being honest. At least you put yourself out there. I never did. I was more into the flavor of the month. I'm not proud of that."

"Maybe not, but you had fun."

His mouth twitched. "Maybe a little."

Their server brought their salads. Zoe picked up her fork.

"Now that I think about it, I sort of remember you having one date for Jen's rehearsal dinner and a different one for the wedding."

"I honestly can't remember."

"We could ask your mom. I'll bet she knows for sure." Her voice was teasing.

"Yeah, let's not do that." He looked at her. "Chad's really gone?"

"As gone as gone can be. I have no feelings for him. Not anger, not anything. I've totally moved on."

"Good to know."

Thursday after Jack was in bed, Jen walked into the kitchen. Her phone was on the counter and she saw she had another text message from Zoe. While part of Jen wanted to stay mad, the truth was she missed her friend. And maybe, just maybe, she *had* been a little too focused on Jack. Not that she was going to stop worrying about him, but it was important for her to maintain her friendships. If nothing else, she needed the support.

I get where you were coming from. Let's meet up next week and talk.

She pushed the send button and felt a little of her ever-present tension ease. She was still furious with her mother, but that was different. It was easier to stay mad at her.

Kirk walked into the kitchen. "You okay?" he asked.

"I've decided to forgive Zoe."

Emotions flashed across his face, but he didn't speak.

"What?" she demanded. "You don't think I should stay mad at her, do you?"

"I don't think you should have been mad in the first place. They're only trying to help."

"By telling me not to worry about Jack? By judging me? How is that helpful?"

"Jen, I don't want to fight with you."

She waited, sensing there was more.

"You are a little obsessed with the baby. We've talked about this."

She stiffened, emotionally slapped by the unfairness of the statement. "I'm not. I'm concerned about a developmental issue. Would you like it better if I wasn't worried? If I didn't take care of things? Maybe we should let him play with matches and drink cleaning solvent. Would that be better?"

"Don't get upset."

"How is that possible? You expect me to take care of him all day long while you're at work, and then you complain about how I do it. Where's the win?"

"I'm sorry I said anything."

"Me, too, but you did. So just finish it. There's more. I know there is." There always was.

"Fine. You want to know what I think? You need to lighten up."

There was that phrase again. Had there been a memo?

"I'm your son's only advocate."

"He doesn't need one. What he needs is a mother who has a life. Interests outside of him. You're in this house too much. Put Jack in day care and get out."

What? She couldn't believe it. "Have you been talking to Dr. Miller behind my back?"

"No. Of course not. Why?" He shook his head. "Dammit, Jen, are you telling me that's what the doctor said? You never mentioned it."

She folded her arms across her chest and told herself she had no reason to feel guilty. She hadn't done anything wrong. She'd been to the pediatrician and there was nothing new to report. "What is there to say? You obviously know everything already."

"I didn't talk to her. Ask Lucas."

"Like I'd believe him."

"What did Dr. Miller tell you?"

She pressed her lips together. "She said there was nothing wrong with Jack and that I should put in him a playgroup or day care so he could socialize with other children."

His eyes narrowed. "You don't think that's something I would want to know?"

"Of course, it's just…"

He waited.

"I knew you'd judge me," she blurted. "You already think I'm losing my mind."

"I don't. I think you're too intense. I think you have too much time to worry. We talked about you going back to work. You wanted to put that off, but I'm wondering if that was a good idea."

She held in a shriek. "He's only eighteen months old. Do you want him with strangers five days a week? How could we trust that? Them? What about all the germs, the diseases? He's our child. We have to protect him."

"We can't keep him cooped up in this house forever. At some point he has to get out in the world."

Kirk didn't get it. She couldn't believe what he was suggesting. It was as if all she'd worked for didn't matter.

"You think he's fine," she said, fighting tears. "What if you're wrong? What if he needs us but we're too busy putting him in day care to notice?"

"What if he *is* fine?" Her husband shook his head. "I don't know, Jen. Are you defining yourself by having a child with problems? I'll ask you the opposite. Who will you be if our son is perfectly okay?"

She would have preferred he slap her, she thought as her heart cracked. "How could you?"

She spun on her heel and ran from the room. She locked herself in the guest bathroom and sank to the floor. Thank goodness she hadn't told Kirk she wanted to have sex with him last week. She was never having sex with him again. Why was he being so mean to her? Why didn't he understand?

Even as she cried, she half listened for Kirk to come to the door and tell her he was sorry. To beg her to forgive him. Only he never did.

Zoe patted Lulu. The Chinese crested had settled on her lap. Today's fashion statement was a lilac sweater dress that came nearly to her butt. The April weather had taken a chilly turn, with low clouds and fog that never cleared. The constant dampness made it seem colder than it was.

Pam poured them each a mug of tea and carried it over to the sofa in her condo living room.

"Have you talked to Jen?" Pam asked, sitting down.

"We've texted. We're getting together this week."

"Good. She and I haven't said a word to each other. That child of mine. She can be so frustrating. I worry about her." Pam grimaced. "I should have listened to you about the intervention. It was a disaster. I never wanted her upset. But of course she won't see that." She sipped her tea. "It's not easy being a parent."

"I'm sure my dad would agree with you."

Pam smiled. "I doubt that. You seem to be a perfectly wonderful daughter."

Zoe appreciated the compliment, even though she wasn't

sure she deserved it. "I have my flaws. He could tell you all about them."

"I'm sure he will," she said, her voice teasing. "I'm seeing him for dinner tonight."

Zoe did her best to keep her mouth from hanging open. "What? I'm mean, oh, wow. I didn't know you were dating." Pam and her dad? Not that Pam wasn't great, but Miguel tended to favor younger women. Although, as he'd pointed out, he hadn't done that in a while.

"Dating?" Pam laughed. "We're not. I can assure you of that. Dating. I don't date. He wants to talk to me about something." Her smile turned impish. "Do you have a birthday coming up? Want me to drop any hints?"

"No birthdays anytime soon."

Miguel wanted to have dinner with Pam? That was unexpected. Maybe he was looking for female friendship. Pam was funny and nice. Occasionally intense, but not in a bad way.

"You'll have to tell me how it goes," she said.

"Promise. Now about why you stopped by... I've been thinking."

Zoe had called Pam a couple of days ago and asked if they could talk about her future. She was feeling a bit at sea these days.

"Me, too," Zoe said. "You go first."

"Your job pays the bills and that's important. So quitting isn't an option. Am I right?"

Zoe continued to stroke Lulu and nodded.

"But your work isn't exactly full-time, so you have time to explore other things. I would suggest you start to think about what else you can do to feel more fulfilled in the short term while you explore your long-term options."

"I hadn't thought of it that way," Zoe admitted. "I was assuming I had to know what to do next. But you're right—I don't."

Pam picked up a pad of paper from the end table. "I did some brainstorming. I hope you don't mind."

"Of course not."

"Short term. You liked certain aspects of teaching but not others. So you don't know if you want to go back or not. Right?"

Zoe nodded.

"What about substitute teaching? You would certainly qualify. You can work a few days a week or a month without making a big commitment. That way you can decide if you really miss it or if you're remembering wrong."

"I never thought of substitute teaching." The idea was appealing. No yearlong commitment and she could try different grades. Maybe see if she had more interest in older or younger kids. "I like that."

"Good. We're just getting started. What about grad school? Is there a subject that interests you? You could audit a few classes at the undergraduate level to help you decide a direction." She glanced down at the paper. "There are online tests to help you determine your interests and give career options. I think taking a few of those would be good for you. Maybe you want to write a book or volunteer or work in your father's company."

They talked for the next hour. Zoe had to put Lulu on the cushion next to her so she could take notes. She knew that Pam worked with women entrepreneurs, but she'd had no idea her friend was so good at brainstorming. By the time Pam had gone through her list, Zoe had filled several pages with ideas and things to research.

"Thank you for this," she said earnestly. "You've given me so much to think about."

"I'm glad. This was fun for me. You're the one who has to do the hard work."

"It will be fun," Zoe told her. "I'm really excited to get

started." There were dozens of suggestions she never would have come up with on her own. "I appreciate all your time."

"My pleasure. I'm glad you asked when you did. I'm going to be out of town for a long weekend with my girlfriends and I wanted to make sure we talked before then."

"Where are you going?"

"Phoenix. These are the women I cruise with. We're meeting on land this time." Pam grinned. "I'm not sure how that is going to go."

"You're so busy. Your work at Moving Women Forward, your travel friends, your life here." Zoe felt boring by comparison.

"Babysitting," Pam added, "although not when Jen and I aren't speaking." She sighed. "I should call her. Despite everything, I miss her and I need to see my grandson."

Zoe put down her notepad. "Do you think there's something wrong with Jack?"

"No. He's fine. He'll talk when he's ready." She wrinkled her nose. "I'm the only one Jen trusts to look after Jack. He's adorable, but she makes it so hard. You wouldn't believe the rules she has. He's on a very rigid schedule, there are food restrictions. I can only run the dishwasher at certain times because of the soap."

"I don't understand."

Pam sighed. "She worries about the soap she uses in the dishwasher, so it can only run after he's in bed at night. Soap is huge in her life. Once I used the wrong detergent in the washer and she was furious."

"I don't think I'm ready for motherhood."

"Trust me—it doesn't have to be that complicated. I love my daughter, but honestly, she needs to take a chill pill." Pam frowned. "No one says that anymore, do they?"

"Not really."

"I'm old. I've embraced it."

Zoe rose. "Thank you again for everything. I have so much to think about."

"I'm glad I could help. Let me know what you decide."

"I will. I promise."

Pam couldn't remember the last time she'd been to The Farm Table. The upscale restaurant prided itself on all things local and organic. They even kept a couple of pigs to eat the table scraps. Jen would be impressed, she thought with a smile as she handed the valet her car keys.

Pam and John had come here occasionally, but it hadn't been one of their regular places. They preferred to dine more casually. Still, it wasn't the kind of restaurant she would go to with girlfriends, so she would enjoy the experience.

Before she could give her name to the hostess, she spotted Miguel.

The man had style, she thought, taking in the dark shirt and darker blazer over black jeans. His hair and beard were neatly trimmed, his skin tanned. He looked elegant. She had no idea what he wanted to talk about but that didn't matter. She was going to have a nice dinner with an interesting man. She would have fun and then return to her regularly scheduled life.

"Pamela." He crossed to her and took her hand in his. "You look lovely."

"As do you."

She'd decided on a dress and heels. Things she rarely wore. She'd taken extra time with her makeup and in the process had realized she needed yet another session with her BOTOX person. The frown lines were back. Pam didn't consider herself particularly vain, but fighting time was definitely an ongoing battle. BOTOX and lots of antiaging skin care products were her personal army.

"Our table is ready," Miguel told her. He held out his arm. "Shall we?"

Pam rested her hand in the crook of his elbow and together they followed the hostess to their corner table.

Despite the fact that it was midweek and off-season, the restaurant was relatively crowded. Pam knew from a few previous experiences that the menu was set for each night and the kitchen frowned on substitutions—all fine with her. She was up for a culinary adventure.

They had barely taken their seats when their server—a young man in his twenties—appeared with two glasses of champagne. A couple of cranberries and a sprig of rosemary floated in each.

"To prepare your palate for tonight's meal," he told them. "Welcome."

"This is going to be fun," Pam said as she held up her glass.

"I'm glad you think so."

They touched glasses, then drank. The herb added a nice earthiness to the sweet bubbles.

"Zoe tells me you have a small dog, as well," he said.

"I do. Lulu's a Chinese crested. Do you know what those are?"

He thought for a second. "The hairless, rock star dogs?"

Pam laughed. "That's her. She has to wear clothes to protect her from the cold and the sun, but I'll admit, I do take things to the next level. She has an entire wardrobe. With all my children grown, it's fun to be shopping for someone small."

"You have a grandson. Isn't he small?"

"Yes, but it's not the same. I hate to say it but boy clothes just aren't that interesting. Lulu lets me indulge my inner Disney princess." She sipped her champagne. "What about you? Mariposa is lovely, but not exactly what I would have expected from a man like you."

He laughed. The sound was low and appealing. She found herself wanting to laugh with him.

"A few years ago, when I started to travel less for work, I decided to get a dog. I wanted a midsized dog. I went to see a breeder about a boxer puppy she had. She also bred papillons. It was summer and I was sitting on the grass. The boxer puppy couldn't have been less interested, but Mariposa came right over and climbed on my lap. She was so tiny, but very determined." He raised one shoulder. "It was love at first sight. I took her home that day."

"She's adorable."

"We'll have to get our girls together."

"I'm sure Lulu would like that." She smiled. "Have you always lived in Mischief Bay?"

"I did when Constance and I were first married. Her family had been here for years."

"Constance?"

"Zoe's mother. My ex-wife."

Pam knew that Zoe's mother had passed away not long after John had died. But being married was different from being divorced, so saying "I'm sorry" seemed odd.

"How old was Zoe when you and Constance split up?" she asked instead.

"Eleven. I'm sure divorce is always hard on the children but we tried to make it as easy for Zoe as possible. We stayed friends." He picked up his glass. "Constance was a lovely, kind person. We simply had nothing in common. I wanted to travel the world and have exotic adventures. She wanted to live where she had always lived, seeing the same people, doing the same things."

"Plus there were all those young women in bikinis," she said before she could stop herself. Not that the Saldivar tequila ads were a secret.

One corner of his mouth lifted. "They were a temptation, I'll admit. But I was never unfaithful to her, if that's what you're asking. Of course, once I had my freedom, I took advantage of the landscape."

Pam wondered what that would be like. To have sex with dozens of different men she barely knew. She honestly couldn't see the point. She wondered how much of that was because she was a woman, how much was about her age and how much was because she'd only ever been with one man. John had been her one true love. Being with him, sexually, socially or any other way, had been wonderful. She was grateful for the time they had together. A string of meaningless encounters sounded awful by comparison.

"I'm not going to ask what you talked about," she said with a laugh. "I'm sure none of it was about conversation."

"It wasn't." He studied her. "You're not going to scold me?"

"Why would I? It's none of my business. There is something about your gender, though. My son-in-law is a detective with the Los Angeles Police Department. His partner is a man who's fifty. According to Jen, he hasn't dated a woman over the age of twenty-five. It's definitely a man thing. Women want more than a pretty face and a firm body."

"You wouldn't date a twenty-five-year-old?"

She grimaced. "Hardly. I have children older than that. I couldn't be less interested."

"I have to agree with you," Miguel told her. "In the past few years, I've found my interests turning elsewhere. As you said, I need someone I can talk to as well as make love with."

There was that voice again, she thought as she felt a slight shiver. What a great evening! It was like dinner and a show, all in one. She was sure that Miguel had his pick of women and even if he'd given up the twenty-year-olds, she doubted he'd gone much older. Not that she was interested. But she had to admit, hanging out with him was fascinating.

"Zoe must be relieved," she teased. "At least your girlfriends won't be asking to borrow her clothes."

He grinned. "That will please her. And speaking of men and women, I noticed Zoe spending time with your son. Did you have something to do with that?"

"I might have given a gentle push."

"Steven seems like a good man." Miguel's mouth twisted. "Unlike her last boyfriend."

She leaned forward and lowered her voice. "I know about Chad. Talk about a nightmare. I can't believe how long he strung her on."

"He's the one who should be strung up," Miguel said. "She tells me to stay out of it, but she's my daughter."

"Of course you feel protective. Steven's father passed away two years ago. While Steven had always planned to take over the company one day, he hadn't thought it would be for years."

She thought about those dark times, how she'd been devastated to the point of being unable to function. "He was there for me, for all of us. John's death changed him. I think Zoe's lucky to have him."

"Said with a mother's love."

"I like to think I'm offering an independent opinion."

"I'm sure you do."

He smiled at her. It was a great smile—full of charm and promise. When he looked at her, it was as if he was genuinely interested. A woman could get used to that kind of thing.

She knew that he was simply being who he was—an actor of sorts. A man used to being the center of attention. His job would have required him to have social flair and he'd been incredibly successful.

Their server appeared with their first course. Delicate scallops on greens with a blood orange reduction. The champagne was replaced with a sauvignon blanc.

"Do you still miss your husband?" Miguel asked.

"Yes, but it's different now. I have a full life I enjoy very much. Friends, my children, my grandson. I have my work at MWF. When John first died, I found it hard to breathe." She picked up her fork. "That sounds so dramatic when I say it now, but I assure you, it was true at the time. I couldn't do anything. For thirty years, I'd been John's wife. Without him, who was I?"

"How did you overcome that?"

"For a while I wasn't sure I ever would. I can't describe what I went through. Just moving forward, living my life, I couldn't do. I was faking being alive every day for the sake of my children."

How odd, she thought. While she didn't keep her past a secret, she wasn't usually so open with someone she barely knew. There was something about Miguel that she trusted, she supposed. Or maybe it was the way he looked at her, as if every word was incredibly important.

"You are a strong woman," he murmured.

"No, I'm not. Or I wasn't." She hesitated, then put down her fork and lowered her voice. "We'd booked a cruise before he died. Afterward, I didn't remember until our boarding passes turned up in his email. I was stunned. I didn't know what to do. At first I was going to cancel, but then I realized the cruise was the perfect escape."

"Escape?"

"From the pain. The emptiness. If I couldn't go on, then I wouldn't. I decided to kill myself. Throw myself off the ship. My children would think it was an accident, and while it would be hard on them, they would get over it." She shook her head. "It's funny when I say the words now. They seem so surreal and ridiculous. But I meant them at the time."

"You obviously changed your mind."

"I did. I met three wonderful women who were also widows. We became friends. I saw beautiful sights and began to understand that I could keep moving forward, even without John. I recognize the irony of the fact that deciding to kill myself was when I started healing. I love him, of course. I'll always be John's wife, but I've found my way without him."

She tilted her head. "Oh, my. I haven't told many people what my real plans were for the cruise. I'm not sure why I told you."

"I will keep your secret, Pamela." His dark gaze was steady. "You are an impressive woman."

She laughed. "I wish that were true. I'm ordinary at best."

"Far from that. I'm sure the men you date tell you that."

"Men?" Was he kidding? "There aren't any men."

"Why not?"

"Because. I'm a grandmother. I'm not interested in that sort of thing."

"We're all interested in that sort of thing. Besides, you're a young woman."

"I'm fifty-two."

"I am nearly sixty. We have many years ahead of us." His expression turned quizzical. "You really aren't seeing anyone?"

"No. Seeing someone?" She shook her head. "I don't date. That would be ridiculous."

Miguel studied her for a second, then pointed to her plate. "You should try the scallop. It's delicious."

The rest of the meal passed quickly. Pam refused the last two glasses of wine. She wanted to make sure she could drive home without a problem. The food was excellent, the company even better. Miguel entertained her with stories of his travels. They talked about their children when they'd been young. She was shocked to find that it was nearly midnight when they finally left the restaurant.

"Lulu is going to be very unhappy with me for leaving her alone for so long," she said as they waited at the valet station for their cars. The night was cool and dark and they were the only ones standing there.

"The leftovers will go a long way to soothing her feelings," he told her.

Pam laughed. "I suspect you're right. Lulu is very sweet, but she's not exactly emotionally deep."

"I had an enjoyable evening with you tonight," he said.

"I did, as well. Thank you again for dinner."

"So how was it?"

"The meal?"

"The date."

Pam opened her mouth, then closed it. "D-date?" Her mind went totally blank.

"When a man asks a woman to dinner with the idea of getting to know her better, it is generally called a date."

"I don't date."

"So you said earlier, but as you have just been on one, I'm going to have to say that you are wrong."

"I... You..."

The valet drove up with her SUV, saving her from babbling more. A date? She'd thought he was going to ask her to help him buy Zoe a present or something. But come to think of it, shopping for his daughter had never come up.

He walked her around to the driver's side of her car and tipped the valet. Before she could figure out what to say or do, Miguel leaned in and lightly brushed his mouth against hers.

"Good night, Pamela. I'll call you in a few days and do my best to convince you to go out with me again."

As she had no reply for that, she got into her car, closed the door, waved and drove away. It was only when she was safely home and soothing a miffed Lulu with bits of duck and scallop that she allowed herself to consider the fact that she very well might have just been on a date. The realization left her feeling guilty and uncomfortable and maybe just the tiniest bit excited about seeing Miguel again.

Chapter Eight

Thursday Zoe showed up with a box of scones and high hopes for her afternoon with Jen. She was also a little nervous, as this was their first post-intervention meeting. While Jen had been friendly enough in their recent texts, maybe all wasn't forgiven and forgotten.

She tapped lightly on the front door. Seconds later, Jen opened the door. The two women stared at each other, then Jen rushed forward and hugged her.

"I'm sorry," Jen said. "For not being a better friend."

"I'm sorry, too. I should never have come over with your mom. It wasn't right."

Jen stepped back and shut the door behind Zoe. "I get why you did it. I'm so focused on Jack all the time. Everyone is telling me to lighten up. I get what they're saying, but hearing the words doesn't make me any less scared about how he's developing."

"I was wrong to judge," Zoe said, and meant it. Sure she thought Jen was overly involved, but that wasn't her call. She thought about mentioning her second thoughts about the intervention but didn't see the point. Not only would it be throwing Pam under the bus, but she had in fact showed up. Therefore she had at least half the blame.

They went into the kitchen. Jen started making tea as Zoe unpacked the scones.

"Tell me what's going on with you," Jen said. "How's work? How's the house? The barbecue was great, by the way. We had such a good time."

"I'm glad. I'm doing okay."

"Just okay?"

Zoe sat at the kitchen table. "I don't know what to do about my life."

"Oh, is that all?"

Zoe smiled. "Yeah, yeah, dramatic much? I get it." She sighed. "I don't know if I made the right decision to give up teaching. I don't want to go back, but I sure don't like what I'm doing now. It's boring and I feel really isolated."

Jen poured boiling water into the teapot, then carried it over to the table. She'd already set out cups and saucers, along with a tea strainer.

"Plus, you thought you and Chad would be married by now, right? Maybe with you pregnant?"

Zoe had to admit that was true—even if now she couldn't imagine why she'd stayed with Chad as long as she had. "I don't know why I thought he was the one. I let him lead me on for years. I was an idiot."

"You were giving him the benefit of the doubt. Any second thoughts about dumping him?"

"No," Zoe said firmly. "We are totally done. I swear. I don't hate him. I don't miss him. I wish him a really good life. Just not with me."

"I'm so glad. I never liked him."

But being a good friend, she wouldn't have said that before. "My dad told me the same thing last weekend. Apparently it was a fan club of one."

Jen picked up a white chocolate chip scone and broke it

in half. "I saw you hanging out with Steven at the barbecue. Are you seeing him?"

"Sort of. Maybe. Yes." Zoe ducked her head. "Is that too weird?"

"That you're dating my brother? No. Before Dad died, I would have warned you off. He was not into relationships. But he's different now. More settled. I think you two would be an interesting couple."

"Interesting?"

Jen grinned. "Yes. And fun. Because everyone wants to be the fun couple, but so few of us can be."

Zoe laughed. This was the Jen she enjoyed. The friend who was interested in everyone around her. The woman who was more than just Jack's mother.

"How are you feeling?" Zoe asked. "Better?"

Jen's smile faded. "No. Kirk and I are fighting. I know you didn't tell him about coming by with Mom, but it's like he was in the room. He's on me to put Jack in day care a couple of days a week. He thinks I should go back to work."

"What do you think?"

"I miss teaching, but how could I leave Jack in one of those places? I want to be the one he spends his time with."

"I don't know enough about babies to have an opinion on that," Zoe said carefully, not wanting to upset their renewed connection. "Do toddlers need socialization with other kids?"

"Yes." Jen sounded more frustrated than happy. "It's an important part of development. So I need him in a playgroup. I just can't find one I like. My mom is the only one I trust to take care of him for me. And I doubt she's going to be willing to do that more than she is now. She's busy all the time."

"So do you *want* to go back to work?" Zoe asked.

"I miss teaching. I miss my students."

Jen had been an elementary teacher when Zoe had met her.

"What about you?" Jen asked. "Is middle school English calling you back?"

"God, no. I can't imagine dealing with that again. But there are elements of teaching I do miss. Maybe I'd like younger kids or older kids more." She took a bite of her scone. "I'm thinking of substitute teaching."

"You're certainly qualified. It would give you the chance to try different ages and figure out if you want to go back. But it can be a pretty thankless task."

"I'm still considering. What are you going to do?"

Jen sighed. "I have no idea. I worry about Kirk and me. I blame Lucas."

"Kirk's partner? Why?"

"He's got all these young chickies in his life. God knows what he's telling Kirk." Jen's eyes filled with tears. "What if he's having an affair?"

"Kirk loves you. He's not the kind of guy to do that." Zoe was sure Kirk had plenty of flaws—everyone did—but she knew how much he loved his wife and son.

"His work is stressful. He's out of touch for hours at a time. He could be doing anything."

"Have you talked about this with him?" Zoe asked.

Jen wiped her eyes. "You mean sat him down and had a rational conversation? Why on earth would I want to do that?"

Zoe smiled. "Being mature is a real bitch, isn't it?"

"Tell me about it." Jen sniffed, then reached for a second scone. "Thank you for being my friend."

"Back at you."

Pam counted down the minutes until her Pilates class finished. She'd been out of sorts for two days now and she knew the reason. The problem was—who could she talk to? She'd finally settled on her friend Shannon. They'd known each other for several years. Shannon had totally been there for her when John had died and, more important, she trusted both Shannon's advice and discretion.

Nicole released them from the plank position and instead of sagging to the floor, Pam scrambled to her feet. Yes, yes, her muscles were whimpering, but she had more important things to worry about. Like getting some advice. Luck was on her side—Zoe hadn't come to the class, which meant Pam didn't have to worry about her overhearing, or wanting to go out for a late lunch. Not that Pam didn't like spending time with Zoe, but Miguel was her father. Talk about complicated.

Shannon, a successful fortysomething who had married for the first time a year and a half ago, walked over. "You were on a tear today. Feeling our oats, are we?"

Pam shook her head. "I need to talk to you about something. Do you have a few minutes before you have to be at work?"

"Of course. Let me get changed and then you can drive me back to my office. There's a coffee place in the lobby."

"Perfect."

Ten minutes later they were making the short drive to Shannon's office building. Although Pam hadn't changed back into street clothes, she had brought a long tunic top to pull over her exercise outfit, so she wasn't totally out of place.

They placed their orders at the coffee shop, then waited for the lattes to be made. Once they had their drinks, they retreated to a couple of chairs in the lobby. Shannon faced her.

"So what's up?"

"Nothing bad," Pam said quickly. "Everyone is fine. It's just…" She drew in a breath. "Remember Zoe who came to class a couple of weeks ago?"

"Sure. Jen's friend."

"We've been hanging out some and I went to a party at her house. Her dad was there."

Shannon grinned. "How very age-appropriate. I see where this is going."

"How can you? I didn't."

"What does that mean?"

"Miguel, her father, is a very handsome man." Pam explained about his role with Saldivar tequila. "He's traveled all over the world, he's…" She clutched her coffee. "It actually doesn't matter about him because he's not the point."

Shannon's lips twitched in obvious amusement. "What *is* the point?"

"We went out to dinner. I thought he wanted to ask me about Zoe or something."

"I love you so much," Shannon told her. "You are always entertaining."

"Stop it! This is important." Pam stared at her intently. "Brace yourself."

"I'm braced."

"Fine. When we were done, he told me it was a date! And then he kissed me."

"That bastard!"

Pam glared at her friend. "You're not taking this seriously."

"That would be true."

"You have to. This is significant. I don't date."

"All evidence to the contrary."

Pam felt frustration building inside of her. "You're not listening."

"I'm hanging on your every word." Her tone gentled. "I get you're upset, but where's the bad here? A handsome man took you to dinner and then kissed you. To me, that sounds like fun. You're single. He's single. Why not enjoy the ride?"

"I'm…" Pam pressed her lips together and did her best to keep from shrieking. "I'm not single."

Shannon touched her arm. "You're not married. You're a

widow. Yes, John was a wonderful man and you were lucky to be with him, but he's been gone a long time. It's okay to—"

"If you say 'move on,' I swear I'll throw this coffee in your face."

"No, you won't."

"I won't. But I'm not dating. And I'm not single. I'm never getting married again. I wouldn't do that to John."

"Okay. That's fine, but there's an entire universe between a first date and marriage." Her friend scooted closer. "Pam, you could live for another forty years. Don't you want to think about the possibility that you might want to share a few of those years with someone?"

"No."

Shannon continued as if she hadn't spoken. "I'm not suggesting Miguel is 'the one.'" She made air quotes with one hand. "But he sounds like a great place to start exploring the possibilities."

Pam couldn't have been more shocked if Shannon had suddenly started singing in Russian. "What about John?"

"Don't you think he would want you to be happy?"

"Not with someone else."

Shannon sipped her coffee before saying, "Really? John would want you to be alone?"

Pam sucked in a breath, then exhaled. "I can't think about this. I'm not going to date anyone."

"Aren't you lonely? Ever? Don't you miss having a man in your life?"

Yes, of course. But the man she wanted was her husband. And if she couldn't have him… Well, maybe she didn't want to say she wouldn't be interested in anyone ever, but it was too soon. Years too soon for her to be thinking about dating.

"I'm not ready," she amended. "And if I were, I wouldn't want to see Miguel. He's too…"

"Handsome? Sexy? Experienced?"

"Yes. I want someone more..."

"Like you?"

"Maybe."

"Then go find him. In the meantime, practice on Miguel. He can be your starter boyfriend."

Pam drew back. "I'm too old to have a boyfriend."

"Apparently not." Shannon grinned. "So how was the kiss?"

Pam thought about the brief, warm pressure. "Nice," she admitted.

"Any tongue?"

She groaned. "I swear I can't take you anywhere."

"And yet, you love me."

"That I do."

The detailed workings of advanced MRI screening machines required Zoe's complete concentration. A little after eleven in the morning, she took a break. Mason was stretched out in the sun, basking, as he always did. She stepped over him and headed for the kitchen to make tea. While the water heated, she would walk around her backyard, which would almost qualify as exercise. Now that she was doing Pilates two days a week, she found herself thinking she should move more in her regular life.

She'd barely made it to the kitchen when the doorbell rang. She glanced at her cat. "Is that the UPS guy? Did you go online and order cat toys, young man? I thought we talked about that."

Mason barely twitched an ear.

"I remember when you hung on my every word," she joked as she pulled open the door. But instead of the UPS guy, Chad stood on her front porch. Chad whom she hadn't seen since the stupid sex incident.

"Hey, Zoe."

He was about six feet, with reddish-blond hair and a winning smile. She remembered how that smile had hit her when they'd first met, on the shoulder of the 405 freeway. Now, as she took in his familiar features, she braced herself for the onslaught of emotions sure to follow.

There was surprise—which was to be expected. A vague sense of *why now*, followed by...nothing. She inhaled and checked again. There was nothing.

"Chad." She leaned against the door. "Why are you here?"

He wore a white T-shirt and jeans. Clothes he would change out of at work where he wore a uniform. She had always loved him in jeans and a T-shirt. They were sexy and so everyman. Today she would admit he looked good, but her heart wasn't racing and she didn't feel those low-in-the-belly tingles anymore. How unexpected. It seemed she might actually be over him.

"I want to talk," he said. "Zoe, aren't you going to let me in?"

Making him stand outside made more of a statement than she wanted, so she moved aside. Mason raised his head, stared at Chad for a second, then relaxed and closed his eyes, as if dismissing the man. Mason had always been an excellent judge of character.

Zoe deliberately sat in one of the living room chairs instead of the sofa. She didn't want Chad too close.

"How can I help you?" she asked.

He frowned. "That's kind of cold. Are you punishing me?"

"I'm working. You dropped by unexpectedly. We're not involved anymore and I don't know why you're here so I'm asking what's going on."

"You're still angry."

"I'm not." Far from it. She was kind of happy about her lack of reaction.

He sat with his elbows resting on his thighs, his hands

hanging loose. "I miss you. I miss us. I want us to get back together. Just tell me what that will take and I'll do it."

She crossed her legs. She hadn't seen this coming and didn't know what to do with the information. She wasn't happy to hear any of it. There was no sense of relief or excitement. Yet more proof that she'd moved on.

Time really did heal. Or maybe it was more than that. Maybe there hadn't been that much to get over. Because looking back, she could see that she and Chad hadn't had much of a relationship.

"Are you going to say something?" he asked impatiently. "You've left me hanging here."

"What does *get back together* mean?" she asked, curious as to what he was offering. "You'd come over a few nights a week. We'd hang out, have sex, then you'd go back to your place?"

"What's wrong with that?" His voice was cautious, as if he sensed a trap but couldn't quite see it.

"Nothing. It's what we always did." She turned the information over in her head. "That's all we did. We rarely went to the movies or even out to eat. We never traveled together."

"It's hard for me to get away. I have work and the kids."

"Right, and they take all your vacation days. And it's not as if I could have gone along. I mean, they barely knew me."

He scowled. "Are you going to keep bringing that up? You've met them. Why isn't that enough? They have to deal with the divorce. They're still adjusting."

She didn't point out it had been almost two years. That whatever was happening between their parents, they were used to it now. Because this wasn't about the kids. It never had been.

"We never had a relationship, Chad. That's my fault as much as yours. We didn't do anything together. We didn't have couple friends. Our relationship was dinner and sex and very little else. I have no idea why I never saw that before."

"Is this about getting married?" he asked, then shook his head. "You're obsessed with getting married."

"I'm not. It was never about the ring, Chad, it was about commitment. It was about being a part of each other's lives." The argument was so familiar. Whenever she tried to take things to the next level, he always deflected her in one way or another.

"And here you are, doing it again. Oh, my God. You've been doing it for years." She was talking out loud, but more to herself than him. "I would push for something and you would distract me with a different argument. Usually about how I was obsessed with getting married. I got embarrassed and immediately pulled back. The argument ended and life went on."

She couldn't believe she hadn't seen that before. "You don't want a relationship. You want a Zoe compartment in your life. An easy booty call with a bonus dinner. Worse, I allowed you to have that. I didn't demand more. Because here's the thing. I'm not wrong to want someone who actually wants to be involved with my life. Maybe it's not what you want, and that's fine, but you don't get to make me feel bad about what's important to me."

She stood. A sense of empowerment left her almost light-headed. Chad grimaced.

"You're not making any sense."

She looked at him. Six months ago she would have sworn she loved this man. But the truth was he'd allowed her to be lazy. For too long, she'd let him be enough. Well, not anymore.

"I don't want to see you again, Chad. We don't want the same things. I wish you every happiness, but it won't be with me."

He stood. "You're going to regret this," he told her. "I was good to you."

She walked to the door and held it open. "Goodbye, Chad."

He looked like he was going to say something else, then shook his head and walked out. She closed the door behind him and glanced at Mason.

"I think that was impressive, don't you?"

She got a tail flick in response.

"I'm going to take that as a yes."

Chapter Nine

Jen pulled into the parking lot of the Learning and Growing Day Care Center on Maness Avenue. The building was large and painted in bright, primary colors. There were trees and lawn and the sound of shrieking children in a big playground off to the side.

According to her research, the day care center had gotten high marks from several parents, it was accredited and none of the employees had criminal records. While that wasn't as much information as she would like, she figured she had to start somewhere.

It was three minutes before ten. She and Jack had a ten o'clock appointment with the director. Even though every bone in her body told her to keep Jack safe at home, a very small part of her brain whispered that it was possible that her son might enjoy hanging out with kids his age. Socialization was an important part of his development, and at the end of the day, it was all about Jack.

She opened the back door of her SUV. Jack smiled and clapped his hands as she unfastened him, then lifted him out. He was a happy, wiggling bundle. She set him on the ground, then took his hand and locked her car.

"This is going to be great," she told him, hoping she wasn't lying. "You'll see. There will be lots of kids and enrichment and you're going to love it."

They walked to the main doors and went inside. There was a small reception area with an unmanned desk to the left and a hallway leading to several large rooms. As she watched, a boy about four wandered down the hall and no one seemed to notice.

Jack started after him. Jen picked him up.

"We're going to wait here for our appointment with Angela," she said cheerfully.

Two minutes later she still hadn't seen an adult, so she started going from room to room. The first two were empty. The third had about fifteen toddlers with only two adults. The noise level was astonishing and chaos reigned.

"Hello," she called. "I'm looking for Angela."

One of the women glanced up. "Her office is at the end of the hall. Aaron, no, don't throw the truck."

"Thanks." Jen glanced over her shoulder. "There's a little boy wandering around out here by himself."

The two women exchanged a look. One rolled her eyes and started out of the room. Just then one of the little boys hit another with a decent-sized toy truck. The blow landed squarely across the bridge of the nose and blood erupted along with shrieks of pain.

"Aaron, what did you do? I've told you and told you."

Jen backed out of the room as the other children joined in the crying. Jack clung to her, looking worried.

No way, she thought grimly. This wasn't day care, this was a badly run institution.

They returned to their SUV. Jen called Angela and got put directly to her voice mail. She left a message, canceling her appointment, then looked at the address of the second place she wanted to visit.

The Learning Academy of Mischief Bay was also accredited

and had plenty of parent recommendations, but it was smaller. Jen had been worried there wouldn't be sufficient staff, but it wasn't like the bigger place had enough people around.

What she wanted to do was drive straight home, to the safety of Jack's ordinary world. But Kirk's words still burned, so she told herself she would give the second place five minutes and then she could be done.

The drive from one day care center to the other took less than ten minutes. This time she found herself in a quiet, residential part of town. The house with the sign in front was across from the playground at Founders Park. There were plenty of trees and nice lawns. The homes were older, but well kept.

Once again she collected Jack and walked to the front door. She rang the bell and was stunned when she heard a dog bark. Who on earth allowed a dog in a day care center? What if the kids were allergic? What if the dog bit someone?

She nearly turned back to her car, but before she could bolt, the door opened and a middle-aged woman smiled at her. "Can I help you?"

"I'm Jen Beldon and this is my son, Jack. Our appointment is at eleven, so we're a little early." Like forty-five minutes early, but Jen wasn't going to admit that out loud.

"Of course. I'm Rose. Come on in."

Jen carried Jack inside.

What had been the living room had been turned into a play area. The big, open space had large windows and a thick mat on the floor. There were shelves filled with toys, a large television against one wall and lots of seating. Small chairs and low sofas, beanbag chairs and a few kid-sized rocking chairs.

"This is one of our play areas," Rose explained. "We have movie afternoons on Monday and Thursday. Otherwise, there's no TV allowed. Our philosophy is that of gentle scheduling." She laughed. "Our goal is to stick to a schedule, but we're dealing with children under the age of five, so we have to be flexible."

Just then a midsize, blue heeler trotted into the room. He had an expressive face, with two brown "eyebrows" and a happy, doggy grin. Despite his wagging tail, Jen instinctively took a step back. Rose motioned for the dog to move closer to her.

"This is Buddy." Rose turned to the dog. "Buddy, can you say hello?"

Buddy raised a paw and gave a low woof. Jen held on to Jack.

"Is it safe having a dog in the house with so many children? What if he bites someone?"

"I certainly understand your concern," said Rose, laying a protective hand on Buddy's head. "He was a service dog for three years. The little girl he was helping passed away and he was devastated. The family and I are friends, so I offered to take Buddy. He's great with the kids here."

Which all sounded fine and well, Jen thought suspiciously, but didn't answer her question.

Rose showed her the dining room that had been converted into a lunch area for the children with smaller-scale tables and chairs. The kitchen looked clean enough. What would have been the family room was also a play area. Jen saw about six toddlers with two caregivers. There were several puzzles on the floor. Outside was a big backyard with plenty of play equipment, large trees, grass and a shady area. Another five or six children played outside and there were two more caregivers with them.

"You're using a lot of your house for day care," she murmured, putting Jack down so he could join the puzzle group.

"My own children are long grown and my husband passed away," Rose told her. "I built an apartment upstairs. I live there and the downstairs is for my business."

Jack walked over and sat down. He reached for a puzzle piece. One of the helpers, a woman in her early twenties, Jen would guess, smiled at him.

"Hi. I'm Holly. Who are you?"

"He doesn't talk," Jen said quickly. "Not yet."

Holly nodded. "That's okay. You'll talk when you're ready. Do you like puzzles? I do. This piece is red."

"Everyone who works for me has a background in either education or early childhood development." Rose pointed to an older woman outside with the other kids. "Mary's been with me nearly ten years. She raised eight children herself, then worked a couple of other places before coming here. Holly is getting her master's in early childhood development. She works here part-time."

Rose talked about how their days were structured and the various programs they offered. A lady came in three mornings a week and taught Mandarin. An older gentleman came and played various musical instruments every Monday and Thursday. But Jen wasn't really listening. Instead she saw that the walls were scuffed and the windows could use a good washing.

She wanted to head back to the kitchen and look at the counters. Were they really clean? Had she seen a jar of peanut butter? Because everyone knew that young children should avoid peanuts. And that dog. She didn't care what Buddy had done before—he was an animal. If a child pulled his tail, he would react.

The little boy next to Jack sneezed. Jen moved toward her son and scooped him up.

She was sure there were sensible questions she was supposed to be asking. On the surface the place was great—if she ignored the dog, the peeling paint and the sick kid.

She felt the familiar tightness in her chest. The one that made it hard to breathe.

Not here, she told herself. She couldn't have a panic attack. Not right now. Later, when she was home. Later, when she was safe. She couldn't do this, she thought desperately. She couldn't leave her child alone in a place like this.

"I have to go," she said, fighting to keep her breath as her chest got tighter and tighter.

Rose looked confused. "Don't you want to fill out an application?" she asked. "I'm going to have an opening in a few weeks. Usually I have a waiting list, but right now I don't."

Jen clutched Jack to her chest. "I, ah, need to talk to my husband. And think about it. I'm just not sure."

She bolted for the door. Rose followed.

"Are you all right?" the other woman asked with concern.

Jen nodded and ran to her car. She got Jack into his car seat, then started the engine. She punched the buttons on the radio until she found the happy children's music Jack liked and turned up the volume. Only then did she start gasping for air.

Her throat was so tight. Her whole body hurt. Tears burned her eyes as she sucked in air.

She told herself she was fine. That she could breathe. That nothing was wrong. Only she knew she was lying. Everything was wrong—and no one would believe her.

What are you doing?

Pam stared at her phone. There was nothing untoward about the message, yet she still felt a strange combination of guilty and naughty as she answered.

Reading.

Would you like some company?

She dropped the phone on the sofa, picked it up again, put it back down, then pressed a pillow against her face and screamed into the soft fabric. Lulu jumped to her feet and stared at her.

"I'm fine," she assured her dog. "It's just… Never mind."

Still looking wary, Lulu curled back up on the sofa.

Pam and Miguel had been texting every day or so since their dinner together. She refused to call it by the other *D* word, despite what Shannon had said. It had been dinner and talking with, ah, the father of a friend. Nothing more.

Even so, her fingers trembled as she typed, sure.

I'll be there in fifteen minutes. I'll bring the limes.

Limes? What did that mean? Was it code for— She groaned. It wasn't code for anything. The man's family made tequila. He probably always had limes on him.

She stood and stared at Lulu. "We're going to have company."

The little dog scrambled to her feet, as if she understood the urgency of the situation, if not the particulars.

Pam scanned her living room. The condo wasn't large— just two bedrooms, a living room and kitchen/dining area. She'd been used to taking care of a much larger place and had no trouble keeping up with the cleaning. She'd dusted and vacuumed just the day before. The guest bath was tidy, the kitchen picked up. There was really nothing for her to do.

She glanced at Lulu. The Chinese crested had on a simple silver T-shirt with the word *Princess* on the back, in shiny letters. Perhaps not Miguel's style, but then she wasn't asking him to wear it. As for herself…

She glanced down, then shrieked again and bolted for her bedroom. She was in a ratty old T-shirt and shorts. While her legs were toned, they were pale and there were a few veins. In her regular life, this didn't bother her, but for some reason, she was suddenly determined to cover up.

She quickly changed into ankle-length pants and a fitted

tank top, then threw on a matching, lightweight, tailored short-sleeved shirt. She left her feet bare, but touched up her makeup, then went into the kitchen and wondered if she should put out some kind of snack.

She tried to figure out how much time had passed. No way she could throw some snacky thing together. Besides, it wasn't as if this was a *planned* meeting. She couldn't be responsible for providing food with no warning.

She'd just about talked herself out of panic when she heard a knock on the door. Lulu gave a little announcement bark, then trotted to the front door, her tail wagging. Pam sucked in a breath, told herself everything was fine, then opened the door.

"Pamela."

The obvious delight in Miguel's voice, the sight of him in worn jeans and a relatively subdued Hawaiian shirt, while looking all manly and handsome, did a number on her breathing. Or maybe she was having a hot flash. She wasn't sure. She had to clear her throat before she could speak.

"Ah, Miguel. Come in."

He smiled at her, then crouched down, offering his fingers to Lulu. "Not until you introduce me to this beautiful girl."

"This is Lulu."

Miguel stroked the side of her face. The Chinese crested let her eyes sink closed for a second before offering a kiss. Pam was almost jealous—the man did have a way with women, she thought. Not that she was interested in that sort of thing. It was simply... All right. Fine. She had no idea what it was, so she would ignore it.

Miguel stepped into her condo and crossed to the large French doors. Beyond the balcony was the boardwalk, then sand, then ocean for as far as the eye could see.

"Beautiful," he said. "You must enjoy watching the ocean and her many moods."

"I do. I lived in a house for years, so I wasn't sure how I would adjust to condo living. Sometimes I feel like my place is a little small but this makes it all worthwhile."

He turned and she saw he had a leather backpack hanging from one shoulder. He took it off and smiled. "I come prepared." He pointed to the kitchen. "May I?"

She nodded, not sure what he was going to do.

Once in her kitchen, he set the backpack on the island counter, then opened it. Inside was a bottle of his family's tequila, several limes, Cointreau and a martini shaker. She started to laugh.

"Seriously? You take that with you everywhere you go?"

"Not everywhere, but many places. Now I need a cutting board and some ice. It's nearly five o'clock."

She got him what he requested. As she filled her small ice bucket, she found a box of frozen mini quiches and pulled them out. If they were going to be drinking tequila, she was going to need food.

While the oven preheated, Miguel crossed to Lulu and lifted her into his arms. He held her easily—not a surprise. He had a small dog himself and would be used to the delicate bones. He cradled her, supporting her and patting her at the same time. Lulu relaxed into the attention.

He took up more space than Pam was used to. Except for her sons, she'd never had a man over to her place and she wasn't sure what to do with herself. Part of her wanted to keep her distance while the rest of her wanted to move closer. Of course, the thought of being too close made her uncomfortable, so she was well and truly confused.

"Have you thought about our dinner?" he asked.

"Some."

He raised his eyebrows, as if questioning her honesty.

She sighed. "All right. Yes, I have."

"Good. I have, as well. You are a beautiful and interesting woman, Pamela."

She laughed. "Oh, please. There's no need to turn on the charm like that."

"You think I'm not telling the truth? How do you see yourself?"

A question that had her totally stumped. How did she see herself? She was a mother, a friend, a wife—although that last role was different now. As for how Miguel had described her, she honestly didn't know what to make of that.

"I don't know how to do this," she admitted, "and I'm not sure I want to. You're very charming and while that's fun, I don't know what you want or expect from me."

She thought that even if they were dating—which they weren't—it was way too soon to be having this conversation. Still, she couldn't seem to stop herself.

"I was married over thirty years. Being with John is all I know. I'm his wife and that is never going to change."

Miguel continued to hold Lulu. "I don't want you to be other than you already are. The person you are today is the woman I find so intriguing. What are you afraid of? Losing your past? You can't. John is with you always. He is a part of you."

Not anything she expected. "If you get that, then why are you here?"

"Because you still have a future, Pamela. Many years ahead of you. I'd like to get to know you better. See where this leads. Now that I understand you haven't felt ready to date, I'll go more slowly." He flashed her a smile. "I'm old enough to appreciate the power of anticipation."

But I'm not interested in you in that way. That was what she meant to say. What she should say. Because she wasn't. Other men weren't on her radar. She wasn't looking for anything other than what she had.

Only she couldn't seem to speak the words. She was confused and sad, but also fighting a very real flicker of, if not hope, then maybe expectation. Miguel reminded her of the best part of her marriage. The connection. Being a part of something. Knowing someone. She hadn't thought she would ever go there again and maybe she still wouldn't. But refusing to consider the possibility no longer seemed so important.

The oven dinged. She slid in the tray of mini quiches. Miguel set Lulu down and walked to the sink. After washing his hands, he turned to her.

"I'm going to teach you how to make a margarita."

"I know how."

The smile returned. "You only think you do. Believe me. I'm a professional. There are secrets that will leave you amazed."

"Highly unlikely, but sure. You can try."

He laughed. "You're not easy, are you?"

"No. I'm also confused and wary, just so you know."

His humor faded. He moved close and stared into her eyes. "Be comfortable saying no, Pamela. At the same time, be comfortable saying yes. Every now and then life gives us an unexpected opportunity. How sad to walk away without sampling what is offered."

Before she could respond, he leaned over and kissed her. Just once and oh so lightly. He straightened and walked to the island.

"The perfect margarita begins with great tequila. I brought you the best."

"You might be a little prejudiced about that."

"I'm not. I've tried all the others and this is by far the most superior tequila ever made. Now the secret to the perfect margarita is proportion and very sweet limes. Do you know how to tell if a lime is sweet?"

She leaned against the counter and smiled. "No, but I have a feeling you're going to tell me."

He winked. "I'm going to show you, Pamela, which is much, much more interesting."

Jen's ongoing research about Jack had finally led her to someone she hoped could help. So Thursday morning she left Jack with her mother and an hour later had parked outside a three-story medical building in Orange County. The outside was a little shabby, but Jen was more concerned about the woman she was meeting inside.

She went up to the third floor and found the office. Deirdre McCallan was an herbalist and nurse practitioner who had rave reviews on several parenting sites. Deirdre specialized in treating autistic children with herbal remedies and other alternative therapies.

Jen had come prepared. She had copies of Jack's medical records, including his most recent blood work and the results of several evaluations. She'd also recorded a few home sessions so Deirdre could see how he interacted.

The reception area was small, with a worn love seat and a single wooden chair. The air smelled of incense and sandalwood. Primitive art decorated the walls. Jen perched on the edge of the wooden chair and told herself everything would be fine. If not this woman, then she would find someone else. She wasn't giving up on her son.

Right at eleven the inner door opened and a tall, thin woman about forty or so came out.

"You must be Jennifer," she said, holding out her hand. "I'm Deirdre. So nice to meet you. Please come back and let's talk."

The private office was about three times the size of the waiting area. There were bookshelves lining two walls and fabric hangings on the others. A large window opened onto the parking lot and the freeway beyond.

The furniture was overstuffed with an Asian influence. There were several carved wood tables and a few low stools along with two sofas. The incense smell was stronger here. A refrigerator hummed in the corner. Next to that was a cabinet with a large lock by the handle.

Deirdre motioned to one of the sofas. "Please, make yourself comfortable."

When they were seated, Deirdre leaned forward. "Tell me what brings you here today."

"It's about my son. Jack. He's nineteen months old." Jen explained how he'd been growing just fine, doing everything he was supposed to do, on time. Until recently. She handed over the records, talked about the tests and finished with, "I know there's something wrong. I'm with him every day and I feel it in my gut. But no one will listen. No one believes me."

Deirdre sighed. "I feel your frustration. Western medicine is excellent when it comes to mechanics. You can't meditate away a broken bone. But with the more subtle issues, especially those involving the brain, it is still in the Dark Ages. If it isn't detailed in a textbook, it doesn't exist." She offered a sympathetic smile. "You're his mother. Of course you would sense what was right and what was wrong about your own child."

She held out her hand and Jen passed over the files. "The human body is a complex organism," she continued. "So many systems interact in unique and unexpected ways. The immune system alone baffles us. What causes cancer? MS? Dementia. We're barely scratching the surface."

Jen listened politely, but honestly had no idea what the other woman was going on about. "I just want Jack to talk."

"Of course you do. To talk and be like other children. It's what all parents want."

"Can you help me?"

Deirdre continued to smile. "I'm going to do my best." She rested her hands on the files but didn't open them. "Let me tell you how my process works. I'll review his tests then arrange for a few of my own. I'll want to have his hair analyzed for toxins. We'll need to do a saliva test, which will be challenging as he's so young, but it's not impossible."

"That's a cheek swab?"

Deirdre shook her head. "He will spit saliva into test tubes at different times during the day."

There was a yucky visual, Jen thought as her stomach lurched. "Okay," she said slowly.

Deirdre set Jack's file on the table, then went to her desk. There she picked up a slim folder and handed it to Jen.

"This will explain the basic toddler package. I suggest we start there. I'll want to start him on supplements right away."

Jen stiffened. The folder slipped from her fingers and fell to the floor. "Supplements. What do you mean?"

"He's low on essential elements."

"You haven't even met him. How can you know that?"

Deirdre's smile was knowing. "Because of where he lives and what he eats. Our food has been robbed of all its nutrients. Your son is in a state of amino acid starvation. Everyone is. With Jack, it's manifesting in his inability to talk."

Supplements? "What's in them?"

"My proprietary blend. I'm afraid I can't tell you what that is. I hope you'll understand."

Jen felt the last bubble of hope pop. She didn't let her son watch TV or eat sugar. There was no way she was going to give him a bunch of mystery supplements.

Deirdre's kind expression never changed. "I know this is difficult. You're confused and afraid. What I'm offering isn't traditional medicine and what we aren't used to can be frightening to us. Take the material and read it. When you're ready, bring Jack to meet me and we'll get started. In the meantime, I would love to check your hormone level. I'm sure they're still out of balance from your pregnancy."

"I just want my son to talk," she repeated. There had to be an answer somewhere. *But not here*, she thought as she rose. She grabbed Jack's file from the coffee table. "How much do I owe you for the consultation?"

"The first visit is always complimentary." Deirdre rose. "I feel your pain, Jennifer. I can help. When you're ready, I'll be here."

If only that information was helpful, Jen thought as she left and made her way back to her car. Once she was behind the wheel, she leaned back and closed her eyes. Hair analysis and saliva tests? Jack wasn't even two. She couldn't do that to him or herself. Whatever the answer was, it wasn't here. Which meant she had to keep looking. She didn't care how long it took or if no one else thought there was a problem. She wasn't giving up on her son. She just wished she wasn't so very alone in her struggle.

Chapter Ten

Zoe pulled into Steven's driveway. His house was slightly larger than hers, and a little older. She could see the roof was new and the yard had been spruced up. Given his background in construction, he was likely to be handy with the remodeling, she thought as she walked around to the passenger side and opened the door.

Steven stepped out onto his front porch, then came down to help. She allowed herself a second to admire him in jeans and an open shirt over a green T-shirt before motioning to the car.

"Don't be frightened," she said with a laugh. "I'm not moving in. I just got a little carried away."

He studied the small Crock-Pot and the two grocery bags. "I think I can handle this much baggage. I'm a tough guy."

With that he put his arm around her waist and pulled her close.

She went easily into his embrace. His kiss was sure and delicious. There was no sense of being rushed, of this being a pit stop on the journey to something better. When he released her, she found herself wanting to keep on kissing him. Her nerves were humming, her girl parts happy.

This was nice, she told herself. Being with him, getting to

know him. So far there weren't any complications or games. No secrets. She appreciated that.

"So what did you bring me?" he asked as he picked up the Crock-Pot in one hand and the bags with the other. She collected her handbag and followed him into the house.

"An asiago cheese dip," she said. "Spicy but one of my favorites. I have crackers, a tortellini salad, cut-up raw veggies and cookies."

Steven pushed open his front door. "I said I was going to make you dinner."

"You are. These are just extras."

The midcentury house had a large living room with a stone fireplace that reached to the ceiling. Big windows opened onto the front yard. She could see the dining room beyond.

"It's a girl thing," she told him as they walked down the short hallway to the kitchen. "We have to bring food."

"I'm not complaining." He set everything on the counter. "All I have is steaks, green salad and some red wine."

"So it all works out."

"It does."

He put his hand on her waist and drew her to him. She went willingly and leaned up against him. Despite their difference in heights, they fit together nicely. He was lean, yet muscled, and he smelled good.

But instead of kissing her, he stared into her eyes. "You're so beautiful."

She flushed. She'd taken extra time deciding on what to wear. She'd settled on a casual dress and flats. Her hair was loose with a slight curl and she was wearing just enough makeup to feel pretty but not so much that she looked like she was trying hard. Nice that he noticed.

He touched her cheek with his fingers, then lightly kissed her lips before stepping back. "What has to go in the refrigerator?"

"The salad. The dip should be plugged in."

They took care of that, then he poured them each a glass of wine. He gave her a quick tour of the house. The hall bath was torn down to the studs. There was a sketch on the bathroom wall, showing what it would look like when it was finished.

"Do you do all the work yourself?"

"I could, but I don't have time. To be honest, while I know how to do tile work, I'm not an expert. So I trade for it. I have buddies who come in and help. In return I show up at their place. It works."

He put his arm around her and led her back down the hall. She saw the guest bedroom had tools stacked in a corner and a pair of sinks by the window.

"I'm going to wait to paint all the bedrooms at once." He gestured behind them. "The master is that way," he said. "Best not to go in there."

"Too messy?"

"Too tempting."

Her stomach clenched. She liked that he was being a gentleman, but not too much of one.

On the other side of the house were two more guest rooms that were untouched and a big bathroom that had already been updated. The quartz countertops gleamed. There was a big walk-in shower and a tub, along with a linen closet. He'd chosen cool colors—white and various shades of gray—but they worked well together.

"Nice," she said. "Did you pick all this out yourself?"

"I wish. My mom helped. She's good with that kind of stuff. I wanted neutral tones. At some point I'm going to settle down. I'm guessing at that time, the lady in question and I will want to get a house together so we can make it our own. This would become a rental property."

He showed her the remodeled family room. A big-screen

TV stood at one end, with comfortable, oversize leather chairs forming a seating area.

"The surround sound is built in," he told her.

She laughed. "Of course it is."

There was a wide sliding door that led to a big backyard. There was a big grassy area, a few scraggly-looking plants and a covered patio with a large barbecue.

"I haven't done much out here," he said. "I landscaped the front last fall and then got busy with the inside of the house. I'll tackle this part in the spring."

"I've always wanted raised planting beds. I want to do some at my house. I'm just not sure how."

"I can help. They're easy."

"That would be nice. Thank you."

They went back in through the kitchen, then around the corner.

"Tell me what you think," he said, stepping back so she could walk into the small half bath.

It was like stepping back in time. The floor and counter were done in 1950s light and dark blue tiles. The ones on the counter were square, but the ones on the floor were six-sided, with the darker tiles on the inside and the lighter tiles as a border. The walls were an even lighter blue. The mirror was round and the toilet was medium blue.

Zoe started to laugh.

"Is that good laughter or bad?" Steven asked.

"I love it."

"Yeah? I'll admit my first thought was to tear out everything and start over. But the longer I live with it, the more it grows on me."

"If we were talking about the kitchen or the master bath I'd tell you to remodel, but this is just a half bath. Why not keep it? It goes with the era of the house and it's actually really appealing."

They went back to the kitchen. Zoe set out the appetizers. She spooned the hot dip into a bowl and they took everything into the living room. Rather than sit on the sofa, they sat on the floor at the coffee table. Soft jazz played from hidden speakers.

"You have a nice setup," she told him. "Is this your first house?"

"It is."

"You did well."

He grinned. "For a man. Admit it. That's what you were thinking."

"Maybe. Of course, you have an unfair advantage. You've been in the construction business for a while. You've been exposed to different styles of architecture."

"I still think beige is a perfectly good color."

She laughed. "Okay, that is very much a guy thing, but you don't think it's the only color."

"That's true."

She looked around. "You don't have Lulu. I know your mom's out of town."

"Lulu is a special girl, but I don't think I'm ready to take her on just yet. She's with my mom's friend Shannon."

"Afraid you'd have to walk her?"

Steven considered the question. "I'm fairly comfortable in my masculinity, but I have to admit, Lulu might be a little too over-the-top for me."

"Maybe if she was wearing something in camouflage."

He grinned. "I think the bigger problem is her wearing anything. She is a dog."

"Not in her heart."

"Mason would never wear clothes," he said.

"Mason's a cat. It's different. I think Lulu looks adorable."

"Then if I have to babysit her, you can walk her."

"In a heartbeat."

"So what's new in the world of work?" he asked. "Any exciting manuals to translate?"

She wrinkled her nose. "No, which is why I've been thinking a lot about doing something else. I'm still at the 'I'm not sure what' stage."

"Any ideas? Still thinking about going into teaching?"

"A question I've been asking myself. I'm thinking about it. Substitute teaching would give me a way to test the waters again, without making a big commitment."

"What age range?"

"I've been checking out the requirements and I'm pretty sure I can handle them all. My degree is in English, so at the high school level I couldn't sub for any of the sciences or PE, but most of the other classes are fine."

He winked. "You'd be that hot new teacher all the guys are after."

She held up both hands. "Thanks, but I doubt that. I'll be the new, awkward teacher who doesn't know what she's doing." She spooned some dip onto a cracker. "Your mom has talked to me about her volunteer work. That sounds interesting, but I don't really have business experience. Still, I'm going to explore some volunteer opportunities. I'm also thinking about grad school. I'm going to talk to a counselor at Cal State Dominguez Hills."

The college was close and had an excellent graduate program.

"That's where I went," Steven told her. "It's a commuter school, but I had a good time."

"I've heard about your wild days. A different girl every night. Any fond memories?"

"Plenty of memories and no reason to go back. That part of my life is over. I'm ready for the next phase."

Which sounded nice, Zoe thought, then reminded herself not to read too much into his words. They were only talking—not making a lifelong commitment. Still, it was nice to hear a man speak about the future at all. Chad never did. There were no specifics with him. No promises, no hopes. At the time, she'd been so sure she loved him. With hindsight, she saw theirs had been a relationship of convenience, nothing more.

"What are you thinking about?" Steven asked.

She searched frantically for some other topic but her mind was blank and she was forced to admit, "My ex."

Steven picked up a slice of red pepper. "In a good way or a bad way?"

"I was just wondering why I stayed with him for so long."

"Didn't you say you lost your mom a while back?"

"Yes."

One shoulder rose and lowered. "That's part of it. Even if you knew he wasn't right for you, how could you make any decision about your love life while you were dealing with the loss of your mother? He'd been a part of your life for a long time."

He paused. "I know what I went through when I lost my dad. Everything changed. It was as if I couldn't trust anything to stay the same. Life seemed fragile. You had to be dealing with something like that. If Chad was the least bit supportive, you would have clung to him. Don't beat yourself up."

The combination of support and insight surprised her. Even though he'd been through the loss of a parent about the same time, his compassion was unexpected. Or maybe that was more Chad leftovers.

"Thank you," she said. "You're right. What's that quote? When I knew better, I did better?"

He nodded. "Now you're doing better."

She looked at him. "I am. I would say I'm doing much better."

He flashed her a smile. "I have no idea if you're talking about me, but I'm going to assume you are. It makes me feel good."

"I am. You're quite the find."

"I'm not all that."

He was, but she had a feeling he already knew, so why keep stating the obvious. He surprised her by moving closer and touching her cheek.

"Besides, if anyone is the lucky one in this relationship," he murmured, "it's me."

He pressed his mouth to hers. She leaned into the kiss and enjoyed the feel of his lips against hers. His arms came around her, she wrapped hers around his neck. They were sitting at awkward angles—with their legs crossed and knees bumping. When he shifted, she relaxed against him and let him lower her to the carpeted floor.

He bent over her and kissed her again. She parted her lips and he brushed his tongue against hers. Heat spiraled out from her belly, warming every part of her. She put her hands on his back and felt the strength of him.

Everything about being with Steven felt right, she thought, her mind fogging over. He was kind and nice and funny and successful. There was no horrible baggage from his past. If he had any deep, dark secrets, Jen would have told her. He was a good guy and he made her tingle in all the right places. Where was the bad?

They continued to kiss. Steven shifted so he was lying next to her on the carpet. One hand rested on her midsection, but he didn't move it higher or lower. Because he was a really good guy, she thought, even as she found herself thinking a little bad boy wouldn't be so terrible.

He raised his head and looked at her. His eyes were bright with passion, his gaze intense.

"I see this going two ways," he said quietly. "We can get going on dinner, or we can move this somewhere more comfortable. It's your call. Either way I'm spending time with you, and to me, that's a win."

Because he wouldn't push. While she was sure he was perfectly capable of seducing the hell out of her, he wouldn't do that. He wouldn't cajole or tease or push. He would want her to walk into his bedroom because that was what she wanted, too, not because it made him happy.

She knew the sensible decision would be to get up and start dinner. That waiting to take things to the next level meant not getting distracted by passion. After all, they'd only been seeing each other a few weeks. She sat up and drew in a breath.

"Dinner," she said, immediately regretting the single word.

He scrambled to his feet before holding out his hand to help her up. "How do you like your steak? I'm good up to medium. If you want it well-done, you might have to scrape off some burned edges."

Just like that, she thought as she stood. No sulking, no pushing, no making her feel bad. Where was the guilt, the whine?

"Medium rare works for me."

He grinned. "That's my best steak."

He started picking up their appetizers. She put her hand on his arm and stopped him.

"Steven, wait."

He looked at her expectantly.

She took his hand in hers. "About the room that was too tempting. I'd like to see it."

She waited two whole heartbeats as her words sank in.

His expression didn't change. "You sure?"

She smiled. "Very."

He kissed her once, then took her hand and led her down the hall.

Saturday night, Pam sat with her friends on the hotel patio. The weather in Phoenix wasn't that much different than the weather in Mischief Bay, but Pam appreciated the opportunity to get away for a couple of days. Not that her life was so taxing, she thought as she sipped her cocktail. It was more that she liked hanging out with her friends and appreciated the opportunity to step back from her life and get some perspective.

They'd started the day with a three-mile hike followed by a late breakfast. After spending the afternoon shopping, they'd returned to the hotel for drinks and dinner. So far no one had suggested they leave their spot on the bar's patio for the restaurant.

"Pam, we've talked about everyone but you," Eugenia said in her Texas drawl. "What's happening on your coast?"

Pam started to say "the usual" only to realize that in the past few weeks, things had gotten a little more complicated.

"Jen is still upset about Jack. A friend of hers and I staged an intervention and that didn't go well. She didn't speak to me for nearly two weeks. That only changed last Thursday because she needed someone to stay with Jack while she went to a doctor's appointment."

Pam thought about the clipped phone call she'd had with her daughter, followed by their brief exchange when Jen had dropped off Jack.

"I don't know what to do about her," she admitted. "I spent three hours with that boy and he's fine. I swear he'll talk when he's ready." She paused. "But what if I'm wrong and Jen is right?"

"Then you'll deal with it," Olimpia, a petite redhead in her late fifties said firmly. "You've raised three children. You have experience. There's something about this new generation of mothers. They think they're the first ones to ever raise a child."

Laura, a tall, full-figured woman groaned. "Don't get me started. My daughters are sticklers for organic. They actually go through my cupboards as if expecting to find a box of cookies labeled Poisonous for Children, But Oh, So Delicious." She shook her head. "I'm not an idiot. I know what I'm doing. But do they think that? Of course not."

"Jen needs to get out more," Olimpia said. "She's not back to work yet, is she?"

"No." Pam thought about their conversation. "She said she checked out day care places but didn't find one she liked."

"Is it possible for one to exist that she would like?" Eugenia asked. "I don't mean that to sound mean, but isn't this the same woman who insisted every item of bedding be natural cotton without dyes?"

Pam winced as she recalled Jen's very detailed baby registry. "That would be her. I just wish I knew what to do. How to help."

"You're there for her," Laura pointed out. "All she has to do is ask."

That was true, Pam thought. She would be there, no matter what. "I suppose it's something that she trusts Jack with me. Not that she has much choice. If not me, then who?"

"Where did we go wrong with our children?" Eugenia asked. "I swear, they all need a time-out."

Everyone laughed. The waitress came over and asked if they wanted another round.

"These are so delicious." Laura held up her glass. "I'm going to speak for all of us and say yes. It's not like we're driving."

Every trip they tried a new cocktail. Sometimes it went well and was their favorite drink for their time together. Other times, it was quickly abandoned. This weekend's suggestion had been a French 75. Pam had never heard of it before, but found she liked the blend of gin, lemon and champagne. It went down very easily, which could be both fun and dangerous.

For a second she wondered what Miguel would think of her friends. She had a feeling he would enjoy their company as much as she did. In turn, he would charm them.

Her evening with him had been a lot of fun. After their margaritas, they'd gone to dinner at McGrath's Pub on the boardwalk. Conversation had been easy. Maybe too easy. Pam wasn't sure she was ready to like Miguel. What if she wanted to keep seeing him? What if she started to actually care about him? That would be far too confusing.

She looked at each of her friends, then asked, "Do any of you date?"

The table went silent.

"That's unexpected," Eugenia admitted.

"I don't," Laura said flatly. "I'm not pining for my late husband. I miss him, of course, but I have to say, I love being single. I get to do what I want, when I want. My kids and grandkids keep me busy. I have no idea where I would find the time." She turned to Olimpia. "Next."

Olimpia smiled. "I date. Some. There's no one special, if that's what you're asking, but I've been known to dine out with a man from time to time."

"Do you want to find someone?" Pam pressed. "Fall in love?"

"Gracious, no. If I felt sparks, I probably wouldn't say no, but casual relationships are plenty for me." She smiled. "Besides even though there are plenty of age-appropriate men around me in Florida, you know what? They still want to go out with someone younger."

They all looked at Eugenia, who sighed.

"I've been seeing someone. He's very nice and we've been together about a year now."

Pam felt her eyes widen. "You never said anything."

"I know. I thought y'all would think I didn't want to be friends anymore and I love our trips. I still want to take every one of them."

"We've never talked about this before," Olimpia murmured. "I wonder why that is."

"We don't want to be judged." Pam spoke without thinking, then realized it was true. "No matter our age. We worry about fitting in. We're all widows. If one of us has a man, does that change our friendship?"

Laura frowned. "I hope not. I'd be happy for any of you if you fell in love again. It's just not for me. Nurses and purses. That's all men want when they get to be our age."

"That's harsh," Olimpia said gently.

"Maybe, but I've seen it happen." She turned to Pam. "What about you?"

Pam thought about Miguel. "I accidentally went on a date."

They laughed. "How was it an accident?" Eugenia asked.

Pam explained about meeting Miguel at Zoe's barbecue. She told them who he was and about Saldivar tequila. "He's so handsome and charming. When he called and asked me to dinner, I thought he wanted to talk about his daughter."

"And he didn't?" Laura asked.

"Not really. He came over a couple of days ago. We had dinner. It was nice."

"And?" Olimpia voiced the question gently.

"I'm mostly confused. About dating. I never thought I would. I wasn't looking. John is still such a part of my life." She held up her hand. "Yes, I know I'm technically not married, but I don't feel single. Given the choice, I would rather be with John than with anyone else. Only no one is offering me that."

Their waitress arrived with their drinks. Conversation shifted to their plans for the next day and their upcoming cruise through Northern Europe.

Later, after more drinks and dinner, they all walked back to their rooms. Eugenia and Pam were on a different floor than the others. They walked off the elevator together and started down the hall.

"About Miguel," Eugenia said. "I know it feels strange. At

least it did for me. Like I was cheating on Roger, or that I hadn't loved him enough. But that feeling goes away."

"I'm not sure I want it to."

Her friend smiled at her. "I thought that, too. It will never be the same, but that doesn't mean it can't be wonderful. You deserve to be happy. You deserve to have someone care about you. That doesn't mean you love John any less. Just be open to the possibilities."

"I'm not sure I'm ready."

"You might not be and that's fine. Just know that the fear is normal. You can ignore it or deal with it, but feeling it doesn't have to mean anything."

"Thank you for that. I am afraid, not to mention uncomfortable. Miguel is just so larger-than-life. I'm totally out of my element."

"That sounds like fun."

"Maybe." Pam was less sure. Still, she felt better than she had earlier. Nothing had to be decided tonight. If she wanted to keep seeing Miguel, that was her choice. If she walked away this second, she still had a perfectly wonderful life of her own.

They reached Pam's room. Eugenia hugged her.

"Sleep well. When you're ready to talk about sex, let me know." Her friend grinned. "It's kind of interesting to do it with someone else."

Pam's mouth dropped open. "Sex? I would never do that!"

Eugenia laughed. "Just you wait. If Miguel is all you claim, then wouldn't it be fun to check him out naked?"

"You're drunk."

"A little, but I'd still say this sober." She waved and continued down the hall.

Pam let herself into her room. Sex with Miguel? Hardly. She was too old. No way she was going to get naked with someone else. Besides, she'd only ever been with John. That was what *they* did. She wasn't going to do that with another man. It would be wrong.

But even as she dismissed the idea, she remembered what it had been like to kiss Miguel. Still, kissing wasn't sex and there was absolutely no way she was ever going there. Ever.

Chapter Eleven

Sunday morning Zoe and Steven walked over to Latte Da to get coffee. Every second of their night together had been magical. Steven was a gentle, passionate lover. They'd eaten late, and then he'd asked her to stay over. The logistics of her not having any of her stuff and having to feed Mason had sent them back to her place where they'd made love again, this time in her bed, and he'd spent the night with her.

Chad had rarely stayed over. Once she'd found out he was married, she'd realized why he hadn't. The apartment he'd claimed as his own had actually belonged to a friend. Later, after the divorce, their pattern had already been set, so he'd always gone home.

She'd spent much of the previous night listening to Steven breathing and reveling in the concept of having a man in her bed for something other than sex.

More than once he'd rolled over and wrapped his arm around her waist, pulling her close. In the morning they'd showered together, then had decided to go out for coffee. Now, as they walked into Latte Da, she admitted that even though things were moving quickly, she liked the direction— and him.

They collected their order, then went outside to sit in the

sun. It was cool, but clear, and the day promised to be beautiful.

"Did you sleep?" he asked, passing her one of the Danishes they'd bought.

"Not much, but that's okay." It had been worth it. "You don't snore."

"Good to know. Was it my imagination or did Mason climb on my chest in the night and glare at me?"

She giggled. "He's trying to claim his territory. He's not used to sharing the pillow."

Steven raised his eyebrows. "The ex didn't sleep over?"

"Not very often."

"Then he's an idiot on several levels."

She smiled.

"What are your plans for today?" he asked.

"Nothing much. I'm going to go see my dad later. What about you? Do you—" She stopped talking when she saw a muscle twitch in Steven's jaw. "What?"

"Nothing."

She replayed her last couple of sentences. "You don't like my father?" They'd only met at the barbecue and she'd thought they'd gotten along fine.

"It's not that." His tone said it was something.

She looked at him and waited.

"I spoke to my mom Friday morning, before she left for Phoenix. She mentioned that your dad had been over the previous evening."

Surprising news, Zoe thought, but hardly reason to be upset. "I don't understand."

"I think they're dating."

Not possible. Pam would have said something to her, wouldn't she? They were friends. Or at least friendly. Of course Miguel was her father, but she was dating Steven, who was Pam's son, and they'd talked about that. All things she would take up with Pam when she was home.

"Why does that bother you?" she asked.

"Because of what you said about him. You said he was a player who dated really young women and never had a real relationship after your mom."

Zoe didn't remember being that specific, but maybe she had been. "He's a really great guy. And the stuff with other women was a while ago." She felt funny defending her father's dating history, but couldn't let Steven think badly of him. "I'm sure he would be—" She paused. "Okay, I have no idea how he would be as a boyfriend, and to be honest, it's not something I want to think about."

"I'm not enjoying this either. We're talking about my mom. The thing is, she hasn't dated since Dad died and they were together from the time she was like seventeen. Miguel is totally out of her league. He's a man of the world." Steven groaned. "I can't believe I just said that. I tried to talk to my mom about it and she wouldn't listen. I'm worried. If he were some accountant who'd been married a hundred years, it would be different."

"Yes, he would be too old for her then."

"You know what I mean."

She did and she was torn. While she appreciated that Steven was the kind of man who looked out for his mother, she wasn't comfortable talking about her father this way. "Dad's not a bad person. He's actually really nice and caring. Despite the divorce, he and my mom stayed friends. We spent holidays together."

"I'm sorry. Zoe, I mean that. I don't want to upset you. I'm just worried about my mom. Can that be okay?"

She nodded. She liked Steven and she didn't want to mess things up by being weird. Her father did have a reputation. She would have to think about what she wanted to do. Talk to him or maybe talk to Pam. Or maybe just mind her own business.

"It's okay." She smiled. "I promise."

Jen had never planned to make Easter dinner a big deal, but somehow, in the past couple years, that was exactly what it had become. The morning started quietly enough, with an Easter egg hunt for Jack in the backyard. As young as he was, he didn't exactly understand what he was looking for, but he seemed happy enough to pick up the toddler-sized plastic eggs they'd left on the grass for him.

After that, the three of them had gone to church. Jen didn't get there as often as she would like, but she enjoyed Easter morning services the best. There was so much hope in the message. A promise for a happy future. The ever-present tightness in her chest seemed to ease just a little.

But once they were home, all bets were off. The family dinner had somehow grown until it was of near-Thanksgiving proportions. There were the three of them, plus Kirk's partner, Lucas, and whatever bimbo he was dating, Steven, who was bringing Zoe, and her mom. Only Pam had called a couple of days ago to say she was bringing Miguel.

Jen was still processing that snippet of information. She told herself the two of them must be just friends, but she couldn't help wondering if they were actually...dating.

"How can I help?" Kirk asked as he walked into the kitchen.

"Do you think my mom and Miguel are dating?"

He took a step back. "No way. I'm not having that conversation. If you want to know, you need to ask her. Speculation will only lead to trouble."

His adamant tone and the hint of fear in his eyes made her laugh. "Why are you so rattled?"

"I'm not getting in the middle of family stuff. I know better."

"Fair enough. What I need from you is to take care of Jack.

I'm going to get cooking." She pointed to where their son sat at his small table. He'd already eaten most of his lunch and was now playing with some seeded cucumber slices.

She would be busy all afternoon. She had the menu prepared—lots of easy appetizers, followed by a sweet corn chowder she'd made in the Crock-Pot. The ham was ready to go into the roaster. Her mom was bringing over scalloped potatoes. There would be a couple of salads and then Junior's Easter Cheesecake she'd ordered from QVC.

Dinner was at five and guests were to arrive about three-thirty. She'd already figured out what serving dishes to use—they were mostly the ones her mom had always put out for her holiday meals—but she still had to set the table, get out the wine, finish up the cooking and not have a panic attack today. Other than that, she was good.

"Anything else?" Kirk asked.

"Taking care of Jack is the most important thing. I'll work faster if he's not underfoot."

"Lucas and Caitlyn will be by about two. Maybe she can help if you need more hands in the kitchen."

Jen held in a scream. There was no point in complaining that Lucas and his girlfriend were arriving an hour and a half early. Kirk would simply look confused and explain Lucas wasn't any trouble. If only that were true.

"I doubt Kaylee is up for holiday cooking," she said instead.

"Caitlyn."

"Whatever."

She saw no reason to learn their names. From what she could tell, the women in Lucas's life were ever-changing. Next week there would be a new one.

Her husband moved close and wrapped his arms around her. "You okay?"

"I'm fine."

She appreciated the question and the hug. While things

weren't perfect between them, they were slowly getting better. Kirk was happy that she'd gone looking at day cares. She was grateful that he would take care of Jack while she got the dinner ready. They were working together as a team. They still weren't doing it, but this was hardly the time to worry about that.

She ushered her two guys out of the kitchen and went to work. While thin slices of French bread toasted as the base for her assorted crostini, she set the table. She prepared the chopped salad with the idea she would add the dressing right before they ate. Zoe was bringing a Waldorf salad. She got the ham in the roaster and started dicing tomatoes for her take on a Caprese topping for the crostini when she heard Kirk calling her. A quick glance at the clock told her it was early, even for Lucas. Which meant he had probably just arrived.

She went out front. Sure enough, the sleek Mercedes had just pulled into their driveway.

"How on earth does he afford that?" she asked. "It has to cost more than he makes in a year." She knew because Steven had paid a crazy amount for his Mercedes SUV and it was nowhere near as expensive as a convertible.

Kirk picked up Jack. "I thought you knew. Lucas has family money. He doesn't need to work. He could walk away from his job anytime he wanted."

"What?"

But it was too late to get answers. Lucas was already out of his car.

As per usual, he was dressed in jeans, a long-sleeved shirt and cowboy boots. He walked around to the passenger side and opened the door. His guest stepped out. Kaylee, um, Caitlyn, had on a dress the size of a handkerchief and spike heels. She was a pretty brunette—all Lucas's women were attractive—and was carrying a bouquet of lilies.

Jen held in a sigh as she forced herself to smile. "Hi," she said as cheerfully as she could. "Thanks so much for coming."

Lucas winked at her. "I can't remember the last time I had Easter dinner. I think I was twelve. What about you, Caitlyn?"

The twentysomething smiled. "Oh, we don't celebrate Easter. My family is Jewish. I looked it up online, though, so I can talk about whatever you'd like." She held out the lilies. "You're Jen, right? Hi."

Jen nodded and shook hands, all the while trying to keep from laughing. Jewish? Then her humor faded as she realized they were having ham for dinner.

"Do you have dietary restrictions?" she asked, wondering if there was time to send Kirk to the store for a chicken.

"I eat pork," Caitlyn told her. "I read that's the traditional Easter meal. It's fine." She greeted Kirk and waved at Jack.

Lucas took the squirming toddler and swung him around. "Happy Easter. Did the Easter Bunny leave you something good?"

Jack laughed as he flew through the air. Jen watched, wondering how someone so inappropriate when it came to his choice in girlfriends could be so good with her son?

Lucas set the boy on the driveway. "All right. What else do I have in here?"

He handed Kirk the requisite six-pack of beer, then opened the trunk of his ridiculous car. "I have something for you, my man."

Jen swallowed her involuntary protest. Whatever it was, it was going to be something that would make her crazy. Like the guitar. It was loud and, of course, Jack loved it. She watched as Lucas lifted out a toddler-sized car. But not just a car, she thought with dismay. A pedal car painted black and white, like a police car.

"There is no way he's old enough for that," she began, but

found herself ignored as Jack rushed to the car and grabbed hold of the sides.

Kirk lifted him inside as Lucas squatted next to him. "Put your feet there, kiddo. Now pedal. You know how to do that?" Lucas leaned in and showed Jack how to start pedaling. It took him several tries but he got the car moving. He squealed as he drove it around the driveway.

Jen couldn't believe it. She could already see the crashes and injuries sure to follow. Dammit, why did Lucas have to always bring the one gift that Jack would love and that would make her crazy? The man had a talent, and not a happy one.

"There's room in the backyard," Kirk said. "Come on, Jack. Drive this way so we don't have to worry about you going out on the street."

Right, Jen thought grimly. Because in the backyard, she only had to worry about him driving through the sliding glass doors.

Caitlyn smiled at her. "Isn't Lucas the best? He's so thoughtful. He ordered the toy car last week and couldn't wait to bring it over." She sighed.

Jen wanted to point out that Lucas was, in fact, old enough to be her father. Her not very young father. But why go there?

"He's the best," she managed, between clenched teeth. She nodded at the flowers. "I should get these in water."

Apparently no one had read Jen's email about what time to arrive because by two forty-five the entire guest list was making themselves at home. She was grateful she'd gone a little crazy with the crostini because people were hungry and there was no way the ham was going to be ready before five.

In a surprising turn of events, Lucas kept close watch on Jack while Kirk supplied everyone with drinks. Jen was in and out of the kitchen. Zoe joined her and handed over a bottle of champagne.

"Your mom has been talking about this drink she tried in Phoenix. A French 75. They've been around forever, but I'd never heard of them. Apparently they go down really smoothly."

"I don't think I should cook drunk," Jen said. "Although I'll admit to being tempted."

"Who could blame you? Or me." Zoe tore off the foil wrapping, then began untwisting the wire around the cork. "I keep telling myself that I shouldn't judge. I'm dating my best friend's brother. Why isn't that just as weird as my dad dating your mom?"

Jen glanced toward the living room where Miguel and Pam sat on the floor helping Jack with a puzzle. "You really think they're dating?"

"They came to Easter dinner together. What would you call it?"

"Two old people hanging out for companionship?"

Zoe rolled her eyes. "Is that what Lucas sees in Caitlyn? Companionship?"

"That's different. He's not as old as..." She did the math and swore. "OMG! Lucas is only a couple of years younger than my mom and he has sex all the time. If they're dating..." She covered her face with her hands. "You don't think they're—"

Zoe pulled the cork out of the champagne. "So you up for trying a French 75 now?"

"Yes. A big one. You didn't answer the question."

"Pam's your mom and my friend. My dad is my dad. I don't want to think about that. Honestly, I think they're just getting to know each other right now but who knows what will happen." She set a bottle of gin on the counter. "Steven's not happy."

"About Mom and Miguel?"

Zoe nodded. "He thinks my dad's a player and your mom will get hurt. I know he used to be, but he's different now.

It's hard. When we talk about it, I get uncomfortable. Like I have to defend my dad or something."

"Then don't talk about it."

"I'm going to take your advice." Zoe got out a martini shaker from the cupboard. "Are you concerned about me dating Steven?"

"No. You're my best friend and he's a good guy. I don't want any details when you guys take things to the next level, but I'm okay with whatever happens." She looked toward the family room in time to see Miguel touch her mother's cheek. "It's so different when it's parents."

Zoe made the drinks and Jen had to admit, they were delicious. The scalloped potatoes went into the oven and she sent Zoe to tell Kirk that Jack needed to eat a snack. But instead of her husband, her brother was the one who carried his nephew into the kitchen.

"Hey, sis. I found this kid wandering around. You want him?"

Jen smiled and took Jack from her brother. She washed his hands, then set him at his small table. After putting out his snack, she sat in one of the small chairs, as well, and motioned for Steven to do the same.

"Are you kidding?" he asked. "I'll break it."

"You'll be fine. Or sit on the floor. The point being, we don't leave him alone here to eat. He's part of the family."

Steven lowered himself to the kitchen floor and eyed the small pieces of cheese and cut-up apple. "That's a good-looking snack you have there, Jack."

The toddler offered a slice of apple. Steven took it. "Thank you, my man. Much appreciated."

Lucas also called Jack "my man" but it was less annoying when her brother did it. She held in a sigh. She was really going to have to get over her dislike of Kirk's partner. If only he didn't date the same type of girl over and over again.

"Did you meet Caitlyn?" she asked.

"Yes. She seems sweet."

Jen raised her eyebrows.

Steven grinned. "She told me she'd looked up the meaning of Easter and was ready to talk about it, if I wanted."

"Did you?"

"I passed." He glanced over his shoulder, then lowered his voice. "Mom brought Zoe's dad."

"I noticed."

"I'm worried about him. He's a player."

"He's nearly sixty."

"Yeah, and Lucas isn't all that far behind, agewise."

Which pretty much confirmed what she and Zoe had been talking about. "Are you really concerned?"

"I am. Mom hasn't dated anyone since she was like seventeen. There was only Dad. She has no idea what she's getting into. What if she falls for him and he breaks her heart?"

"You'll beat the crap out of him?"

Steven grimaced. "I'm serious."

"So am I. Kirk will help. I think the pair of you could take him."

"Is this you helping?"

"No, it's not. Steven, Mom is a capable adult. Let her screw up before you start trying to run her life."

"So you're perfectly fine with her going out with Miguel?"

"I don't know. I miss Dad. It's weird to see her with another man, but that's my problem, not hers. Look at this from her perspective. She's always been a loving, supportive mother. Maybe it's time we started acting a little bit more like her and accept what's happening."

"What *is* happening?" he asked.

"She's moving on."

Two days after Easter, Zoe dropped by her dad's place. Mariposa met her at the front door. The little dog danced in circles as she barked and jumped to show her joy at the visit. Zoe dropped to her knees.

"Hey there, pretty girl. How are you?" She picked up the dog and cuddled her. Mariposa smelled of bubble gum. "Did you just get a bath? You smell nice."

That compliment earned her a doggy kiss. Still holding the papillon, she walked through the kitchen and found her father making coffee.

"Hi, Dad."

Her father got out two mugs. "Do you need money?"

"What? No. Why would you ask that? I haven't come to you for money since I left college."

"You texted me and said you wanted to talk. What was I supposed to think?"

"That I love you very much and wanted to see you?"

"Uh-huh. You saw me on Sunday, at Jen's house."

The family dinner had been interesting. Good food and fun company, but an odd mix of people. Plus there had been the distraction of watching her father with Pam. They weren't overly affectionate but still, there was a definite undercurrent. Steven had been tense and that had put Zoe on edge. While she appreciated that he was worried about his mother, the reason for his concern was *her* father. Talk about awkward.

"The dinner was good," she said as he poured them each coffee.

"It was."

"Pam is nice."

Her father shook his head without looking at her. "Don't go there. It won't end well."

Zoe felt herself flush. "I have no idea what you're talking about."

He glanced at her. "You're about to make a comment about me seeing Pam. I love you, Zoe. I would die for you, but you do not get to comment on who I'm seeing. Pam is a lovely

woman. I like her very much. You're not going to come between us."

"I don't want to."

He raised an eyebrow.

"Dad, I don't. I agree. Pam *is* lovely, and you're charming
and I'm just…" She drew in a breath. "She hasn't dated much.
I don't want you to hurt her."

"And what if she hurts me?"

"That doesn't seem very possible, but okay. I don't want
either of you to get hurt."

"We're adults," he told her. "We'll handle it. We don't
need your help." He picked up a mug. "Zoe, for five years I
watched you with Chad. Everything about the relationship
was a disaster. You put your dreams on hold for him and at
the end you were left with nothing. We could all see it, but
you loved him so I kept quiet. I respected your choices, even
if I didn't agree with them. I'm asking you to extend me the
same courtesy."

His words shamed and embarrassed her. She ducked her
head. "Okay. I won't say anything."

"Thank you. How much of this is Steven and how much
of it is you?"

She looked at him. "What do you mean?"

"I know Pam's your friend, but you've never cared about
who I was dating. Is Steven behind these questions?"

"Um, maybe."

He shook his head. "Maybe it's time to start thinking for
yourself, Zoe."

Chapter Twelve

"We are burning rubber today," Jen said cheerfully as she spotted a parking space by the dry cleaners. "Look at how many errands we got done and it's not even lunchtime. Yay us."

She came to a stop and glanced at Jack in the rearview mirror. He grinned at her.

"It *is* impressive," she said. "Later, we'll celebrate. What do you say we take that new car of yours for a spin around the neighborhood?"

Jack shrieked with excitement. She laughed. She had to admit that at first she'd been upset about the pedal car, but Jack was enjoying it so much. He'd caught on really fast and an article she'd read said the combination of having to move his feet while steering was good for motor skill development. And it was a fun way for them to get exercise together. While he pedaled around, she was able to get in some walking.

She unfastened her seat belt but before she could get out of the SUV, her cell phone rang. She glanced at the screen and saw Kirk's name.

"It's Daddy," she said as she pushed the talk button. "Hi. What's up?"

"Jen, there's been a shooting."

It took a second for Kirk's stark words to sink in. Her heart stopped beating and she couldn't hear anything. There was an awful sense of drowning, of losing control, of terror.

She had to clear her throat before she could speak. "Are you okay?"

"I'm fine," he told her. "It's not me. It's L-Lucas." His voice cracked. "Jen, he took a bullet for me. It's bad. It's really bad. Can you come to the hospital? I need you."

"Of course. I'll be there." She dug for a pen and wrote down the information. "I have to find someone to watch Jack," she said. "I'll call as soon as I'm on my way."

"Thanks."

She hung up and did her best to catch her breath. Lucas was shot. Lucas had taken a bullet for Kirk. Kirk was okay but Lucas had been shot.

She was shaking so hard, she couldn't use her phone. She started the car and used the Bluetooth system to call her mom. Pam agreed to meet her at the house.

Twenty minutes later Jen was on her way to the UCLA Medical Center in Westwood. She was still trembling and fighting panic with all she had. Later, she told herself. She would fall apart later. Right now Kirk needed her.

It took her over ten minutes to find parking. She ran into the emergency room and asked for Lucas. The admitting guy wouldn't tell her anything, so she called Kirk and he told her he would come get her. As she waited, she saw dozens of LAPD officers walking into the hospital. They were here to watch over one of their own.

"Jen!"

She turned and saw Kirk hurrying toward her. He was pale, with blood on the front of his shirt. Her stomach heaved and the edges of the room seemed to fold in on each other. She sucked in air as he hugged her tight.

She hung on to him, feeling the warmth of his body against

hers. Kirk was fine, she told herself over and over again. Her husband was fine.

"What happened?" she asked.

He put his arm around her and led her through the labyrinth that was the ER department. "We were checking out a lead when we heard a call about officers in trouble. We went to back them up. One second it was quiet and the next all hell broke loose. There were bullets flying everywhere. I was nearly hit. Lucas pushed me down. We both returned fire. It was only a couple of seconds later I realized he'd been hit."

The trembling returned in full force. She had trouble walking along with him. It could have been Kirk, she thought, trying not to breathe in the hospital smell.

"I called for an ambulance. They got there fast, but there was so much blood."

He led her to a bank of elevators. "He's already gone up to surgery. We're waiting there." Tears filled her husband's eyes. "They asked about family, you know, like they always do. Lucas doesn't have anyone. His parents are dead and he was an only child. There isn't anyone to call."

Jen thought about all her resentments. How she'd assumed Lucas was a player, a cowboy who lived for danger. But he'd saved her husband's life, risking his own at the same time.

"He has us," she told Kirk as they stepped onto the elevator. "We'll be there for him."

They got out of the elevator and walked toward a waiting room. There were several LAPD officers there in uniform along with other men and women Jen assumed were detectives. She knew a few, but Kirk hadn't been on the force long enough for her to have met them all.

One of the guys walked over and shook Kirk's hand.

"He's in surgery," the other man said. "He's got a couple of gunshot wounds. None are life threatening, but one's through his shoulder. He's going to have a hell of a recovery."

They continued to talk in low voices. Kirk held on to Jen's hand so tightly that her bones ached. But she didn't complain. She knew that he was going to have to leave soon to give his statement. That he was only able to be in the hospital for now because Lucas was his partner—but there would be paperwork. She knew that once he left, it would be hours until he could come back.

She pulled him to the corner. "I'll stay," she said. "When you have to go do your thing, I'll stay here until he's out of surgery."

Kirk's gratitude was visible. "Thanks, Jen."

"I want to be here. And when he gets out of the hospital, he can come stay with us."

"You sure about that?"

She grimaced. "It's not like his flavor of the month is going to stay with him. You'll feel better knowing he's taken care of, and Jack adores him. It will be fine."

And the least she could do, she thought grimly. Because she'd misjudged Lucas and now she owed him.

"Returning women are the most successful demographic at college," Janice said. "I joke it's because they've felt the fear and are ready to change their lives." She smiled. "While you don't fit that profile, given how successful you've already been, I think you would do well here."

"I appreciate the vote of confidence," Zoe told her. Her head was spinning. She'd made an appointment to talk to one of the counselors in the graduate school office and had been blown away by all the various programs. There were so many choices.

Janice stapled a business card to the folder she'd filled with information. "This is just an overview. There's a lot more material online. You have our schedule, with application dates

right on top. My email address is on the card. I'm here if you
have any questions."

"Thank you. I'm sure I will, once I figure out a direction."
Zoe shook hands with her, collected the folder and walked
out of Janice's small, cluttered office.

Once in the hallway, she paused to catch her breath. She'd
come in hoping to be inspired. She hadn't realized her bache-
lor's degree qualified her for so many different grad programs.
She could pursue education, if she wanted to go in that direction and stay in the K–12 schools. She could get her master's in a specific subject, if she was interested in teaching at
a community college. There were even some Masters/Ph.D.
combined programs, if she was feeling especially ambitious.

She headed for her car. The campus was large and sprawl-
ing, with low, older buildings, newer multistory buildings and
massive parking lots. It had been built back when land had
been cheap. Over time she was sure parking garages would
be added, but for now, the Cal State Dominguez Hills campus was in transition.

She felt better now that she'd taken action. Thinking about
what to do with her life wasn't very satisfying. Equally trou-
bling was the fact that it had taken her dad to get her moving
forward. His comment about putting her dreams on hold because of Chad had stung. Probably because he'd been right.

She *had* put aside what she wanted—hoping that Chad
would finally pop the question. She'd been so sure she wanted
to be with him. That he was the man of her dreams. Now
that he was out of her life, she was shocked at how easily
she'd been able to move on. Shouldn't it have taken longer?
Been harder? Sure, there'd been that one afternoon of stupid
sex, but she'd regretted it the second it had happened and she
hadn't been tempted to do it again.

Seeing him a couple of weeks ago had convinced her she
wanted nothing to do with him. She was healed. But while

she might be over him emotionally, she still had to deal with the consequences of her relationship.

She'd quit her job for a man. The reality was humiliating and awful, but there was no escaping the truth. She could pretty it up by saying there had been another opportunity or that she wasn't sure she had loved being a teacher, but the truth was she'd changed careers because of Chad. Because she'd assumed they were going to get married and she wanted to work at home when they had children. WTF?

Now, looking back, she could see the giant red flags that she'd so cheerfully ignored. The fact that he never spent the night at her place. That he rarely wanted her to visit him at his. That they didn't talk about the future, go on vacation or spend time with his kids. She'd been a fool. Worse, she'd wasted five years of her life being a fool. And she'd always thought she was so smart.

Zoe started across the parking lot. The afternoon was sunny and warm. Perfect late-April weather. She told herself the day was too beautiful for her to dwell on the past. She wasn't going to beat herself up for her poor choices. Instead she was going to move forward, making better decisions. She'd already filled out the paperwork to be a substitute teacher. It would take a while for that to be processed, but she was looking forward to working with kids again. That should help her figure out if leaving teaching had been the right decision or not.

She'd nearly reached her car when her phone rang. She dug it out of her bag and smiled when she saw Steven's name on her screen.

"Hi," she said.

"How did it go? Did you get the information you needed from the counselor?"

"I did. To be honest, I'm overwhelmed by everything she told me. I'm going to have a lot to think about before I can make a decision."

"Want some company while you're contemplating?"

His question caused her toes to curl in her shoes. She and Steven had been seeing a lot of each other. Ever since they'd "taken things to the next level" so to speak, they'd been hanging out a lot. She liked being with him.

"I would love some company."

"Good. I still have to fix your stairs. I'll bring my toolbox and take care of that." He chuckled. "I've been putting it off because I wanted to have an excuse to come by. I guess I'm feeling more secure in our relationship."

She stopped by her car and stared at her phone. Had he really just said that? Admitted he'd been nervous about them?

"I'm glad," she told him. "You should."

"Good. You should, too. I'll see you at about five."

"See you then."

They hung up. Zoe allowed herself a second of pure happiness and did a little two-step before getting into her car. It wasn't the L word, but it was them moving forward. Easily. Normally. No secrets, no agenda. Just two people finding out that they liked each other. And it was really, really nice.

Sometime close to four, Pam looked up as Steven walked into Jen's house. He crossed to her and pulled her to her feet before hugging her.

"I just got your text about Lucas. Have you heard anything?"

"No." Pam sank back on the floor next to Jack. "He's still in surgery and will be for hours. They've heard it's going well. His shoulder is the biggest problem. I guess they have to pin the bone or something. It's going to be a long recovery. Jen should be home in a bit. She wants to get Jack through the evening herself, then she'll head back to wait for Lucas to wake up."

Steven sat on the carpet, across from his nephew. "Hey, big guy. How's it going?"

Jack beamed at him, then pointed to the puzzle pieces on the floor.

"That's a tough one," Steven told him. "Look how green that cat is. What a funny cat. Where do you think this piece goes?"

Jack took it and tried it in several spots before setting it into the correct slot.

"Good for you," her son said. "What a smart guy."

Pam held in a smile. Steven was good with Jack. If things worked out with Zoe, he could have a couple of little ones of his own, and wouldn't that be nice? She wanted more grandchildren—a point she made whenever it seemed appropriate. She didn't want to push, but she wanted to make sure her children understood that she had needs.

"How's Jen holding up?" Steven asked.

"She's upset. It could have been Kirk."

Something any wife would be panicked about, Pam thought, although Jen seemed to worry more than most. Ever since she'd had Jack, she'd been living on the edge. Not that Pam was going to discuss that with her now.

"You said she wants to go back and sit with Lucas after Jack's in bed?" he asked. "I could come stay with him."

Pam raised her eyebrows. "Have you babysat him before?"

"No, but he'll be asleep. I'm pretty sure I can handle that. If he wakes up, I'll call her."

"You're a good man."

"I have my moments."

Jack reached for another puzzle piece. She glanced at her son. "Speaking of moments, how are things going with Zoe?"

"Good."

She waited. "That's all I get?"

"Pretty much. I like her. I'm enjoying spending time with her. I'm going to stop by in a little bit and see her."

Which meant what? They were just friends? They were falling in love? She desperately wanted to ask, but knew the danger of getting too involved. She'd set things in motion and now she had to sit back and wait. It wasn't fair, but it was the right thing to do.

Steven handed Jack another puzzle piece. "Speaking of dating, how's Miguel?"

She pressed her lips together. "That is none of your business."

"Oh, you get to ask about my love life but I can't talk about yours?" His voice was teasing, but she wasn't sure how he felt. He'd already warned her off Miguel once.

"I'm your mother. It's for the best if we don't discuss me and other men."

His humor faded. "There are other men?"

"I didn't mean it like that."

"Then how did you mean it?" He turned until he was facing her. "Mom, this is a big deal. I worry about you. You were with Dad for your entire adult life. Dating has changed."

Was he serious? "How on earth has it changed?"

"I've been doing some research. Did you know that the fastest growing demographic for STDs is people over fifty-five? It's because you didn't grow up using condoms. When you were young, all you had to worry about was getting pregnant. It's different now. There are all kinds of diseases to think about."

She couldn't decide if he was incredibly sweet or if she should box his ears.

"You're lecturing me?"

He winced. "I'm trying to prepare you for what you're facing."

"Diseased men?"

"Maybe. Miguel has been dating a lot longer than you. There have been a lot of women. When you sleep with him, you're sleeping with them, too."

She could see the flush of color on his cheeks and the tension in his jaw. Having this conversation wasn't easy for him, which should have made her feel compassionate and yet did not.

"And here I thought a threesome would be adventurous," she murmured.

Steven muttered something under his breath. "Mom, I'm serious."

"Maybe I am, too." He flinched and she decided to take pity on him. "All right. Thank you for that odd and slightly gross bit of information. I will keep it in mind, should that ever become an issue. And while you don't deserve to know this, I will share it anyway. You can relax. I'm years away from getting that involved with anyone."

Her son looked at her intently. "Mom, you don't know that. Things happen. You could be swept away."

Pam was saved from commenting on that by Jen's arrival. Jack stood and ran over to her, his arms outstretched. She scooped him up. "How's my best boy?" she asked, then looked at Pam and smiled. "Thank you for helping."

Pam stood. "I was happy to be here. How's Lucas?"

"Out of surgery. It went much faster than they first thought, which is great. He's going to be in recovery a few hours, then they'll take him up to his room. The surgeon said everything went really smoothly. He's going to have a long road until he's back to normal, but he should get there."

Steven joined them. "Mom said you'll want to go back to the hospital tonight. I can look after Jack once he's in bed, if you want."

"Are you sure?"

"He'll be sleeping. I can handle it."

She nodded, obviously exhausted. "I appreciate it." She set Jack down and glanced at the clock. "Can you be back around nine?"

"I'll be here."

Pam allowed herself a moment of pride in her children. John would have loved this moment. She wasn't sure what he would have thought about Steven giving her dating advice, though. Of course if he was around to voice an opinion, she wouldn't have needed it, and wouldn't that have been nice.

"Mom, you okay?" Jen asked.

"Yes. Just mulling over your brother's worries about me getting involved with other men."

She waited for her daughter to shriek, but Jen only set Jack in his small kitchen chair and started preparing dinner for him.

"You should listen. You were with Dad forever. The world is different now."

Which was annoyingly what her son had said. "I'm perfectly fine."

Jen pulled chicken out of the refrigerator. "Mom, if our situations were reversed, you'd be giving us advice. We only want to make sure you stay safe."

There were a thousand things she could say. She could get angry, be sensible or she could shut them down. The latter seemed the best choice for her.

She smiled. "I gave birth to both of you. I pushed you each out of my vagina. When you can say the same about me, I'll listen."

With that, she picked up her bag and left.

Steven arrived right on time, but the second Zoe let him in the house, she could tell something was wrong. He looked tense and more than a little trapped.

"What?" she asked.

Steven set his toolbox on the floor of her entryway and leaned against the wall. "My mother. I can't do it. I can't give her any more dating advice. No matter how carefully I try to explain things, she won't listen. And in the end, I'm the one who's cringing. I don't know how she does it, but she always wins."

Zoe held in a grin as she moved in front of him. "Did she torture you?"

"I can't talk about it. I swear if I repeat what she said, I'll never get it up again."

"That would be extremely sad." She put her hand on his arm. "If it makes you feel better, I talked to my dad and that didn't go well either."

"I doubt he used the word *vagina*."

"Um, no. He told me to mind my own business."

"Good advice." He looked at her. "You okay with us staying out of it?"

She made an X on her chest. "I swear that I am."

He leaned in and kissed her. "Good. Because I'm not ready to stop making love with you."

Words designed to warm a girl's heart—and other places.

He picked up his toolbox. "I'm ready to tackle those stairs for you."

"This way."

They walked to her small hallway. Steven carefully lowered and raised the stairs a few times before putting sandpaper on a block. He asked her for an old sheet to protect the floor, then went to work, sanding the side of the old wooden stairs.

"I should probably ask what you're doing so I can fix the stairs myself next time," she said as she watched.

"Please don't. Then I won't feel important and necessary. If you can do everything yourself, what do you need me for?"

She laughed. "Assuming your mom didn't damage you permanently, I have several ideas."

"I want to hear all of them." He flashed her a grin, then returned his attention to his work.

She liked how he focused on what he did. How he was good with his hands. Her dad had always told her to find a man who was more than just interesting or fun to hang out with. That she would probably get stuck with the cooking and cleaning, and any man in her life needed to contribute, too. While Chad had been more than capable, he'd never actually helped much around the house.

"What are you thinking?" Steven asked unexpectedly.

"That my ex was more flash than substance."

"Should I be worried that you're thinking about him?"

"No. I've been thinking that he was never especially good for me. He worked as a master mechanic, but he never helped around the house. Like what you're doing with the stairs." She raised a shoulder. "I was thinking that I was really lucky to have met you."

"Good. Keep thinking that." He winked.

"I should probably reward you with dinner."

"You probably should." His smile faded. "Have you talked to Jen today?"

"No. I had a missed call from her but I didn't want to call back while she was feeding Jack. Is everything okay?"

"Lucas was shot."

"What? Oh, my God! When? What happened? Is Kirk okay?" Steven filled her in on the basics of the shooting.

"She must be totally freaked," Zoe murmured.

"She seemed all right when I saw her a bit ago, but she has to be scared. She wants to go back to the hospital tonight. I told her I'd come over and stay with Jack after he went to bed."

"Want company?" Zoe asked. "I'd be happy to hang out with you. Plus I'd like to see Jen, even for a couple of minutes."

"That would be great. With you along, I don't have to worry if Jack wakes up."

Zoe wasn't sure she could handle the toddler any better than he could, but at least they would have each other. She thought about her friend and how terrified Jen must be right now—dealing with the fact that her husband had almost been shot. Saved only by his partner's actions.

The world could be a scary place. Maybe Jen was right to fuss about things all the time. Maybe taking that much control was a reasonable way to feel safe.

Chapter Thirteen

"Are you ready?" Pam asked as she parked in front of the large Spanish-style house a mere two miles from her own condo. She looked down at the dog in her lap. "We're going to meet a new friend. She's a papillon named Mariposa. She's very pretty but not as pretty as you. Just so we're clear."

Lulu looked up, her ears forward, as if listening attentively.

"Are you nervous? I'm nervous." She glanced at the house. Lush plants grew all around the front. The windows looked original and there was a beautiful tile roof. The neighborhood was upscale and older, with families who had lived in the area for generations.

She drew in a breath and smiled at Lulu. "You're right. This is just a stall tactic and not a very good one. Let's go."

She picked up her little dog and got out of her car, then walked around to the passenger side to collect her bag. She set Lulu down on the front path and told her to go potty. Better to do that now than risk an accident in all the excitement.

Her business done, Lulu sniffed a few plants before returning to Pam and presenting herself, butt first, in the classic *pick me up* position. Pam drew her close. On the bright side, having her dog with her allowed her to focus on something other than her nerves.

"It's just lunch," she told herself. She would be fine. Miguel was a friend, nothing more.

She reached the wide, tiled front porch. The front door opened before she could knock. Miguel smiled at her.

"You came."

He was as good-looking as she remembered. Just as appealing was the way he was holding Mariposa. The two dogs caught sight of each other and strained to start sniffing.

"Shall we?" he asked.

"I'm sure it will be fine."

They both lowered their dogs to the foyer floor. Lulu stood her ground while Mariposa trotted toward her. They stared for a second, then did a quick butt-sniff exchange. Mariposa dropped to the puppy-play position—front end down, butt in the air, tail wagging. Lulu glanced at Pam, as if asking if it was okay.

"Go have fun," she said. Lulu barked once and went running toward Mariposa, then the two dogs took off.

"They look good together," Miguel said. "I like her sweater."

Pam had dressed Lulu in a lightweight knit top that wouldn't get in the way of romping, but would still keep her warm and protect her from the sun.

"The color looks good with her eyes," Pam joked.

Miguel smiled. "You look lovely, as well."

A simple compliment, but when delivered in that chocolate-velvet voice, she found it difficult not to swoon.

"The weather is warm enough for us to eat on the patio," he said. "It's this way."

She followed him through a large, open living room to a huge kitchen. The Spanish influence was everywhere—from the high beamed ceilings to the tile throughout. She would guess the house had been built in the 1920s. The window casings were deep and several of the doorways were arched.

The kitchen itself blended modern touches—upscale stainless steel appliances and quartz countertops—with old-world elegance. The cabinets were heavy dark wood, roughly finished. There were open shelves and the backsplash was a blend of colorful tiles she would guess were hand painted.

What was it Laura had complained about? That older men were only interested in nurses and purses? From what Pam could tell, Miguel wasn't hurting financially and he seemed healthy enough.

He led her to a covered patio with glassed-in walls and a glass roof. The space was part sunroom, part gazebo. A round table had been set for lunch. She smiled when she saw two dog beds by the door. One looked well used while the other was obviously new. It was, she had to admit, an incredibly thoughtful touch that got past her defenses far more easily than any smooth compliment.

He held out her chair. She sat down and looked past him to the huge garden beyond. He had to have at least a half acre, maybe a little more, all landscaped. The back wall was stone and covered in bougainvillea.

"Beautiful," she breathed. "Your house is lovely."

He sat across from her and poured them each a drink from a glass pitcher filled with what she assumed was juice, sliced limes and ice.

"I like to think that while an ocean view is wonderful, my small garden has its own kind of charm."

"It's hardly small and it does." She took a sip and nearly choked. "This is a margarita!"

He raised one shoulder. "Did you expect less?"

"A lot less. It's barely noon."

"Tequila can be enjoyed any time of the day." One corner of his mouth turned up. "If you aren't comfortable driving home, we'll call an Uber. I'll get your car back to you later today."

Which was the correct response, she thought. Offering her safe transportation rather than inviting her to stay until she sobered up. She was torn between wondering if she'd misjudged him and the fact that he was far more experienced at this than she was. While she'd wanted to dismiss every ridiculous thing Steven had told her, she'd been unable to forget his horrifying statistics on STDs in people her age.

Not that she ever planned on having sex with Miguel, but still. The news had been off-putting.

Lulu and Mariposa came tearing through the patio and raced out onto the lawn.

"They're getting along well," she said.

"I'd hoped they would." He rose. "Let me get the first course. I'll be right back."

First course? So there was more than one?

Miguel walked into the kitchen. Seconds later he was back with a beautiful salad of spring greens and tropical fruit. The dressing was both sweet and spicy and she had to admit the margarita only made everything taste more delicious.

"This is wonderful," she said. "So you cook?" He hesitated just long enough for her to start laughing. "Never mind. I have my answer."

"I never learned to cook," he admitted. "I have neither the interest nor the talent. Someone comes in a few days a week to care for the house. She cooks for me, as well."

"Of course she does," Pam said with a laugh. "You have quite the life here."

"I try to be comfortable."

"I know you divorced a long time ago. No remarriages?"

"I was busy with work and travel."

She speared a piece of papaya. "And young women."

"One or two."

"That's not what I heard. My son is very concerned about

your worldly ways. I wasn't sure I should listen to him, but I'm beginning to wonder if he's right about you."

She was partially teasing and partially testing the waters, so to speak.

Miguel put down his fork and leaned toward her. "What would you like to know?"

"To be honest, I'm not sure."

"Then I will tell you things and you can decide if there is more you need to know."

That seemed fair.

"Constance and I were not well suited. I enjoyed my work and the travel and she was more content to stay home. At first she went with me, but she was shy and it was torture for her. When Zoe came along, she said she couldn't travel anymore— not with a baby. I told her we would hire a nanny, but she didn't want that, so our lives went in separate ways. By the time we divorced, we were already single, if that makes sense."

"It does."

"She was a good woman. A wonderful woman and a kind friend. I think I loved her more after we divorced than I did before. We were able to raise our daughter together, to stay in touch, all without the fights or expectations." He reached across the table and touched her hand. "What are you thinking?"

"That I hear the words and I can't begin to relate to them." She smiled. "But it's nice that you and Constance stayed friends."

"It was. She was an anchor in a way. Her and my daughter. I always knew when it was time to come home and see my girls."

The affection in his voice made her like him more. She was glad that he and his ex-wife hadn't hated each other. It spoke well of them as people. She understood that marriages failed, but it bothered her when there was so much anger between couples. It spilled over into everything else in their lives and hurt the children.

"You, on the other hand," he said, "were married to the same man for how long?"

"Thirty-one years. I met John when I was a teenager. We had three children together." She pulled back her hand and tucked it on her lap. "I thought we would grow old together. His death was very unexpected."

Miguel nodded. "I would imagine you were devastated. With Constance, we knew the end was coming, yet it was still difficult. Losing a loved one is always hard, regardless of the circumstances. I still miss her."

"I miss John, as well. Everything is so different now, yet he's still a part of things." She picked up her fork. "I have the friends I travel with, my wonderful grandson, my children. My life is full."

"John is always with you."

"I know. I take comfort in that."

She supposed her friends would tell her this was truly awful conversation for what was supposed to be a date. But if she and Miguel couldn't talk about their pasts, then they didn't have much of a future. She was who she was today because she had been with John for so long.

"You're strong," he told her.

"I suppose I am. I was always fairly competent, but I'm not sure I would have said I was strong. Now I've had to learn to be. I bought my condo and I've moved on."

"Do you regret selling the family house?"

"I didn't sell it. I gave it to my daughter. She lives there with her husband and her son. So I get back all the time." She laughed. "Every now and then I want to complain about the changes she's made, but then I have to remind myself that it's not my house anymore. So if she wants to paint or replace the carpet, I keep my mouth shut."

He chuckled, then rose and cleared the salad. Pam looked out in the yard. Both Mariposa and Lulu were stretched out in the sun, as if they'd exhausted each other playing.

Miguel returned with the main course. "Grilled chicken with polenta cakes," he said as he refilled her glass.

Pam thought about stopping him, then decided she would enjoy herself. There was always Uber.

She took a drink. "You never thought about remarrying after Constance?"

"No. I wasn't interested in settling down."

"Too many beautiful women?" she asked, her voice teasing.

"Yes. There was that. Also, I didn't want to have regrets. I know I hurt Constance and Zoe when I left. We recovered, but there is still a wound. Falling in love again seemed more of a risk than I was willing to take."

"I know what you mean. I can't imagine ever caring about anyone the way I cared about John. He was my world. I don't think I would risk that again." She was starting to feel the tequila. It was the only explanation for her suddenly blurting out, "I'm not getting married again. I'll always be John's wife."

Her words hung out there for several seconds. Pam felt her cheeks heat, but didn't call back the statement. While she knew that a couple of dates didn't mean she and Miguel had progressed past casual acquaintances and there was no reason to suspect he would ever want to be more, she couldn't help needing to be clear to him and maybe to herself.

He looked at her, his dark gaze steady. "Yes," he said slowly. "I can see that." He pointed to her plate. "Try the polenta. I think you'll like it. Louisa does an excellent job with it."

She took a bite. "It's delicious." She waited to see if he had more to say about her proclamation, but when it seemed he didn't, she said, "Tell me about where you enjoyed traveling the most."

"Anywhere tropical." He smiled. "And not because of the young women in bikinis."

"Did I say anything?"

"You were thinking it. I could tell."

She laughed. "I wasn't, but I am now."

They talked about his travels and hers. She told him about the cruise she was taking with her friends in a few weeks. They didn't discuss Constance again, or John, but Pam felt as if she'd been clear on her feelings. Apparently he was fine with them. Maybe this dating thing wasn't so very hard after all.

Zoe waited at the bottom of the little kid slide in the park while Jen helped Jack into position.

"You ready?" Jen asked, her tone light. "I'm going to let go."

Jack waved his arms, then shrieked with laughter as he made his way down the slide. Zoe caught him and helped him to his feet. He pointed to the slide and raced back to the short ladder, indicating he wanted to go again.

He really didn't talk, Zoe thought. Jen wasn't imagining that. But he made himself understood, so that was good. She was careful not to say anything. Jen was barely holding it together. She'd been spending all her free time at the hospital with Kirk's partner. Zoe had stayed with Jack twice already and Jen's family was helping out when they could.

"You going back to the hospital tonight?" Zoe asked.

Jen shook her head. "Kirk wants me to stay home and get some sleep." She covered a yawn. "I'm not going to say no. I'm exhausted. But Lucas is getting better and that's what matters." She released Jack, who slid to the ground and giggled. "I've ordered a hospital bed and one of those rolling tables for him. The wound in his leg is healing pretty quickly so he should be able to get around a little." She wrinkled her nose.

"I'm grateful. I'm happy to take care of him but I don't think either Lucas or I want me to be helping him with a bedpan."

"That would be awkward. When does he get released?"

"Tomorrow sometime. Kirk and one of the other detectives will bring him home. He's going to need to stay with us at least three weeks. Maybe longer."

"Let me know how I can help."

"You've been great," Jen told her. "This has been really hard for me." She grimaced. "I used to resent Lucas and worry he was leading Kirk astray. Now I worry that Kirk is out there with a temporary partner who might not be so willing to take a bullet." She drew in a breath. "I guess this is a lesson to be grateful for what I have."

Jack ran around to climb the slide again.

"Enough about me," Jen said firmly. "How are you? How are things with Steven?"

"Good. I'm doing my best to take things slow and be sensible. I don't want to make any Chad-like mistakes."

"You won't. Steven's nothing like Chad. He's really grounded and he's lousy at keeping secrets."

"Excellent qualities in a man."

Jen helped Jack into position, then released him. He slid into Zoe's arms.

"So, you two do the deed yet?"

Zoe laughed. "Are you sure you want to know? He *is* your brother."

"Good point, although the way you answered means yes." She wrinkled her nose. "I've always been able to ask for details, but now I can't. That's not fair. As the best friend, I have certain rights."

"Let me know what you decide and I'll go with it."

Jen nodded. "Are you happy?"

Zoe thought about the question. There was a lot going on right now. She wanted to have more people in her life. She wanted to figure out the next step for her, careerwise, and she was starting what seemed to be a great relationship with a wonderful guy.

"I am. I'm in a really good place right now and I'm grateful."

Later, when Jack had tired of the slide and swings, Jen took him to her SUV and got him in his car seat. She and Zoe hugged.

"I'm around," Zoe told her. "Whatever you need."

"Thank you. When all this calms down, I want to go have lunch or something. Just the two of us."

"I'd love that."

Zoe walked over to her car. She was about to get in when her cell phone rang. She glanced at the number. While it looked familiar, she couldn't place it.

"Hello?"

"Zoe Saldivar?"

"Yes."

"This is Amanda from Dr. Herron's office. Do you have a second to talk?"

Zoe couldn't imagine why her gynecologist's office would be calling. She'd had her annual five months before and everything had been fine. She went in every three months for her birth control shot and had her next appointment lined up.

"Sure. What's going on?"

"I'm so sorry to be calling you. It's just we've heard from the pharmaceutical company that manufacturers your birth control injections. There was a problem with several batches, including yours. We need you to come in as soon as possible. We want to give you a pregnancy test and assuming all is well, give you another shot."

Zoe stood by her car and let the words sink in. Confusion was followed by disbelief, then panic.

"The shot isn't working?"

"No. I'm sorry."

Sorry? *Sorry?* How did that help? "But I've been having sex."

"If I could schedule you to come to the office, we can figure out the next step in your treatment."

The next step? She felt her heart pounding in her chest. Oh, God. She'd had sex with Steven just a few days ago. They'd used a condom but that wasn't always—

Her breath caught in her throat. No, she thought in horror. Steven wasn't the problem. She'd had sex with Chad nearly two months ago and she hadn't used anything. Because they'd both been tested and they weren't sleeping around and she'd assumed she was on birth control.

"No," she whispered. "No."

"I'm sorry. Can you make it in the day after tomorrow?"

Zoe nodded, then realized the other woman couldn't see her. "Yes. What time?"

"Eleven-fifteen."

"I'll be there."

Zoe hung up and leaned against her car. No, she told herself. This wasn't happening. Or if it was, she wasn't pregnant. She couldn't be. They'd only done it once, she told herself. Just that one time. What were the odds?

She got in her car and started the engine, but she didn't pull out of her spot. Instead she rested her head on the steering wheel and tried to catch her breath. She was fine, she told herself firmly. Fine and not pregnant. She had to be. Because there was no way she was going to have a baby with Chad.

Chapter Fourteen

Jen double-checked the guest room. The regular bed was out in the garage and the rented hospital bed was in place. There were clean towels in the en suite bathroom and fresh flowers on the dresser. Kirk had brought in a TV and set it up in the corner. Jen had borrowed a walkie-talkie set from friends so Lucas could call for her if he needed help.

She wasn't concerned about the extra work having Lucas in their home would mean. She was more nervous about having to deal with him day after day. Whatever would they talk about? She barely knew the man and what she knew she didn't like. But he'd saved Kirk and she owed him. So she would nurse him back to health and bite her tongue when she wanted to say what she was thinking.

On the bright side, Jack adored him and a visiting nurse would come in a couple of times a day for the first week or so, relieving Jen of any *intimate* tasks.

A little after one o'clock, Kirk pulled up in his sedan. His friend Matt was with him. Together they got Lucas out of the car and moving toward the house.

They went slowly, one man on either side of Lucas to support him. Lucas had a huge sling on his left arm—probably to keep his shoulder stable. His right leg was bandaged from knee to groin. He was pale and sweating. By the time they reached the front door, Jen was sure he was going to pass out.

"Can you carry him?" she asked as they made it into the foyer.

"I'm fine." Lucas's words came out from between clenched teeth. "This is nothing. You should see me on New Year's Day. Talk about a hangover."

"You're gray and your eyes are about to roll back in your head," she told him. "You're already a hero." She turned to her husband. "Carry him."

Matt shrugged, then put his arm around Lucas's waist. Kirk did the same. Lucas swore at them both, making her grateful her mom was keeping Jack for a few hours. They lifted him and in less than a minute they were in the guest room.

Jen moved to pull back the covers, then looked away as they settled Lucas in the hospital bed. He groaned as he shifted to get comfortable.

"What about his pain meds?" she asked Kirk.

"They gave him a shot right before we left the hospital." Her husband handed her a bag of pills. "He needs them on a schedule. Can you take care of that or do you want me to—"

"I can handle my own damn pills," Lucas growled. "I don't know why I'm here. I would be fine at home."

"Oh, please." Jen shook the bag. "You wouldn't last a day and we all know it." She looked at Kirk. "I'll write up a schedule for the pills so we can all know what he gets when. I can set the timer on my phone for the night ones."

"I can take my own goddamn pills," Lucas muttered again as he closed his eyes.

Jen eyed the gray cast to his skin and hoped he wasn't going to pass out. She knew basic first aid, but nothing more.

She left the guys to talk to their friend and went to the kitchen. She opened Excel and created a grid for a week's worth of meds, then printed out three copies. She'd just finished when Matt and Kirk came into the kitchen.

"He says he wants to sleep," Kirk told her. "I'm going to run Matt back to the station."

Jen's stomach knotted. She wanted to cling to her husband and tell him not to leave her alone with Lucas. But this had been her idea and she was going to have to figure out how to deal with him sooner or later.

"I know you have paperwork," she said cheerfully. "Stay and do that. I'll see you at dinner."

"You sure?"

"We'll be fine. If he starts to bug me, I'll slug him in the shoulder."

Kirk kissed her. "That's my tenderhearted girl."

They left. Jen filled a pitcher with water and carried it and a glass into the guest room. Lucas opened his eyes but didn't speak.

She set the water on his table and showed him the walkie-talkie. "All you have to do is push the button, and then speak. I'll hear you." She set the pill schedule on the dresser. "I should probably handle the meds for the first day or so."

"You're bossy."

"You're in no position to complain." She put her hands on her hips. "Are you able to focus? Because I'd like to go over some ground rules."

Lucas managed a shaky smile. "I figured we'd get to those. Sure. Fire away."

"No drinking, no smoking, no women. I'm happy to cook food you like, within reason. Just tell me what you want. There's no swearing around Jack. He doesn't eat sugar or junk food and he can't watch TV."

"Jesus, that kid's going to be in therapy for the rest of his life."

She glared at him. "You have no idea what you're talking about. There are studies that show—"

He cut her off with a wave of his hand. "I'm sure there are. I know you're trying to be a good mother, Jen, but give it a rest. You wind yourself so tight, one day you're going to snap."

Even though she told herself she didn't care, his words stung. "You don't know anything about me."

"I know plenty. What are you so damned afraid of?"

"I'm not."

"Yeah, you are. I don't get it. You have it all. A great husband, a beautiful house and Jack. Why do you always go looking for trouble?"

Her chest got tight and her eyes burned. "You don't get to talk to me like this."

"Babe, I'm high as a kite. I can say anything I want. You're afraid every second of every day. I wish I knew why. I'm sure you do, too. But that's not the real problem. The real problem is Jack can feel it. So can Kirk. He worries."

She swallowed. "What do you mean?"

He shook his head, then closed his eyes. "You think I'm leading him astray, but you're wrong. I'm fighting for your marriage, but man, is it an uphill battle. You don't make it easy, you know that? Jack's a good kid. He's going to be fine. You're the one I worry about. I swear if you don't get this figured out, you're going to end up in an asylum or divorced. But hell. What do I know? I'm just some…"

She waited but there weren't any more words. It took her a second to figure out he'd fallen asleep. Just like that.

"Don't worry," the nurse said with a smile. "These don't hurt at all."

Zoe nodded, as if physical pain from an ultrasound was her biggest concern. It wasn't. The fact that she was having one was a much bigger deal.

Nothing about this was fair, she thought. She'd just started to get her life in order. She had a plan—or at least the beginning of one. She was going to substitute teach and look at grad school and maybe quit her job. And what about Steven? He was a great guy. She liked him a lot. How on earth was she supposed to tell him she was pregnant?

She was having a baby and that baby was going to ruin everything. Her life would never be the same. Steven wouldn't understand. How could he? She didn't understand. They were just at the good part. The sparkly beginning where they'd figured out there was potential. And now she was going to lose him forever.

She lay on the padded table and felt the warm gel on her belly. Tears filled her eyes and ran down into her hair. This wasn't right, she thought frantically. This wasn't fair. She didn't want to be pregnant. But four at-home tests had confirmed that sex had consequences. Now she was going to find out how far along she was.

Part of her hoped that the baby was Steven's. While that would be a nightmare, it would be a better one than being pregnant with Chad's baby. She didn't want to be involved with him. She didn't want a child with him. But she and Steven had used a condom, so the odds were—

"There we are," the nurse said, her voice caring and happy. "Your baby has settled in very nicely. Look, you can see the heartbeat."

Zoe turned and looked at the monitor. All she saw was a mass of shapes, some light, some dark. There were—

She saw the steady beating of a tiny heart.

Emotions welled up inside of her. Fear, hope, anger, excitement, resignation. There was a baby and it was real. And the fact that she could see the heartbeat meant that she was way more than two weeks along. The baby was Chad's. Tears continued to pool in her hair. She clutched her hands together and wondered what on earth she was going to do now.

Forty minutes later she was dressed and in her doctor's office.

"I'm sorry," Dr. Herron said with a sigh. "We have several patients affected by this problem and three of them are pregnant." Her expression was kind. "I know you weren't expecting this. You're still early along. We can certainly terminate the pregnancy with no problem. I can do it this afternoon."

Zoe blinked. An abortion. Of course. Because she hadn't planned on this happening. In fact, she'd taken steps to prevent it. She was firmly pro-choice. This was her right.

"I'm having the baby," she said. The words were involuntary, but she couldn't seem to call them back. "I wasn't expecting this and I'm not with the father and it's a mess, but I'll carry him or her to term."

After that, she was less sure. Adoption was an option. Or she could raise her baby herself. Only that meant being involved with Chad. He might be a lousy boyfriend but he was a really attentive father. But jeez, Chad?

Her doctor nodded. "That's entirely up to you. Based on the dates you've given us and the ultrasound, you still have a few weeks to change your mind. In the meantime, let's talk about how to have a healthy, happy pregnancy."

Zoe drove home with piles of papers and pamphlets. She was going to have to change her diet, give up alcohol and caffeine, get more rest, start exercising regularly and basically live life as her baby's vessel. Her head hurt and her stomach threatened trouble.

None of this was fair, she thought. None of it was right. She'd done nothing wrong. Okay, yes, she'd had stupid sex with her ex, but was she supposed to pay for that for the rest of her life?

When she got home, she found Mason sleeping on her bed in a patch of sun. She picked him up and held him close. For once he didn't squirm to get away. She breathed in the scent of his fur and listened to the soothing sound of his purring.

"I'm pregnant," she told him.

His green-eyed stare wasn't the least bit judgmental.

Still fighting tears, she walked over to her computer and logged on. She searched *I want to give up my baby for adoption.* Twenty minutes later she had a working knowledge of what was required and knew there was no way she could do it. She might not have planned this, but she was perfectly capable of having a baby on her own. She had a good job, supportive friends and family. As for Chad—well, she couldn't think about that right now.

Her cell rang. She looked at the screen and didn't recognize the number. "Hello?"

"Zoe Saldivar?"

"Yes."

"I'm calling to see if you'd be available to substitute teach tomorrow. It's a fifth grade class."

The question was so incongruous when compared with what she'd been dealing with. Substitute teach? How could she?

She was about to say no when she realized that pregnancy wasn't the end of the world. Life still went on. It might not be as she expected, but either she moved forward or she stayed stuck.

"Yes, of course. Happy to."

"Good. I'll email you the information right now."

Filia's daughter, Marta, was nearly ten and just as pretty as her mother. She smiled shyly at Pam, then took her book over to a corner chair and started to read.

"I'm sorry," Filia said for the third time. "My sister looks after her, but she's sick."

"Don't worry about it," Pam told her. "This won't take long."

Filia had come through with a business plan to expand her salon. Pam had already reviewed it and had been pleased to see it was realistic and detailed. Filia had a firm grasp on the amount of start-up capital she would need as well as the time it could take to build a loyal client base.

They discussed the plan and Filia showed Pam the work sheets that supported her numbers.

"How long until you have to give your landlord a commitment?" Pam asked. She knew that Filia wanted to rent the space next to her nail salon.

"Six weeks. He hasn't heard from the current tenant yet, but I know he plans to vacate." Filia put her hands on the table. "I can do this. I know I can. I feel it inside. I'll work hard. I'll work every day. This is my dream and I want to make it happen."

Pam wanted that for her, as well. "Then let's do that. I've got a few notes for you on your plan. Places to add a little more information. I've also brought along some bank applications. These are for two banks we've worked with before. They are very supportive of local businesses. When you're ready to make an appointment, let me know. I want to come with you." Pam handed over two business cards. "I've worked with both of these people before. If things don't work out there, we can try the Mischief Bay Credit Union. You'd be pushing the upper limit of their business loans, which is why I don't want to start there."

She was also going to talk to Bea about some of the angel funds they had access to. Angel funds were a group of private investors who offered low interest loans or even grants to new businesses. Tech was hot right now and getting most of the attention, but Pam thought she might be able to swing a little cash Filia's way if necessary.

"I'll get these finished this week," Filia promised. "Then I'll call you so we can schedule before your trip."

"Excellent. I look forward to it."

Pam watched Filia and her daughter leave the offices of MWF. She might not be saving the world with her volunteer work, but she liked to think she was making a small difference. Each action was like ripples in a pond, or so she told herself. Now if only little Jack would start talking and Zoe and Steven would get serious, her life would be perfect.

Zoe parked in the Mischief Bay Elementary School parking lot and told herself everything was fine. She was doing great—the lack of sleep meant nothing. She would get by on grit. Maybe if she could have gulped down a couple of cups of coffee, she would have felt better, but that wasn't possible. She was going to have to will her way to alertness. At least her caffeine headache had gone away the previous day. That was something.

She collected the tote that held her purse, her lunch and some ideas for what she could do with her class, told her stomach to calm down, and got out to face her first day of substitute teaching.

Even as she walked purposefully, she felt the nerves running up and down her body. There was a slight tremor she was going to ignore and a pressing need to burst into tears. She didn't know how much the latter was because of hormones and how much was about terror, and she wasn't sure it really mattered. Later, when she had her sense of humor back, she would think about the really sucky timing of all this—getting her first teaching gig literally the day after she found out she was pregnant with her ex-boyfriend's baby—and laugh. But today was not that day.

She made her way to the administration office, signed in and was escorted to her class. On the way, the office secretary told her about lunch, where the teacher's break room was, the teacher's bathroom and a bunch of other information that simply flowed in one ear and out the other.

"Sandy Russell, across the hall, also teaches fifth grade. Ask her anything."

They stopped in front of an open classroom door. This was it, Zoe thought in disbelief. She'd really done it. She was expected to be a substitute teacher for the whole day. To a room full of fifth graders she'd never met.

What had she been thinking? She knew nothing about the primary grades. That was Jen's department. Zoe had always taught middle school. She knew what to do with a snarky thirteen-year-old girl. How different were they at ten? She hadn't been ten in a really long time. Things had probably changed. She doubted a single girl in her class had a Spice Girls doll in her closet.

The secretary was still talking. Zoe did her best to tune in, then gave up and just smiled until there was silence.

"That's a lot to take in," she murmured, hoping it was a somewhat appropriate comment.

The other woman laughed. "You'll get it. I'm in the office if things get really bad. Have fun."

Uh-huh. Because that was so very likely.

Zoe stepped into the room. It was big with windows along one wall. There were—she counted—twenty-eight desks. That wasn't so bad. She had a list for roll call, a schedule for the day and somewhere in this room was the mythical sub tub. The place where she would find lesson plans and ideas, notes on what to expect and how to control the class.

She located the tub in a back closet, but when she opened it, there was nothing inside except for three DVDs. *Sky High, Escape to Witch Mountain* and *Mulan*.

Zoe went cold. No, no, no. There had to more than that. Everything she'd read online said that the regular teacher always left a tub filled with information and ideas and things to do and...

She looked back in the closet, but there wasn't a second tub. Or a box. Or anything. She searched the desk up front. It was mostly empty. She had an entire day with kids she didn't know and nothing but three movies? They were kids' movies. They weren't even two hours long!

She was just about to bolt when the first of her students arrived. Three boys walked in together. They took one look at her and grinned, but not in a happy way. More as a challenge. Or a promise. She swallowed.

"Hi. I'm Miss Saldivar."

"That's a stupid name," one of the boys said.

His friends laughed.

Zoe felt herself flush. She looked away so they couldn't see, and told herself they were testing her. Testing her and winning.

She greeted the rest of the students, wrote her name on the blackboard, and then called roll. She stumbled through more than one pronunciation before that task was finally done, then glanced at the clock. It was eight-forty. She had the students until three. Even with lunch and two recesses, that was still nearly six hours.

"I don't have a lesson plan," she said with what she hoped was a friendly smile. "Who wants to tell me what you were studying? And if you could say your name, too, that would be great."

One of the first boys to arrive waved his hand. As no one else did the same, she was forced to point at him.

"Math," he said with a wicked grin. "I'm Cameron."

How incredibly helpful. "What kind of math?"

"The one with numbers."

Several students laughed. A couple of the girls rolled their eyes. One of the girls raised her hand.

"I'm Meagan. We're working on fractions. Adding fractions with unlike denominators."

"No, we're not," Cameron said. "No one needs to know that."

"We can learn it now or learn it later. It's not like they're going to change what we need to know to graduate out of fifth grade just because we have a substitute."

"You don't know that," Cameron told her.

"Of course I do. Everyone does."

Cameron's friends started yelling. Meagan's friends joined in and soon the whole class was arguing about whether or not the material was necessary.

Zoe called for attention and was ignored by all of them. She walked to the front of the room and started counting. When she reached twenty, someone asked what she was doing.

"Figuring out how long you're going to have to wait after the bell rings for recess until you can leave," she said sweetly. "Bad behavior adds time. Good behavior subtracts it."

The room went silent.

Zoe asked about other subjects and got a general idea of what was going on. But she had no material herself. She figured she could fake her way through a lot of things, but fractions wasn't one of them. A little after nine, she surrendered to the inevitable and put on *Sky High*.

When the recess bell rang, the students surprised her by waiting the fifteen seconds they had on the board before racing out of the room. Zoe stared at the empty desks and told herself that feeling like a failure wasn't the same as being a failure, even if the subtleties of that statement eluded her at the moment.

"Hi. I'm Sandy Russell," a petite, fortysomething redhead said as she walked into the classroom. "How's it going?"

"Not that great. I don't have a lesson plan or anything."

Sandy nodded knowingly. "You're subbing for a new teacher. I've told her she's got to get her sub tub together, but she's scrambling still. Let me guess. Movies?"

"We're watching *Sky High*."

"Want to be doing something else?"

"I would love to be doing nearly *anything* else."

Sandy laughed. "You're smart to qualify that statement. Give me five seconds. I'll be right back."

Sandy returned as promised. She carried a huge plastic tub over to the desk and opened it.

"There are a lot of good games in here. Right now we're really working on our vocabulary, so I would say to focus on that." She pulled several folders, blocks and smaller boxes out of the bin. "Here you go."

Zoe took the stack of cards along with a clear plastic bag filled with bean bags. The cards had a word on one side and a definition on the other.

"Like a bean bag toss," she said. "This is great."

Together she and Sandy went through the other options. Zoe borrowed a couple of folders with different ideas in them.

"I appreciate the help," she said sincerely. "I was dying."

Sandy shook her head. "Don't worry about it. I know it's hard to step in, especially this far into the school year. Routines are set and while the kids say they like a play day, they really miss their regular schedule."

"I'll return everything at the end of the day," Zoe promised.

By the time her students were back from recess, she'd moved all the desks and set out the vocabulary cards. Some showed the word, others showed the definition. She divided the students into teams and they took turns tossing the vocabulary words. She put down a second set and they had another round.

Time passed quickly and before she knew it, they were heading off to lunch. She used that time to write a series of fraction equations on the board and then covered them with large sheets of paper. She had a few minutes to wolf down her sandwich and grab some water before the kids were back.

This time she let them pick their own teams. They rotated through the various fraction stations and when that was done, she totaled up the points. Silly prizes, from Sandy's tub, were awards. There were stickers proclaiming things like Most Awesome and Totally Great. She finished up the day by having her students pull pieces of paper from a bowl. On it was a topic. They had to talk on it for three minutes. Subjects ranged from favorite pets to would you rather have a baby brother or sister. There was lots of laughing and starting over, but everyone had fun and the afternoon flew by.

When the final bell rang, Zoe knew more than half the kids' names and had managed to go several hours without Cameron making a smart-aleck remark. Two things she considered a victory. She stood by the door and thanked each student for helping her out that day.

Cameron stopped in front of her. "I'm sorry I was a butthead before. You're a really good teacher. I hope we get you again."

"Thank you, Cameron. Best not to say the *B* word."

He flashed her a grin. "Hey, I have a reputation I have to worry about."

She laughed, not sure if he was going to turn into a professional criminal when he grew up or run for elected office.

By three fifteen she'd returned Sandy's sub tub to her and thanked her another fourteen times. By three thirty her room was clean and she was signing out of the school. It was only after she got in her car that she realized how incredibly exhausted she was. She hurt from her head to her toes. Her feet ached, her back was sore and there was a throbbing just behind her eyes.

First thing in the morning she was going to send Sandy Russell thank-you flowers. The second thing she was going to do was spend some quality time online, looking at activities to do with children of various ages. She couldn't count on being rescued again, which meant if she was going to continue substitute teaching, she needed her own sub tub.

Mason greeted her with several pointed meows, as if explaining he wasn't used to her being gone all day and he really didn't like it. She sank to the floor and pulled him close. His soft purr eased the tension in her chest.

She desperately wanted a glass of wine, she thought, wondering what she had in her pantry. A nice merlot or a margarita. Did she have limes?

She was about to go investigate, when she suddenly remembered there would be no drinking for her. Because she was pregnant with Chad's baby. Pregnant! Her!

Reality crashed in on her. She lay on the floor and stared at the ceiling while Mason kneaded her belly and purred.

"I'm pregnant," she said aloud. "I'm going to be a single mom. It's real."

She didn't want to be pregnant, which was slightly different from saying she didn't want the baby. At least she hoped it was. Somehow she was going to have to figure out what she was doing. There were logistics. The single mom part bothered her. She was totally on her own. Oh, she could ask for help and she had people who would be there, but it wasn't as if she was madly in love with the baby's father.

Which reminded her that she was going to have to tell Chad at some point. And her father. And—

She sat up and grabbed Mason. "I have to tell Steven!"

Her cat blinked at her. She set him on the floor and groaned. "I can't. What am I supposed to say?"

The truth seemed the obvious choice, but that wasn't going to happen. *Hi, Steven. Just calling to let you know I'm pregnant with Chad's baby. How are you?*

She had to tell him the truth, which meant losing him. Losing *them.*

She covered her face with her hands and gave in to the tears. Crying turned to sobs as she thought about all she was about to lose. Steven was everything she'd been looking for. He was a great guy. They could have...

Mason rubbed against her and purred. She sniffed, then stroked him.

"It's over," she whispered. "All of it. He's going to leave and I can't blame him. There's going to be a baby, Mason."

He mewed, which she took to be a few cat words of support. She wiped her face. While she wanted to wait to tell Steven the truth, she knew that was wrong. Better to just get it over with quickly. Like ripping off a bandage. The pain would last a lot longer, but there was no avoiding that.

She picked up her cell phone and called Steven. He picked up on the second ring.

"Hey, I was just thinking about you," he said. "How was your first day of substitute teaching?"

Her eyes filled with more tears as regret poured through her. Steven had remembered. Of course he would. He was a good guy. Funny and kind and smart. He was good to his mom, handy around the house and damn good in bed. How on earth was she ever going to find someone like him again?

"It went okay," she said, hoping he couldn't hear that she'd been crying. "Look, Steven, I need to tell you something. This thing between us. It's not going to work out. I'm sorry." She had to swallow before she could keep talking. "It's not you. I know people say that all the time but this time, it's really t–true."

She sucked in a breath. "You're great. All of this has been amazing. I just can't see you anymore. I'm so sorry."

She hesitated, hoping he would say something but there was only stunned silence.

"Okay. Well, I, um, wish you the best. Goodbye." She ended the call, then looked at Mason. "I hate my life."

Mason meowed his agreement, then wound his way around her legs. She staggered to the sofa and sank down just as the tears returned.

She cried for what felt like forever, then forced herself to wash her face before boiling water for herbal tea. None of this was fair, she thought as she worked. She hadn't done anything wrong. She should probably get a lawyer and sue the hell out of the company that had messed up the shots. Which all sounded really proactive and great, but didn't help right now.

What was she going to do? How was she going to get through this?

She should make a list, she thought. Figure out who she had to tell and when she was going to do that. She would work up to Chad because there was no way that was going to go well. Pregnant!

She brewed her tea and tried to get excited about dinner. The headache was gone, thank goodness, but she still felt crappy. She was so not used to standing all day and she already missed Steven. She wanted to talk to him, to hold him, to see his smile. How long until that ache got better?

She fed Mason, then sat down with her tea. She would make a plan, she told herself. Figure out what steps she had to take and in what order. Then she would eat a salad with a lot of chicken for protein, then go to bed early. In the morning she would take the first step. Until then, she got to feel sorry for herself. She was going to wallow in missing a wonderful man. There had been so much promise, she thought sadly. So much—

Her doorbell rang.

Zoe frowned as she wiped away tears. She wasn't expecting anyone. Maybe it was that guy from Publishers Clearing House, telling her she'd won twenty million dollars. While the money wouldn't solve all her problems, it would help.

She sniffed and walked across the living room. Steven stood on her porch.

Chapter Fifteen

Zoe's heart jumped, her breath caught and she half expected to be imagining Steven. But there he stood.

"What are you doing here?" she asked, wondering how mad he was and if he was going to yell. Only he didn't look mad. Handsome, sexy and maybe confused, but not mad.

"I don't break up over the phone," he told her as he stepped into the house. "I want you to tell me to my face and I want to know why."

She would have sworn she didn't have any tears left. Yet they filled her eyes and spilled down her cheeks.

"I didn't want to," she blurted before she could stop herself. "I had to."

He glanced around. "You're being held hostage and if you break up with me, they release you?" There was no amusement in his voice. "Come on, Zoe. I deserve better than this. No one is making you do anything. What happened? I thought things were going well between us. I thought we had something. Was I wrong?"

He was being rational, she thought. She might have been wrong about him being angry, but he wasn't letting his emotions control her. Instead he was asking mature questions. Like a grown-up.

She closed the front door and walked over to the sofa. He followed and sat across from her. Humiliation burned, but there was no avoiding the truth. Not that he wasn't going to find out eventually.

"I'm on birth control," she said. "I get a shot every three months."

He frowned. "Okay. What does that have to do with anything?"

She swallowed and knew she had to just spit it all out. Then make sure she wasn't standing between him and the door so she didn't get mowed down when he bolted.

"Two months ago I had sex with Chad. It was after we broke up. It wasn't planned and it was a mistake. But it happened. A couple of days ago I got a call from my doctor's office. There was a problem with my last shot. The batch was bad or something. The bottom line is I wasn't protected, like I thought." She raised her chin. "I'm pregnant. With Chad's baby."

She pressed her lips together. There was no point in saying anything else. Steven wasn't going to be around to hear it. Only as the silence stretched between them, she noticed he didn't seem to be moving.

He looked at her. "And?"

"And what?"

"Why did you break up with me?"

She raised both hands then let them fall into her lap. "I'm pregnant with Chad's baby. I didn't plan for this to happen and I certainly don't want to have a baby with him, but here I am. Doing it."

"Are you getting back together with him?"

"What? No! Of course not. Never. But I'm going to have to tell him at some point. And deal with him like forever." Her stomach flipped over a couple of times, making her wonder if she was going to throw up. She drew in a breath.

"You've decided to keep the baby," Steven said.

She nodded. "My doctor said it was early enough for me to get an abortion, but I don't want to do that. As for adoption, that's not going to happen either. I'm having a baby."

Words she knew to be true, but still couldn't seem to grasp. "I'm sorry." She ducked her head and told herself she wasn't going to cry again. She was going to hold it together. And then eat salad.

Steven crossed to the sofa and sat next to her. He looked into her eyes. "That's a lot."

She sniffed.

"You okay?" he asked.

"No. I'm not. I'm confused and scared and I didn't want to mess things up this way. I liked what we had together. I thought…" Well, she couldn't say what she thought because she wasn't sure, but there had been something special between them. "I'd hoped things would be great between us." She told herself to be strong and brave and that she would be rewarded. At least at some point. "You don't have to stay."

"I'm going to ignore that last comment," he told her. "Tell me if I understand this. You found out that you're pregnant with Chad's baby. You're sure it's Chad's?"

"I had an ultrasound. I'm two months along."

"Okay. You had sex with your ex one time."

She nodded vigorously and held up a hand. "I swear. It was such a mistake. You have no idea how I regret it. No matter what, Chad and I are not getting back together."

"I believe you. So you're going to have the baby and work out some kind of parenting plan with Chad."

"Yes on the baby and I have no idea on the other part."

"You broke up with me because you assumed I wouldn't want to be with you now."

She blinked away yet more tears. "Yes."

He stood and crossed to the other side of the room. Once

there, he faced her. "Why didn't you just tell me what had happened?"

"I haven't told anyone. I don't know what to say. I was embarrassed and sad and upset."

"I get that. Now I want to ask you a favor."

She waited.

He looked at her. "Let me screw up *before* you decide I'm in trouble."

"What?"

"You assumed I wouldn't want to stay together once I knew you were pregnant. You made the decision before me. But you have no idea what I'm thinking. Hell, I don't know what I'm thinking. But I do know this—I'm not walking away. I need to think about everything and figure out what I want. I need some time."

She honest to God couldn't believe what he was saying. "You're not running?"

"Not yet."

"You might not run?"

He smiled. "I'm thinking I could maybe handle this. I'm not sure. It's a lot to take in. But so far, it's not out of the question."

She told herself not to hope. That if she started to believe, it would hurt too much if he decided he was done. But she couldn't help feeling just a little bit better than she had before.

"Take as much time as you need," she told him.

He returned to the sofa. "You said no one else knows. Who are you going to tell next?"

"My dad, I guess. Jen." She thought about Pam and had a feeling Steven's mother wouldn't be as understanding as her son.

"I'll tell my mom," he said, as if reading her mind. "But let's wait a few days on her."

"Thank you. I'm going to have to tell Chad, too. I'm not looking forward to that conversation."

"I'll be there if you want."

"While I appreciate the offer, I'm going to have to tackle that one on my own."

He took her hand in his. "You're really strong."

"I'm a mess. I can't stop crying and I'm seriously bitter about the lack of coffee and alcohol in my life."

"Want to go get dinner?"

"Yes. I'd like that a lot."

He smiled. "Me, too."

Jen got through the first three days of Lucas's stay by trying not to spend any time with him. A logistical challenge, given that he was in their house and she was the one mostly taking care of him. She was still wrestling with his drug-induced assessment of her and her life. While she wanted to defend herself and her actions, she kept coming up against the fact that he might have been telling the truth.

By the end of the first week, they'd gotten into a routine. Lucas was able to join her and Jack for breakfast. Despite her concerns about him being inappropriate around her son, Lucas was only patient and attentive when it came to Jack. He talked to the boy, played with him, read to him and in return, Jack adored him. More than once Jack had insisted on giving Lucas his precious Pooh bear for the night.

Jen had managed to spend some time on the computer, researching depression and anxiety. She wondered if she was suffering from some form of both. Within a two-year period, she'd gotten pregnant, lost her dad, had a baby, moved and had to deal with her husband changing jobs. That was a lot for anyone. On her good days she told herself there had to be a way out. On her bad days, she wondered if she was going to slip into madness.

One of the bright spots of having Lucas around was that her panic attacks happened less frequently. Maybe it was knowing there was someone else in the house. Maybe it was that he provided a distraction. She wasn't concerned with the why, only the fact that she was able to get through more of the day without feeling like she was about to die.

They spent mornings outside as much as they could. The late-April weather was perfect—warm and sunny with the lightest of breezes. Jack drove around the patio in his car or played on the grass. Lucas sat in the shade, watching, talking some. He had more color and was only napping once a day. Basically he went down when Jack did. A thought that amused her.

She sat on the grass, letting the sun warm her back. Jack was in front of her with several trucks and some blocks. He carefully loaded the blocks and moved them around her to her other side, where they were dumped onto the ground.

"You have construction in your blood, little man," Lucas said. "Like your uncle and your grandfather."

"How do you know about my dad?"

He winked. "I know things."

Which meant Kirk had told him. She wondered what else her husband had shared, but was nervous about asking. Knowing Lucas, he would tell her the truth—something she was pretty sure she couldn't handle.

His cell phone buzzed. He pulled it out of his sweatpants pocket and glanced at the screen. She'd thought it might be the visiting nurse, confirming her visit, but when he put it back in his pocket without answering, she knew it was someone else.

"Caitlyn?" she asked.

He scowled. "Leave me alone."

"You should let her visit you."

"You said no women."

Oh, right. She had. "She can come over. Just don't—" She glanced at Jack. "Make noise."

"So we can do it but we have to be quiet?"

She blushed. "I don't want Jack scarred."

"I didn't plan for him to be in the room. Besides, there's no way I'm ready for that right now. I'll see her later. Or not at all."

"Don't you miss her? She's your girlfriend."

"She's a woman I date. There's a difference."

True enough. The lack of committed relationships in his life was the reason she'd insisted he stay with them. "I don't mind if she comes by. There are other reasons to see a woman than that."

"Not many good ones." He tilted his head. "Present company excluded."

She laughed. "Oh, right. Because I'm so dazzling to be with."

"You're actually pretty fun. When you're not hysterically imagining the worst."

She was about to snap at him when she reminded herself he was trying to get a rise out of her. She wouldn't give him the satisfaction. "I've been doing some research online. I might have anxiety."

"You think?"

The sarcastic tone made her bristle. She was about to snap back when he stunned her by saying, "I'm sorry. That was rude. It's a reflex and not a good one."

Lucas apologizing? To her? "Um, it's okay."

"It's not. I'd play the 'I'm wounded' card, but why state the obvious." He looked at her. "You have something going on, Jen. I'm sure you have some mental issues, but there's some physical stuff, too. Chemicals out of whack or whatever. You should see someone about it."

She was still stuck on his claim that she had mental issues. "Oh, and I suppose you have a name?"

"Yeah, I do."

She opened her mouth, then closed it. "Excuse me?"

"There are a couple of people who help out guys on the force when things get tough. It's a combination of traditional drugs with supplements."

"I've already seen a crazy supplement lady, thank you very much. I don't need my hair analyzed."

"Good, because these people don't do that. They run a bunch of blood work, talk to you and then put together a program." He jerked his head toward the house. "There's a card in my wallet, on the dresser. Call them. They can help. They're used to dealing with cops and their significant others. They know what you're going through."

"That's really nice. Thank you."

"You're welcome. Now go call them. I'll watch the kid."

She hesitated a second before standing. "I'll be right back."

"When you've made your appointment, you can go buy me cigars."

She rolled her eyes. "That is so not happening."

"You need to learn how to have fun."

"You need to accept your limitations. Ten days ago you were shot. You're still on all kinds of drugs. Enjoy those while you can. Cigars. As if."

"Killjoy."

"Bite me. Oh, wait. I'm too old."

He laughed. "I might be willing to make an exception."

"Liar."

His phone buzzed.

She pointed to it. "Answer it and tell her to come over. I'd rather have her in the house than a cigar."

He grinned. "What if we make noise?"

She walked to the house. "I'm ignoring you. Totally and completely."

The cold, gray overcast day suited Zoe's mood perfectly. There wasn't rain, but the skies were not happy. The temperature was cool enough to require a jacket or sweatshirt. In her case, she'd chosen a bright pink Minnie Mouse one, thinking the adorable Disney character would brighten her mood. But despite her magical powers, there were some problems a high-heel-wearing mouse couldn't solve.

Zoe sat on a bench by the carousel. Despite the fact that it was midafternoon on a Wednesday, there were plenty of people at the Pacific Ocean Park. Mostly mothers with young children. Lots of mothers and even more children.

Zoe had never paid much attention to them. They were part of the landscape. After Jen had had Jack, they'd come here, first with him in a baby carriage and later with him in a stroller. In the past few months, he'd been big enough to ride one of the horses. Jen strapped him in carefully, then stood watch. Zoe had always thought she was being overprotective. Now she wondered how she would feel the first time her child came to the POP and rode a horse.

She waited for a second, wondering if emotion would appear. There was nothing. It was like asking herself how she would feel if she lived in an African village that just got its first clean water well. She could imagine. She could pretend. She could fake it but she couldn't actually *know*. Because it hadn't happened. At least not yet.

She touched her stomach. From what she could tell, there weren't a lot of changes in her body. Her breasts might be a little more tender and she felt more bloated than usual. But other than that, she was who she had always been. At least on the outside. On the inside, she had something the size of a lima bean that was going to change her forever.

She hugged her arms to her chest, trying to find comfort in Minnie, then stood when she saw Jen approaching. She'd texted her friend and asked if they could meet. She was surprised when Jen had suggested midafternoon. It was usually

Jack's nap time. Even more startling, Jen didn't have her son with her.

"Hi," Jen said as she hugged her. "Are you okay? What's going on? You said you needed to talk."

That was exactly what Zoe had said because announcing she was pregnant via smartphone seemed tacky.

"Where's Jack?" The question was more delay tactic than a request for information.

Jen sat next to her and wrinkled her nose. "You're not going to believe it. I barely believe it." She paused dramatically. "I left him home with Lucas."

"What?"

"I know. It's incredible. But he's down for his nap and they adore each other. Lucas is getting around okay and swears he can get him up from his nap. I told Jack so he wouldn't be surprised and he was fine with it."

"Lucas? The same Lucas who dates twenty-year-olds and just got shot?"

"That's the one." Her expression softened. "I'm going to continue to shock you by saying I'm starting to like him. He's really a good guy hiding under his bad boy facade. He took two bullets for Kirk. I will owe him forever."

Jen looked like she was going to say more, then shook her head. "Enough about me. What's going on?"

Zoe angled toward her friend and drew a knee to her chest. There was no good way to say this. "A little over two months ago I had sex with Chad." She held up her hand. "I know it was stupid and I have no one to blame but myself. It was over, I got lonely and I caved. Which would have been okay, except I got a call from my doctor's office last week and there was a problem with the batch of birth control shots I use." She looked Jen in the eye. "I'm pregnant."

Her friend stared at her. "Oh, God."

"I know. I've had an ultrasound. I'm two months along."

Jen blanched. "Oh, God. Pregnant! With Chad's baby. Who knows? Have you told Steven? Are you okay?"

"Yes, and I don't know." When her friend looked confused, Zoe clarified. "I'm okay. Sort of. I'm still in shock and trying to take it all in. Steven knows. He's not running, which I would do if I were him. He still might, but for now he's thinking about what this all means."

A fact that made her grateful—and on edge. Because every time her phone rang, she wondered if it was him, breaking up with her. So far, he hadn't. She wasn't sure if the passage of time was good or if he was simply putting off the inevitable.

"Does my mom know?"

Zoe shook her head. "Steven's going to tell her."

Jen grimaced. "That's not going to go well."

That was what Zoe was afraid of, too. She considered Pam a friend, but with Steven involved, she had a feeling that all bets were off.

"Pregnant," Jen breathed. "Are you keeping the baby?"

"I have to." She drew in a breath. "I know I could have an abortion, but it doesn't feel right. Not for me. There's no reason I can't have a child on my own."

"What about Chad?"

"I haven't talked to him yet. I know I have to tell him, but it's not like he can do anything until it's born. I don't want him involved at all. In a perfect world, he would simply go away."

"Do you think that's going to happen?"

Zoe dropped her head to her chest. "My luck isn't that good. I wish it were. I briefly thought about giving up the baby for adoption, but I doubt he would go for that. So here I am, unexpectedly expecting." She looked at her friend. "What are you thinking? Are you mad?"

Jen hugged her tight. "I love you. Why would I be mad?" She drew back and smiled. "I know this isn't about me, but

I'm super thrilled that you're going to have a baby. I've been the only one of my friends with a kid. I think it will be fun to have that to share. I can tell you all about pregnancy and a newborn. I want to help however I can."

Zoe wasn't ready for any actual information, but knowing she had a supporter was a big help.

"What's next?" Jen asked.

"I'm going to go see my dad. Then I have to suck it up and tell Chad. I'm not looking forward to that."

"You think he's going to want to be involved with the baby?"

Zoe glanced toward the carousel and back. "I know he is. He has a lot of flaws, but he loves his kids. Of course, maybe he just loves those two. Maybe he'll want to ignore mine. Wouldn't that be great." Not having to deal with Chad would make things much easier. "I'm going to look online and find out what's involved with a father letting go of his parental rights."

"If he doesn't want to do that, he's going to have to pay child support," Jen pointed out. "That might scare him into going away. If that's what you really want."

Zoe held up a hand. "I'm totally over him. I swear. I would like nothing more than to have him gone." She would rather have to deal with her child on her own than have to work things out with Chad.

"I'll keep my fingers crossed," Jen promised. "Let me know how I can help. Lucas might know a good lawyer who can help, if it comes to that. Or some of my mom's friends. She knows a lot of people."

Jen hugged her again. "Poor you. What a mess. Just know that once you have your baby, it's all worth it."

Zoe hugged her back and hoped she was telling the truth.

Zoe left the POP and started for home. At the intersection by her house, she went left instead of right, then turned down another street and drove a mile into the older part of Mischief Bay. She parked outside her father's house and called on her cell.

"Zoe! I was just thinking about you. How are you?"

She had planned on saying she was fine. Of course, she was fine. She was...

Unexpected tears burned in her eyes and her throat burned. "D-Dad," was all she was able to get out.

"What's wrong? Where are you? Zoe? Have you been in an accident?"

She shook her head, not that he could see. "I'm okay. I just... Can I come talk to you?"

"Of course. I'm home. Where are you? I'll come to you."

"I'm out front."

She was going to say more, but there was a click and she knew he'd disconnected the call. Seconds later, the front door opened and her father barreled toward her, Mariposa at his heels. He ran to her car and pulled open the driver's door.

"What's wrong?" he asked as he drew her to her feet. "Are you hurt?"

She gave in to the tears and hung on. Her dad was big and strong and he'd always been there for her. She trusted he would be now, although she was terrified to tell him what had happened. What if he was mad at her? What if he rejected her?

Her heart whispered that wouldn't happen, but irrational fear was stronger than love and common sense.

Mariposa jumped up and down next to them, barking, as if also concerned. Zoe finally drew back enough to scoop up the little dog.

"Group hug," she said, stepping close to her father again, the little dog tucked between them.

When she'd finally caught her breath, she sniffed, then wiped her face. Mariposa licked her cheek, as if offering her own kind of comfort.

"I'm okay," Zoe said.

"Let's go inside."

They walked into the house. She sank onto the living room sofa, Mariposa settling next to her. Miguel pulled up an overstuffed chair. He sat with his forearms on his knees, his gaze intense.

"Tell me."

For the third time she explained about Chad and the stupid sex and the failure of her birth control.

"I'm sorry, Daddy," she whispered. "I'm pregnant."

Her father groaned. "Is that all? I thought you were dying."

"I'm perfectly healthy, but there's going to be a baby."

Miguel crossed to sit next to her. "A baby is a good thing. Look what you grew into."

That made her laugh. She angled toward him and leaned back into the corner of the sofa. "I'm scared, Dad. And confused. I don't want to deal with any of this, but I have to."

"You're feeling okay?"

"I feel fine. No morning sickness, nothing. I feel stupid, but that's not the baby's fault."

"You didn't do anything wrong."

"I had sex with Chad. I knew better. I knew it was over. But he'd been calling and I caved. This is a really high price to pay for a moment of weakness."

"You'll be fine. Who else knows?"

"Jen and Steven. I haven't told Chad yet."

"You're going to have to."

"I know. I just wish I didn't have to. It's one thing for me to have this baby on my own. It's another to have to deal with him." Forever, she thought grimly. No matter what—for the rest of their lives, they would have to deal with their child. It was a horrible thing to consider.

"You should marry him."

Zoe stared at her father. "Excuse me?"

"He got you pregnant. It's the right thing to do."

"No way. You hate him. You said he was terrible for me and you were glad when we broke up."

"That's true, but now you're pregnant. It's different."

"This isn't 1880. I'm not marrying Chad." She shuddered. "He was a horrible boyfriend. He would be a worse husband." She narrowed her gaze. "Don't you dare say that I should have thought of that before."

"I wouldn't. I only want you to be happy. Zoe, being a single mother is going to be hard."

"Mom did it."

"You weren't an infant and I was there."

"I have support, too. I'll be fine."

Marry Chad. As if. Jeez. "I liked it better when you thought I was dying."

"I'm sorry. I shouldn't have said that. What can I do to help?"

"Stop telling me to marry Chad. Other than that, just be my dad. I'm confused and scared and I'm going to have a baby. That's a lot."

"It is." He sighed. "I can't even offer you a margarita."

"Tell me about it. I had to give up coffee, as well. It's horrible."

He chuckled, then looked at her. "A baby. I'm going to be a grandfather."

She grinned. "So much for the younger women."

He waved his hand. "I gave them up years ago. Still, a grandfather." He laughed. "I like it."

Chapter Sixteen

Pam tossed her phone on the sofa. She hadn't heard from Miguel in three days. They'd been texting regularly and suddenly he'd gone quiet. She didn't know what to do with that information. Was he sick? Had he met someone else? Not that they were actually dating-dating, so she shouldn't care who he was seeing. Although she had to admit she had been enjoying his company. More than she thought she would.

Worse, she felt funny. Unsettled. Confused. She hadn't felt this way since she'd been sixteen and had a mad crush on a boy who never noticed her. She was far too old to have those kinds of feelings. Maybe it was the flu.

She got up and walked into the kitchen to check on the spinach dip she had heating in the oven. Steven had called to say he wanted to stop by. Company business, she thought as she put tortilla chips on a plate. She'd invited him to dinner, but he'd told her he couldn't stay. Still, she'd made snacks.

She set out the chips, along with some cut-up fruit. She knew that Steven worked out and she was sure he tried to eat right, but she doubted he got any fruit at all.

She buzzed him in shortly before five and met him at the door.

"Hi," she said, surprised he didn't have his briefcase with him. "Aren't I signing papers?"

"What? No. This isn't about work."

She raised her eyebrows. "Why not?"

He kissed her cheek. "Because everything at the office is fine."

"Oh." Then why was he here?

He picked up a barking, dancing Lulu and rubbed the side of her face. "How's my rocker chick girl?" he asked. "Feeling good? I like the shirt."

It was a lavender one proclaiming Lulu as a Hot Babe. Probably not politically correct, Pam thought, but she liked it.

They walked into the kitchen. Pam got Steven a beer and poured a glass of white wine for herself. She pointed to the table.

"You must be hungry."

He eyed the food. "You didn't have to go to any trouble."

"I don't mind. It's nice to cook for someone."

Her son hesitated a second before sitting down. When she was settled across from him, she sipped her wine. "So what's up?"

Time and practice allowed her to read her children fairly well. She could tell whatever Steven wanted to talk about, it wasn't horrible, but he was nervous. If not work then…

Zoe, she thought, doing her best not to smile. Of course. They'd fallen in love. It was serious and he wanted her to know.

While it seemed a little quick, she wasn't surprised. They were great for each other. She'd guessed that from the start. Now that Zoe was over horrible Chad, she could get involved with Steven. Maybe he wanted to get engaged! She would like another wedding in the family. Plus, with no mother of the bride, she could help. She'd loved being a part of planning Jen's wedding.

"It's about Zoe," Steven began.

Pam did her best to wait patiently. "Uh-huh?"

"I like her a lot."

"I'm glad. She's lovely. Smart, kind. She and Jen have been friends for years."

"I know." He looked at her.

For a second, she was reminded of how much he looked like John at that age. If only her husband was still with them, she thought with a combination of love and pain. He would be enjoying all of this.

"I see a lot of potential with her," he continued. "I think she might be the one."

"It's a little soon for that, isn't it?" she said before she could stop herself. "How well do you know her? I like her and she's been Jen's friend forever, but you have to be sure before you jump in."

Steven grinned. "Oh, Mom, it's nice to know that some things never change."

"I'm sure I don't know what you're talking about."

"I'm sure you do. How you love to assume the worst about any situation. At least we all know where Jen gets her crazy from."

"I'm not crazy."

"I know, I know." He held up both hands. "I'm simply pointing out you go right for the worst-case scenario. And you know what? Sometimes things work out for the best."

She pressed her lips together but didn't speak.

His smile faded. "For what it's worth, I'm going to take it slow with Zoe. I just want you to know, she's important to me."

She liked all that he was saying, but there was still something. "What aren't you telling me?"

He paused for a second, and then said, "She's pregnant."

"What?" She nearly came out of her chair. Lulu looked up from her bed, as if concerned there was a crisis. "That's not possible. Did you do it the first day? What—aren't you wearing a condom?"

"Mom. Stop. You're not listening."

"Pregnant? Are you sure?" Pam felt her stomach drop. No. That wasn't possible. Zoe being pregnant so quickly would ruin everything.

"It's not my baby."

Pam blinked. Not his? No... "It's Chad's baby? She had sex with Chad? When? They were supposed to have broken up? Did she cheat on you?"

"Stop talking," he said gently. "Let me finish before you start jumping to conclusions."

"How can I not jump?" She pressed her lips together. "Fine. Talk."

"A couple of months ago, Zoe and Chad hooked up. It was a onetime thing."

He kept talking, explaining about a birth control shot gone wrong and an unexpected pregnancy. Pam listened, as he'd requested, but every new statement hit her like a slap.

Zoe had told her that she'd had sex with her ex, but at the time, Pam hadn't cared. Things were different now. Zoe was dating her son. And pregnant with another man's child. It was totally unacceptable.

"Is she keeping the baby?"

A ridiculous question, she thought the second she asked it. Of course she was. Otherwise, why would anyone need to know?

"She is."

Of all the... Pam drew in a breath as a more horrifying thought occurred to her. "Why did you tell me you liked her? You're not staying with her, are you? You can't keep seeing her."

"Mom," he began.

"No. Listen to me, Steven. You don't need this kind of trouble. You don't want to have to deal with someone else's kid. Do you know how difficult that will be? Chad will be in your life every single day. You won't be able to escape him. You won't even be the baby's father. Chad will get his say and you'll have to do whatever he wants. Plus, she slept with him once. How do you know she won't do it again?"

"Mom!"

"I'm simply pointing out she's obviously not as over him as we all thought. Who's to say she won't go back to him?"

"She won't."

"So she says now. I don't like this, Steven. It's not right. You deserve better." There was so much danger, she thought frantically. How could he not see that? He could be hurt—desperately hurt. Zoe and Chad would have all the power and Steven would have nothing.

He stared at her. "I thought you liked Zoe."

"I do, but this is different. You're my son." She sensed he wasn't listening. Or if he was, he wasn't understanding. "I'm serious. You don't need this kind of hassle. No one does. Walk away while you still can. Let her go. You'll find someone else. There are lots of attractive, smart women out there who would be thrilled with you."

Her son's expression hardened. "Stop it. I mean it. I appreciate that you want to take my side in this, but you really need to stop talking before you say something we'll both regret."

"What does that mean?"

"I'm not giving up Zoe. I meant what I said. I think we have something special and I want to see it through."

"Even though she's pregnant with someone else's child? Even though you'll never really be that baby's father? Even with Chad and their past?"

"Yes."

"You're wrong. I can't believe you don't see that. Steven, listen to me. I know people who have divorced and remarried. It's never easy. There are always adjustment issues. Why would you sign up for that? You have to reconsider."

"I don't." He stood. "Mom, I knew you'd take it badly. I hoped I was wrong, but I see that I wasn't at all. Even so, I hoped for something else. Something supportive. I guess that was my mistake."

"Steven!"

He put down his beer and walked out. Before she could go after him, she heard the door close and he was gone.

Jen shook the pills out onto her hand and paused before shrugging and downing them all with a big gulp of water. She'd been to see the specialist Lucas had recommended. She'd met with Alana, who had listened sympathetically then arranged for blood work. While that was being processed, she'd started Jen on a mild antianxiety medication and some general supplements. Nothing scary. Just normal, friendly sounding vitamins with a few other things—all available at her neighborhood health food store—along with the single prescription.

She'd also insisted that Jen drink at least sixty-four ounces of water a day, write down five things for which she was grateful and spend fifteen minutes sitting in a quiet room. Not meditation, Alana had insisted when Jen had rolled her eyes. Just quiet. So she could start to remember what it was like to listen to herself.

None of the instructions were especially onerous or even surprising, yet after only a few days, Jen already felt different. Slightly more in control and less panicky. She knew that the medication would take a few weeks to reach the proper dosage in her body, but she was happy to experience the placebo effect. Whatever worked.

She put the orange juice container back in the refrigerator, then began clearing the kitchen table. Breakfast had become a bigger deal. Lucas could go all day without eating, but he did enjoy a big breakfast. Kirk would happily eat any kind of egg dish put in front of him, and Jack seemed to thrive on the extra male attention.

With Lucas in the house, Jen no longer fed her son at his small table for breakfast and lunch. Instead she used the high chair at the kitchen table. Lucas was happy to keep Jack company. Like now. The two of them were hanging out in the sunroom. Lucas reading the paper while Jack played with one of his toy trucks. Jen could keep an eye on both of them from the kitchen.

Kirk came in, dressed for work. "I gotta go," he said. "Court this morning, then casework this afternoon."

She smoothed the front of his dress shirt—required attire for a court appearance. "Have fun."

He kissed her, then pulled her into the walk-in pantry. "How are you doing?" he asked, his voice low. "It's been a couple of weeks. Lucas says things are fine, but what do you think?"

She smiled. "I'm good. Seriously, it's okay having him around. I'll admit I was nervous, but he's pretty low-key. Now that he can move around on his own, he's a big help with Jack and I enjoy the company."

Lucas was brutally honest. While she didn't always like what he had to say, she had to admit he usually had a point. And the referral to Alana had worked out.

Kirk kissed her again. "Should I be worried that you two are getting along so well?"

She laughed. "He's not my type and you know it. Besides, even if I was pining, I'm way too old for him."

Her husband chuckled. "He might make an exception for you."

"As if." She put her hands on his shoulders. "I swear you have nothing to worry about. I'm feeling better and that's plenty for me."

"Good. I'll see you tonight."

He left. Jen finished in the kitchen, then made all three beds before returning to the front of the house. She walked into the sunroom.

A square throw rug covered the tile floor. There were large windows that could be opened to allow in a cross breeze, or removed completely in the summer. Rattan furniture covered with thick cushions gave the space a tropical feel. Jack sat on the rug while Lucas was in the chaise closest to the open play area.

"You have a doctor's appointment today," she reminded Lucas as she sat in one of the chairs.

He groaned. "I don't want to go."

"That's mature. We need to leave in an hour." She eyed the sweatpants and T-shirt he'd taken to wearing. Both were easier for him to manage as he recovered. "Did you want to get changed? I guess I could help."

"I'm not your kid. I can dress myself."

"Someone has attitude this morning." Lucas was normally pretty even tempered. Even when he was in pain, or telling her what exactly was wrong with her, he never snapped, didn't yell.

"Are you concerned that he'll want you to start physical therapy?" she asked. "I don't mind driving you."

He turned his cold, green gaze on her. "I'm perfectly capable of driving myself."

Uh-huh. Jen had her doubts about that. Lucas's leg was still healing. There was no way he was going to get into that ridiculous car of his. If he thought he was ready to drive, did he think he was ready to be on his own?

She thought about all he could now do by himself. The day nurse no longer visited and he didn't need Kirk's help to get in and out of the shower. He was down to over-the-counter pain meds, except at night. So what was the problem?

"Do you want to leave or are you worried I want to kick you out?" she asked, deciding to be as blunt as he had been with her.

"Both."

Funny how it was the first time she thought maybe he was lying to her. Which meant what? She knew that if Lucas wanted to go, he would be gone. Which left her only one option.

She walked over to the foot of his chaise and sat down. "Lucas, I like having you here. Okay, at first I only invited you because I was grateful for what you did, but it's different now. You're so good with Jack and while your advice isn't exactly gently delivered, it's usually dead-on. Stay as long as you want. I mean that."

His mouth twisted. "With no cigars and no women? I don't think so."

She laughed. "Until they become a more pressing need, don't worry about it. You're good for Jack and you're good for me."

"Thank you." He cleared his throat. "Why haven't you gone back to work? It's past time. What are you waiting for? There's nothing wrong with your kid."

And just like that, her warm fuzzies evaporated. "You really have to work on your bedside manner."

"I'm the one who was shot, not you."

"You've been playing that card a little too long."

"Answer the question."

She wanted to say she didn't have to, but instead told herself that it was easier to talk to him about this kind of thing than nearly anyone else.

"I still worry about Jack."

He groaned. "Give it up."

"I can't. He's my son."

"You hover. The kid doesn't talk because you anticipate his every need. Next?"

Would it be horribly wrong to slap him? "I don't want to put him in day care. I've visited a couple of them and they're awful. I asked my mom if she would look after him, but that didn't go well."

"What a surprise. You mean she doesn't want to give up her life to take care of your child? Shocking. You should disown her. Why even have a mother if she's going to act like that?"

"Sarcasm doesn't suit you."

"Sarcasm suits everyone." His voice gentled. "It's time, Jen. Go be normal. You'll like it."

As quickly as it had formed, her irritation disappeared. Mostly because in that moment, Lucas reminded her so much of her dad that she wanted to fling herself at him and be held in an embrace only a father could give. But Lucas wouldn't understand and he wasn't her father, so she pushed the urge away and stood.

"Let me know if you want to get changed and need help," she said.

"Not happening."

"And be ready to leave in an hour."

"Or what?"

She smiled. "Trust me. You don't want to push me."

"I'm not worried." He grinned. "Don't forget I know you. You're all talk, kiddo."

She walked back into the house. She knew that Lucas hadn't been trying to hurt her, but his parting shot had stung. Was he right? Was she all talk? And if she was—how could she not want to change?

Zoe was starting to think she should simply have cards printed up explaining she was pregnant with her ex's baby. Maybe something from Vistaprint. She could upload some text, a few pictures and stop having to tell the same awful story over and over again.

A plan that would work just fine with many of the people in her life, but not with Chad, she thought grimly. He was going to have to hear the entire sordid tale directly from her. Which was why she'd asked him to stop by after work.

She'd spent the entire afternoon trying to figure out what she was going to say. Oh, she knew the facts, but the order she said them mattered. In a perfect world, he would simply sign away the rights to his child and she would never have to deal with him again. But knowing how Chad felt about his kids made her less hopeful. Although he might not want any more children and there was the issue of child support. Maybe he would be happy to walk away.

The lawyer she'd gone to see had warned her the chances of that were unlikely. In California, signing away parental rights wasn't as easy as they made it look in the movies. As a rule, the fathers who got to escape their responsibilities were minors—usually well under the age of eighteen. The state took a dim view of capable adult males weaseling out of fatherhood.

Zoe paced her living room and checked the time every fifteen seconds from four thirty until five fifteen, which was when Chad had told her to expect him. She'd debated serving drinks and snacks, and then had decided once she'd shared her news and made her case for him signing away rights, they weren't going to linger over chips and salsa.

She let him into her living room and motioned to the sofa.

"What's up?" he asked as he took a seat.

She settled as far away from him as she could. She felt sick to her stomach, which could have been either nerves or the pregnancy. Why did it have to be like this?

"We're not getting back together," she began, then wondered if she should have started somewhere else.

Chad started to stand. "I don't need this crap," he said.

"Why did you want to talk to me? I already got it, Zoe. You want some fairy-tale relationship. Fine. That isn't me. What we had was good, but you're too stubborn to see that."

"Wait. I'm sorry. I shouldn't have said that. Please sit down. This is important."

He reluctantly settled back on the sofa and stared at her. She sucked in a breath.

"I'm pregnant."

Chad stared at her. Nothing about his expression changed. His jaw tightened a little but otherwise he didn't move. She waited until he finally asked, "You're sure?"

She told him about the shot not working. "I had an ultrasound. There's a baby."

"And it's mine?"

She told herself not to get angry. They'd split up. It was a reasonable question. "Yes. I understand that you'll want confirmation of that. I would prefer to wait until after the baby is born so we can do a cheek swab. Any other testing at this point is too invasive."

He turned away and then looked back at her. "You're pregnant and you're keeping the baby?"

She nodded and waited. He didn't say anything else and she still couldn't read his expression. He looked calm, which surprised her. She'd thought there would be screaming and accusations.

"This isn't what either of us wanted," she began, her voice deliberately quiet and calm. "It's a shock and you need time. I get that. Like I said, I'm keeping the baby. Anything else isn't an option for me. But you already have two kids you love very much. If you want to sign away your rights, I'm okay with that. I have a lawyer who can—"

"No." His gaze was direct. "No, I won't sign away my rights." He stood and wiped his palms on his jeans. "I have to think this through. I have to figure this out. I wasn't expecting—" He crossed to her small kitchen, then walked back. "Hell, Zoe. Pregnant?"

She shrugged.

"I need to think," he told her. "Let me get back to you."

She stood. "Sure. There's plenty of time. I'm only two and a half months along. There's nothing to be done right now."

"Okay. I'll call you." He crossed to the door, then turned back to her. "You're doing all right?"

"I'm fine."

He nodded and left. She stood by the door for a few seconds, in case he came back. When she heard the sound of his car, she walked into her kitchen.

Mason sat on the wide windowsill. He blinked as if asking how things had gone.

"I don't know," she admitted. "He didn't yell, which is always good. I don't think he's going to give up the baby, which means we're stuck with him for a very long time."

Mason walked over to rub against her. She stroked his cheek before picking him up. The sound of his soft purr calmed her.

"I love you, too," she whispered.

Chapter Seventeen

Pam found that reminding herself that Zoe hadn't gotten pregnant on purpose did less to alleviate her anger than she would have hoped. What on earth had the girl been thinking? Worse, Pam knew she was partially to blame. Oh, not for the pregnancy. That was all on Zoe and Chad and possibly the inept drug company that had failed to do one seemingly simple job. No, her culpability came from the fact that she'd been so sure she knew best. She'd been so sure that Zoe and Steven would be a great couple. *She'd* thrown them together, and look! It had worked. Now they were dating and despite Zoe's pregnancy, Steven still thought he might stay with her.

Pam had sent him several long, logically written emails explaining why being with Zoe was a huge mistake. She'd pointed out all the reasons he would regret it later. So far he'd ignored her—well, except for a brief text telling her that while he loved her, she needed to back off. Now she had a whole truckload of anger and nowhere to put it.

She thought about talking to Jen but was concerned her daughter would take her friend's side. There was no way Pam could speak to Zoe herself. She would start shrieking and that never went well.

She cleaned her condo, worked on several projects for

MWF, then took Lulu for a walk. While they were out, she got a text from Miguel, asking if he could stop by. They agreed he would be at her place in twenty minutes.

She didn't rush home. There was no point in checking her makeup or putting out food. His wasn't a social call—not the way it had been before. She guessed he wanted to talk about Zoe and Steven—parent to parent. The problem was going to be that they were on opposite sides.

He was waiting in the building lobby when she and Lulu returned. He smiled at her in that charming way of his. Her feckless stomach seemed to flop over, which the rest of her ignored. This was not a time to be flirtatious, she reminded herself. This was war. Or at the very least, a pending skirmish.

"How have you been?" he asked as they rode up in the elevator together.

"Fine. And yourself?"

"Excellent."

They reached the top floor. Pam led the way to her condo and they went inside. She opened the patio slider, but stayed in the living room. Lulu drank from her water bowl, then got into her bed, as if prepared to enjoy the show.

Miguel, as handsome as ever, damn him, waited for her to take a seat before he did the same. Then he smiled again.

"It seems we have something to talk about," he began. "You know about Zoe?"

"If you mean that she's pregnant, then yes."

"Good. I thought you'd been told." He paused to study her. "You're not happy with the news?"

"Are you?"

"I am." The smile returned. "I'm going to be a grandfather and what man wouldn't want that? I'm hoping for a little girl. Just like her mother. Although a boy would be nice, too. The toys are more interesting." He raised a shoulder. "I'm easy to please."

Pam realized she hadn't thought about Zoe *having* a baby. Oh, she'd been dwelling on the pregnancy for days now, but not the actual baby. The sweet smell and shape of a newborn, the soft skin, the little hands. Her wall of determination started to crack, but then she reminded herself about what this would mean to Steven and her resolve strengthened.

"What about Chad?" she asked.

"Zoe should marry him."

"What?" Pam's voice was a yelp. "You want her to marry Chad?"

"Of course. He's the father of her baby."

"He's a jerk. You can't be serious. He cheated on his first wife for years. He lied about being married. He refused to let Zoe get to know his children. He strung her along for five years. Why on earth would you want a man like that in your daughter's life?"

Miguel stared at her as if she'd grown a second head. Or maybe a third. A blurt too late, she realized maybe Zoe hadn't exactly shared all that with her father. Because what daughter would?

"Pretend I didn't say that," Pam muttered, feeling her cheeks flush.

Miguel's jaw clenched. "She didn't tell me all that."

"I'm sorry. I wasn't thinking. I've been upset. I shouldn't have said any of it." She felt horrible for betraying a friend's confidence. She never did that. Zoe being pregnant didn't excuse her.

"I never liked Chad, but things are different now. I thought…" Miguel muttered something under his breath. "This complicates things."

"I agree. Zoe needs time to figure out what's best for her."

His head snapped up as he glared at her. "What does that mean?"

"Just that she has a lot on her mind."

"You're worried about Steven."

"Of course. He's my son."

"Zoe's my daughter."

"She and Steven haven't been going out very long. It doesn't make sense for them to stay together, considering her change in circumstances."

"You'd rather he abandon her?" Miguel's voice was deceptively soft.

"Why does it have to be abandoning? Why can't they just break up? Like it or not, Chad is going to be in her life forever. The child is going to be Chad's, not Steven's. Being a stepparent isn't easy. Why would he take that on? It's not like he's the one who got pregnant."

Oops. Wrong thing to say.

"You blame my daughter?"

"She is the one who had sex with her ex."

"It was a mistake. You've never made one?"

"Not like that." She felt her temper rising and tried to keep calm. "Look, Zoe's great. I really like her. But I'm also worried about Steven. He's thinking about this idealistically and has no idea what he's getting into. Neither of us think Chad is a great guy, but he's the father and his rights will always come first. He will always have the final say over another man. Steven and Zoe barely know each other. I think they both need time to assess where they are."

"You're protecting your son."

"Yes."

"As I will protect my daughter." He studied her. "Where does this leave us?"

"You mean can we get past this to still be friends?"

He nodded.

Oh. She hadn't thought of that. "Do you want to?"

"I don't know."

An honest response that hit her like a slap. She wasn't sure what she felt about Miguel. He was very handsome and interesting, and when she was with him, she was reminded that there were still possibilities. Not that they were involved in that way, she told herself. Still, she'd enjoyed her time with Miguel and didn't want to see it end.

"After all, this is so new," he told her. "It doesn't make much sense for us to keep seeing each other, considering our change in circumstances."

He was using her own words against her. Before she could figure out what to say in return, he stood.

"Goodbye, Pamela."

And just like that, he was gone and she was alone—again.

Although Steven had warned her that Pam wasn't in a good place about the pregnancy, Zoe was determined to talk to her about it. Whatever happened with Steven, she and Pam were still friends. At least she hoped they were. So she dressed for Nicole's class and made her way to Mischief in Motion. Maybe sweating together for an hour would give Zoe the courage to approach Pam.

When she arrived at the exercise studio, she found Pam was already there. The other woman stiffened when she saw her, as if surprised. She gave a tight smile before turning away. Not exactly the warm greeting Zoe had been hoping for, but at least Pam didn't disappear.

Fifty minutes and much muscle trembling later, Zoe gathered her limp self together and walked over to Pam.

"Hi," she said, hoping she sounded braver than she felt. "I know this is awkward, but I really miss us hanging out. I was hoping we could figure out a middle ground."

Pam collected her tote. Zoe did the same and they walked out together.

"I'm not sure there is any," Pam told her when they reached the sidewalk. "My main concern is Steven."

Which kind of hurt but made sense. "He's your son. I get that. You know I didn't plan this, right? It wasn't supposed to happen."

"You still slept with Chad. You could have used a condom and you didn't. I thought only my generation was irresponsible."

The unfair judgment made her eyes burn. "Is that what you think?"

"I don't know what I think," Pam told her. "Are you going to marry Chad? It's what your father wants."

"Why are you talking to me like this? Why aren't you being my friend?"

"Because at the end of the day, Steven is family and you're not. I have to take care of him. I have to keep him safe. I want him to be happy and that can't happen with you. I'm sorry, Zoe. Bringing you two together was a mistake. One I wish I could undo."

Zoe told herself the pain was just hormonal and that she didn't actually care what Pam thought. Sure they'd become friends, but for what? Five minutes? She had other people. She didn't need Pam.

Only Zoe had come to see Pam as a surrogate mother. Jen was Zoe's best friend. Was Pam going to get between them, as well? Because Pam was making it clear she was going to try to keep Steven from making what she saw as a huge mistake with his life.

"I didn't plan this," Zoe repeated. "I didn't do it on purpose."

"No one thinks you did. My problem is I know what it's like to have a child, Zoe. I know how things change. There's no way this is right for Steven. I'm sorry you're going to have to go through this alone, but that's the way things are."

Lulu popped her head out of Pam's tote just then and gave a little bark. Zoe didn't know if the dog was greeting her or telling her off. Based on how things had gone thus far, it wasn't hard to pick.

"Pam, please," Zoe pleaded. "I really need you. I want us to stay friends."

Pam's expression hardened. "It's better if we don't. I'm sorry, Zoe. Goodbye."

If Jen could just figure out a way to have sex with her husband, her life would be perfect. Okay, not perfect. If Jack could talk *and* she could figure out a way to have sex with Kirk, *then* her life would be perfect. Seriously. But neither was happening, and to be honest, she was starting to be more concerned about the sex.

She couldn't remember how long it had been. That wasn't happy news. And if she couldn't remember, he couldn't either. Unless he was getting it somewhere else.

"Don't go there," she told herself as she peeled off the brightening facial mask she'd applied twenty minutes before. Lucas would have said something. God knew he wasn't afraid of speaking the truth.

So if Kirk wasn't having sex with some chickie, then she could win him back. She rubbed the leftover serum into her skin and decided that "winning him back" wasn't the right phrase. She could reignite the spark.

Which was what this morning was about. Kirk was off and he and Lucas had taken Jack to the POP to give her some alone time. She'd put it to good use. She'd shaved her legs, done the mask and was now going to apply the scented body lotion Kirk liked. They had the whole day together. She planned to be flirty and fun, with just enough touching to leave him panting. Okay, maybe not panting, but *in the mood*. That was what she wanted for today. The promise of good things to come tonight.

As she applied her makeup, she thought about the other

changes she wanted to make in her life. To be honest, the staying at home with a toddler thing was starting to get to her. A few months ago she'd been terrified at the thought of going back to work, but sometime in the past few weeks, she'd really started to miss teaching. Maybe it was hearing about Zoe's substitute teaching. She'd always enjoyed her students and the challenges of making sometimes boring material interesting. She liked having summers off. But going back to work meant putting Jack in day care and that was a problem she had yet to solve.

She dressed. Early May wasn't stiflingly hot, but the temperature had definitely gone up by a couple of degrees. She decided on light blue crop pants with a matching tank. She slipped on a crisp, white, short-sleeved shirt and left it open, then pulled the hot rollers out of her hair.

"And we're done," she whispered.

She thought she looked pretty good. Not fancy, but rested and pretty. The mask had worked its magic on her skin. She was more wholesome than sexy, but Kirk was a girl-next-door kind of guy and that should appeal to him. Later, she could show him her bad girl moves.

She went into the kitchen and downed as much water as she could without gagging. While she hated to admit it, the simple instructions Alana had given her seemed to be working. She'd taken to having her fifteen minutes of quiet time while Jack napped. Just being still and letting her mind wander was much more refreshing than a frantic attempt to get her mile-long list of chores done. Her blood work had come back showing she was low on several vitamins, including iron and D, which would make her tired and more prone to anxiety.

She liked that she was taking care of herself. It felt good. She'd been so focused on Jack for so long that she'd somehow gotten lost. There had to be a place somewhere between being self-consumed and being a martyr, and she hoped she'd found it.

She prepared the marinade for the flank steak they were barbecuing that night, then checked the clock. "The boys" were due back by eleven-thirty. She'd already made chicken salad for lunch. She would guess that Lucas was going to be exhausted by the outing and would crash for the afternoon. Hmm, Jack would take a nap, as well. Maybe the seduction didn't have to wait until tonight.

She heard the sound of the SUV pulling into the garage and felt a little quiver low in her belly. She touched the spot and grinned. There was a blast from the past, she thought happily. Nice to know she still had those feelings for her husband.

She walked toward the mudroom to greet everyone. Kirk came in first, Jack in his arms. She took one look at Kirk's happy expression and started to laugh.

"What?" she asked. "You're pleased about something. What is it?"

Lucas stepped around him. "You'd be lousy at poker, bro. This is a family thing. I'm going to my room."

Jen had no idea why Lucas felt he had to leave, but she let it go. She hurried over and took her son, who held out his arms for her and laughed. She pulled him close.

"Well?"

Kirk pulled her into the family room and onto the sofa. "Look!" He pulled out his phone and spooled up a video.

Jack squirmed to get down and ran over to sit by his low toy box. He began pulling out his trucks and cars. Obviously he wasn't the least bit impressed by whatever Kirk wanted to show her.

"Here." Kirk pushed a button on his phone and a video began to play.

She stared at the screen. Jack was running around at the POP, on the grass. Not by the playground, but off to the side.

A woman walked by with two dogs. Labs, she would guess. Jack clapped and pointed.

"Dogs. Big dogs. See, Daddy?"

Her heart stopped. Actually stopped beating. The world went dark, then bright, bright white before tilting and finally righting itself. Relief was warm and sweet and so very welcome.

She stared at Kirk, who was watching her happily.

"He spoke?" Tears filled her eyes as she looked from the video to her son, then back at Kirk. "He spoke?"

"He did."

She began to laugh and hurried to Jack, then dropped down beside him. "You can do it! I knew you could. Oh, Jack!" She hugged him tight, then tickled him. He laughed and put his arms around her. "Big kiss."

He pressed his tiny toddler lips to hers, then squirmed away. She pointed to the truck. "What is that, Jack? Can you tell Mommy what that is?"

He smiled at her, then put his fingers against his mouth in a motion she knew to mean he was hungry.

"You want lunch? Okay, we can eat. But can you tell me what that is?" She pointed to the truck again.

He only smiled.

"I don't understand," she said to Kirk. "Why won't he talk?"

"Why does it matter? There's more on the video, Jen. He chatted up a storm. He can talk. That's the important thing."

She knew he was right, but still, why was Jack silent now?

"He'll talk when he's ready," Kirk assured her. "It'll be any second now."

She nodded, but was less sure. Jack was her baby. Shouldn't he talk around her the most?

She got lunch ready and called Lucas to join them. All through the meal, she tried to get Jack to talk, but he only smiled and waved and did his gesturing that was so clear to her. She understood him completely, but still, she wanted the words.

After his nap, she sent Kirk in to wake him. She waited in the hall, where Jack couldn't see her. Kirk pulled their son out of his crib.

"Did you have a good nap?"

"Yes!"

Jen's heart fluttered as she heard the word. She stepped into the room.

"Hi, sweetie."

Jack grinned and waved, but didn't speak.

By eight that night, she had to accept the truth. Her son would talk—just not around her. With her he used their special physical communication.

"I don't get it," she told Kirk when they'd retreated to their bedroom. "What am I doing wrong?"

"You're not doing anything wrong. He doesn't need to talk to you, Jen. You know exactly what he wants. But at least we know he *can* talk."

How could he not see that wasn't good enough? "So you think I hover. That I'm keeping him from talking."

"I don't mean it like that. You're a great mom."

"No, I'm not. A great mom wouldn't have a son who won't talk to her. A great mom would have figured this out weeks ago. I'm terrible and useless. Everything is awful."

She knew she was saying everything wrong and that she would regret saying all this later, but she couldn't seem to stop herself.

"I've made this happen," she continued. "I'm the problem. You and Lucas have him for fifteen minutes and suddenly he's fine. I'm with him all day long and I couldn't fix anything. I hate this. It's not fair. It's not right. What's wrong with me?"

She hurried out of the room. But there was nowhere to

go, she thought grimly as she brushed away tears. She wasn't about to run out on her family. She had her husband and her son. Her son, whom she loved more than anything on earth. Her son, who would talk to anyone but her.

Chapter Eighteen

Zoe told herself to live in the moment. To not ask questions when she was hopeful but also terrified of the answer. Still, when a handsome man showed up with a bottle of sparkling cider, the nonalcoholic kind, and settled in as if he planned to spend the evening, it was hard not to hope.

They were out on the small patio, sitting in lounge chairs next to each other. It was about an hour until sunset and the sky was that perfect blue right before the orange color. Mason lay in a patch of sun, his tail flicking every now and then, as if he, too, wanted to know.

Zoe glanced at Steven. "Not that I don't appreciate the company, but why are you here?"

He chuckled, then drank some of his cider. "I wondered how long it would take you to ask."

"Still waiting."

He reached for her hand. "I heard you talked to my mom."

She grimaced. "I'm not sure I would call it a conversation." The memory still hurt. She'd honest to God thought that she and Pam were friends. She couldn't have been more wrong.

"I'm trying to see her side," she said with a sigh. "You're her son and she loves you. She's looking out for you. But wow, was she very clear on her thoughts. She really doesn't like me."

He squeezed her fingers before releasing her hand. "She likes you fine, but she's worried about me."

"That woman has some serious Mama Bear in her. I would not want to get between her and one of you ever."

"Does that mean you're going to do what she says? You're going to break up with me?"

She put down her drink and turned until she was facing him. She put her feet firmly on the ground. Mostly to steady herself but also to be able to flee if necessary. Because sometimes a girl had to bolt. What with being pregnant and all, she could pretend she was going to throw up, and wasn't that convenient?

"It's not my decision to make," she said carefully. "You said you needed time. That's about you, not me."

"And if I still want to see you?"

Her heart gave a little thud. "That would be nice."

He smiled. "I was hoping for more than nice." The smile faded as he turned toward her. "Zoe, I do want to keep seeing you. I've thought about what you told me. I know it's not going to be easy. You're dealing with a lot. The pregnancy is complicated but not a deal breaker. I like you. I think we have something special and I don't want to lose that."

What on earth had she done to deserve a guy this great? she wondered. Maybe she'd saved kittens in a previous life.

"Are you sure? Because I don't know what's going to happen with Chad and everyone else. Your mom is going to be really mad. I don't want her hating me. Or you, although I guess she really wouldn't hate you for long. You're her son. But I'm pregnant. You have to get that, Steven. I'm going to get fat and my ankles are going to swell and we won't be able to have sex for a long time and when all that is done, there will be a baby and while I'd love for you to be involved, I don't know how much you want and you're not the biological father and I don't know if that matters."

She paused for breath. While she was inhaling, he leaned in and kissed her.

"That's a lot," he whispered.

"It is. I want you to be prepared."

"There's no preparing for that." He kissed her again. "I'm going to have to wing it."

He leaned back in his chaise. "What about those raised plant beds you were talking about? We should get on that. You'll want fresh, organic fruits and vegetables for yourself and later for the baby. Do you have a tape measure? I need you to show me where you want them. I need to do some research to be sure, but I'm guessing the supplies are easy enough to get at the hardware store. The local nursery should have organic soil, but we'll have to make sure we get the right kind for growing food." He looked at her. "Unless you're going to use it for flowers?"

She blinked. "No. I was thinking vegetables and maybe some berries."

"That's what I thought."

She shifted until she was stretched out again and did her best not to ask yet again if he was sure. Steven had decided. For reasons not the least bit clear to her, he wanted to stay involved. She told herself to simply accept him at his word and be happy.

Still, she couldn't help asking, "What are you going to tell your mom?"

"I don't think she has an opinion on your plant beds."

"Steven!"

He shrugged. "I'll talk to her. She's not going to make me choose, Zoe. She's a smart lady. She'll come around."

"And if she doesn't?"

"Let's worry about that if it happens, okay?"

"But that's so logical."

"Take a walk on the wild side."

"I did that once and now I'm pregnant."

He laughed. "Speaking of that, when's your next doctor's appointment?"

"I have my very first official visit on Monday. When I went before, it was more of an assessment than a *hey, you're having a baby* kind of thing."

"Can I come with you?"

She looked at him. "To the doctor?"

"Uh-huh. I want to be there through everything."

"Why?"

He reached for her hand again. "Zoe, I care about you. Haven't I been clear on that? You're pregnant. I'm going to do what I can to help." He swore. "Do we have to wait for the visit to make love?"

She felt her mouth drop open. She consciously closed it before telling herself that bursting into tears would only frighten him. Stupid hormones. But how else was she supposed to react to a man who not only wanted to keep dating her, he wanted to go through the pregnancy with her *and* have sex with her?

"We're allowed to do it," she told him. "It's okay."

"Do it?" He raised his eyebrows. "Is that how you think of our emotional and physical joining as we become one? I'm just a sex toy? An object? I don't matter at all?"

She held in a giggle. "I believe the correct phrase is boy toy. A sex toy generally has a battery."

He pulled his hand away and sighed heavily. "You're using me for sex. I'm crushed."

"Too crushed to get it up?"

He turned toward her. "Never that. Should I prove it to you right now?"

She put down her drink and held out her arms. "Yes, please."

Pam decided the world had gone mad. There was no other explanation. Despite knowing better, Steven had yet to call her and apologize for what he'd said. She hadn't heard from

Miguel and as for Zoe, well, she wasn't going to think about her anymore. Zoe was the source of all the trouble.

After feeling at loose ends for several days, Pam decided she needed a little time with her favorite grandson and went over to Jen's. Her daughter opened the front door.

"Hi. Did I know you were coming by?"

"No. I should have called. Is this a bad time?"

Jen let her and Lulu into the house. "It's fine. Jack is down for his nap and Lucas is watching some horrible daytime television. He's become totally addicted to those weird talk shows where everyone overshares."

They walked through to the family room. Pam crossed to the slider and let Lulu out. Her little girl had gone potty before they left, but she didn't want to take a chance. Not with Jen being so uptight about keeping the house perfect.

Pam sat in the sunroom. Jen had changed out the cushions last summer. The new pattern was nice. Not what she would have chosen, but still very pretty.

Jen picked up a few of Jack's toys and put them in the toy box. Her movements were deliberate, as if she had something on her mind. Pam knew her children well and could guess that Jen was once again going to obsess about Jack. Pam decided to speak before Jen could get started.

"Have you talked to Zoe?" she asked, hoping she sounded more casual than she felt.

"What? Not in the last day or so. I did before. Why? Is everything okay?"

"How would I know? I'm not speaking with her."

Jen frowned. "Why would you say that? Because she's pregnant? Mom, you know it's not her fault, right?"

"She had sex with Chad."

"So? It was a post-breakup thing. It happens." Jen studied her. "You didn't say anything to her, did you?"

"I said she should stay away from Steven. That he deserved better."

"Oh, my God!" Her daughter stared at her. "Tell me you're kidding."

"I'm not. Why would I be? You know it's going to be a nightmare. Chad won't go away. She was in love with him before. What if she decides she's still in love with him? Then where will Steven be? He's better off ending things now. Before they get out of hand."

"Is that what you really think?"

"Why are you surprised?"

"Because it's mean and not like you at all."

Pam shifted in her seat. Her daughter's steady gaze seemed very judgy. "I'm doing what's best."

"No, you're not."

"Stop looking at me like that."

Jen shook her head. "I honestly don't know what to say. Steven can take care of himself, Mom. We all can. You made sure of that. You should trust him." She hesitated. "Is this about Dad?"

"What does your father have to do with anything?" Pam thought about adding that John would agree with her, only she was suddenly less sure about that.

"You lost him suddenly. It was hard on you." Her voice gentled. "You can't protect us from the bad stuff in life, Mom. Steven knows what he's doing. You should be on his side in this and on Zoe's."

"Steven's family. Zoe is not."

"Zoe's my friend. I thought she was your friend, too."

"You're looking at this all wrong," Pam told her, frustrated that she couldn't make anyone understand why this was so important. "They've only been dating a few months. So what if they break up? It was probably going to happen anyway. It's not like Steven has a great track record when it comes to relationships, and based on Chad, Zoe's taste can't be trusted."

"What on earth is wrong with you, Mom? You sound so vicious and heartless."

"I'm being practical."

"You're being a bitch."

Pam stared at her daughter. "You don't get to speak to me that way."

"Then stop acting so awful. What's wrong with you? Zoe made one mistake and now she's dealing with it. She could have had an abortion, but she decided to keep the baby. I would think you would respect that and her. She's a good person. If she and Steven fall in love, then they're both really fortunate to have found each other."

"You couldn't be more wrong. Steven has no idea what he's doing."

"He's a grown man. Leave him alone. I have to say, I'm totally shocked by what you're saying."

"I'm protecting my family."

"Is that what you're calling it?" Jen shook her head. "You always taught us to think about other people. To imagine what they were going through and to act out of compassion. I guess that was all a load of crap."

Pam shifted in her seat. "This is different."

"It's not. It's exactly the same. Zoe's my friend, Mom. Whatever happens, I'm going to be there for her. If you don't like that, I'm sorry. You couldn't be more wrong about this. About all of it." She rose. "You need to be careful. Because if you push Steven too hard, you risk losing him. I mean it, Mom. This is bad."

Pam felt herself flush. She didn't like being talked down to by anyone. She wasn't wrong. She knew exactly what she was doing and saying.

"Steven needs someone to get him to see sense," she said as she stood.

"Is that your plan?" Jen asked, putting her hands on her hips. "Before you try and possibly ruin your relationship with your son, let me remind you that the only reason he would consider taking on Zoe and the baby is because of what you and Dad taught us. You always said we were to see the best in people and give them a chance. I guess that's more crap, right?"

Lulu trotted into the sunroom. Jen scooped her up and held her. "It's been a hell of a week, Mom. There's stuff going on here that—" She kissed Lulu, then handed her over. "Never mind. I don't want to know what you think about anything. You're wrong about Zoe and you're wrong about Steven. But you're going to have to figure that out for yourself."

Pam took her dog and started for the front door. "I can't believe you're taking her side in this."

"That makes two of us who are shocked right now."

Pam got into her SUV and put her hands on the wheel. She was shaking and felt a little sick to her stomach. What was wrong with Jen? Why couldn't she see the impending disaster? Was everyone blind but her?

She paused and glanced upward, once again missing her husband. If John were here, he would know what to say. He would get through to Steven and convince him no woman was worth years of unhappiness. John would tell him—

For a second Pam had the thought that John might very well be telling her something very close to what Jen had said. That she needed to back off. That no matter how she tried, she couldn't protect her children from everything and that they had to be free to live their lives. Even if that meant walking into what was—at least to her—a disaster waiting to happen.

"No," Pam said aloud. "I won't. If Steven refuses to see the obvious, I have to show him why he's wrong."

Whatever it cost to keep him safe, the price would be worth it.

★ ★ ★

Jen stretched out on the grass in her backyard. The day was sunny, the air warm, the sky blue. She told herself to revel in that. To enjoy the moment, to be one with nature.

Which was all a bunch of nonsense. She was furious. There wasn't a cell in her body that wasn't vibrating with rage and the worst part was she had absolutely nowhere to put the anger. She couldn't be pissed at her son. Jack was a toddler and doing his toddler thing. Kirk was only the messenger. What had happened wasn't his fault either. She'd tried to tell him that, but they'd both known she wasn't happy. Her great dreams of seduction had burned up in a fire of resentment. All these days later she was still dealing with too much emotion and a lot of self-loathing.

Jack knelt next to her, moving his truck over the recently mowed grass. Next to him was the ridiculous guitar that he loved. Lucas dozed in the sunroom. Zoe sat next to her on the grass, her gaze fixed on the video Jen had showed her.

"I don't know what to say," her friend admitted. "You must be relieved." The words were more question than statement.

"You can say it," Jen told her. "We're all thinking it."

"No."

"Yes. It's my fault. I'm so attentive that he doesn't need to talk around me. I went online and read about the phenomenon. Usually it happens between siblings who are close in age. The older sibling can read what the younger one wants and takes care of things. So the baby doesn't have to talk. I've done that with Jack." She sat up and covered her face with her hands. "I'm a helicopter mom."

"You're not."

"Pretty close. I hover. I anticipate. I worry. I'm the reason Jack won't talk."

"But he does talk."

"Not to *me*."

Jen had tried all weekend. She'd withheld toys a second or two, hoping to get Jack to ask for them. There hadn't been a single word. She'd left him with Lucas for a couple of hours and Lucas's guilty expression upon her return had told her that the boy had chatted up a storm.

"I'm a failure."

Zoe hugged her. "You're a wonderful mom and he's lucky to have you. You take really good care of him."

"I'm smothering him. Learn from my mistakes. I mean that. I'm a disaster."

So much for meditating and drinking water, she thought grimly. Those practices might be helping her, but they weren't doing anything for her son.

She lowered her voice. "I really hate this. I have so much negative energy and I can't find a place for it. I'm terrified I'm going to snap or something."

Zoe shook her head. "You're going to be okay. Now that you understand what's going on, you can relax about Jack. Then you can start to relax about everything else. The big picture issue is solved. Can you hang on to that?"

Jen nodded even though she was lying. The truth of what had gone wrong circled in her head like a hamster on a wheel. She couldn't escape it. But that didn't mean everyone else wanted to talk about her problems. She shifted so she was sitting cross-legged.

"You're right about the big picture. Jack can talk. That's what matters most." She faked a smile, convincingly she hoped. "Enough about my stuff. What's new with you? How are you feeling? Still good?"

"I haven't been sick at all. I feel kind of guilty about that."

Jen laughed. "Be grateful. Hormones are powerful little suckers. Don't worry. There is plenty of unpleasantness to be had in the rest of your pregnancy. Enjoy this part of it while you can. Did you see the doctor?"

"Yesterday." Zoe's mouth twisted. "Since we know the exact date of conception, it wasn't hard to calculate my due date. I've already had the first ultrasound and everything looks good. She told me to continue gestating and be happy."

Easy advice for the doctor to give, Jen thought. She suspected it was more difficult for Zoe to take.

"How are you doing with that last one?"

"Being happy? I don't know. Things are complicated. Chad wants to talk to me."

"He knows?"

"Yeah. I told him. He said he needed some time to think about it. I told him I was okay with him giving up his child, but I don't think he's going to go for that. I've spoken to a lawyer. If Chad's staying in my life, I want to get the parenting plan in place as early as possible. While the baby is still a theory."

"Less is more?" Jen asked.

Zoe hesitated. "I want to be fair, but less would be great. He doesn't have custody of his other two children. I don't think he'll want custody of ours. He sees them every other weekend and for part of the time on the holidays. So I'm hoping for something similar."

"Will he want to spend every other weekend with a newborn?"

"I don't know and as I plan to breast-feed, I don't know how he can. We'll have to figure it out." Zoe plucked at the grass. "Are you mad at me?"

"What? No! Why would I be? You're my friend. I'll support you in every way I can." She pointed to the stack of books she'd put out in the sunroom. "Would I be offering you my well-read collection of pregnancy books if I was mad?"

Zoe smiled. "No, and I had no idea that you owned so many."

Jen looked at the pile of over a dozen books. "I guess it is a lot. Maybe start with two or three. I'll show you my favorites."

"Steven already bought me *What to Expect When You're Expecting*. It's very detailed."

"A great resource, though. You'll love that one. They walk you through your pregnancy, month by month."

Jack stood up and waved at her. Jen opened her arms and her son ran to her. She pulled him close, turning him so he sat between her crossed legs.

"So, you're still seeing Steven," she said, as casually as she could.

"Yes." Zoe eyed her. "What are you thinking?"

"That you're far too good for him." Jen smiled. "Seriously, I'm happy. Dad's death changed us all. Steven finally had to finish growing up. He's given up his bimbo-of-the-week dating and has been looking for someone for a while. I'm glad he found you."

Zoe didn't look convinced. "Even though I'm pregnant with Chad's baby?"

"Even though. I know there will be issues, but every relationship has problems. You two know what you're getting into and can plan accordingly. Everyone I know who has stepkids says the worst part is they didn't have any say when the kids were young. Steven will be with you and the baby from birth. He'll be a part of things."

If he and Zoe got serious enough to get married and later there was a divorce, then Steven would be screwed. Stepfathers rarely got to see their stepkids again. But her brother was a smart guy—he would know the risks. If he wanted to be with Zoe, then she was going to support that.

"Thanks for that," Zoe told her. She tickled the bottom of Jack's bare foot. He laughed and she smiled. Then the smile faded.

"Your mom doesn't share your generous spirit."

Jen grimaced. "She's being quite the *beyotch* right now and I have no idea why."

"She's protecting her son."

"I find it fascinating that you're making excuses for her. If I were you, I'd be egging her car."

Zoe grinned. "Not my style." The humor faded for a second time. "I honestly don't know what to say to her. She's so determined to see this as bad for Steven. For you, too, I'm guessing."

Jen wasn't going to talk about her recent fight with her mother. "You were the maid of honor at my wedding. Our relationship is important to me and my mom doesn't get a vote."

"I don't want to cause trouble."

"You're not. Trust me. It's all good." Jen looked at her. "You're dealing with so many things right now. Pregnancy takes a lot out of your body. You have to take care of yourself and surround yourself with people who will be there for you. I want to be one of them and it sounds like Steven does, too. So go with it. As for my mom—" she shrugged "—I hope she eventually gets it, but if she doesn't, you'll still have us."

Chapter Nineteen

So far there weren't a whole lot of physical disadvantages to being pregnant, Zoe thought as she crossed her living room and opened the door. But there sure were logistical ones.

"Hello, Chad."

"Zoe."

Having to deal with her ex was the biggest one. As much as she didn't want to see him, she knew she was now in a position where she had to take his calls. And when he'd asked to see her, she had said yes.

It was the middle of the day, which meant he'd stopped by on his lunch break. Something she was grateful for—they could hardly get into anything significant in the forty-five minutes he had off.

He had on his usual uniform of jeans and a white T-shirt. She found it strange that she had once thought him handsome. She supposed that came from seeing him differently. She'd never been able to depend on him—not the way she depended on Steven. He'd been such a relatively small part of her life. Now she only saw him as someone she used to know. What they had seemed so long ago—all baby evidence to the contrary.

She motioned to the sofa and he took a seat. For a second

she allowed herself to hope that he'd decided one more kid was more than he could handle and that he would give up his rights. Not that she was really expecting that to happen. So far her luck hadn't been that good.

"How are you feeling?" he asked.

"Fine. I saw the doctor and everything is going well with the baby."

"Good." He rubbed his hands together, then stood and walked to the far side of the room. He faced her. "I've been thinking."

Oh, please, oh, please, she chanted silently.

"About us and the baby. The thing is…" He swallowed, then moved close and sat next to her. He smiled. "Marry me, Zoe. We can make it work." He took her hand in his. "I mean it. Marry me. You always wanted that, right? Well, now you can have it. The ring, the wedding. Whatever. You've got a really nice house. It should work for the baby. I'll probably keep my apartment, you know, for when I have my kids. But that's okay."

She drew back her hand and told herself this wasn't happening. Chad hadn't just proposed.

Marry him? There was no way. They couldn't… She couldn't…

"Zoe?"

"Chad, no. We're not getting married."

"Why not?

"For one thing, we don't love each other. We didn't have a relationship. We had something that was convenient to both of us."

"But you always wanted us to get married. You talked about it. You said it was why you bought this house."

Something she would always regret. Not the house—wanting to marry him. "Things have changed. I see now that I was wrong. You don't love me. You don't even want to give up your apartment. You never wanted anything more than what we had. You were right. We aren't good together."

"But we're having a baby. When a couple gets pregnant, they should get married."

Jeez, he sounded like her father. "That doesn't change anything. I'm not marrying you, Chad. I'm sorry. You're sweet to ask, but no."

He shifted back on the sofa, then stood. "I thought you'd want to."

"I don't."

"I'm not giving up my kid. I want to see him or her."

She held in a sigh. Disappointing but not surprising. "I figured. You were always very devoted to your other children. We'll figure out a parenting plan that works for both of us. It will be a little complicated while the baby is breast-feeding, but we'll make it work."

He shook his head. "I thought this was what you wanted," he repeated.

"I know. I'm sorry."

"I was going to buy you a ring."

"I appreciate that."

"Is there someone else?" he asked.

She nodded. "He's a great guy. You'll have to meet him at some point."

She thought there might be some kind of reaction but Chad only sighed. "My ex remarried over the holidays. What is it about you women and locking down some guy?"

Zoe opened her mouth, then closed it. "Your ex-wife got married and you didn't tell me?"

"I didn't think it was important."

But they'd been together when it had happened. He should have—

She mentally put on the brakes. Not her problem, she reminded herself. None of this was anymore. Chad would always be Chad. It was why she wasn't with him anymore.

She rose and crossed to the door. "We'll talk again soon. I'll get the parenting plan started with my lawyer. I don't know if you want representation, as well. You should probably think about it." She thought about mentioning the fact that she wouldn't want him in the delivery room with her, but they were a long way from that happening. Months and months. Anything could happen. Well, anything except her getting back together with Chad.

He walked to the open front door and stepped onto her porch. "You're sure?"

"I am. I'll talk to you later."

"Okay."

She didn't wait to close the door. There was nothing left to say. When she heard his car drive away, she returned to her office and sat in front of her computer. But she didn't start typing right away. Instead she leaned her head back to keep her tears at bay.

She'd totally messed up. Everything about this pregnancy was so unexpected. She put her hand on her stomach.

"Even you," she whispered. Especially the baby. Still, there were blessings. A year ago, she would have jumped at Chad's proposal. Talk about a disaster. She didn't want to marry a man who talked about keeping his own apartment, not that his inability to fully commit was even the biggest problem. They didn't love each other. She was pretty sure he'd never been in love with her at all. As for herself, she had no idea when her feelings had faded. All she knew was that they were gone now.

She was going to have a baby and Chad was going to be the father. She couldn't seem to escape either fact. There would be a parenting plan and visitation and child support. None of which pleased her, but it was the price of doing business, so to speak. Because she *was* having this baby.

Her phone chirped. She glanced down at the screen and saw she had a text from Steven. It was a picture of a page for an organic seed catalog.

The accompanying text read: Can't wait to see you tonight. I'll be the guy with the promise of butter lettuce.

She laughed. Looking forward to it.

She put down her phone. At least the Steven part of her life was going well, she thought. How could she resist a man who tempted her with organic lettuce seeds? It was physically impossible and she would be a fool to try.

Pam usually battled with mixed feelings when she left on a trip. Of course she was excited to see her friends and whatever the cruise ports would be, but she also felt a twinge at leaving her family behind. But this trip was different. With the exception of missing Lulu and her friends, she was grateful to be leaving Mischief Bay for three weeks. She needed the time away. Maybe being somewhere else for a while would help her clear her head.

She'd texted all three of her children, reminding them of her trip. Brandon, who knew nothing about the Zoe issue, had responded with a friendly phone call. The other two had texted back, wishing her well, but nothing more. A far cry from their usual chitchat about where she was going and what she would be seeing.

She knew that Steven and Jen were still upset with her, even though she was right and they were wrong. Well, fine. Let them stew while she was gone. Things would be different when she got home.

She left her plane at JFK and walked toward baggage claim. Olimpia's flight from Orlando was due in about the same time and they had arranged to meet up and share a cab to their hotel. Laura and Eugenia should have already arrived. In the morning the four of them would fly to Copenhagen where they would spend two days before boarding their ship.

Pam found her two large bags, then checked her phone for a text from her friend. Olimpia was only a couple of carousels away. She sent a message back, explaining where she was and they started to walk toward each other.

Pam spotted Olimpia first. At the sight of her friend, she felt her control start to slip. By the time they were hugging, Pam was in tears.

"What's wrong?"

"Everything's a mess. Steven, Zoe, Miguel. It's because of Zoe. Okay and maybe me. I'm the one who set her up with Steven. If I hadn't done that, none of this would have happened. Of course if she hadn't slept with Chad, things would have been okay, as well. I thought I was doing the right thing, but it's a disaster."

Olimpia patted her back. "That's quite a list. Let's get a cab and you can tell me about it on the way to the city. We'll meet up with the girls. You'll feel better after cocktails."

"But I don't know what to do."

"Pam, you're going to Europe. You don't have to do anything until you get home."

An hour later they arrived at the Peninsula Hotel in midtown. Pam had explained everything to Olimpia, including how the world seemed to be siding with Zoe, even though there was a very good chance she was going to break Steven's heart.

They checked into their rooms and agreed to meet in a half hour. Pam only bothered with one of her bags. She'd put everything she would need before the cruise in one case. The second suitcase would be unpacked on the ship.

She went down to the Bar at Clement where she found her friends waiting for her. Based on their expressions, she knew that Olimpia had already shared her troubles. At least she didn't have to go over it all again.

"I don't want to talk about my ridiculous family," she announced. "How is everyone else?"

"We're good," Eugenia said as they hugged.

Laura shifted over to give Pam room on the bench seat, then scowled. "Dear God, you are in such good shape. It's annoying. How often do you exercise?"

"A few times a week."

She thought of the workouts at her friend Nicole's studio. Workouts that Zoe had joined her for. Which probably wouldn't be happening now. Pam felt a twinge of regret. Not that she wanted to be friends with Zoe anymore—she didn't. But Pilates would be good for Zoe's pregnancy. There was something so magical about seeing a woman's body change and knowing there was a new life waiting inside. Bouncing back from a pregnancy was hard enough—if Zoe continued to practice Pilates, she would find it easier.

Someone should tell her, she thought wistfully. Only Zoe's mother had passed away and Pam wasn't sure Jen would think to mention it. There were other things...

Pam reminded herself she wasn't on Zoe's side anymore so she shouldn't care about how well she did or didn't do after her pregnancy. Still, if circumstances had been different, she would have enjoyed having another baby in her life. She loved them when they were newborns. That sweet smell, the way they relaxed so completely in her arms. There was nothing quite so wonderful as rocking a newborn.

"Earth to Pam," Laura said. "Are you still with us?"

"What? Oh, sorry." She looked at her friends. "What were we talking about?"

"We were discussing our cocktail schedule," Eugenia told her. "The cruise is just too dang long for us to have a single drink we depend on."

Olimpia looked amused. "Did you just say dang?"

"My Texas is showing," Eugenia said with a laugh. "Sorry. My gentleman friend and I have been spending more time together than usual and his accent rubs off on me. My point being, we need to rotate what we're drinking."

"We'll be in Russia for a few days." Laura smiled. "We should definitely have a vodka-based drink. It's only polite."

"We don't have to decide now." Olimpia looked around the table. "As long as we have our New York cocktail decided. Agreed?"

They all nodded.

"I believe it was my turn." Eugenia drew in a breath. "Bellinis. Champagne is always appropriate, especially before a trip like the one we're going on."

"Bellinis it is," Laura said, and flagged the server.

They placed their order. Their server left small bowls of nuts and olives for them. When he'd left, Olimpia glanced at them.

"So how is everyone doing? Any news?"

Laura shrugged. "I'm good. Pam, should we be worried about you, with everything going on?"

"I'm fine. Just trying to figure things out."

"Poor Steven." Laura's expression was sympathetic. "He's got some tough decisions to make. I know you're staying neutral, but on the inside, you must be dying to tell him what you think."

Pam opened her mouth, then closed it. She realized that while she'd told Olimpia what was happening, she'd neglected to mention that she'd done more than simply listen. She'd hardly stayed neutral. She'd not only told Steven what to do, she'd fought with her daughter and ended things with Miguel. Or maybe he'd ended things with her. She wasn't sure.

"Obviously Steven needs to break things off with Zoe." Eugenia shrugged. "I don't mean to sound harsh, but there's no way he wants to take on another man's baby. Not if Chad's going to stay around." She looked at Pam. "Is he?"

"That's what I understand."

Before she could thank her friend for seeing things so clearly, Olimpia spoke up.

"How can you say that?" Olimpia asked. "Break up with her? The pregnancy wasn't her fault. It simply happened. And for that she should lose a wonderful man like Steven? Of course he'll stay with her. If they care about each other, they'll figure it out. Besides, he wasn't raised to run from a problem like that. We all know Pam and what she believes. She's an honest, fair, wonderful person. Steven has to be exactly the same. There's no way he's going to turn his back on Zoe."

While Pam appreciated the compliment, she wasn't sure she deserved it. According to her children, she wasn't very nice these days.

Laura shifted in her seat. "Zoe did sleep with the ex. That's kind of tacky."

"Agreed," Olimpia said. "But come on, it happens. And she thought she was protected. Nothing Zoe did was irresponsible. We all talk about raising our children to be good people. To look past the superficial to the person inside."

"A baby isn't superficial," Eugenia pointed out. "It's a life changer. Why would Steven want that?"

"Why wouldn't he? He's a good guy. Yes, a baby complicates things, but so what? Are you saying if he met someone who was divorced and had a couple of kids you would tell him to run? Why is this different?"

"She's pregnant," Laura said slowly. "I see your point and I get the divorced thing. How interesting that her being pregnant makes it seem like more of a complication. I can't explain why."

It was as if her friends had become the voices in her head, Pam realized. They were having the argument for her.

"My friend Shannon married a man with two children," Pam said slowly. "There were adjustments but it's working out."

"See." Olimpia sounded triumphant. "Did you tell her to run from him?"

"Of course not." Pam remembered how difficult it had been for Shannon when she'd met Adam. Getting to know the children had been a challenge. But she'd gotten through it and now they were blissfully happy. Not to mention fostering five-year-old twin boys.

She smiled. "In fact, Shannon keeps Lulu for me when I travel. My little girl is in doggy heaven with a whole pack of kids to boss around."

"Jen doesn't…" Laura held up a hand. "Never mind. Until dogs come germfree and totally organic, she can't have her around too much. I remember. My daughters would be so proud of her."

The Bellinis arrived. They each took one and raised them as they toasted each other.

"To us," Laura said. "And our wonderful trip."

They touched glasses and took a drink. Laura put hers down.

"Do you think I'll be able to find a pashmina anywhere we're going? My black one is so tired. I would love something new and fresh."

"We've got an extra day in Copenhagen," Eugenia said. "We'll shop after we see the sights."

"I have a pale silver one I brought," Pam told her. "You can borrow mine."

Laura grinned. "I'd be careful, if I were you. If I love it, I might not want to give it back."

They all laughed. Pam drew in a breath as she felt herself relaxing. These were her friends and they loved her. They had been there for her from the first day she'd met them. They supported her and trusted her. Only now she wasn't completely sure that trust was warranted.

While she hadn't meant to keep the whole story from them, it seemed she had. They knew the facts, but not her reaction to them, and she couldn't help wondering if they would like her just a little bit less if they knew everything that had happened.

Jen backed out of the driveway. She told herself that she didn't have to go through with this. That she could change her mind. Only she knew she couldn't—not really. Jack still refused to talk to her. He was loving, eager, happy and totally silent. As he'd chatted with his dad, Lucas and even the mailman, she knew that she was the problem. Which meant she had to be the solution. If only she didn't feel as if she were seconds from having a panic attack.

She ignored the tightness in her chest. Her medication should keep the symptoms at a manageable level, she told herself firmly. Which meant there was no reason not to move forward with her plan. Step one—get Jack into day care. To that end, she had an appointment with Rose. She would fill out the paperwork and get Jack enrolled.

"You okay?" Lucas asked from the passenger seat.

"No, but I will be."

"It's just day care."

"Children have died in day care."

"Exaggerate much?"

She glared at him. "It's happened. I've seen stories on the news."

"These are the same people who brought us alien landings, I'm sure." He held up a hand. "Yes, it's happened. Once, maybe twice. The odds are in your favor." He grinned. "Actually I believe the correct phrase is *may the odds be ever in your favor.*" He chuckled at his own joke.

"Yes, yes, very funny. You've quoted *The Hunger Games.*

Later you can recite some lines from *The Godfather* and we'll all have a good laugh."

"Someone's a little high-strung this morning."

She was and she didn't need him pointing that out to her.

"I'm hungry," Lucas said as she turned onto Choppy Avenue. "Let's go to In-N-Out Burger. We have time."

"Are you insane? A burger place? Do you know what they serve there?"

"Burgers?"

She really, really wanted to slap him. Hard. The problem was she had a bad feeling Lucas would slap her back. Not only would that change things, but it would be a bad thing for Jack to see.

She glanced in the rearview mirror and saw her son was calmly playing with his stuffed raccoon.

"Jack doesn't eat fast food."

"It's a burger, Jen. Not rat poison. They serve good quality stuff."

"Like French fries."

"Yes, that's a traditional accompaniment."

"Jack doesn't eat fries."

"Poor kid."

She tightened her grip on the steering wheel. Despite her medication, she could feel her heart pounding. The familiar tightening began to coil around her chest. She hadn't had a panic attack in over a week. They'd been lessening in strength and number. Why was she having one now?

"We can't go there," she said quietly, willing herself to keep breathing.

"Why the hell not?"

"You swore in front of Jack," she shrieked.

Lucas muttered something under his breath. In the backseat, Jack began to cry.

"See! Look what you did."

"Me?" Lucas's voice was a growl. "I'm not the one wound so damned tight I'm going to explode."

His words hit her hard. She wasn't wound tight. She'd been doing so much better. Except she really couldn't catch her breath and Jack was crying. Up ahead she saw the familiar In-N-Out sign and swung into the parking lot. She parked and pointed to the door.

"Take him outside. Now!"

For once Lucas did as she asked. He got out and collected Jack. The two of them walked over to the grassy area beside the outdoor seating. Jen stayed in the car and tried to steady her breathing. She felt both cold and hot and her chest was so very tight.

She hung on to the steering wheel and concentrated on her breath. "If I can talk, I can breathe," she said aloud, knowing the act of speaking would make her understand that she was okay.

After a few minutes, she started to calm down. What on earth had happened? Lucas was right—it was just a French fry. Why was she so hysterical?

She supposed a lot of the problem was Jack talking to everyone but her. She was filled with guilt over that. Plus the idea of putting him in day care had her on edge. But she knew she had to keep moving forward. She didn't like where she was in her life right now. She didn't like who she'd become. She had to get things in perspective.

She sucked in one last breath, then grabbed her bag and got out of the car. Jack was fine, playing with his toy raccoon, but Lucas seemed wary.

"Better?" he asked, keeping his distance.

"Yes. I'm sorry. Of course we can have lunch here. I like their food."

As for Jack, well, she would simply have to deal with any consequences.

They went inside and ordered. Lucas got a Double-Double, while she chose a regular hamburger. They agreed to split fries. She asked for water and Lucas got a vanilla shake with an extra cup and spoon.

She gave Jack a small portion of her burger, then put three fries on a napkin. He seemed more interested in pointing at cars driving by the window than eating.

She took a bite and nearly groaned. "I haven't had one of these in forever. I'd forgotten how good they are."

Jack ate some of his burger, then nibbled on a fry. He seemed to enjoy what he had but left the other two fries on the napkin. Because he was a kid and had access to tasty food all the time, she thought sheepishly. One fast-food lunch wasn't any big deal. Life was all about balance, she reminded herself.

"I'm sorry I swore," Lucas said unexpectedly. "I've been trying not to do that in front of Jack."

"I know and I appreciate the effort. I guess I can be annoying."

"You think? Maybe you should get your meds checked."

She grinned. "That bad?"

"Not all the time. You're loosening up, but you could stand to unwind a little more."

"I know. I'm doing better. The talking thing threw me."

"It would be hard on anyone."

"Thank you." She sipped her water. "You're really good with Jack. Ever think about having kids of your own?"

Lucas glared at her. "Way to ruin the mood. No. I'm not the father type."

"I don't believe that. Of course, you're too old, but given the age of your girlfriends, at least one of you would be around to see him or her graduate from college."

"I'm ignoring you."

"Then nothing has changed."

He winked at her. "Sass. I like it."

They finished their lunch. Jack ate one more fry, then had a spoonful of Lucas's milk shake.

"Ready to brave the infested, germ-house of a day care center?" Lucas asked.

"Ha-ha. It's not that bad."

"That's not what you were saying before."

She stood and collected their trash. "I know, but it's different now. The marvels of the modern pharmaceutical era."

Lucas grabbed her arm. "It's not the meds, Jen. It's you. You've been working the program. Give yourself credit. You deserve it."

"Thank you." The unexpected compliment gave her a little boost. "That's nice."

"It's true, and we both know I don't do nice."

"Is it too old, too?"

He grinned and scooped up Jack in his good arm.

They walked to the SUV. Lucas buckled her son in his car seat, then closed the back door. He opened the driver's door for her.

"I'm going to head home tomorrow."

It took her a second to realize what he meant. "You're leaving?"

"I've already started physical therapy. I'll be back on the job in a week. I'm perfectly capable of taking care of myself."

Which was all true, but so what? "I don't want you to go," she blurted. "I like having you around."

"You need more to do with your day. Go back to work. Have another kid. Stay busy. You're happier when you're busy."

He was right, but she knew her wanting him to stay wasn't that general. "Lucas, you're family."

His green gaze settled on her face. "Thank you for that. I feel the same way. But you're cramping my style."

She knew he had to get back to his regular life, but still.

"We'll all miss you." Funny how she started not liking Lucas at all and now she didn't want him to move out of her house.

"You'll see me all the time. I promise."

"Good."

She got in the car and they drove to the day care center. This time, when she parked out front, she saw the neighborhood was family focused. Across the street was the playground at Founders Park. The trees were mature, the lawns well kept.

"Nice," Lucas said as he climbed out. "Do they take the kids over to the park?"

"I don't know. We'll have to ask."

She got Jack out of his car seat. He seemed to remember the house and ran up to the front door. Jen and Lucas followed.

Rose answered, Buddy right behind her.

"Mrs. Beldon. How nice to see you again." Rose turned to Lucas. "Mr. Beldon? A pleasure."

Jen held in a chuckle at Lucas's look of panic. "Please call me Jen," she said. "And this isn't my husband. This is Lucas. He's a friend of the family. Kirk's working, so he offered to come along."

She helped Jack up the single stair, then crouched down. "Jack, honey, do you remember Buddy?"

Jack laughed and reached for the dog. Buddy bent his head, as if making himself more toddler-size. Jack squeezed his neck.

"Buddy used to be a service dog," Jen told Lucas. "He's good with the children."

Lucas raised his eyebrows but didn't say anything.

Rose took them on a tour. This time Jen tried to look past the mess made by children. She found the windows were plenty clean, as were the toys. Rose showed her everything from the cleansers she used to the bathrooms. There was a security system in place, along with a Nanny-Cam set up that allowed parents to log in and watch what was happening at the house.

"It's a secure network," Rose told her. "We can't have just anyone watching our babies."

Jen got a copy of the schedule, which included what would be served for lunch and snacks, along with the movies that would be shown and academic subjects to be covered. While he was here, Jack would be introduced to the concept of letters and colors, along with shapes and numbers. By the time the three of them left, she'd signed up Jack and paid for the first month of day care. She was starting him at three mornings a week. If that went well, she would expand the time.

"How are you holding up?" Lucas asked as they walked back to the SUV.

"It's scary, but I know it's the right thing to do."

"Jack's going to love it there."

"I know. He'll be around other children and that's important. Children need to learn to socialize."

"What about you, Jen? What do you need?"

She sighed. "I think I need to learn to get over myself."

Chapter Twenty

Zoe was beginning to think that meeting her dad for break-fast had been a bad idea. Despite the fact that she needed to get more protein in her diet and she didn't like cooking eggs at home, she wasn't sure the delicious omelet had been worth the lecture.

"He's the father of your baby," Miguel said, his voice intense.

"I'm so very aware of that."

"Do you want me to talk to him? Tell him what's what? I could do that—man-to-man."

Something she knew would not end well. She supposed most people would be worried about their dad. But Chad, for all his flaws, would fight fair. Miguel would not. Not exactly the normal quandary, Zoe thought as she sipped on her herbal tea. "I miss coffee."

"Don't change the subject."

"I wasn't. I was making an observation. Dad, I love you. You're very sweet to worry about me, but I'm fine. And I'm not marrying Chad."

"Because you don't want to or because he hasn't asked?"

She groaned. If they weren't at the restaurant in the Inn at the Pier, she would start banging her head against the table. There was absolutely no way she was going to tell her father that Chad had proposed. Miguel would latch onto that tidbit and do his best to convince her all her problems were solved.

"For a man who has traveled the world several times over, you're shockingly old-fashioned," she said. "I miss Mom." And way more than coffee, she added silently.

Her father's eyes widened. "Why do you say that?"

"Because she would talk some sense into you. She would tell you to stop badgering me and start being supportive." Plus, when a woman was pregnant for the first time, she wanted her mom around, Zoe thought wistfully.

"I'm not badgering you."

"I feel badgered."

"Then I'll stop."

"Really?"

"For now."

She laughed. "Thank you for being honest."

"I try. How are you feeling?"

"Great. I've been very lucky so far. Minimal morning sickness. Work is going well. Steven has been very supportive."

Her father grimaced. "I don't know how I feel about Steven."

"Then it's probably for the best the two of you aren't dating."

"Very funny."

"Thank you. I think I have a future in stand-up."

Her father shook his head. "You take after your mother. You know that, don't you?"

"I like to think so, and thank you for the compliment. Not that you're not wonderful, too."

"I worry about you."

"I know, Dad. But I'm fine. I'm going to have a baby without Chad. At least as little Chad as possible. I hope you'll be supportive of that."

"I'll try. Where does Steven fit into the picture?"

"We're still figuring that out." She clutched her mug of tea. "I like him a lot. If I wasn't pregnant, I would be drinking champagne and planning vacations to Hawaii. As it is, I'm cautiously optimistic, but taking things slow. There's more than just me to consider. I have to worry about my child."

And Steven, she thought, but knew better than to mention that to her dad.

"You think he can handle it? You having a baby?"

A legitimate question, Zoe thought. "He's doing okay so far, but right now it's just theory. We'll see what happens when I start to swell up like a watermelon."

"Your mother was beautiful the whole time she was pregnant with you."

"You're sweet to say that." She put down her tea. "How are you doing, Dad? What's been going on?"

"Not much."

"What happened with Pam?"

Zoe knew their last conversation had gone badly but she hadn't heard very much about her father and Pam.

"She and I disagreed."

"Oh, you agree on one thing," she said. "You both want me to marry Chad."

He surprised her by shaking his head. "Actually she doesn't. She disapproves of Chad very much and would be disappointed that I mentioned you marrying him."

"What?" Pam taking her side. "I thought she hated me."

"She doesn't. In fact, my guess is Pamela's reaction has nothing to do with you at all."

Like she was going to believe that, Zoe thought, choking down another swallow of herbal tea.

"She lost her husband unexpectedly," her father continued. "She suffered greatly and didn't know how to deal with the grief. Pamela wants control so she can keep those she loves safe. With you pregnant by Chad, there is no way for her to protect Steven. That's why she's lashing out."

Zoe stared at her father. "Oh. My. God. Have you been watching daytime television?"

He frowned. "You disrespect me. I'm disappointed."

"Dad, come on. That's not fair. I can't believe you're being so emotionally deep and understanding." She groaned. "That came out wrong." Note to self: breakfast with Dad was a very bad idea. "What I meant is, you've really been thinking about this."

"I have. You should do the same. Be more understanding."

"Is this before or after I marry Chad?" she grumbled. "I'm the one who's pregnant. Shouldn't she be more understanding of me?"

"Yes, but that is not going to happen, so it's up to you."

"I hate being the mature one in a relationship."

He smiled. "I'm well aware of that, yet you continue to rise to the occasion."

"So you're okay with her attitude."

His humor faded. "Not at all. She hurt you and that makes me angry. But I'm trying to understand why."

"You must really like her."

"I find her...intriguing."

Zoe wasn't sure what to do with the information. For a while she'd been all in when it came to her dad and Pam. She'd been a little flummoxed by her dating Pam's son and Pam dating her father, but this was Los Angeles and she was sure things like that happened all the time here. But her pregnancy had changed everything.

"Are you going to pursue things?"

Miguel flagged down the waitress and asked for more coffee. "You want more tea?"

"No, I'm good." She was awash in herbal deliciousness. At least for now.

She waited, knowing her dad would return to the subject at hand. Sure enough, when the waitress was gone, he said,

"I haven't decided what to do about Pamela. We'd only gone out a few times. I thought there was some potential, but now I'm less sure." He smiled. "You're my daughter. I will always be on your side."

"Thank you for that." She wanted to say that Pam was a bitch and they should all ignore her. Except she knew that Pam was actually a really nice person. She'd seen it for years. This was the first time she'd been on the receiving end of anything that wasn't supportive and positive. Maybe she was an idiot, but she was willing to think her dad was right and that she should give Pam the benefit of the doubt.

"She's very protective of her son," she said. "Looking at it from the girlfriend perspective, I was upset. But I suspect my thoughts on that will change when I have my own child to worry about."

Which was as close to "go for it" as she could get right now.

"There's nothing to be done at this moment," Miguel pointed out. "Pamela is on her cruise. I'll decide what to do when she gets back."

"Waiting for a sign?" she asked, teasingly.

"One never knows. Stranger things have happened."

Zoe believed that. After all, she'd been given a bad birth control shot and was now pregnant with her ex-boyfriend's baby. That definitely fell into the "strange" category.

Pam stood on the corner with her friends and stared down at the double brick line that marked where the Berlin Wall had once stood. There were shops and restaurants and behind them the beautiful Berlin Ritz-Carlton Hotel. It was hard to believe that less than forty years ago, they would have been standing in the no-man's-land between the two halves of the city.

She looked at the poster showing what it had been like before, then glanced around her. There were cars and buses.

They were only a few steps away from luxury shopping. Her mind simply couldn't reconcile the images.

"This is my favorite stop," Laura announced, as she took pictures with her phone.

Olimpia laughed. "You say that at every stop. Each one is your favorite."

"That's not true."

"Oh, but it is," Eugenia confirmed. "Two days ago, Oslo was your favorite. Before that, Copenhagen. I'm sure when we get to St. Petersburg, that will be your favorite."

Laura sighed. "Now I have to stop speaking to all of you. It's very sad."

Everyone laughed. Pam joined in, but more out of social politeness than because she thought the comment was funny. Not that it wasn't. The problem wasn't them, it was her.

Ever since leaving Mischief Bay, she'd felt strange. Off, somehow. Not sick, just out of sorts. Not that she knew what sorts were, but she was out of them for sure. Or sad. No, she wasn't sad. She knew what that felt like. She'd lived and breathed it after she'd lost John. This was different.

She missed her kids. She knew that for sure. She kept wanting to text Jen or Steven to find out how they were. She'd specifically added the international plan to her cell phone so that wouldn't be a problem. But what was she going to say? It wasn't as if they'd parted on happy terms.

"That place looks great," Eugenia said, pointing to a café. "Let's get lunch there and then poke around town. We've got three hours until we head back to port."

They'd already been on a city tour and had seen most of the sights, including the Brandenburg Gate and Checkpoint Charlie. Now they were on their own until it was time to get back on the bus that would take them to the train station and from there, their ship.

They crossed the street and went into the restaurant. It was open and cheerfully lit with plenty of big windows.

"It's Germany," Olimpia pointed out. "I say we drink beer to celebrate being here."

"I'm in," Eugenia said.

Pam nodded, then excused herself to use the restroom. She walked by the bar. There were several posters on the wall, all of them advertising various liquors. She turned the corner and came face-to-face with a poster for Saldivar tequila that featured a very handsome man she happened to know.

The photograph was maybe ten or fifteen years old, she would guess. Miguel stood by a bar in a tropical setting. His smile was knowing, his posture inviting. She could practically hear his sexy voice murmuring, "Pamela."

She blinked against unexpected tears, then hurried to the bathroom. On the way back to the table, she looked away from the poster. She'd barely settled in her seat when Olimpia took one look at her and asked, "What happened? Are you all right?"

Her friends stared at her.

"Tell us," Eugenia said gently. "Aren't you feeling well?"

Pam pressed her lips together. "I'm fine."

"Uh-huh." Laura leaned back in her chair. "We ordered a beer for you, by the way. I hope you like it. And no, we're not changing the subject. Something's up. You've not been yourself since we left New York. Now talk."

Pam drew in a breath. "I can't. You won't like me anymore."

The other three women exchanged glances. "I doubt we're that shallow," Olimpia said gently. "But if we are, you're well rid of us."

Pam felt her eyes fill with tears. She blinked quickly and vowed she would not cry in a foreign country.

Their waitress returned with four large mugs of beer. The women toasted each other and drank before looking back at

Pam. She understood that unless she could come up with a convincing lie in the next fifteen seconds, she was stuck with the truth.

"Jen and Steven aren't speaking to me," she finally said, staring at the coaster on the wooden table. "I told Steven he was making a huge mistake about Zoe. That he should walk away. I said that getting involved with her would ruin his life. Or words to that effect. Jen told me stay out of it, but I didn't listen. Plus Zoe is her friend. So she's mad at me, too. And I'm starting to think maybe she has every right to be."

Pam looked up at her friends and saw them watching her with expressions of compassion and understanding. "I don't mean to be a bad person. I don't. I try to see other people's sides of things. I like Zoe. I wish her only the best. It's just... Chad was such a disaster and she's stuck with him. I don't want that for Steven. I don't want him raising someone else's child. I want him to have what his father and I had. His own baby. No one else's. I just know this is all going to end badly and Steven will be hurt. I want to keep him safe and I can't because no one will listen."

She drank her beer again, then put it down. "But he won't believe me or listen. He thinks I'm overreacting and then we fought. I said some things..." She shook her head. "I'm so confused and I miss them all."

"What about Miguel?" Eugenia asked softly.

"Oh, that went badly, too."

"What do you want?" Laura asked.

"I honestly have no idea. I think for now I'd like to not talk about it."

"Then we won't," Olimpia told her.

They ordered their lunches. Conversation turned to what they'd seen that morning and how the city had changed so completely.

"I want to go to that chocolate shop we saw," Laura said. "We'll get dessert there for sure."

Everyone agreed. Pam thought she might like to take some cocoa home. Lunch came and she ate. Conversation flowed around her. She was quiet, but knew that was okay with her friends. She needed to think right now. She trusted them to give her space.

Before they left, she walked back to the bar and took a picture of the poster of Miguel, then sent it to him with a simple text.

It seems you are everywhere.

It was two in the afternoon in Berlin, so maybe seven in the morning in Mischief Bay. Even so, it took only seconds for his reply to come in.

Is that good or bad?

She hesitated before answering. She wasn't sure what he was thinking or what she wanted or anything else. She just knew she needed a connection to home and right now Miguel was all she had.

Good, she wrote back. Then she rejoined her friends.

The teacher of the Mischief Bay High School AP English class also didn't have a sub tub for Zoe. Instead she'd left a detailed lesson plan, a list of which students could be counted on to help and some notes to guide the discussion.

"Guess we're not watching *Sky High* here either," Zoe murmured to herself as she went over the information.

The class was studying Shakespeare. Students were allowed to pick their project, as long as it was comprehensive. Either one of his plays or a collection of his poetry. Although she'd taken a class on Shakespeare in college, Zoe had a feeling the AP students were going to challenge her. Something she looked forward to.

The school schedule was in blocks, with different subjects studied on different days, but for longer periods of time. It wasn't a format Zoe was familiar with. She had two and a half hours with the AP English class this morning, followed by two hours of regular English after lunch. The latter was taking an essay test, followed by an hour of reading a short story collection.

Right on time, her AP students filed into class. They eyed her curiously, but weren't overtly hostile. She introduced herself, then took roll. She only mangled a few names and a couple of the students helped out with the pronunciation.

Zoe leaned against her desk and glanced at the notes she'd been left. "Jefferson, you're starting today's discussion." She looked down at the paper. "You're reading *A Winter's Tale*, I believe."

Jefferson, a tall teen, opened his laptop and typed on a few keys. "I am. It's been interesting because of the change in tone." He looked at her. "You've read it, right?"

She held in a smile. "I have."

A long time ago, but she was pretty sure she remembered enough to be able to fake her way through a conversation.

"So there's this part." He began to read.

"Sir, the year growing ancient, Not yet on summer's death, nor on the birth
Of trembling winter, the fairest flowers o' the season—
Are our carnations and streak'd gillyvors, Which some call nature's bastards: of that kind
Our rustic garden's barren; and I care not to get slips of them."

He looked up. "It got me to thinking. There are a lot of flower references in Shakespeare."

Several students groaned. A dark-haired girl in the front row shook her head. "I'm sorry," she said cheerfully. "Jefferson loves spreadsheets. It's like an addiction for him. He's probably made up a spreadsheet for every flower reference in every Shakespeare play." Her mouth twitched. "Consider yourself warned."

Jefferson ignored her. "I did a search online and then put the flower related quotes into a grid."

There was a second group groaning.

"What?" he demanded. "It's interesting. He even mentions flowers in the Henrys. They're everywhere."

"Dude, like flowers?" another guy asked. "It was the olden times. They didn't have a lot to talk about. Nobody texted."

"It's more than that," Jefferson insisted, brushing his dark hair off his forehead. "Flowers meant something back then. They had significance. Different flowers represented emotions. Or hardships. Like this part from *A Winter's Tale*." He cleared his throat, then read again.

"And with him rises weeping: these are flowers of middle summer, and I think they are given to men of middle age."

Jefferson looked up. "The flowers are women, right? Girls. Young girls given to old guys. The flowers of middle summer references a time in life, not the real summer."

He pointed to the girl at the front of the room. "There are flowers in your play."

"What are you reading?" Zoe asked.

Jefferson rolled his eyes. "*Romeo and Juliet*. It's crap. But the part about the flowers."

"'A rose by any other name would smell as sweet'?" Zoe asked.

"Right. More flower references. See, I think the flowers are everything. They survive the winter, they're seen as God's blessing. 'They neither toil nor do they spin.'"

"I think Jefferson hit his head," one of the guys joked.

"Go ahead and think that," Jefferson told him. "And when I get accepted at Harvard, we'll see who's laughing."

"Anyone else have flower theories?" Zoe asked.

Conversation flowed easily among the students. Zoe enjoyed the exchange of ideas. The time flew by quickly. When class ended, Zoe stopped Jefferson by the door.

"You know, now I'm going to have to go back and reread *A Winter's Tale*."

He grinned. "It's not my favorite play, but it's interesting."

At lunch, Zoe went into the teacher's lounge. She'd brought her lunch and found a place at one of the tables. The other teachers were friendly and welcoming. She had to admit today was more interesting than teaching at the elementary school had been.

While her afternoon block took their test, she reviewed the book of short stories and thought about what it had been like when she'd been teaching middle school. Some of her students had been interested in the subject, but most had not. She'd struggled to make the material interesting to them so they would be engaged.

At the time she'd thought she wasn't cut out for teaching and there had always been the draw of the elusive Chad. That one day he would come to his senses and realize they were meant to be.

Events had conspired. She'd had the opportunity to expand her "help pay the bills" second job into a full-time opportunity with shorter hours and better pay. Her mom had been sick and Zoe had wanted to be there for her. She'd been frustrated with her teaching. Or maybe her life. Regardless, she'd quit teaching and had started translating manuals full-time.

Her path had been so clear, she thought as she turned pages in the book. She'd been so sure. Her mom's illness had distracted her from the going nowhere-ness of her relationship with Chad. Her mother's death had devastated her. It wasn't until she'd been trapped alone in her attic that she'd realized how empty and boring her life had become.

She didn't know exactly what she wanted for her future, but she knew that translating manuals wasn't it. She wanted more. Engagement with other people. An exchange of ideas. She missed teaching. And while she could accept that, what bothered her the most was that, as her father had pointed out some weeks ago, she'd totally changed her life for a man.

Like many people, she'd been distracted by the beauty of the flower, rather than the substance of it. Or lack of substance.

She held in a smile. Okay, things were bad if she was mixing metaphors with flowers and Chad and Shakespeare. She supposed the point was, she wanted more days like today. Days where she could hope that an unexpected discussion about how words have meanings and meanings change over time would stay with a student for years. She wanted to get back into the occupation she had once loved.

The question was how and in what capacity. Being pregnant would make scheduling a new job difficult. Plus, she wanted to be home with her baby for the first few months. And to be honest, she wasn't excited about returning to middle school.

She thought about her meeting with the counselor at Cal State Dominguez Hills. Graduate school would give her more options. She could look at teaching high school or even community college.

She knew she had some decisions to make. She'd been blessed

with the luxury of options and she was grateful for that. As for what had happened with Chad—she was determined to learn from her mistakes. Whatever she decided going forward, she would choose based on what was right for her and her baby. Not Steven or Chad or any other man. This was her life and she needed to be the star of it. And while she was being decisive...

She pulled out her cell phone and began an email. It took a couple of false starts before she figured out what she wanted to say.

Dear Pam—I'm sorry you're so upset about my pregnancy and what it means as Steven and I continue to see each other. I'm not sorry I'm pregnant. I'm confused. I'm terrified. I wish anyone but Chad were the father, but I'm not sorry. I refuse to be sorry. This baby is a blessing—however he or she came to be. And while I'm sorry you're not happy, I won't apologize for what happened. Not now, not ever.

I had thought...hoped really...that we could stay friends. I thought you were my friend. But I see now I was wrong. I understand why you're choosing your son over me—what I regret is that you feel there has to be a choice. That you can't be happy for him and for me. I would never hurt him. I'm not saying he won't get hurt. Life means taking risks. The only way to keep that from happening is to live in a cave and never talk to anyone.

It's funny. I always saw you as this perfect person, living a perfect life. Now I realize you're just like everyone else. Mostly good, some bad and a lot of faking it to get by. This information could have brought us closer. Instead, it comes too late. I'm sure you won't believe me, but I really do wish you all the best.

Zoe sent the email before she could change her mind. She didn't know if it was the right thing to do or not, but it was too late to change her mind now. Maybe that was the solution, she thought as she put her phone back in her bag. Burn bridges so there's no chance of changing your mind and trying to turn around.

Chapter Twenty-One

Saturday afternoon Jen finished her fifteen minutes of quiet mind time, as she thought of it, and opened her eyes. The house was still. Kirk was working and Lucas had moved back to his place. Jack was asleep, although he should be waking up from his nap any second now.

She let herself enjoy the peace. To see it as simply what was. Not the absence of anything. Irrational panic poked around, as if looking for an opening. That happened every now and then, but she was learning to observe rather than feel.

The meds were helping. As was knowing that there actually wasn't anything wrong with her son. Or if there was, it was her. That truth was one she'd yet to come to terms with. Mostly she alternated between fury and guilt, with guilt generally winning. *She* was the reason her son wasn't talking. It was her fault. Just hers. In her attempt to be the best mother possible, she'd totally screwed up. All the organic food and nonchemical cleaning didn't make up for that.

When her mom got back from her cruise, Jen was going to ask Pam to take Jack for a few hours to confirm that he really was talking to anyone but her. He would start day care on Monday. She would get a daily report for the first week.

She knew in her gut that the report would say Jack was talking up a storm.

"Something I'll be happy about," she promised herself as she stood and straightened the bed.

She went into the kitchen and confirmed she had everything she needed for dinner, then looked at the clock and frowned. Jack should be awake by now. He pretty much kept to his schedule, especially during the day.

She walked into his room. Although the curtains were drawn, there was still plenty of light to see. She crossed to his crib.

"Hi, sweet boy. Ready to wake up?"

Jack barely stirred. Jen flipped on the lamp and saw that he was flushed. When she touched him, his skin was burning hot.

"Jack," she said, keeping her voice calm as she lowered the side of the crib, then scooped him up in her arms. "Honey, can you look at me?"

He was limp in her arms and barely stirred as she lifted him. She carried him into the hall bathroom and then shifted him to one arm as she opened the drawer that held the thermometers.

She used the forehead one first. It took a second to turn on, then she brushed it across his skin. The reading sent panic racing through her—103.7.

"It's okay," she said, more to herself than him. "It's okay. We'll try this again."

She used the ear thermometer next and got the same reading. Still holding Jack she ran to her bag and pulled out her cell phone.

It took her two minutes to work her way through her pediatrician's answering system so she could leave a request for an immediate callback. Once she'd put the phone down, she grabbed clean dish towels and dampened them. She carried her son to the sofa, then used the damp cloths to lightly stroke Jack's face and arms. His eyes opened and then closed. He barely moved, even when she sang to him.

Her stomach was a solid knot of fear. She thought about starting a bath, but didn't want to do anything until she heard from the doctor. That included giving him medication. Better to know if she had to take him to the ER first.

Five incredibly long minutes later, her phone rang.

"Hello?"

"Mrs. Beldon, I'm Dr. Wilson. I'm on call this weekend. Tell me about Jack."

"He's not very responsive. I wanted to wait to give him anything. I'm wiping him with a cool, damp cloth, but didn't know if I should start a bath or what."

"Take his temperature again, please."

She pulled the thermometer out of her jeans pocket and ran it across his forehead. "It's 103.8."

"You're going to have to take him to the emergency room. Can you do that or do you want to call an ambulance?"

She thought about how far she had to go. "I'll get there just as fast," she said. "I'll go now."

"Where are you going?"

"Mischief Bay Memorial."

"I'll call ahead and let them know you're coming. They'll be ready."

"Thank you."

Panic rushed in, but she ignored the sensation. No matter how bad she felt, she knew in her head she *was* breathing. She didn't have time to worry about anything but Jack.

She shoved her feet into shoes, grabbed her purse and then picked up Jack. His head rolled back as if he were unconscious. She did her best not to scream in fear and checked his breathing. His chest rose and fell and she could feel his hot breath on her cheek. She ran to the SUV and buckled him in his car seat.

"Be okay, Jack, honey. I love you so much. Please be okay."

She opened the garage door, then backed out carefully. She didn't want to get into an accident on the way to the hospital.

The drive was less than three miles. She focused on her driving, even as she wanted to call Kirk. Better to do that from the hospital, she told herself. She had to get Jack to the doctors. Then he would be fine. Everything would be okay.

She parked in front of the ER, ignoring the red zone. She pulled Jack from the car and ran inside. She saw the admitting station and raced over.

"I'm Jen Beldon. My son, Jack, is twenty months old. He has a high fever and now he won't wake up. Help me!"

The woman behind the desk took one look at the limp child in Jen's arms and immediately called for help. A nurse came running, a doctor right behind him. They took Jack from her and started down the hall. She followed.

Once they were in the examination room, the doctor peppered her with questions. She pulled out her phone and read off the dates of Jack's last immunizations. The nurse took his temperature while the doctor asked about allergies. They hooked up an IV and began meds and fluids, and took blood. A volunteer came in and asked for her car keys so she could move Jen's car to the parking lot. Jen stepped into the hallway and got out her cell phone.

Her hands were shaking so much that she had trouble pushing the button that automatically dialed Kirk's number. When she finally got it to work, her call went directly to voice mail.

"It's me," she said, her voice thick with tears. "I'm at the hospital. Mischief Bay Memorial. It's Jack. He spiked a fever. We're at the ER. Call me."

She hung up and tried Lucas, but was immediately put

through to voice mail, as well. Which meant they were working somewhere they couldn't get calls.

She tried her brother, then Zoe, but no one answered. Her mother was in Europe.

Jen returned to the small examination room and sat next to Jack. He looked so tiny, lying there. She touched his cheek and was relieved to feel a little less heat. The meds must be working. But why wouldn't he wake up?

The nurse came and checked on her every few minutes. The doctor returned to say they were checking his blood test.

"At this point my best guess is some kind of virus," the doctor told her. "We'll know more soon."

Jen didn't know how long she sat next to Jack, talking to him, praying for him. Her whole body hurt and she wrestled with more fear than she'd ever felt in her life. But she kept it together—she had to. She was all Jack had.

Drama unfolded around them. She heard other people come into the ER. The staff wheeled equipment while technicians performed tests of all kinds. It was loud and busy and she wanted to be anywhere but here.

After what felt like hours, Jack's eyes opened. He turned his head and smiled at her.

"Hey, you," she whispered. "How are you doing? We're in the hospital. You were sick but they're going to make you better."

The nurse came in. "Look at that. He's awake. Are you thirsty, honey? Want some water?"

Jack nodded weakly. Jen helped him into a sitting position, then held the small cup while he took a couple of sips. She lowered him back down and held his tiny hand in hers.

She opened the storybook app on her phone and read to him. About an hour later, the doctor returned to say they were looking at a viral infection rather than a bacterial one.

By then, Jack's fever had dropped below 101. She'd barely absorbed the news when Kirk called to say he was on his way.

She assured him that Jack was okay, then went back to reading the story to her son.

By the time Kirk and Lucas arrived, Jack was sitting up and playing with a couple of toys one of the nurses had brought in. He was still a little flushed, but obviously feeling better. Kirk rushed into the examination room and hurried over to her. He held her tight, then turned to Jack. Lucas followed him and Jen was surprised to find herself hugged tight by her husband's partner.

"How is he? What does the doctor say?"

Jen brought them both up to date.

"What about you?" Kirk asked anxiously. "Are you all right?"

"I'm fine."

As she spoke, she realized that she was still shaky but she'd been telling the truth. She *was* fine. She'd gotten through the crisis on her own. She'd held it together, had taken the right steps. She'd been strong.

Maybe her own medication and quiet mind time had helped. Maybe she'd muscled through because she was Jack's mother and she'd done what she'd had to so she could save her son. At this point, she wasn't sure it mattered. Knowing she was capable was its own kind of power.

She wasn't going to assume that all would be well now. That some miracle had healed her. There would still be challenges and moments when she wanted to curl up and keen. But knowing she could count on herself in a crisis was something she planned to hang on to for a very long time.

One of the great joys of coming home was being welcomed. As Pam wasn't sure what Steven or Jen would say when they saw her, she took even more pleasure than usual in Lulu's exuberant greeting. Her little dog danced around her when she picked her up at Shannon's, crying and yipping, then huddled close on the drive home. She refused to be parted for even a second and jumped into the suitcase every time Pam took something out.

"I'm not leaving," she reassured her pet. "I'm back. That's why things are coming out, not going in."

Lulu didn't seem convinced and instead watched Pam with a steady stare.

"I have guilt," Pam admitted, picking her up for maybe the fourteenth time in as many minutes. "Does that make you feel better?"

Lulu swiped her chin with a kiss, then snuggled close and sighed.

"I'm glad we're back together, too."

When she was done unpacking, she checked her email. A lot had piled up while she'd been gone. Although she'd had access to the internet on the ship, she hadn't logged on after being hit by an email from Zoe. It had come in shortly after the cruise ship left Berlin and had kept Pam awake for more than a few nights. She'd been forced to consider what Steven's girlfriend and someone she'd once called a friend had said.

She cleared out the junk, then went through what was left. She had a couple of e-bills and a note from Filia, wanting to set up an appointment as soon as Pam was able. Pam sent her back several dates, and then looked at Lulu.

"No one has texted me," she told the dog.

Lulu watched her anxiously.

"It's fine. I get that everyone is busy. I'm not the center of the universe. But still..."

Usually she heard from at least one of her children, welcoming her home. And there hadn't been any more messages from Miguel. Not after their brief exchange in Berlin.

Was it up to her? Should she be the one to get in touch with them? Should she—

Her phone chirped. She picked it up and saw a text from Brandon. He asked about her trip and mentioned he wanted to come visit her later that fall. At least one of her children cared.

She answered him, then made a list of what she was going to need at the grocery store. Not that she could go this afternoon. Lulu would freak out at being left alone and taking her into the grocery store would cause problems. People were very fussy about having dogs where they bought food. A reality Pam found annoying. Had they seen how dirty some children were?

"Speaking of dirty," she said as she picked up her dog. "Let's get you a bath, little girl. Then we'll get snuggly in our pajamas and have an early night. Tomorrow we'll run errands and maybe go see Jen."

Lulu wagged her tail in agreement.

In the morning Pam texted her daughter and asked if she could come by.

You're already back! Welcome home. For some reason I thought you weren't getting in until this afternoon. Yes, please, come by. I could use the company.

Pam picked up Lulu and headed for the door. "I'm guessing we have yet another crisis to deal with."

She collected the presents she'd bought, then they drove over to Jen's. Pam carried her tote bag and Lulu up to the front door. Jen opened it before she got there and hugged her.

"How are you?" her daughter asked. "How was your trip? I have to say, of all the cruises you've been on, that's the one I envy most. All those great places. Maybe someday."

"We had a terrific time." Pam set Lulu down. "I gave her a bath yesterday."

"On your first day back? You didn't have to do that on

my account." Jen crouched down and patted Lulu. "How are you this morning, young lady? I'm sorry Jack isn't here to play with."

It was only then that Pam realized Jen wasn't holding her son. And her leaving him alone in a room was out of the question. "What? Where is he?"

"Day care. He goes three mornings a week."

Pam felt her mouth drop open. "When did this happen? I've only been gone three weeks."

"I know. Come on. I'll make you some coffee."

They went into the kitchen. Pam looked around and was surprised to find the counters weren't as perfectly cleaned as usual and there was actually a stack of books on the coffee table in the family room.

While the coffee brewed, Jen pulled a handful of cookies out of a plastic container and set them on a plate. The two of them sat at the table, while Lulu settled on the cushion of a third chair. Pam spent a few minutes talking about her trip.

"I'm putting together a digital photo album that I'll send you in a day or so," Pam said. "I also have a few things for you and Kirk, and of course, Jack."

She got her tote bag and pulled out a large bottle of vodka. "I know, I know. Not a surprise, but we tasted a lot and this is very good. I got you these."

She set the Matryoshka on the table. The traditional Russian nesting dolls were hand painted with a beautiful floral design.

"Oh, Mom, they're amazing." Jen unpacked the dolls and studied them. "I love them. Thank you."

"You're welcome. This is for Jack. I bought it in Stockholm. It's all organic. The wood is organic, the varnish is food grade."

She set the small, hand-carved car on the table. It was a simple curved design, with bright green wheels.

"He's going to have fun with this for sure," Jen said, coming around the table and hugging her. "Thanks for thinking of us." Jen returned to her seat.

Pam studied her daughter. "What's going on? You're different."

"Am I?" Jen laughed. "Let's see. I honestly have no idea where to begin." She picked up her coffee. "Lucas has moved out and he's back at work. Half days for now, but he'll be full-time soon enough."

"I'm sure you appreciate having your house back."

"Mostly. It turns out he's pretty easy to be around. Who knew? What else? Well, I told you Jack's in day care."

"A surprise." Pam would have bet there wasn't a single day care center in the state that would meet Jen's incredibly high standards. "Are they local?"

"Yes, in the older part of Mischief Bay. It's pretty wonderful and he's enjoying himself." She moved her cup around on the table. "I've been seeing someone. Not a therapist, exactly. More of a nutritional expert who does some counseling. I'm taking some supplements and a mild antianxiety drug. It's helping. I've been looking at my life and I've realized I have to change."

She drew in a breath. "Jack can talk."

"What? That's wonderful. Since when? Oh, my goodness, you must be thrilled." Pam had known there wasn't anything wrong with him, but she was pleased to have confirmation. "Just words or whole sentences? Do you have it on video?"

"I don't, but Kirk does. He talks to Lucas and at the day care center." Jen's mouth twisted. "He won't talk to me."

"I don't understand."

Her daughter grimaced. "Jack will have a conversation with everyone but me. I guess I know him too well. He can tell me what he wants by not speaking. Apparently it's not uncommon."

"I thought it mostly happened with siblings close in age."

"It does, but here we are."

Pam knew that Jen struggled with so many issues. She worried that some of them were her fault. She, too, had been an anxious mother—at least with her firstborn. By the time the boys had come along, she'd calmed down. But Jen hadn't had a second child yet.

"Are you all right?" Pam asked.

"I'm dealing. I temper my frustration with the knowledge that he's perfectly fine. I ask him to use his words and one day he will. Later, when he's a teenager and sassing me, I'll remember his not talking and be nostalgic."

"You're so calm," Pam admitted. "It's impressive."

"I believe the word you're looking for is *surprising*." She shrugged. "The medication helps, I'm sure. I'm also taking some supplements and taking a few minutes every day to clear my head. Eventually the little things start to add up. At least that's what I'm telling myself."

It was like her daughter had finished growing up while she'd been away, Pam thought. And while she was happy that Jen was figuring it all out, she had to admit she felt a little left by the wayside.

"The day care decision was a part of the talking?" she asked.

"It was more the realization that Jack has to have more to his life than just me," Jen admitted. "I really do need to go back to work."

Pam remembered their heated conversation when Jen had asked her to take care of Jack full-time and she'd refused. "I could look after him some," she began.

Jen shook her head. "Mom, it was wrong of me to ask you to be responsible for my son. Kirk and I need to handle the situation. You've always been generous with your time and I appreciate that. I'm not saying I'm never going to ask. Of course I am. You and Jack have a great relationship. But I need to expand my child care circle, so to speak."

"You're doing so well."

"I'm mostly faking it, but I'm moving forward. That's what we're supposed to do, right? Nothing stays the same."

Pam knew what her daughter meant but still felt oddly judged by the statement. As if Jen's progress pointed out how her life hadn't changed much at all in the past couple of years. After John's death there had been nothing but change. Since settling into her new routine, there had been a lot of sameness.

She'd told herself stable was good, however, listening to Jen, she found herself questioning the assumption.

"How's your brother?" she asked, to distract herself.

"Brandon's great. I talked to him last week."

Pam picked up a cookie and broke off a small piece for Lulu. "Very funny."

"Oh, you mean Steven. He's great—so is Zoe."

Pam waited. Jen smiled at her.

"You're not going to talk about them?" Pam asked.

"Nope." Her humor faded. "You're wrong to get between them, Mom. I think Steven's serious about Zoe. I know you're worried about him getting hurt and you have legitimate concerns about what it means for her to be pregnant with another man's baby, but here's the thing. What if it all works out? What if they fall madly in love and get married? For the rest of their lives, they'll look back on this time and remember how you weren't there for them. Is that what you want?"

Pam folded her arms across her chest. "He's going to get hurt." She said the words as firmly as she could, yet there seemed to be a bit of a question in her voice. A whispered... *what if Jen was right and she was wrong?*

"Fine. Let's say he is. So what? He's a big boy. He'll get over it. Better to be supportive of him now than wait to say 'I told you so' later. You love him, Mom. Be there for him."

"I'm not sure I agree with you. If he wants to be safe…"

"He doesn't, Mom. He wants to be in love with Zoe."

Pam pressed her lips together. There were so many things she could say, so many responses. But how many of them made sense in the face of Steven falling in love?

"I just don't know," she admitted. "He's wrong. I feel it in my bones."

"You have to let it go. I beg you—at least think about what I said. You've always been close with each of us. I'd hate for that to change."

Pam sniffed. "Are you telling me that my son will choose that woman over me?"

"In a heartbeat, Mom. In a heartbeat."

Chapter Twenty-Two

Zoe had to admit that watching a good-looking guy do manual labor on a spring afternoon was a great way to spend her time. Steven had already completed two of the raised beds in her garden and was just finishing up the third. Next up would be a simple irrigation system that would allow her to water the beds with a single turn of a handle. Between now and the project being finished, all she had to do was figure out exactly what she wanted to plant.

"Is Mason going to use this as a giant litter box?" Steven asked as he screwed the last board in place. "Or is that okay in the world of organic produce?"

Zoe sat on a blanket in the shade, Mason next to her. She stroked her cat. "Mason is a litter box kind of guy. He doesn't do dirt. I guess no one taught him that the outdoors is basically a giant cat litter box, so we're safe from him." She smiled. "My neighbors are mostly dog people, so I think it's going to be okay."

"Good." He reached for one more screw.

Not exactly a romantic conversation, but one that was practical. She watched Steven work, grateful he was concerned about her and the garden.

"I've got a friend who owns a pickup," he told her. "I'll

borrow it to pick up the dirt this week. The guy at the nursery said it would be in Tuesday."

"Thank you. I'll finalize what I want to plant tonight and place my order."

"My little farm girl," he teased.

"That's me. I need to buy something in gingham. Maybe a big straw hat."

"You need the hat to keep out of the sun." He stood and surveyed the three raised beds. "All right. There you go."

He collected his tools and other supplies, then joined her on the blanket. She handed him a glass of lemonade.

"I really appreciate you doing this for me," she told him. "Seriously. It means a lot."

"I like working around the house. At the office I'm pretty much stuck behind a desk. Every now and then I get to a job site, but mostly when there's a crisis, so that's no fun."

"Do you miss being one of the guys?"

"Sometimes." He smiled at her. "I remember the first time my dad took me with him to a construction job. I was maybe six. I had my own tiny tool belt and a hard hat. All the guys called me Sport or Buddy. I thought I was so cool."

"You never wanted to do anything else?"

He shook his head. "I knew I would go into my dad's business. Brandon was never interested, nor was Jen. It worked out."

"But you would have liked to wait awhile to take charge."

"Yeah. Not just because I miss him but because it was a lot to take on."

She thought about all he'd been through. How he could have balked at having to take over such a large company. But he hadn't. He'd given his all and he'd been successful.

She shifted so she was sitting cross-legged. "I have to tell you something."

"Okay." His dark gaze settled on her face.

She drew in a breath. "Chad proposed. I told him no," she

added quickly, then stopped talking to give Steven time to process the information.

His gaze didn't waver. "Are you sure?"

"Yes. I don't want to be with him. I've done a lot of thinking about our relationship. I know why I was interested in him and I know why it didn't work. I'm as much to blame for all of it as he is. Maybe more. Rather than look at who he was and who I was when I was with him, I played a game of pretend. It was all going to be better someday. I wasn't realistic."

She felt herself flushing, but kept talking. She wanted to tell him everything. She didn't want any secrets with Steven.

"I kept telling myself that everything would be okay if he and I got married. What I couldn't see or didn't want to see was that the problem wasn't tying him down. It was that he didn't want to be that involved with me. I think I was close to figuring it all out when my mom died."

He nodded. "That makes sense."

Because Steven understood what it was like to lose a parent. In fact, he'd been the one to first bring up the theory of how her mother's death had impacted her relationship with Chad.

"You were right before," she continued. "I felt so vulnerable and alone. Chad was there. What we had was familiar. So I hung on for a couple more years. I wish I hadn't. I wish I'd been stronger." She lightly touched her belly. "I want to be clear, Steven. I don't regret the baby. I regret the how and that it's Chad's, but I'm not sorry I'm pregnant. I can't be. This is my child."

"I know that, Zoe. You could have gotten rid of it and no one would have known. But you didn't. I respect that."

"Thank you. I've talked to my lawyer. We're working to have the parenting plan agreed to before the baby's born." She hesitated. "I'm going to ask for full custody with Chad only having visitation rights. He has that with his ex-wife, so I don't think it will be a problem. So I will be the full-time parent."

He tilted his head. "You think that's a surprise? I didn't expect anything else from you." He leaned toward her. "Zoe, I get it. You're having a baby and that baby is going to be around all the time. Are you trying to scare me away?"

"No. I'm hoping you'll stay. I just want you to know what you're in for."

"I'm in this for you." He brushed his mouth against hers. "Now that I know he's not going to poop in the vegetables, I'm in it for Mason, too."

She laughed. "Thank you. You've been so great. I really like what we have together."

"Me, too."

"Your mom still hates me."

He straightened and made a noise in the back of his throat. "You and me both."

"That's a problem."

"No, it's not."

"You say that now, but she's your Mom. You love her. You don't want to make her unhappy."

"Are you saying I have to choose?"

"I'm not, but she might." She held up a hand. "Steven, I really don't want to lose you, but I also don't want to make trouble."

He put down his lemonade and shifted on the blanket so he could lower her to the ground. As he bent over her, he smiled. "Zoe, you're sweet. Thank you for that. Let me be clear. I'm in love with you."

Her mind went totally blank. She couldn't speak, could barely breathe. He loved her? He loved her!

One corner of his mouth turned up. "Yeah, it shocked the hell out of me, too."

When she opened her mouth, he touched his fingers to

her lips. "Don't say anything back. I want you to think about it. I want you to think about us and what we could be together. I love you. I want to be with you. I want to be a part of this baby's life and all the other babies you have. I have a lot of plans for us. But first you have to be sure. So take all the time you need."

She wanted to tell him that she loved him, too, but understood what he was saying. They both had to be sure she wasn't just reacting to his wonderful declaration.

She kissed him. "This probably means I could get some right now."

He started to laugh. "It probably does. Is that what you want?"

"Always."

"This is Desire."

Jen smiled at the young woman standing beside Lucas. Seriously? Desire? "Nice to meet you."

Desire, a platinum blonde who was maybe twenty-two, dimpled. "Lucas had told me so much about you and your little boy. We're very excited to babysit tonight."

Knowing how well Lucas and Jack got along, Jen thought that might actually be true. But she was surprised that her husband's partner wanted to include babysitting a twenty-one-month-old in his dating repertoire. Still, Kirk's last-minute suggestion they go out to dinner had left her scrambling for child care. She'd been about to talk to Rose at the day care place to see if one of the child care providers could fill in when Kirk had offered Lucas.

Jen knew that a short three months ago, she would have thrown herself off a cliff before letting Lucas anywhere near her son. Now she knew better.

Lucas followed Desire into the house. As he passed Jen, he leaned in and whispered, "I promise we won't have sex in front of him."

She laughed. "I actually believe you on that. I don't care if you drink, but no cigars in the house."

"Agreed. What about TV?"

"No porn."

Lucas chuckled. "Not my style, but thank you for the clarification." He studied her for a second. "You're looking good."

She brushed the front of her dress. "Thank you. I haven't worn this in a while."

"No, I meant you. Not the dress. How are you feeling?"

"Good. Better. Thank you for all your—"

He shook his head. "Don't go there, Jen. Don't thank me. We're family. This is what we do for each other, okay?"

"Then I won't thank you but can I at least set you up with a woman in her thirties? Just once? You could try it."

He winked. "Maybe in a few years. When I'm older."

She groaned. "Fine. I'm going to go finish getting ready. Kirk's in the shower. We should be out of here in about twenty minutes."

She turned as Jack came running into the living room. He took one look at Lucas and shrieked happily, then held out his arms. Lucas picked him up and swung him around.

"Hey, look at you, my man. You're so big." He drew Jack against his chest. "Jack, this is Desire. Can you say hi?"

"Hi," Jack said with a smile. "Pretty."

Desire smiled. "Thank you. You're very charming."

Jen did her best to enjoy the moment. She occasionally heard Jack talking. He still wouldn't talk directly to her, but that was okay. Annoying but okay.

"Give us a few minutes," she called as she went down the hall toward the master.

She'd done her makeup earlier and curled her hair. All she had to do was put on lipstick and her shoes. Kirk should be out of the shower by now and—

She'd barely stepped into the bedroom when her husband

grabbed her and pulled her close. With one hand he closed and locked the door, with the other he reached for her breasts. At the same time he claimed her with a deep kiss that had her bones melting.

"What are you—" she managed between kisses.

"God, I've missed you. Missed us."

It was only then that she realized he was completely naked. And aroused.

Still kissing her, he backed her up toward the bed. She went willingly, grateful she hadn't put on dressy jeans for their night out. She only had to unzip her dress for it to fall to the floor. He immediately had her bra off and she pushed her panties to the floor. Then they were on the bed and he was touching her everywhere.

Hunger burned. She stroked his back and tangled her legs with his while he rubbed her breasts, before easing his hand between her legs. His fingers found her clit and in seconds, she was breathing hard.

They continued to kiss, tongues rubbing, arousing. She supposed she should care that Lucas and Desire were out in the living room. That Jack was still awake. But screw it, she thought, then giggled at the double entendre.

"What?" Kirk asked.

"I love you," she told him, and pushed him onto his back.

He sucked in a breath. "You on top?"

It was his favorite position—one she rarely wanted to do for an assortment of reasons that all seemed really stupid right now. He liked it, she came faster and who cared if she bounced around like a fool? Sex wasn't supposed to be dignified, right?

"Me on top."

She straddled him, then lowered herself onto him. He filled her so deeply, she groaned. He reached for her breasts and squeezed her tight, sensitive nipples. She lowered her hand so she could rub between her legs even as she raised and lowered herself on his erection.

It didn't take long, she thought, barely able to breathe as she went from *take me* to *I'm coming* in less than a minute. The combination of his hands and hers, his dick and her circling herself pushed her right to the edge. She opened her eyes and saw him watching her.

"Do it," he growled. "Come on, Jen. Let me see you come. All of it."

She moved faster and faster, rode him up and down then gave in to the inevitable. She cried out as she came, her muscles contracting around him. She kept her eyes open the whole time, letting him see what he'd asked. All of her. All of them.

She stopped touching herself and leaned forward, bracing herself on her hands. He moved to grip her hips. Her climax continued, lighter now, with only the internal stimulation. He moved faster, harder. Their eyes locked until he, too, lost himself in the pleasure.

When they were done, he rolled her onto her side.

"You're so sexy," he whispered. "I've missed you."

"I've missed you, too." She smiled and kissed him, then looked at the clock. "Four minutes. I'm not sure that's a personal best for us, but it's close."

He chuckled and hugged her. She held on to him.

"I want to do this more," she whispered into his chest, listening to the rapid beating of his heart. "A lot more."

"Me, too. I love you."

"I love you, too."

He smiled at her. "I'm starving. Ready for dinner?"

"Yes, but we should probably get dressed first."

Kirk laughed. "You might be right."

Pam arrived ten minutes early for her meeting with Filia, but the other woman was already there. Pam took one look at Filia's anguished face and knew the news wasn't good. Before she could say anything, she noticed Filia's ten-year-old daughter sitting next to her.

Filia rose. "I'm sorry. Marta asked to come with me and I didn't want to refuse her. I like that she's interested in my business. She won't be any trouble. I hope that's all right."

"Of course it is," Pam told her gently. "There's a conference room next to my office. She can sit in there and be perfectly safe while we're talking."

It only took a few minutes to get Marta settled. Pam led Filia next door and positioned her chair so Filia could see her daughter through the glass walls of the conference room. Pam sat at her desk.

"Tell me," she said, knowing Filia had set up meetings while Pam was gone.

"The banks turned me down. The second one wouldn't even make an appointment with me. They said I didn't qualify." Color stained her cheeks. "I work hard. Sometimes I work seven days a week. I know what I'm doing. I'm a good risk. I started with nothing and I built my business into what it is today. I don't understand. Is it because I'm a woman? That I wasn't born in this country? What is it?"

"I don't know," Pam said honestly. "I'm sorry you went through this and I'm really sorry I wasn't here." Not every client got every loan they applied for, but they usually got a meeting and some consideration. "I'm not giving up. I hope you feel the same way."

"I'm not. I'm determined. I—"

"Good morning, Pamela."

Pam looked up and saw Miguel in the open doorway to her office. He was so unexpected and he looked so good. Her heart fluttered, her mouth went dry. She knew she couldn't speak, so it was for the best that he glanced from her to Filia and shook his head.

"My apologies. I didn't know you were with someone. I'll come back."

She hadn't seen him since before the cruise. She didn't know why he was here now, but she wanted to make sure she had a chance to talk to him.

"Should I leave?" Filia asked.

"No," Pam and Miguel said together.

Miguel nodded. "I'll wait, if that's all right?"

"It is." Pam waited until he was gone before turning back to Filia. She gave herself a single heartbeat to hope that his appearance meant he hadn't completely given up on her, then pushed him from her mind so that she could focus on her meeting. "I'm so sorry for the interruption."

Filia smiled. "Your friend is a very handsome man. I feel as if I've seen him before."

"He gets that a lot. Now about your determination."

"I'm very determined. I'm worried about getting a loan, but I'm not giving up. So many people have told me *I can't* over and over again. That I couldn't come to America. That I couldn't start a business. That I couldn't make it success-ful. All my life I was told I dream too big. But I was raised to be strong and to believe in myself. I'm going to make this happen."

"I know you are," Pam told her, impressed by Filia's resolve. "Those banks were just the first round. We have many more options. I want to try the Mischief Bay Credit Union next. They like to make loans in the community." There were also grants and the angel funds, but Pam had to make sure that conventional funding had been attempted first.

"Now that I'm back, I'll come with you to your meetings."

"I'd appreciate having you there," Filia told her. "Thank you so much. As soon as you get me the information, I'll set up the appointment."

"Give me two minutes. I'll go pull the forms right now."

She walked back to the file room where they kept the information on banks and credit unions. Pam found the files on the one she wanted. As she walked back to her office, she saw Miguel talking to Filia's daughter. No, not talking, she realized with a start. He was letting the girl paint his fingernails.

The sight of the strong, handsome man of the world with the little girl melted her heart. It also gave her hope. Hope she hadn't realized she'd been wishing for. Not that she was ready to get involved with Miguel romantically. Only she did want to see him and talk to him, and well, if he kissed her again, that might be all right, too.

She returned to Filia and they went over the various forms. While Filia would submit them online, Pam wanted to make sure she understood everything the credit union was looking for. Thirty minutes later, Pam hugged Filia.

"I'm with you," she promised. "However long this takes, I'll be with you and we'll make this happen."

"Thank you."

They went through to the conference room. Pam smiled when she saw that Marta had used some kind of glitter polish on Miguel's nails.

"Oh, no!" Filia sounded mortified. "I'm so sorry. You're going to need nail polish remover to get that off. I don't have any with me, but I can certainly pay for some."

Miguel winked at her. "I like it," he said, his voice teasing. "Don't worry. I have a daughter, too. I can handle this."

Filia left with her daughter. Pam waited until they were gone before ushering Miguel into her office.

"I have nail polish remover at home," she said, trying not to focus on the incongruity of the broad-shouldered man with the pink, glittery nail polish.

"So do I," he told her. "Actually I have some acetone in the garage, which is about the same thing. Don't worry about it." He glanced toward the door. "Is she all right?"

While Pam appreciated his concern about Filia, she couldn't discuss a client. "She's fine. Um, how are you?" A statement more polite than the "I wasn't sure I ever expected to see you again," which was what she was really thinking. Along with, "Wow, I missed you so much more than I thought I would."

"I'm good. You had a nice cruise?"

"Yes. The weather was perfect and my friends and I enjoyed seeing the sights."

His dark gaze settled on her face. "Thank you for the text. I'm glad I was on your mind, however briefly, Pamela."

The words spoken in his low, velvet voice, made her squirm. She honest to God didn't know what to say. Or think. Or feel. He confused her on so many levels, plus there was the whole Zoe situation, which was starting to seem less clear that it had been.

"You have something on your mind," he told her.

"I'm not sure why you're here. You're the one who walked out."

One shoulder raised and lowered. "I did. You were being unreasonable so rather than fight, I left."

"Do you always walk away when you're upset?"

He smiled. "Men don't get upset, Pamela."

"Fine. Do you always walk away when you're angry?"

"No. I stay and fight."

"But you didn't. You left." A fact that had upset her more than she'd realized at the time. "I'm sure it's very satisfying to be the one who simply gets to walk away, but it's not fair to the other person. I thought we were friends."

"Did you?"

She suddenly felt stupid. Had she made a mistake? Was he simply toying with her? "Why are you here, Miguel?"

"You reached out to me when you were in Europe. I want to do the same, now that you're home."

She thought about her email from Zoe. The one that had

made her feel so bad about herself and the situation. Had she been wrong to assume it was best for Steven to break up with Zoe? She wanted him to be the father of any child he was involved with. She wanted him to know what that was like. How was it possible to love Chad's baby as much as his own?

"I can hear you thinking from here," Miguel said.

"I'm hoping you can't hear *what* I'm thinking."

"Unfortunately, no."

"It's for the best. Trust me on that. My mind is a confusing place."

"Then let me help by clarifying a few things."

"All right. Although it's difficult to take you seriously while you're wearing glitter nail polish."

"I trust you're up to the task." He studied her for a second. "Zoe is my daughter and I love her very much. I won't choose between the two of you, just like you won't choose between me and Steven."

"Of course not."

"Then there's only one solution."

She nodded, shocked at how much disappointment she felt. She barely knew Miguel—she shouldn't care if they ever saw each other again. And yet she was upset to know that she would never have the opportunity—

"You'll have to get over your unreasonable stance on what's happening."

She felt her mouth drop open. "Excuse me?"

He didn't say anything, leaving her to close her mouth and consider what he'd said. "You want me to change my mind."

"I want you to be reasonable. Not just for me, Pamela. For yourself, as well. Steven and Zoe are still together."

Something she would know if she and Steven were currently speaking. They'd never not been close, she thought regretfully. She didn't like that Miguel knew more than she did about what was happening with her son.

He rose. "Think about it. I believe you have the heart of a lioness. You will protect your children with all you have. But sometimes the right thing to do is nothing. We have to let them grow and make their own mistakes. Perhaps they are meant to be together, perhaps not. Only time will tell. What I do know is that giving ultimatums helps no one. I hope you'll agree with me on that."

She gave the tiniest of nods.

"Good. Then I hope I will see you soon."

Before she could ask him what he meant, he walked out of her office. She glared at the place he had been, then deliberately turned away.

"Annoying man. I don't need you in my life."

Only the words didn't ring true and Pam was left with a sense that something very important was missing—if only she could figure out what.

Chapter Twenty-Three

"Meerkats," Jen said firmly as they passed through the entrance of the Los Angeles Zoo. "I love the meerkats."

"They're lazy," Lucas told her. "They've gone Hollywood. What happened to standing at attention to protect each other in the…" He frowned. "What are they? A herd?"

Kirk laughed. "That's grazing animals, my friend."

"Yeah? If you're so smart what are a group of meerkats called?"

Kirk looked at Jen. She laughed as she pushed Jack's stroller. "I didn't start this," she protested with a grin. "I just want to see them."

"They're a mob or a gang," Desire told them. "The babies are called pups. So they're not cats at all." She dimpled. "I used to watch *Meerkat Manor* when I was little."

Jen moved close to Lucas. "Uh-oh. She's smart. How on earth did that happen? You must be horrified. And here I thought the two of you might last a month."

"You are such a smart-ass," he whispered back, then sighed. "Damn. I hate it when they're secretly smart."

"Imagine the nightmare if she was also secretly old."

"Not a chance of that. I make sure to check their driver's license early on."

"Now you're going to also have to ask for SAT scores. Or maybe just their high school GPA."

"Dating is such a pain."

"But necessary if you want to get laid. You could start using call girls."

He pressed a hand to his chest. "I don't pay."

"Oh, honey, you're so paying for what you're getting. It's your own personal underground economy."

He chuckled and moved back to Desire's side.

"My point being," he said as he took her hand, "the meerkats used to do their on-guard thing. Now they just lie in the sun and wait for audition calls. The zoo should fly raptors over the enclosure and put the fear of God into them."

"I believe that would be the fear of death," Jen corrected. "Unless you think God is a raptor."

Kirk put his arm around her. "She got you, bro." He kissed her cheek.

"And here I thought today was going to be a good day," Lucas grumbled.

They made their way up the wide path toward the meerkats. The morning was sunny and warm, the zoo relatively quiet on a Thursday. Jen was happy to spend time with her husband and son on a rare day off for Kirk. Having Lucas and Desire along was fun, too.

"You're getting along better with Lucas," Kirk said quietly. "I'm glad."

"He's grown on me," she admitted. "He's like the big brother I never had." She rolled her eyes. "He has hideous taste in women, but that's okay. One day he'll wake up and see the light."

Kirk dropped his hand to her butt and patted it. "Or find himself alone. We'll have to build an apartment for him over the garage."

"He'll need one of those automatic chair lift thingies," she said with a laugh. "So he can get up the stairs."

They reached the meerkat exhibit. Jen took Jack out of the stroller and held him in her arms.

"Oh, can I?" Desire asked.

"Sure." Jen passed him over.

Desire and Lucas walked closer to the exhibit. Jen could hear the twentysomething talking to Jack. Her son chatted back.

"He still won't talk to me," she said, trying not to take it personally. "I know, I know. It will happen eventually. I created the problem and I have to fix it by being patient."

Kirk shifted her so she was facing him, then put his hands on her hips and drew her close. "You didn't create the problem. It just happened."

"You're sweet. A liar, but sweet." She stared into her husband's eyes and felt the love swelling inside of her. "You're a really good guy. I'm lucky to have married you."

"Yes, you are and I'm lucky right back."

She smiled and they kissed. When they drew apart, she turned to look at Desire and Jack. So much had changed in the past few months.

"I need to go back to work," she said, returning her attention to Kirk. "I've talked to my old principal and there should be a spot for me in September. One of her teachers is going to have a baby this fall and wants a year off."

"Are you sure? You've really liked staying home."

"I have, but it's been hard on me, too. I'm making progress. I want to keep it that way. I think working for the year will be good for me. We can save money and we have a great day care place for Jack." She raised her eyebrows. "We can work on getting me pregnant around the end of the year. I think it's time for that second baby, don't you?"

He smiled. "I do. Very much. I want a girl."

"That would be between you and your sperm. I'm simply the vessel."

He chuckled. "We should probably keep practicing on the whole baby-making front. Just to make sure we're doing it right."

"I would love that."

"Me, too."

She stepped toward Jack. He was trying to say the word *meerkat* fairly unsuccessfully. When he saw her, he reached for her.

"Are you having fun?" she asked. "Do you like the meer-kats?"

Rather than say yes, he waved his arms in his happy way, communicating the message without words. Jen drew in a breath and refused to give in to frustration or guilt. Jack *could* talk. That was what was important.

"The kids' section next," she said. "We're going to Muriel's Ranch. It's a petting zoo. We can brush the Nigerian Dwarf goats."

"Someone's been on the internet," Lucas said.

"Yes, I have. Because it's okay that I'm smart."

"I love little goats." Desire clutched her hands in front of her. "The way they jump all around and their little tiny hooves. It's magical. If I had to come back as an animal in my next life, I'd want to be a little goat. Or a kitten. Or a walrus, because nobody cares if a walrus gets fat. Or a dancing horse. That would be great."

Jen leaned close to Lucas. "Maybe less smart than we thought?"

"I can only hope."

He moved next to Desire and continued the animal reincarnation discussion with her. Jen thought about all he'd done for her and for Kirk. She knew her husband had been kidding about his partner moving into an apartment above the garage, but she hoped whatever happened, they would always be close. Over the past few months, Lucas had become a part of their family. He had been there for both of them and she knew they would always be there for him.

She had a feeling that when Jack reached his "I hate my parents" stage of being a teenager, Lucas would be someone he could turn to. And even then, she would still worry about Lucas being the wild one in the relationship.

A quality kind of problem, she thought happily as they crossed into Muriel's Ranch.

"I see goats," Desire cried out.

"At least it's not dead people," Kirk murmured, and Jen laughed.

Zoe stretched out on a chaise in her father's backyard, Mariposa on her lap. She played with the little dog's silky ears and let the sun warm her body.

She was in a good place, she thought with more than a little surprise. Yes, she was pregnant and who could have seen that coming? She was also still up in the air about her future. But she was making progress and, well, there was Steven, who said he loved her.

She still hadn't said the words back. She'd tried after they'd made love, the last time she'd seen him, but he'd told her to wait. To be sure. With everything going on, he didn't want her to feel pressured. Which only made her love him more.

Her dad walked out with a pitcher and two glasses, then settled on the chaise next to hers.

"Herbal tea," he told her. "Organic. For what this costs, I could have bought a steak."

"I'm allowed to eat steak," she said with a grin.

"Very funny. You need to appreciate the fact that I'm not drinking coffee in front of you."

"I do. Very much." She smiled at him. "You're very good

to me. In fact, everyone is being really nice to me. This getting pregnant thing has an upside."

"Very funny. I'm always good to you."

"Yes, you are."

She took the glass he offered her. Mariposa raised her head, as if expressing interest. Zoe laughed. "You would so not like this, little girl."

She held out the glass. Mariposa took one sniff, then visibly recoiled and eyed her. The message was clear: "How on earth could you drink that stuff?"

"She would have liked the steak, as well," Zoe teased.

"I'm sure that's true." Miguel stretched out on the chair next to her. "What have you decided?"

"I'm keeping my job and I'm signing up for grad school. I should be able to take at least a couple of classes over the summer. I'm not sure about fall. I would be really close to my due date. But maybe I could take one class and arrange to take the final early."

A decision she didn't have to make today, she told herself. "My attorney is working on the parenting plan. I hope to have that to Chad by the end of the month. Steven's going to paint the baby's room for me."

"Has Chad proposed again?"

"No. I think he feels he did his duty and now we can move on." She glanced at her father. "You're not going to pressure me on that again, are you?"

"No, I'll let it go." He looked at her. "Because you're my favorite daughter."

"I'm your only daughter."

"That, too. And because you've convinced me Chad wouldn't make you happy." His gaze intensified. "I want to pay for graduate school and I don't want you to argue about it."

"Dad, no."

His brows rose. "This would be you arguing."

"I know, and while I appreciate your generous offer, I'm paying for my own grad school. I'm a big girl. I can afford it."

"You have to save for the baby. What about college?"

"Do you know the baby's the size of a radish?"

"Radishes grow up and need to go to college."

"Fine. Then put my grad school fund toward that."

He drew his brows together, then relaxed. "All right. I will. But if you need anything, I'm here."

"I know. Thank you." She drank more of her tea.

"I can't decide if I want you to have a girl or a boy."

Which was just so like him. "You do realize you, in fact, don't get a say?"

"I understand basic biology, yes." He reached for her hand. "I wish your mother were alive to see this."

The unexpected words made her eyes fill with tears. She squeezed his fingers. "Me, too."

"She would be so happy."

Zoe nodded. "Then she would go beat the crap out of whoever made the mistake at the pharmaceutical company."

"I would join her in that."

Zoe was going in another direction. She'd already been approached by several attorneys representing other women who were also dealing with unexpected pregnancies from the faulty shots. While she was fortunate enough to be in a position to deal with her situation, she knew there were other women whose lives had been completely shattered by what had happened. The only way to make sure that sort of thing didn't happen again was to band together.

She released her father's hand. "What else is new?" she asked, mostly to distract him. "Have you seen Pam since she's been back?"

"How did you know she was back?"

"I knew the dates of her trip."

"I told her she had to make peace with you before I would see her again."

"Because you're all that and she'll change her mind for you?"

Zoe spoke lightly in an effort not to let him know how much Pam's reaction still stung. Telling herself over and over again that Pam was right to protect her son didn't take away the hurt of having someone she considered a friend reject her. It seemed to her that middle ground wouldn't be all that hard to find—but Pam wasn't interested in that.

"I am all that, as you put it. But that isn't the reason she'll change her mind. She's a good person. She'll figure out what she's doing is wrong. When she does, will it be too late?"

"You mean will I hold a grudge?"

"Yes."

"I'm less sure about her seeing my side of things than you, but yes, if she stops seeing me as the devil, I want to be friends with her."

"Thank you."

She smiled. "No offense, Dad, but I'm not saying that for you. I'm saying it for me. I need to be able to let go. It's the right thing to do and best for the baby."

"I still get to be proud of you if I want."

She smiled. "Later I'll finger paint some flowers and you can hang them on the refrigerator."

"Now you mock me."

"Only with love, I swear."

Over the next week, Pam kept busy. She went with Filia to her appointment with the business loan specialist at the credit union. The meeting had gone well. Filia had received preliminary approval with final approval to be decided in the next few days. As all Pam had done was sit quietly while Filia spoke, she knew she couldn't take credit for anything except providing moral support. Still, Filia was thrilled and Pam couldn't wait to be there for the grand opening of her expansion.

Pam tended her container garden, texting pictures of her thriving bush monkey flower to Ron at the nursery. His quick reply of, I'll never doubt you again should have been satisfying, but wasn't. Mostly because she couldn't seem to settle in her life. Or maybe her skin.

It was all Steven's fault, she thought as she drove to her daughter's house. Or Zoe's. It was the two of them together. Whatever had she been thinking when she'd set them up? From what Pam could glean, the two were as close as ever. Which meant Steven hadn't taken her advice. He also wasn't speaking to her. Not really. Oh, sure, he would respond if she texted him, but he hadn't been by to see her since her return and they hadn't spoken on the phone. She knew she could invite him over, but in her heart of hearts, she was terrified if she asked he would say no.

So instead she went to see Jen, who at least was still speaking to her.

Jen answered the door with a smile. "Perfect timing." She held up her flour-covered hands. "I'm trying to knead bread and it's not going well. Jack is thirsty. Could you get him some juice, please?"

"Of course. Or I could knead the bread for you."

"I have to conquer it. Dough is not going to get the best of me."

Pam and Lulu walked inside. Jack lit up when he saw them and ran over. He held out his arms and cried, "Grandma!"

Pam swept him up into her embrace. "Hello, Jack. How are you?"

"Good." He pointed at the dog. "Ruru."

"Close enough." Pam walked into the kitchen. "He's really talking."

Jen worked the dough. "That's the rumor," she said, her voice resigned.

Pam sighed. "Still not to you?"

"Nope. I'm dealing with it." She wrinkled her nose. "My counselor says to be patient, which is good advice that's hard to follow. Still, progress and all that."

"You're still seeing a counselor?"

"Uh-huh. I've cut back to every other week. I'm going to stay on the meds through the first few months of the school year, then see if I can cut back on them. I'm already at a low dose. Honestly, I think the meditation, getting enough water and sleep are helping just as much. Being mindful of taking care of myself."

Pam got Jack his drink and sat with him at his small table.

"That's great," she said. "I'm glad you're feeling better."

"Me, too. Plus I know the anxiety will get better as I get older. It did for you."

Pam picked up Lulu and held her close. "I don't know what you mean."

Jen didn't bother looking up from her dough. She turned it over, shrugged, then plopped it in a bowl and covered it with a dish towel. "Now you have to rise. Don't let me down." She washed her hands, then turned to Pam. "You know how you were so tense when we were little. Worried about every little thing. That went away as we grew. I wonder if it's hormone based. I'll have to look that up."

"I wasn't worried about everything," Pam told her firmly.

Jen laughed. "Yeah, you were. You were always creating disaster scenarios. You still do. Like with Steven and Zoe. I understand there's a risk, but all of life is like that. Yes, they could get a divorce and he would be heartbroken, but they could also stay together for the next eighty years."

Pam wanted to say that they wouldn't live that long, but

she was too busy processing what her daughter had said. No, what her daughter thought of her.

"You think I was a nervous mother?"

"Oh, Mom, don't. We all have our thing. Yours was keeping us safe. You were worried and that was nice. We knew you cared. I'm a lot like you. I worry, too. It's just you could manage yours on your own and I needed help."

Pam had the sense that her daughter was trying to make her feel better, which wasn't working at all. She still couldn't believe how Jen viewed her. It was so different from how she saw herself.

"I have a very full life."

"I know you do. You really took care of yourself after Dad died. We wondered how you would go on and you impressed all of us. The way you help women in business and travel with your friends? I want to be like that someday."

Jen sat on the floor next to Jack. "Hi, sweetie."

He grinned at her.

"Are you drinking water?" she asked.

Jack nodded.

"Can you say *water*?"

Jack just laughed.

Jen sighed. "One day," she told him. "One day you'll talk to me and you won't stop, right?"

He giggled.

She patted her lap and Lulu jumped onto it. Jen stroked her. "About your dog," she said. Lulu looked at her. Jen rubbed the side of her face. "Yes, I'm talking about you, little girl." She looked back at Pam. "I can keep her when you travel. If Shannon can't."

The entire world had gone mad, Pam thought. "You want to keep Lulu?"

"Uh-huh."

"Do you know she's a dog? She'll pee and poop in the yard."

"And I'll make Kirk clean it up. Yes, I know, Mom. I should have offered before. Jack loves her, she's a good girl and I'm sure there will be times when Shannon can't deal with her around. I'm saying I can."

"You've certainly changed."

"I hope so. I'm trying. I'm going back to work in September. I can't wait to be with my class again. Kirk and I are going to start trying to get pregnant again close to Christmas. With luck this time next year, I'll be about six months along."

"That's wonderful. I'm so happy for you."

"Thanks. We're happy, too. Jack is going to be a great big brother."

They continued talking, but Pam wasn't really paying attention. She was caught up in the sense of things changing and her having to struggle to keep up. Jen was so together now. So in charge of everything happening in her life. Pam felt superfluous by comparison.

"Do you talk to your brother much?" she asked.

"Brandon?" Jen set Lulu on the floor and pulled Jack onto her lap. "Or Steven?"

"Of course Steven. I can talk to Brandon anytime I want."

"Why can't you talk to Steven?"

"I don't know. He hasn't called me."

"Have you called him?"

I'm not the one in trouble. Words she thought but didn't say. And the way things were changing so fast, she had a feeling Jen would disagree with her assessment.

"I've been busy," Pam said defensively, not liking the sense of being in the wrong. "Besides, he's my son."

"And you're his mom." Jen's tone was gentle. "He respects you and wants you to be happy for him. If you want to blame someone for what he's doing, then be mad at yourself and

Dad. You were the two teaching us to accept people and be understanding of what they were going through."

Which was close to what Steven had said the last time she'd spoken to him.

"This is different."

"It's not." Jen looked at her. "You know Zoe didn't get pregnant on purpose."

"Yes, I know. I know. Everyone keeps saying that. It doesn't change anything."

"It changes *everything*, Mom. She didn't plan on this, didn't expect it to happen, yet there she is, taking responsibility. She's going to be a great mother, but she's got to be scared. Plus, she has to deal with Chad and that's not going to be fun. It's a lot. You had Dad when you got pregnant with me. I was planned. You were both happy. She doesn't have any of that. With her mom gone, I'm the only one she can ask about having a baby and it's not like I did a great job with Jack."

"You did an amazing job. You're an excellent mother."

Jen's smile turned rueful. "Thanks, but my only child will talk to everyone but me. I'm guessing that means I don't qualify for mother of the year."

"You're being too hard on yourself."

Jen hesitated a second, drew in a breath and said softly, "Maybe you're being too easy on yourself."

Pam jerked her head as if she'd been slapped. She started to stand, then forced herself to stay in place. She was already fighting with Steven. Did she really want to be on the outs with Jen, too?

"I'm not a bad person," she insisted. "I care about my children."

"So much that you won't accept what Steven wants. Funny how your son won't talk to you either, Mom."

Pam felt herself flush. She reached for Lulu and then stood. "I don't know what to think."

Jen rose and set Jack on his feet. "I love you, Mom. I hope you're not mad."

"I'm not. I'm…" She bit her lower lip. "I have no idea what I am." A nervous mother who was alienating her children? That was so not how she saw herself. She sucked in a breath and told herself she wouldn't cry. Not until she was home by herself. "What do you want from me?"

"For you to love me and my family, and for you to let us love you back. Oh, and get off Steven and Zoe. They need your support, your wisdom and in time, your babysitting. Let it go, Mom. Steven's a grown man. Don't make him choose."

Which was what Miguel had said to her. To not make him choose. Only she understood Miguel choosing his daughter, but Steven…

Steven would choose the woman he loved, because that was what you did when you wanted to be with someone. A child was different. You always had to side with your child, but a parent was… Not disposable, she thought. A parent could be left behind.

Steven would leave her. He would choose Zoe and leave her. While he went on with his life, she would be forever out of his inner circle. She would be excluded from all that was precious to him.

The pain of that image cut through her until she thought she couldn't breathe. It was one thing to not be speaking but if that became permanent, then what? John would be so very ashamed of her.

The truth of that slammed into her, leaving her weak. Funny how she thought of John so much and yet had never considered what he would say about Steven and Zoe. She could hear his familiar voice even now.

It's not our decision to make, Pam. Fuss all you want, but at the end of the day, Steven's going to do what he's going to do. Trust him to make the right decision, then get out of the way.

The words were so clear, she glanced around to see if he was in the room with them.

"Mom? Are you okay?"

Pam nodded, then picked up Lulu. "I'm fine. I was just thinking about your father."

"I miss Dad, too."

"I know you do." She drew in a breath and smiled. "For what it's worth, you're not disqualified from mother of the year."

"Okay." Jen looked confused. "What does that have to do with what we were talking about?"

"On the surface, nothing." Pam hugged her daughter, then kissed the top of Jack's head. "I love you both and I'll see you soon."

"Are you okay?"

"Yes. Don't worry."

With that, Pam left. When she got to her car, she hesitated for a second, then realized where she had to go and what she had to do.

Chapter Twenty-Four

Pam drove to the quiet neighborhood and parked in front of Zoe's house. She picked up Lulu and went to the front door. Once there, she tried to think about what to say. When nothing came, she knew she either had to wing it or walk away, and leaving was no longer an option.

She knocked and waited, thinking about the email Zoe had sent, hoping Zoe really did wish her the best. Zoe answered a few seconds later. Her eyes widened with surprise.

"Pam. What are you doing here?"

Pam looked at her, searching for signs of the pregnancy. Her cheeks were a little fuller, but that was pretty much it. Zoe's loose shirt didn't hint at her growing tummy.

"I thought we should talk," Pam admitted. "Now that I'm here, I don't know what to say. Except maybe that I want to be the person you thought I was. Before. I want to be friends."

Zoe didn't look convinced. "Is this because of me or because of Steven?"

So she knew they weren't speaking? Of course—Steven would have told her what was going on.

Pam never thought she would be one of those mothers who resented her children forming intimate connections. For a second she remembered when she'd been the one Steven had run to so she could brush away his tears and fix whatever was wrong. Those days were long gone. He was a man now, with a man's heart. One he'd obviously given to Zoe.

"Can I say both?" she asked quietly.

Zoe smiled. "I appreciate your honesty. Come on in."

They went out onto her patio. Pam spotted Mason sunning himself by a raised garden bed. She set her little dog down and Lulu trotted over to inspect the feline. Mason opened an eye, then closed it. Lulu glanced back at Pam, then inched closer to Mason and collapsed next to him.

"And here I was expecting drama," Zoe admitted. "So much for dogs and cats not getting along."

"Lulu's pretty well socialized. It takes a lot to rattle her."

They sat on chairs in the shade.

"How are you feeling?" Pam asked. "Any morning sickness?"

"Not really. I had a few days of reacting to different smells, but that's gone. So far things are easy." She held up crossed fingers. "I'm hoping it stays that way."

"You're through the worst of it. After about twelve weeks the hormones calm down. I always assumed they were too busy growing the baby to bother with me."

"I like that idea."

Pam thought about all that had happened. All the things she'd said and hadn't said directly. She decided the only way to make things right was to say all the things that had to be said.

"If you marry Steven and then get a divorce, he has no rights over the baby," she began. "Even if he raised the child and loved him or her, he gets nothing. He has to walk away. What if it's a little girl who adores him and he needs her in his life? What if it's been ten years or fifteen? He'll be destroyed."

Zoe drew in a breath. "Chad isn't going to sign away his rights. Steven can't adopt the child."

Not news, but disappointing all the same. "That's what I

worry about. Him getting hurt. Chad will always be the father." Her mouth twisted. "I remember how excited John
was when I told him I was pregnant for the first time. We
went through all that together. He and I. We'd created a life.
It was something we shared—would always share. Steven
doesn't have that either."

Zoe wiped away tears. "You want me to let him go. I don't
think I can."

Pam searched her heart before answering. The easy answer
was yes, they should break up. But she'd lived long enough to
understand there weren't usually easy answers. "No, I want
you to understand that however much you've loved your baby,
I've loved Steven just as much, but for longer. Years and years.
I look at you and see a young woman I like very much. But
I'm so afraid."

"Afraid enough to stand between us?"

"I've already tried that," she admitted. "It didn't work out
well. I've tried to keep him safe and that's not working either. Now I have to accept what you two want." She angled
toward Zoe. "I'm happy if you love him. It's everything else
that concerns me. I was wrong to judge you. I'm sorry about
that. I'm sorry I tried to convince him not to see you anymore. But I won't apologize for worrying about Steven. It's
part of my job."

"Because you're his mom."

Pam nodded. "Can we make peace with all that between
us?"

Zoe's eyes were bright with tears. "I think we should try."

Zoe spent the afternoon researching fume-free paint and
looking at furniture for babies. After Pam's visit, there was
no way she was going to get any work done. About four, she
went outside and looked at her garden, at the tiny plants so
recently planted. She put her hand on her belly and knew that

in a few short weeks, she would feel the first stirrings of life growing inside of her.

Pam hadn't been wrong. The truth was a bitch, but there it was, staring her in the face. Pam hadn't been wrong to worry, to question, to want to protect Steven. Her points were all good ones. If she and Steven kept going the way they were going—if they were in love, it was reasonable to think they could get married. And then what? This child that he would help raise from birth would never be his. If the worst happened and they broke up, the most Steven could hope for was some kind of visitation. And the odds were against it. Which meant he was putting more on the line for her than she was for him.

She knew she was getting ahead of herself. That things were still really new between them, but she also understood what he was looking for and she couldn't help hoping he'd found it with her.

The baby complicated everything and yet she couldn't wish it away.

Funny how so much had changed so quickly. Six months ago, she was breaking up with Chad and wondering what she was supposed to do without him. Now she had a new career path, a baby on the way and a wonderful man who loved her.

She felt something brush against her calf and glanced down. She smiled. "And you, Mason. I still have you."

Her cat meowed at her, as if telling her not to forget that.

"Do you think you're going to like children?"

The slow green-eyed blink could easily be interpreted as a yes, she thought with a chuckle.

"What's so funny?"

She turned and saw Steven walking toward her. He held two reusable grocery bags in his hands. Cut flowers were sticking out of one.

She hurried toward him. After taking one of the bags, she raised herself up on tiptoe and kissed him. "You're early."

"I know. I kept thinking about you, so I ducked out of work and here I am." He raised the bag he still held. "Ingredients for a garden salad, along with cut fruit, all organic. Free-range chicken and a recipe for a quick marinade that my mom texted me. She says it's delicious."

He put his arm around Zoe and guided her toward the house. "I've been pissed at her and haven't talked to her since she's been back, and then she goes and texts me marinade recipes. I'm a bad son."

"You're not. You've been very protective of me and I appreciate it."

"I love you, Zoe. What else would I be?"

What else indeed?

They'd reached the kitchen. She put down her bag, then took his and set it on the counter, as well. Then she took his hands in hers and led him to the kitchen table.

"We have to talk," she told him. "I have to say a few things."

His dark gaze never left her face. "Should I be worried?"

"No. It's not like that. I want us to be sure."

They were sitting close enough for their knees to touch. She studied his face—the handsome lines, the strength of him. He was calm, capable and affectionate. He loved his family, his country and he took care of his employees. He was, by all definitions, a good man.

"I love you," she began.

He smiled. "Yeah?"

She nodded, but when he reached for her, she shook her head. "Let me finish. I love you, Steven. I'm so lucky to have found you." She raised a shoulder. "Or rather I'm so lucky your mom threw us together. You've been wonderful. But the baby complicates things."

"I'm okay with the baby."

"I believe you. We've talked about it so many times. I know you understand in your head what's going to happen, but I'm less sure about your heart. I need you to be completely sure that you're willing to do all this because you love me and not because you want to be a hero."

She'd thought he might get mad or push back, but Steven being Steven, he only nodded slowly.

"That's a fair point," he said. "I am the guy who wants to be a hero, but not this time. I'm here because of you, Zoe. If things keep going, then I know I'm taking a chance. I'm willing to do that."

She drew in a breath. "If things keep going the way they're going, I'm willing to take a chance, too. I'm going to have a parenting plan in place for Chad before the baby's born. There's no way he's going to give up the rights to the baby, so you couldn't be the adoptive parent. But if we, um, well, I'm not saying we're going to but, if we, you know, took things further, then we could do some kind of...you know...plan."

She stumbled to a stop, not sure how to say what she was trying to say. Because jeez, it wasn't like he'd proposed or anything. Heat burned on her cheeks. Would it be too weird to suddenly stand and suggest they get going on that marinade?

He touched her cheek. "You're saying if we get married then we could do the same kind of thing. Like a prenuptial visitation agreement." He smiled. "You're not the only one looking things up online."

Relief eased through her. "Yes, a visitation plan."

"I'd like that." He leaned in and kissed her. "Zoe, I love you."

"I love you, too."

He kissed her again. "We're good?"

"We're the best."

★ ★ ★

Pam had one more stop on her apology train. She'd been to see Zoe, she'd spoken with Steven. Now there was just Miguel to deal with.

Taking a page from the brave young women in her life, she'd texted him and asked him to meet her at the pier for a drink. He'd said yes, and now here she was, walking into a restaurant bar to meet a man.

Not just any man either. A complicated, handsome man who had kissed her.

She still didn't think she was ready to start dating. But she also wasn't willing to walk away from Miguel. Which left her shaking oh-so-slightly.

He'd arrived before her. She saw him at a corner table by the window. When she approached, he stood and smiled at her.

"Pamela. How beautiful you look. Such a pleasure to see you."

That voice. It wasn't fair he had that voice. It was smooth and silky and made shivers dance up and down her spine.

When she was seated, he flagged the server. "May I?" he asked Pamela.

She nodded and he ordered margaritas on the rocks, made with his family's tequila. Of course.

She'd dressed carefully in a dark red dress that was tighter than she normally wore her clothes. It was sleeveless and just to her knee. Her low heels gave her a bit more height, but not so much that she wobbled when she walked. She'd done her hair and makeup, sprayed on a light mist of perfume, and then worried her nerves were going to make her throw up and wouldn't that be an impression?

"I spoke to Zoe," she blurted, figuring she might as well get the apology part over with. "I was wrong to get between her and Steven and I told her that. I also explained why I was worried about what could happen if they broke up. But it's not my decision to make. I see that now. I can't protect him from everything. I have to trust him to make the right choices for him."

"How did she take it?"

"You know she was totally gracious and forgiving."

He smiled. "I had hoped she would be, but one never knows for sure. So all is well?"

"It is. I hope it is. I don't know. Is it?"

"Ah, Pamela." He studied her. "You're an interesting woman."

Interesting? *Interesting!* No! She wanted to be intriguing or mysterious. An article on global GDP was interesting.

"Do I still frighten you?"

"I, ah, you..." She cleared her throat. "Yes."

"As you do me."

"Do I?"

The smile returned. "You are more complicated than I'm used to. And there is the issue of you being John's wife."

"You remember that."

"It is impossible to forget."

"I can't change who I am."

"You can change a little. We all just saw that, but I know what you mean. I admire the faith of your love. In my way, I feel the same about Constance. She was special and will always be a part of me. We had Zoe together, just as you had your children. So where does that leave us?"

The server returned with their drinks. Miguel waited until she picked up a glass then touched his to hers.

"I suggest we toast to possibilities and the promise of what might yet be," he said.

"To possibilities."

She took a sip.

"And good sex," he added.

She started to choke. After she finished coughing and put down her glass, she stared at him. "Are you serious?"

He winked. "Never more so."

A thousand thoughts swirled through her mind. Then a million. There was fear, confusion, worry and the tiniest kernel of anticipation. She'd been alone for two years. While she would never stop loving John, she was close to accepting that the world kept turning and dragging her along with it.

"You'd have to wear a condom," she said primly. "I've heard that people over fifty are the fastest growing demographic for STDs."

Miguel leaned back in his chair and laughed. The hearty, happy sound came from his belly. She smiled, more than a little smug at his response.

"Oh, Pamela, you are unexpected in so many ways." He raised his glass again. "To us."

"To us, Miguel."

The sound of the baseball game blaring on the TV competed with conversation, laughter and Lulu and Mariposa playing some game that involved lots of running in and out of the house, not to mention barking. Jen had long since given up keeping control over the party and decided she was just going to go with it.

Fourth of July in Mischief Bay had dawned clear and warm, with the promise of a perfect evening for fireworks. Jen and Kirk were hosting a barbecue until sunset, then everyone would walk over to the beach to watch the fireworks.

"Let me get the guys to carry out the kitchen table," Pam said. "Then we'll put in the leaves and it can be the buffet table."

"Perfect. I have paper plates in the pantry."

Her mother raised her eyebrows. "Paper plates?"

"They're biodegradable. I got the good ones."

Jen also got the point. She didn't like paper plates. She didn't like loud parties and dogs running through her house. Or at least she hadn't. Part of getting better was learning to let go. It had taken her a while but she'd finally figured out that when she stopped trying to control the world, she had a whole lot less anxiety.

Oh, it hadn't gone away. There were still nights she woke up from a dead sleep with her heart pounding and the horrible sensation of being unable to breathe. But those events were more and more rare. Every day she practiced her coping skills. She took care of herself, had her quiet mind time and took her meds. Sometimes it really did take a village to get through life.

Kirk and Steven carried the table outside. Her mom put down a plastic tablecloth, then set out the paper plates. Jen got the platter of raw hamburgers from the refrigerator and took it outside.

"We have meat," her husband called. "Meat because we are men." He took the tray, then kissed her. "And women."

Desire sat in the shade with Zoe and Miguel. Lucas walked by carrying Jack fireman style. Her son shrieked with laughter.

"Careful," Jen said with a tilt of her head. "Someone might be trying to steal your girlfriend."

"Miguel's too into Pam," Lucas said without looking. "We all know it."

They did. The older couple, while discreet, was obviously taking things to the next level. Not that she wanted to know what that meant. Let Steven deal with the whole old people having sex if he was so concerned. And speaking of her brother, things were going well with Zoe. Her mom had calmed down and accepted what seemed to be the inevitable.

They were all in a good place, she thought happily. Kirk was loving his job and she was dealing with it. They were making love regularly now. It was as if that one explosive moment had broken through whatever had been keeping them from each other.

She returned to the kitchen to get the hot dogs. Steven followed her.

"Jen, can I ask you a favor?"

"Sure." She handed him the hot dogs, then went into the pantry to collect the buns. When she stepped back into the kitchen, her brother had put down the plate. His expression was serious.

"What? What's wrong? Are you sick? Is everything okay with the baby?"

"Relax. You sound like Mom."

"There are worse things. What is it?"

"I want some help." He glanced over his shoulder. "You can't say anything, but I want to get Zoe a ring." His grin turned sheepish. "An engagement ring."

"What?" Her voice echoed through the kitchen. She lowered it to whisper, "Sorry. You're going to propose?"

"I am."

She flung herself at him. "Good for you. That's so great. Yes, of course I'll come with you. She's going to want to wait until after the baby's born to get married. Just so you know."

"You've talked about it?"

"No, but it's a girl thing." She hung on to him. "My little brother getting married. You're so grown-up."

"Thanks." He looked at her. "You can't tell anyone. I mean it. Except Kirk. Promise?"

"I swear."

"Good." He grinned. "I'm really happy."

"Me, too."

He took the hot dogs and buns out onto the patio. Jen did a little dance in her kitchen. When she turned she saw Jack smiling at her. He gestured to the refrigerator. She dropped to a crouch.

"Hey, little man. Are you thirsty? What would you like? Use your words, please."

Because that was what all the articles said. To ask for words. So she did, a dozen times a day, all to no avail.

Jack pointed to the refrigerator again, then smiled at her. "Milk, Mommy. Peas."

She dropped onto her butt and stared at him. Her brain replayed the statement. He'd said *milk*. He'd said *Mommy*! He'd said *please*. At least she was pretty sure it was *please* and not *peas*.

She wanted to grab him close and hug him and scream to the world: *My son spoke to me!* Only the voice in her head said not to make a big deal of it.

So she smiled and stood. "Milk it is."

She poured milk into a sippy cup and handed it to him.

"Tank you."

"You're welcome."

Together they walked out of the kitchen and joined the party.

★ ★ ★ ★ ★

Discussion Questions

*Note: The questions themselves contain spoilers, so you should
wait until you've finished the book to read them.*

1. The three heroines—Zoe, Jen and Pam—have three distinct
   story lines, but they impact each other. Talk first about
   each heroine's character arc, and then discuss the points at
   which they intersect. How do the events of one character's
   life change the events of another's? Which story created
   the most emotion in you? Why?

2. Why do you think Jen was so convinced there was
   something wrong with her son? Did you applaud her
   efforts to get him help, or did you think she should have
   done something different? Did your feelings change
   throughout the course of the story?

3. Do you think the relationship between Zoe and Jen was
   a friendship of equals? Why or why not? What about the
   friendship between Zoe and Pam?

4. Did your feelings about Pam change because of how she
   behaved after she found out that Zoe was pregnant? What
   made you understand why she felt the way she did, if
   anything? What do you think made her come around?

5. Toward the end of the book, Pam says of her son Steven,
   "I can't protect him from everything." How was this theme

illustrated in the story? Did you recognize any other themes as you read?

6. Discuss the line between protective and overprotective. How did the characters cross that line? Have you ever gone too far when trying to protect the people you love?

7. What did the characters learn because of what happened in the story? Which character grew or changed the most? Do any of those lessons apply to your life?

8. Discuss the men in the book—Steven, Kirk, Miguel, Lucas and Chad. Did each heroine end up with the right man? Why or why not? Which man did you like the most, and why?

9. What did you think of the relationship between Jen and Lucas? Did you expect something different to happen? Did you like the way this relationship was handled? Why or why not?

10. Pam's story began in *The Girls of Mischief Bay*. Did you read the first Mischief Bay book? If not, do you want to go back and read it now? If some people in your group did read the first book and others did not, discuss how your perception is different.

Suggested Book Club Menu

Miguel's Steak Fajita Quesadillas

Black beans

Chips and salsa

Margaritas (of course!)

Recipe

Miguel's Steak Fajita Quesadillas

2 ribeye steaks, sliced 1/4-inch thick, then cut into 1-inch pieces
Marinade:
Juice of three limes
1/2 cup tequila (too bad you can't use Saldivar tequila!)
2 tbsp triple sec or other orange-flavored liqueur
1 jalapeno, seeded and diced
3 cloves garlic, minced
2 tsp salt
2 tsp cumin

8 oz Monterrey jack cheese, shredded
8 flour tortillas

Mix together the marinade ingredients, then pour over the steak. Marinate for 2–3 hours, stirring occasionally. Drain and discard marinade. Cook beef pieces on the stove in a heavy-bottomed pan over medium-high heat for 2–3 minutes per side. Set aside and wipe out the pan with a paper towel. Lower heat to medium-low. Place a flour tortilla in the pan, sprinkle with cheese. Place one-quarter of the steak pieces on it, then top with more cheese and another tortilla. When the cheese on the bottom has melted, carefully flip over and cook another minute or so. Cut the quesadillas into wedges and serve warm.